W9-ACV-253

Also by Richard Ford

A Piece of My Heart (1976)

The Ultimate Good Luck (1981)

The Sportswriter (1986)

Rock Springs (1987)

Wildlife (1990)

Independence Day (1995)

Women with Men: Three Stories (1997)

A Multitude of Sins (2002)

The Lay of the Land (2006)

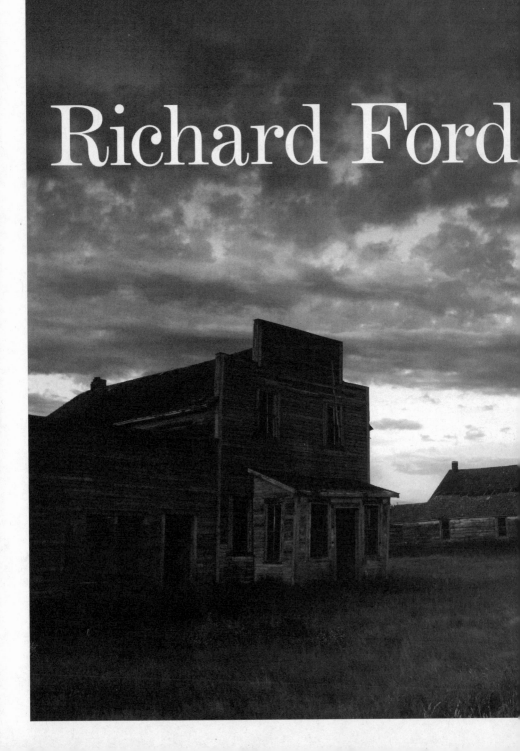

Richard Ford

Canada

HarperCollins Publishers Ltd

Canada

Copyright © 2012 by Richard Ford.
All rights reserved.

Published by HarperCollins Publishers Ltd

First Canadian edition

No part of this book may be used or reproduced in
any manner whatsoever without the prior written permission
of the publisher, except in the case of brief quotations embodied in reviews.

HarperCollins books may be purchased for educational, business, or sales
promotional use through our Special Markets Department.

HarperCollins Publishers Ltd
2 Bloor Street East, 20th Floor
Toronto, Ontario, Canada
M4W 1A8

www.harpercollins.ca

Library and Archives Canada Cataloguing in Publication
information is available upon request

ISBN 978-1-44341-111-0

Designed by Suet Yee Chong
Frontispiece photography © iStockphoto.com/Andrew Penner

Printed and bound in Canada
9 8 7 6 5 4 3 2 1

Kristina

Canada is a work of the imagination. Every character and event in it is fictitious. No resemblance to real people is intended or should be inferred. I've taken liberties with the townscape of Great Falls, Montana, and also with the prairie landscape and with some particulars of the small towns in the southwest of the Province of Saskatchewan. Highway 32, for instance, was unpaved in 1960, although as I've written about it, it is paved. Beyond that, all outright errors and omissions are my responsibility.   RF

Part One

1

FIRST, I'LL TELL ABOUT THE ROBBERY OUR PARENTS committed. Then about the murders, which happened later. The robbery is the more important part, since it served to set my and my sister's lives on the courses they eventually followed. Nothing would make complete sense without that being told first.

Our parents were the least likely two people in the world to rob a bank. They weren't strange people, not obviously criminals. No one would've thought they were destined to end up the way they did. They were just regular—although, of course, that kind of thinking became null and void the moment they did rob a bank.

MY FATHER, Bev Parsons, was a country boy born in Marengo County, Alabama, in 1923, and came out of high school in 1939, burning to be in the Army Air Corps—the branch that became the Air Force. He went in at Demopolis, trained at Randolph, near San Antonio, longed to be a fighter pilot, but lacked the aptitude and so learned bombardiering instead. He flew the B-25s, the light-medium Mitchells, that were seeing duty in the Philippines, and later over Osaka, where they rained destruction on the earth—both on the enemy and undeserving people alike. He was a tall, winning, smiling handsome six-footer (he barely fitted into his bombardier's compartment), with a big square, expectant face and knobby cheekbones and sensuous lips and long, attractive feminine eyelashes. He had white shiny teeth and short black hair he was proud of— as he was of his name. Bev. Captain Bev Parsons. He never conceded that Beverly was a woman's name in most people's minds. It grew from Anglo-Saxon roots, he said. "It's a common name in England. Vivian, Gwen and Shirley are men's names there. No one confuses *them* with women." He was a nonstop talker, was open-minded for a southerner, had graceful obliging manners that should've taken him far in the Air Force, but didn't. His quick hazel eyes would search around any room he was in, finding someone to pay attention to him—my sister and me, ordinarily. He told corny jokes in a southern theatrical style, could do card tricks and magic tricks, could detach his thumb and replace it, make a handkerchief disappear and come back. He could play boogie-woogie piano, and sometimes would "talk Dixie" to us, and sometimes like Amos 'n' Andy. He had lost some of his hearing by flying the Mitchells, and was sensitive about it. But he looked sharp in his "honest" GI haircut and blue captain's tunic and generally conveyed a warmth that was genuine and made my twin sister and me love him. It was also probably the reason my mother had been attracted to him (though they couldn't have been more unsuited and different) and unluckily gotten pregnant from their one hasty encounter after meeting at a party honoring returned airmen, near where he was re-training to learn supply-officer duties at Fort Lewis, in March 1945—when no one needed him to drop bombs anymore. They were married immediately when they found out. Her parents, who lived in Tacoma and were Jewish immigrants from Poland, didn't approve. They were educated mathematics teachers and semiprofessional musicians and popular concertizers in Poznan who'd escaped after 1918 and come to Washington State through Canada, and became—of all things—school custodians. Being Jews meant little to them by then, or to our mother—just an old, exacting, constricted conception of life they were happy to put behind them in a land where there apparently were no Jews.

But for their only daughter to marry a smiling, talkative only-son of Scotch-Irish Alabama backwoods timber estimators was never in their thinking, and they soon put it out of their thinking altogether. And while from a distance, it may seem that our parents were merely not made for one another, it was more true that when our mother married our father, it betokened a loss, and her life changed forever—and not in a good way—as she surely must've believed.

MY MOTHER, Neeva Kamper (short for Geneva), was a tiny, intense, bespectacled woman with unruly brown hair, downy vestiges of which ran down her jawline. She had thick eyebrows and a shiny, thin-skinned forehead under which her veins were visible, and a pale indoor complexion that made her appear fragile—which she wasn't. My father jokingly said people where he was from in Alabama called her hair "Jew hair" or "immigrant hair," but he liked it and loved her. (She never seemed to pay these words much attention.) She had small, delicate hands whose nails she kept manicured and shined and was vain about and gestured with absently. She owned a skeptical frame of mind, was an intent listener when we talked to her, and had a wit that could turn biting. She wore frameless glasses, read French poetry, often used terms like "cauchemar" or "trou de cul," which my sister and I didn't understand. She wrote poems in brown ink bought through the mail, and kept a journal we weren't permitted to read, and normally had a slightly nose-elevated, astigmatized expression of perplexity—which became true of her, and may always have been true. Before she married my father and quickly had my sister and me, she'd graduated at eighteen from Whitman College in Walla Walla, had worked in a bookstore, featured herself possibly as a bohemian and a poet, and had hoped someday to land a job as a studious, small-college instructor, married to someone different from who she did marry—conceivably a college professor, which would've given her the life she believed she was intended for. She was only thirty-four in 1960, the year these events occurred. But she already had "serious lines" beside her nose, which was small and pink-ish at its tip, and her large, penetrating gray-green eyes had dusky lids that made her seem foreign and slightly sad and dissatisfied—which she was. She possessed a pretty, thin neck, and a sudden, unexpected smile that showed off her small teeth and girlish, heart-shaped mouth, though it was a smile she rarely practiced—except on my sister and me. We realized she was an unusual-looking person, dressed as she typically was in olive-color slacks and baggy-sleeved cotton blouses and hemp-and-cotton shoes she must've sent away to the West Coast for—since you couldn't buy such things in Great Falls. And she only seemed more unusual standing reluc-tantly beside our tall, handsome, outgoing father. Though it was rarely the case that we went "out" as a family, or ate in restaurants, so that we hardly noticed how they appeared in the world, among strangers. To us, life in our house seemed normal.

My sister and I could easily see why my mother would've been at-tracted to Bev Parsons: big, plank shouldered, talkative, funny, forever wanting to please anybody who came in range. But it was never com-pletely obvious why he would take an interest in her—tiny (barely five feet), inward and shy, alienated, artistic, pretty only when she smiled and witty only when she felt completely comfortable. He must've somehow just appreciated all that, sensed she had a subtler mind than his, but that he could please her, which made him happy. It was to his good credit that he looked beyond their physical differences to the heart of things human, which I admired even if it wasn't in our mother to notice.

Still, the odd union of their mismatched physical attributes always plays in my mind as part of the reason they ended up badly: they were no doubt simply wrong for each other and should never have married or done any of it, should've gone their separate ways after their first passion-ate encounter, no matter its outcome. The longer they stayed on, and the better they knew each other, the better she at least could see their mistake, and the more misguided their lives became—like a long proof in mathematics in which the first calculation is wrong, following which all other calculations move you further away from how things were when they made sense. A sociologist of those times—the beginning of the '60s—might say our parents were in the vanguard of an historical moment, were among the first who transgressed society's boundaries, embraced rebellion, believed in credos requiring ratification through self-destruction. But they weren't. They weren't reckless people in the vanguard of anything. They were, as I said, regular people tricked by circumstance and bad instincts, along with bad luck, to venture outside of boundaries they knew to be right, and then found themselves unable to go back.

Though I'll say this about my father: when he returned from the theater of war and from being the agent of whistling death out of the skies—it was 1945, the year my sister and I were born, in Michigan, at the Wurtsmith base in Oscoda—he may have been in the grip of some great, unspecified gravity, as many GIs were. He spent the rest of his life wrestling with that gravity, puzzling to stay positive and afloat, making bad decisions that truly seemed good for a moment, but ultimately misunderstanding the world he'd returned home to and having that misunderstanding become his life. Again it must've been that way for millions of boys, although he would never have known it about himself or admitted it was true.

2

OUR FAMILY CAME TO A STOP IN GREAT FALLS, Montana, in 1956, the way many military families came to where they came to following the war. We'd lived on air bases in Mississippi and California and Texas. Our mother had her degree and did substitute teaching in all those places. Our father hadn't been deployed to Korea, but been assigned to desk jobs at home, in the supply and requisition forces. He'd been allowed to stay in because he'd won combat ribbons, but hadn't advanced beyond captain. And at a certain point—which happened when we were in Great Falls and he was thirty-seven—he decided the Air Force was no longer offering him much of a future and, having put in twenty years, he ought to take his pension and muster out. He felt our mother's lack of social interests and her unwillingness to invite anyone from the base to our house for dinner may have held him back—and possibly he was right. In truth, I think if there'd been someone she admired, she might've liked it. But she never thought there would be. "It's just cows and wheat out here," she said. "There's no real organized society." In any case, I think our father was tired of the Air Force and liked Great Falls as a place where he thought he could get ahead—even without a social life. He said he hoped to join the Masons.

It was by then the spring of 1960. My sister, Berner, and I were fifteen.

We were enrolled in the Lewis (for Meriwether Lewis) Junior High, which was near enough to the Missouri River that from the tall school windows I could see the shining river surface and the ducks and birds congregated there and could glimpse the Chicago, Milwaukee, and St. Paul depot, where passenger trains no longer stopped, and up to the Municipal Airport on Gore Hill, where there were two flights a day, and down the river to the smelter stack and the oil refinery above the falls the city took its name from. I could even, on clear days, see the hazy snowy peaks of the eastern front, sixty miles away, running south toward Idaho and north up to Canada. My sister and I had no idea about "the west," except what we saw on TV, or even for that matter about America itself, which we took for granted as the best place to be. Our real life was the family, and we were part of its loose baggage. And because of our mother's growing alienation, her reclusiveness, her feeling of superiority, and her desire that Berner and I not assimilate into the "market-town mentality," which she believed stifled life in Great Falls, we didn't have a life like most children, which might've involved friends to visit, a paper route, Scouts and dances. If we fit in, our mother felt, it would only increase the chance we'd end up right where we were. It was also true that if your father was at the base—no matter where you lived—you always had few friends and rarely met your neighbors. We did everything at the base—visited the doctor, the dentist, got haircuts, shopped for groceries. People knew that. They knew you wouldn't be where you were for long, so why bother taking the trouble to know you. The base carried a stigma, as if things that went on there were what proper people didn't need to know about or be associated with—plus, my mother being Jewish and having an immigrant look, and being in some ways bohemian. It was something we all talked about, as if protecting America from its enemies wasn't decent.

Still, at least in the beginning, I liked Great Falls. It was called "The Electric City" because the falls produced power. It seemed rough-edged and upright and remote—yet still was a part of the limitless country we'd already lived in. I didn't much like it that the streets only had numbers for names—which was confusing and, my mother said, meant it was a town laid out by pinchpenny bankers. And, of course, the winters were frozen and tireless, and the wind hurtled down out of the north like a freight train, and the loss of light would've made anybody demoralized, even the most optimistic souls.

In truth, though, Berner and I never thought of ourselves as being from anywhere in particular. Each time our family moved to a new place—any of the far-flung locales—and settled ourselves into a rented house, and our father put on his pressed blue uniform and drove off to work at some air base, and my mother commenced a new teaching position, Berner and I would try to think that this was where we'd say we were from if anyone asked. We practiced saying the words to each other on our way to whatever our new school was each time. "Hello. We're from Biloxi, Mississippi." "Hello. I'm from Oscoda. It's way up in Michigan." "Hello. I live in Victorville." I tried to learn the basic things the other boys knew and to talk the way they talked, pick up the slang expressions, walk around as though I felt confident being there and couldn't be surprised. Berner did the same. Then we'd move away to some other place, and Berner and I would try to get situated all over again. This kind of growing up, I know, can leave you either cast out and adrift, or else it can encourage you to be malleable and dedicated to adjusting—the thing my mother disapproved of, since she didn't do it, and held out for herself some notion of a different future, more like the one she'd imagined before she met our father. We— my sister and I—were small players in a drama she saw to be relentlessly unfolding.

As a result, what I began to care greatly about was *school,* which was the continual thread in life besides my parents and my sister. I never wanted school to be over. I'd spend as much time inside school as I could, poring over books we were given, being around the teachers, breathing in the school odors, which were the same everywhere and like no other.

Knowing things became important to me, no matter what they were. Our mother knew things and appreciated them. I wanted to be like her in that way, since I could keep the things I knew, and they would characterize me as being well-rounded and promising—characteristics that were important to me. No matter if I didn't belong in any of those places, I did belong in their schools. I was good at English and history and science and math— subjects my mother was also good at. Each time we picked up and moved, the only fact of life that made moving frightening was that for some reason I wouldn't be allowed to return to school, or I would miss crucial knowledge that could assure my future and was obtainable nowhere else. Or that we'd go to some new place where there would be no school for me *at all.* (Guam was once discussed.) I feared I'd end up knowing nothing, have nothing to rely on that could distinguish me. I'm sure it was all an inheritance from my mother's feelings of an unrewarded life. Though it may also have been that our parents, aswirl in the thickening confusion of their own young lives—not being made for each other, probably not physically desiring each other as they briefly had, becoming gradually only satellites of each other, and coming eventually to resent one another without completely realizing it—didn't offer my sister and me enough to hold on to, which is what parents are supposed to do. However, blaming your parents for your life's difficulties finally leads nowhere.

3

WHEN OUR FATHER TOOK HIS DISCHARGE IN the early spring, we were all of us interested in the presidential campaign then going on. They agreed about the Democrats and Kennedy, who'd soon be nominated. My mother said my father liked Kennedy because he imagined a resemblance. My father profoundly disliked Eisenhower for reasons having to do with American bombers being sacrificed to "softening up Jerry" behind the lines on D-Day, and due to Eisenhower's traitorous silence about MacArthur, who my father revered, and because Ike's wife was known to be "a tippler."

He disliked Nixon as well. He was a "cold fish," "looked Italian," and was a "war Quaker," which made him a hypocrite. He also disliked the UN, which he thought was too expensive and allowed Commies like Castro (who he called a "two-bit actor") to have a voice in the world. He kept a framed photograph of Franklin Roosevelt in our living room on the wall above the Kimball spinet and the mahogany and brass metronome that didn't work but came with the house. He praised Roosevelt for not letting polio defeat him, for killing himself with work to save the country, for bringing the Alabama backwoods out of the dark ages with the REA, and for putting up with Mrs. Roosevelt who he called "The First Prune."

My father maintained a strong ambivalence about being from Alabama. On the one hand, he pictured himself as a "modern man" and not a "hill-William," as he said. He held modern views about many things—such as race, from having worked alongside Negroes in the Air Force. He felt Martin Luther King was a man of principle and Eisenhower's civil rights act was badly needed. He felt the rights of women needed a fairer shake, and that war was a tragedy and a waste he knew about intimately.

On the other hand, when our mother said something slighting about the South—which she often did—he grew broody and declared Lee and Jeff Davis to be "men of substance," even though their cause had misled them. Many good things had come from the South, he said, including more than the cotton gin and water skis. "Perhaps you could name me one," my mother would say, "naturally excluding yourself, of course."

The instant he quit putting on his Air Force blues and going to the base, our father found a job selling new Oldsmobile cars. He felt he'd be a natural at selling. His warm personality—happy, welcoming, congenial, confident, talk-a-blue-streak—would attract strangers and make what other people found difficult easy for him. Customers would trust him because he was a southerner, and southerners were known to be more down to earth than silent westerners. Money would start coming in once the model year ended and the big sales discounts kicked up the values. For his job, he was given a pink-and-gray Oldsmobile Super-88 to use as a demonstrator, which he parked in front of our house on First Avenue SW, where it would serve as good advertising. He took all of us for drives out to Fairfield, toward the mountains, and east toward Lewistown and south in the direction of Helena. "Orientation-explanatory-performance checks," he called these day trips—though he knew little of the country in any direction and actually knew very little about cars except how to drive them, which he loved doing. He felt it was easy for an Air Force officer to land a good job and that he should've left the service when the war was over. He would be way ahead now.

With our father out of the Air Force and working, my sister and I believed our life might finally achieve a permanent footing. We'd been in Great Falls four years. My mother caught a ride each school day out to the little town of Fort Shaw, where she taught the fifth grade. She never talked about teaching, but she seemed to like it and sometimes spoke about the other teachers and remarked that they were dedicated people (though she seemed to have little other use for them and would never want them visiting our house any more than people from the base). At the end of the summer I could foresee starting Great Falls High School, where I'd found out there was a chess club and a debating society, and where I could also learn Latin, since I was too small and light to play sports and had no interest in any case. My mother said she expected Berner and me both to go to college, but we would have to go on our wits because there would never be enough money. Though, she said, Berner already had a personality too much like hers to make a good enough impression to get in and should probably just try to marry a college graduate instead. In a pawn shop on Central Avenue she found several college pennants and tacked these to our walls. They were articles other kids had outgrown. Furman, Holy Cross and Baylor were my three. Rutgers, Lehigh and Duquesne were my sister's. We knew nothing about these schools, of course, including where they were located—though I had pictures in my mind of what they looked like. Old brick buildings with heavy shade trees and a river and a bell tower.

Berner, by this time, had begun not to be so easy to get along with. We had not been in the same classes since grade school because it was considered unhealthy for twins to be together all the time—though we'd always helped each other with our schoolwork and done well. She stayed in her room much of the time now, read movie magazines she bought at the Rexall, and *Peyton Place* and *Bonjour Tristesse,* which she smuggled home and would not say from where. She watched her fish in her aquarium, and listened to music on the radio and had no friends—which was true of me also. I didn't mind being away from her and having a separate life with my own interests and thoughts about the future. Berner and I were fraternal twins—she was six minutes older—and looked nothing alike. She was tall, bony, awkward, freckled all over—left-handed where I was right-handed—with warts on her fingers, pale gray-green eyes like our mother's and mine, and pimples, and a flat face and a soft chin that wasn't pretty. She had wiry brown hair parted in the middle and a sensuous mouth like our father's, though she had little hair anywhere else—on her legs or arms—and had no chest to speak of, which was true of our mother as well. She usually wore pants and a jumper dress over them that made her look larger than she was. She sometimes wore white lace gloves to cover up her hands. She also had allergies for which she carried a Vicks torpedo inhaler in her pocket, and her room always smelled like Vicks when you came near her door. To me, she resembled a combination of our parents: my father's height and my mother's looks. I sometimes found myself thinking of Berner as an older boy. Other times I wished she looked more like me so she'd be nicer to me, and we could be closer. Though I never wanted to look like her.

I, on the other hand, was smaller and trim with straight brown hair parted wide on the side, and smooth skin with very few pimples— "pretty" features more like our father's, but delicate like our mother. Which I liked, as I liked the way our mother dressed me—in khaki pants and clean, ironed shirts and oxford shoes from the Sears catalog. Our parents made jokes about Berner and me coming from the postman or the milkman and being "oddments." Though they only, I felt, meant Berner. In recent months, Berner had become sensitive about how she looked, and acted more and more disaffected—as if something had gone wrong in her life in a short amount of time. At one moment in my memory, she'd been an ordinary, freckle-faced, cute, happy little girl who had a wonderful smile and could make funny faces that had made us all laugh. But she now acted skeptical about life, which made her sarcastic and skillful at spotting my defects, but mostly made her seem angry.

She didn't even like her name—which I did like and thought it made her unique.

AFTER MY FATHER had sold Oldsmobiles for a month, he was involved in a minor rear-end traffic accident while he was driving too fast in his demonstrator, and was also back on the base where he had no business being. After that, he began to sell Dodges and brought home a beautiful two-tone brown-and-white Coronet hardtop with what was called push-button drive and electric windows and swivel seats, and also stylish fins, gaudy red tail-lights and a long whipping antenna. This car likewise sat in front of our house for a period of three weeks. Berner and I got in it and played the radio, and my father took us on more drives and we let the air rush in with all four windows down. On several occasions he drove out the Bootlegger Trail and let us drive and taught us to back up and how to turn the wheels correctly for skidding on ice. Unfortunately he didn't sell any Dodges and came to the conclusion that in a place like Great Falls—a rough country town of only fifty thousand, brimming with frugal Swedes and suspicious Germans, and only a small percentage of moneyed people who might be willing to spend their money on fancy cars—he was in the wrong business. He quit that then and took a job selling and trading used cars on a lot out near the base. Airmen were always in money scrapes and getting divorced and being sued and married again and put in jail and needing cash. They bought and traded automobiles as a form of currency. You could make money being the middle man—a position he liked. Plus the airmen would be apt to do business with a former officer, who understood their special problems and didn't look down on them the way other townspeople did.

IN THE END, he didn't stay long at that job either. Though on two or three occasions he took Berner and me out to the car lot to show us around. There was nothing for us to do there but wander among the rows of cars, in the shattering, hot breeze, under the flapping pennants and the silver flashers-on-wires, gazing at the passing base traffic from between the car hoods baking in the Montana sun. "Great Falls is a used car town, not a new car town," our father said, standing hands on hips on the steps of the little wooden office where the salesmen waited for customers. "New cars put everybody in the poorhouse. A thousand dollars is gone the second you drive off the lot." At about this time—late June—he said he was thinking of taking a driving trip down to Dixie, to see how things looked there, among the "left backs." My mother told him this was a trip he'd make on his own and without his children, which annoyed him. She said she didn't want to get close to Alabama. Mississippi had been enough. The Jewish situation was worse than for coloreds, who at least belonged there. In her view, Montana was better because no one even knew what a Jewish person was—which ended their discussion. Our mother's attitude toward being Jewish was that sometimes it was a burden, and other times it distinguished her in a way she accepted. But it was never good in all ways. Berner and I didn't know what a Jewish person was, except our mother was one, which by ancient rules made us officially Jews, which was better than being from Alabama. We should consider ourselves "non-observant," or "deracinated," she said. This meant we celebrated Christmas and Thanksgiving and Easter and the Fourth of July all the same, and didn't attend a church, which was fine because there wasn't a Jewish one in Great Falls anyway. Someday it might mean something, but it didn't have to be now.

When our father had tried to sell used cars for a month, he came home one day with a used car that he'd bought for himself, and had traded away our '52 Mercury for—a white-and-red '55 Bel Air Chevrolet, bought off the lot where he'd been working. "A good deal." He said he'd arranged to begin a new job selling farms and ranch land—something he admitted he knew nothing about but was signed up to take a course on in the basement of the YMCA. The other men in the company would help him. His father had been a timber estimator, so he was confident he had a good feel for things "out in the wilds"—better than he did for things in town. Plus, when Kennedy was elected in November, a period of buoyancy would dawn, and the first thing people would want to do was buy land. They weren't making more of it, he said, even though there seemed to be a lot of it around there. The percentages in selling used cars, he'd learned, were stacked against anybody but the dealer. He didn't know why he had to be the last person to find these things out. Our mother agreed.

We, of course, didn't know it then, my sister and I, but the two of them must've realized that they'd begun to draw away from each other during this time—after he'd left the Air Force and was supposedly finding himself in the world—and to recognize they saw each other differently, possibly begun to understand that the differences between them weren't going away but were getting larger. All the congested, preoccupying, tumultuous, moving around base after base and raising two children on the fly, years of it, had allowed them to put off noticing what they should've noticed at the beginning—and it was probably more her than him: that what had seemed small had become something she, at least, didn't like now. His optimism, her alienated skepticism. His southernness, her immigrant Jewishness. His lack of education, her preoccupation with it and sense of unfulfillment. When they realized it (or when she did)—again, this was after my father accepted his discharge and forward motion changed—they each began to experience a tension and foreboding peculiar to each of them and not shared by the other. (This was recorded in various things my mother wrote, and in her chronicle.) If things had been allowed to follow the path thousands of other lives follow—the everyday path toward ordinary splitting up—she could've just packed Berner and me up, put us on the train out of Great Falls and headed us to Tacoma, where she was from, or to New York or Los Angeles. If that had happened, each of them would've had a chance at a good life out in the wide world. My father might've gone back to the Air Force, since leaving it had been hard for him. He could've married someone else. She could've returned to school once Berner and I had gone to college. She could've written poems, followed her early aspirations. Fate would've dealt them improved hands.

And yet if they were telling this story, it would naturally be a different one, in which they were the principals in the events that were coming, and my sister and I the spectators—which is one thing children are to their parents. The world doesn't usually think about bank robbers as having children—though plenty must. But the children's story—which mine and my sister's is—is ours to weigh and apportion and judge as we see it. Years later in college, I read that the great critic Ruskin wrote that composition is the arrangement of unequal things. Which means it's for the composer to determine what's equal to what, and what matters more and what can be set to the side of life's hurtling passage onward.

4

M OST OF WHAT I KNOW THAT WENT ON NEXT—
from the middle of the summer, 1960—I know
mostly from various unreliable sources: from what I
read in the *Great Falls Tribune,* which carried stories about our parents
that made it seem that there was something fantastic and hilarious about
what they did. I know other things from the chronicle my mother wrote
while she was in the Golden Valley County jail, in North Dakota, awaiting trial, and later in the North Dakota State Penitentiary in Bismarck. I
know a few things from what people told me at the time. And, of course,
I know some particulars because we were there in the house with them
and observed them—as children do—as things changed from ordinary,
peaceful and good, to bad, then worse, and then to as bad as could be
(though no one got killed until later).

FOR ALMOST THE WHOLE TIME my father had been stationed at the
base in Great Falls—four years—he'd been involved (though we didn't
know it) in a scheme to provide stolen beef to the officers' club, for which
he received money and fresh steaks we ate at home twice a week. The
scheme was well established at the base, handed down from supply officer
to supply officer as they passed through their assignments and out. The

scheme involved doing illegal business with certain members of the Cree Indian tribe, who lived south of Havre, Montana, on reservation land and were experts at stealing Hereford cows from local ranchers' herds, butchering the cows in secret, then transporting the beef sides down to the base all in a night's work. The meat was stored away by the officers' club manager in the club's cold box and served to the majors and colonels and the base commander and their wives, who knew nothing about where it came from and didn't care as long as no one got caught and the beef was good quality—which it was.

Obviously this was a small, penny-ante scheme, which was why it had easily gone on for years and everyone expected it to go on permanently. Only, a misunderstanding arose on the base, and parts of the scheme that involved billing practices in the supply and requisition office came embarrassingly to light, and several Air Force people were disciplined, and my father lost his rank of captain (of which he was proud) and became a first lieutenant again. He may have been one of the parties who caused the swindle to come to light, but that was never stated. The whole episode—which no one in our house ever discussed and Berner and I didn't know about—almost certainly contributed to his decision to leave the Air Force. It's possible he was forced to retire, although he received an honorable discharge certificate, which he framed and hung up in our living room above the piano, beside his FDR photograph. The picture was there after our parents were arrested, when my sister and I were alone in the house and no one came to see about us. In several moments during that time, I stood and perused it ("Honorably discharged from the United States Air Force . . . a testimonial of Honest and Faithful Service . . .") and thought that what it said wasn't true. I considered taking it with me when I left. But in the end I forgot about it, hanging in our abandoned house for somebody else to make fun of and eventually throw in the trash.

What my father did—and this is in my mother's chronicle ("A Chronicle of a Crime Committed by a Weak Person" was her title; she may have intended her story to be published someday)—what my father did, while he was unsuccessfully trying to sell Oldsmobiles, then Dodges, and then trading used cars and motorcycles to airmen, was again seek out the Indians south of Havre and try to establish a new business in beef sides. He believed the Indians had lost a profitable outlet for their line of work. And if he could find someone or someplace new to supply meat to, everything could start up again and even be better than before, because the Air Force wouldn't be involved, and he'd have no one to split his proceeds with. Once again, it was such a third-rate, badly considered connivance that it could've been comical had it not been life altering: our father and our tiny, stern Jewish mother in their modest rented house in Great Falls, these hapless Indians and the rustled cows slaughtered in the middle of the night in an old semi-trailer. Common sense should've dictated none of this ever take place. But no one had access to common sense.

After realizing he wouldn't make enough money to support our family while he learned the farm and ranch business—even with his two-hundred-eighty-dollar Air Force pension and my mother's salary from the Fort Shaw school—my father set out to find someone who could be a new customer for stolen beef, someone he would be the middle man for. There wouldn't be many such possibilities in Great Falls, he knew. Columbus Hospital. The Rainbow Hotel—where he knew no one. One or two steakhouse clubs he might've known about, but which were watched by the police because of illegal gambling. What his eye fell on was the Great Northern Railway, which ran the Western Star passenger train through Great Falls on its way to Seattle, then back in two days to Chicago, and that had a steady need to supply the dining cars with first-class food, coming and going. Our father believed the provider of prime beef could be him, again in association with the Indians near Havre. He knew about an airman who'd sold ducks and wild geese and venison (all illegal) to a Negro who worked for the railroad and was a head waiter in the dining car service. It was to this black man our father paid a visit (went to his house in Black Eagle) and proposed to sell him beef that he (our father) would supply from the Indians he said were his associates.

This Negro man—his name was Spencer Digby—was positive to the proposal. He'd been involved in other such schemes over the years and wasn't afraid of them. The railroad, it seemed, wasn't that different from the Air Force. I remember my father came home one afternoon and was in a rising jolly humor. He told my mother he'd formed an "independent business partnership" with "people on the railroad," which was going to supplement our income while he learned the ins and outs of the farm and ranch game. It wouldn't change everybody's life and fortunes forever, but it would put things onto surer ground than they'd been on since he'd left the base.

I don't remember what our mother said. What she wrote in her chronicle was that she'd been thinking about leaving my father for some time and taking my sister and me to Washington State. When he'd described to her the arrangement for selling stolen meat to the Great Northern (which he apparently wasn't embarrassed about), she wrote that she'd opposed it, and had right away begun feeling a "terrible tension," and decided— because everything seemed to be going very wrong—that she should leave with us very soon. Only she didn't do that.

Of course, I don't know what she actually thought. It was certainly true that our mother—a young, educated woman with good values (she was thirty-four)—didn't think of herself as having anything in common with small-time criminals. It's possible she didn't know about the previous Air Force connivance, since our father went off to the base every morning like it was any other job, only you wore a blue uniform. He may not have talked to her about what went on there, since she would probably have opposed it then, too, and he might've known she was more and more disenchanted at still finding herself an Air Force wife.

She may have thought she was near the end of that particular life by then, and that better things would be possible once Berner and I were old enough, and divorce was finally thinkable. She could've left him the minute he told her about the Great Northern scheme. But again she didn't. Therefore, all that might've happened if she'd never met Bev at a Christmas party, the poems she'd have written and published, the small-college teaching possibilities, the marriage to a young professor, the different children from Berner and me—*all* that which might've happened to her in a revised life, didn't happen. Instead, she lived in Great Falls, a town she'd never before heard of (so confusable with Sioux Falls, Sioux City, Cedar Falls), lived in one world taken up with us, feeling isolated, not wanting to assimilate, and thinking only frustratedly, complicatedly of the future. And all the while our father existed in another world—his easy scheming nature, his optimism about the future, his charm. They seemed the same world because the two of them shared it, and they had us. But they weren't the same. It's also possible that she loved him, since he unquestionably loved her. And given her general unoptimistic frame of mind, given that she might've loved him, and that they had us, she conceivably couldn't face the shock of going away and being just alone with us forever. This is not an unheard-of story in the world.

5

FOR A WHILE, MY FATHER'S DEALINGS WITH THE Indians and the Great Northern must've gone smoothly. Although my mother wrote in her chronicle that at this time—it was mid-July—she began to experience "physical ennui," and for the first time in years began to talk to her parents on the telephone when my father was out learning about selling ranches and overseeing the delivery of stolen beef. Our grandparents had never taken any part in our family life. My sister and I had never even met them, which we knew was unusual, since we were aware of people in our school who saw their grandparents all the time and went on trips with them, received cards and gifts and money on their birthdays. Our Tacoma grandparents had opposed their intelligent daughter with a decent college degree marrying a slick, smiling Alabama ex–fly boy, who set off alarms in their insular immigrants' world in Tacoma. They had offended my father by letting their disapproval be known. He was insulted by being undervalued, and as a result he never encouraged us to visit them or them to visit us, though I don't think he ever specifically forbid it—not that they would've come to any of the places we lived. Texas or Mississippi. Dayton, Ohio. They had the idea our mother should've entered "the professions," should've lived in a sophisticated city and married a CPA or a surgeon. Which my mother told Berner she never would've, since she always wanted—being the rare person as she knew herself to be—a more adventurous life. But her parents were pessimistic and fearful and inflexible—though they'd been in America since 1919. And they found it permissible to turn their backs on their daughter and her family and let us all disappear off into the interior of the country. "It would still be nice for you to know your grandparents before they die," she said to us a few times. She kept a framed black-and-white photograph, taken at Niagara Falls—three bespectacled, miniature people who looked alike, each wearing a rubber raincoat, looking miserable and mystified, posing on the gangplank of a boat (the *Maid of the Mists,* I now know, having since ridden it myself) that made tours right into the roaring downspout of the falls. It was her parents' return trip across the continent on their twentieth wedding anniversary, in 1938. Our mother was twelve. Woitek and Renata were their names. Vince and Renny, their American names. Kamper wasn't their name either. Kampycznski. My mother's name, Neeva Kampycznski, was a name that fit her better than Kamper, or even Parsons—the second one not fitting her at all. "*There's* a real cataract, there, kids," she said, staring at the cracked photograph, which she'd fetched out of her closet for us to see. "You'll both see that someday. It makes these puny falls here look like a joke. They're not great falls—unless they're all you know, like these hicks who live here."

I believe our mother expressed to her parents her dissatisfactions and possibly talked about leaving our father and taking Berner and me with her to Tacoma. Before that, I didn't know Seattle and Tacoma were so close. I had known about the Space Needle from our weekly school newspaper, and that it would soon be built. I wanted to see it. The World's Fair seemed brilliant and dazzling contemplated from Great Falls, Montana. I have no idea if our grandparents were sympathetic to our mother's complaints or would've welcomed us home with her. It had been fifteen years that she'd been gone, without their blessing. They were old—

rigid, conservative, intellectual people who'd saved their own lives at a bad time and wanted life to be predictable. They merely *could've* been receptive. Though neither, as I've said, do I believe leaving would've been a simple matter for her—even as out of place as she was. In that way she may have been less unconventional and more conservative than I give her credit for being. More like her parents than she knew.

I WAS BY THEN extremely interested in beginning Great Falls High School and wished it could start long before September, so I would be out of the house more. I'd found out the chess club met once a week through the summer in a dusty, airless room in the school's south tower. I rode my bicycle over the old, arched river bridge, all the way up to Second Avenue South, to be an "observer" of the older boys who played against each other and talked cryptically about chess and about their personal strategies and power sacrifices and tossed around famous players' names I didn't yet know—Gligorish, Ray Lopez, even Bobby Fischer who was already a master and admired by the club members. (He was known to be Jewish, which I took some unreasonable, silent pride in.) I had no idea about how to play. But I liked the orderliness of the board and the antiquated appearance of the pieces and how they felt in my hand. I knew a person needed to be logical to play and be able to plan moves far in advance and have a good memory—at least the other boys said as much. The members didn't mind my presence, and were arrogant but friendly, and informed me about books I should read and about the monthly *Chess Master* magazine I could subscribe to if I was serious. There were only five of them. No girls were members. They were the sons of lawyers, and doctors at the hospital, and talked pretentiously about all sorts of things I knew nothing of but was fiercely interested in. The spy plane incident, Francis Gary Powers, the "Winds of Change," the revolution in Cuba, Kennedy being a Catholic, Patrice Lumumba, whether the executed murderer Caryl Chessman had played chess instead of having his last supper, and whether it was right or wrong for baseball players to have their names on their jerseys—conversations that made me realize I didn't know much that was going on in the world, but needed to.

My mother encouraged my playing. She told me her father used to play in a park in Tacoma against other immigrants, sometimes competing in several games at once. She thought chess would sharpen my wits and make me more at ease with how complex the world was, and make confusion not be a thing to fear—since it was everywhere. With what I'd saved of my dollar-a-week "bat-hide" allowance, I'd bought a set of Staunton plastic chess pieces at the hobby shop on Central, along with a roll-up vinyl board, which I kept permanently set up on my dresser top, and also bought an illustrated book the club members recommended to teach myself the rules. This I kept with my Rick Brant science mysteries and the Charles Atlas muscleman books that had been left in the house and I'd read. I specifically liked it that all the chess men looked different, slightly mysterious and had complicated responsibilities that required them to move only in predetermined ways for specific strategic missions, which my book described as representing how real war went on at the time when chess was invented in India.

My mother didn't play. She preferred pinochle, which she said was a Jewish game—although she had no one to play it with. My father didn't like chess because, he said, Lenin had been a chess player. He preferred checkers, which he claimed was a more natural game that required subtle, deceptive skills. This made my mother sneer and say it was only subtle if you were from Alabama and couldn't think straight. When I got my set, I laid it out and showed her how the men moved. She tried to execute some of these, but grew uninterested and finally said her father had ruined it for her by being too demanding. I found out from my book that players all played chess against themselves for practice and would spend hours studying how to beat themselves so that when they played against a real opponent in a tournament, the game became just something you played in your head—which appealed to me, though I couldn't figure out how to do it and made rash, uninformed moves the club members would've hooted at. Several times I tried to convince Berner to sit on the opposite side of the board, on my bed, and let me perform moves that I read straight out of the *Chess Fundamentals* book, and which I would then instruct her how to answer. She did this twice, then also got bored and quit before the game had barely begun. When she was disgusted with me, she would stare hard at me and not speak, then breathe through her nose in a way that was meant for me to hear. "If you ever were any good at this, what difference would it make?" She said this as she was leaving. I, of course, thought this wasn't the point. Everything didn't have to have a practical outcome. Some things you only did because you liked doing them—which was not her way of thinking about life by then.

BERNER WAS, of course, my only real friend. We never endured the rivalries and bitter disagreements and belligerence brothers and sisters can suffer. This was because we were twins and seemed often to know what the other was thinking and cared about, and could easily agree. We also knew the life with our parents was very different from other children's lives—the children we went to school with, who we fantasized as being regular people with friends, and parents who acted normal together. (This, of course, was wrong.) We also agreed that our life was "a situation," and waiting was the hard part. At some point it would all become something else, and it was easier if we simply were patient and made the most of things together.

As I've said, Berner had lately come to advertise a more severe temperament and didn't talk to anyone much and was often sarcastic even to me. I could see my mother's grave features living in her flat, freckled face—her rounded nose, large, pupil-less eyes with thick eyebrows, large pores in her pimply skin and dark, wiry, heavy hair that started near her forehead. She didn't smile any more than my mother did, and I once heard my mother say to her, "You don't want to grow up to be a tall gangly girl with a dissatisfied look on her face." But I don't think Berner cared who she would grow up to be. She seemed to live entirely in the present moment, and thoughts about what would happen to her later didn't displace the feeling that she didn't like how things were now. She was physically stronger than I was and would sometimes take hold of my wrist with her large hands and rub my skin in opposite directions and make the "Chinese burn," while she told me that because she was older than I was, I had to do what she said—which I did almost all the time anyway. I was very much unlike her. I mused and fantasized about what would happen later—in high school, about chess victories, and college. It might not have appeared to be true, but Berner was probably more realistic in her skepticism than I was in my own views. It might've been better for her, given how her life turned out, to have stayed in Great Falls and married some good-hearted farmer and had a lot of children who she could've taught things to, which would've rendered her happy and taken the sour look off her young face—which was, after all, just her defense against being innocent. She and my mother kept a silent closeness between them that had nothing to do with me. I accepted and appreciated this closeness for Berner's sake. I felt she needed it more than I did, since I thought I was better adjusted at the time. I was supposedly close with my father—which was what boys were expected to be, even in our family. But it wasn't possible to be very close to him. He was away from the house much of the time—first, at the base; and then when that fell away, being cast off in the world, selling then not selling cars, then learning to sell farms and ranches, and eventually middle manning stolen beeves to be trucked by larcenous Indians down to the Great Northern depot, a plan that would be his undoing. All our undoing, finally. In truth, we were never very close, although I loved him as if we were.

IT SEEMS POSSIBLE, I suppose, to look back at our small family as being doomed, as waiting to sink below the churning waves, and being destined for corruption and failure. But I cannot truly portray us that way, or the time as a bad or unhappy time, in spite of it being far out of the ordinary. I can see my father out on the small lawn of our rented, faded mustard-yellow house with white shutters, my tiny mother seated on the porch steps, hugging her knees, wearing her blousy, sailcloth shorts; my father in snappy tan slacks and a sky-blue shirt and a yellow-diamond snakeskin belt and new black cowboy boots he'd bought for himself after his discharge. He is tall and smiling and un-self-aware (although with secrets). My mother's dense hair is pulled back careless and bushy with a scarf. She is watching him inexpertly putting up a badminton net in our side yard. The '55 Chevrolet is at the curb in the stalky elm shade under the soft Montana sky. My mother's small eyes are focused estimatingly, her features pinching into her nose behind her glasses. My sister and I are helping unspool the net—since it's for us that the badminton is being erected. Suddenly my mother smiles and raises her chin at something he says: "Nothing's foolproof around me, Neevy," or "We're not very good at this," or "I know how to drop bombs, but not how to put up nets." "We know that," she says. Then they both have a laugh. He had his good sense of humor, and so did she, though as I've said she rarely felt the impulse to avail herself of it. This was typical of them and all of us at that time. My father went off to work that summer at one place or other. I began to read my book about chess and also about keeping bees, which I'd decided would be my other project in high school because no one else, I thought, would know about bees—which were an interest, I felt, likelier to be found in rural schools where there was FFA or 4-H. My mother had begun reading European novels (Stendhal and Flaubert); and since there was a little Catholic college in Great Falls, she'd begun going out there and attending a summer class once a week. My sister had suddenly, in spite of her severe views of the world and bad temperament, discovered a boyfriend—whom she'd met on the street walking home from the Rexall (which upset my father, though he soon forgot about it). My parents didn't drink alcohol or fight with each other or to my knowledge have other lovers. My mother may have felt a "physical ennui," and thought increasingly of leaving. But she always thought more about staying. I remember she read a poem to me at around this time by the great Irish poet Yeats, which had in it the line that said, "Nothing can be sole or whole that has not been rent." I've taught this poem many times in a life of teaching and believe this is how she thought of things: as being imperfect, yet still acceptable. Changing life would've discredited life and herself, and brought on too much ruin. This was the child-of-immigrants viewpoint she'd inherited. And while hindsight might conclude the worst about our parents—say, that there was some terrible, irrational, cataclysmic force at work inside them—it's more true that we wouldn't have seemed at all irrational or cataclysmic if looked at from outer space—from Sputnik—and would certainly never have thought we were that way. It's best to see our life and the activities that ended it, as two sides of one thing that have to be held in the mind simultaneously to properly understand—the side that was normal and the side that was disastrous. One so close to the other. Any different way of looking at our life threatens to disparage the crucial, rational, common-place part we lived, the part in which everything makes sense to those on the inside—and without which none of this is worth hearing about.

6

EVEN THOUGH OUR FATHER'S NEW SCHEME TO
sell stolen beef to the railroad went—at least at first—as
he planned it, the story later published in the *Tribune*
clearly disclosed it had been a more complicated scheme than the one he'd
conducted at the base. There, the Indians trucked the meat in through the
main gate. The guards were alerted to let them pass. They drove straight
to the rear of the officers' club, unloaded the beef, and got paid, possibly
by my father, in hard dollars right on the spot. He and the officers' club
manager, a captain named Henley, held back an agreed-to share of the
Indians' money and took home their choice of tenderloins to feed their
families. Everybody was satisfied.

The Great Northern Railway transaction, however, had to be different because the Spencer Digby Negro turned out to badly fear and
distrust Indians and was also of a skittish nature about his job—a well-
paid union job with a high seniority status in the dining car service. This
Digby would let the Indians drive their panel truck—which had the sign
of a Havre carpet company on its side—to the loading dock at the Great
Northern depot and would take delivery of the contraband. But he refused
to pay the Indians on the spot—again, for reasons having to do with fearing and distrusting them, and because of needing to check the quality of

the meat. Both of these reasons insulted the Indians, who didn't like doing business with a Negro. An arrangement had to be made, therefore, for our father to come to the depot and receive the money from Digby, but not until a day had passed and Digby had secured the money to pay and had satisfied himself that the meat was of a high enough quality to serve in the dining cars. Digby wanted the two transactions—accepting the beef and paying out the money—kept separate, as if the money wasn't really *for* the meat (in case he was caught), and as if my father was the actual provisioner and the Indians only worked for him as laborers. At the heart of schemes like this there's always something unreasonable, the explanation of which is that human beings are involved.

THIS ALTERATION in the original air-base scheme put my father into a precarious position. He liked the role of middle man because it made him feel and look competent, and he didn't see it as precarious (until it was too late). But the new scheme meant that for a day or more the Indians no longer had possession of the beef they'd stolen and butchered at grave risk to themselves, then driven down to Great Falls and delivered in more or less full view—after having already put themselves at risk by cruising through town with a truck full of beef that didn't belong to them, at a time in history when the Great Falls police would've gladly arrested an Indian for no reason, and also generally kept their eyes on any Negroes, since they were then causing trouble down South. In return for these risks, however, the Indians were not able to take prompt possession of the money they were fully entitled to—$100 per beef side (beef was cheap then). And even more perilous in their view, they had to wait conspicuously around town to get the money from my father, who they only partially trusted. Before, they'd trusted the Air Force because one of them had once been an airman, and Indians always tended to trust the government to take care of them because that's the way it'd always happened. In that way they were not so different from my father.

The danger of the new scheme—an arrangement my father worked out, believing it would please everyone—was that he was in the middle between parties who were both criminals, and who didn't trust or like each other, but who he himself had decided he *could* trust, if not actually like. And worse, each time beef was delivered, he immediately owed money to Indians who no one would want to owe money to or be owed money *by* because they possessed well-respected violent tendencies. Two of them, the *Tribune* later said, were murderers, and another was a kidnapper. All three had been in Deer Lodge Prison for more than half their lives. Looked at all these years later it is a ridiculous scheme that should never have worked even once. Except it did and is no more ridiculous than robbing a bank.

One day in mid-July my father got up in the morning and told us all he was planning to drive out to Box Elder, Montana, on the highway north toward Havre to inspect a piece of prime ranch land his new company was hoping to sell at a big profit. He wanted my sister and me to go with him, since he said we'd been Air Force brats all our lives and knew nothing about where we lived and spent too much time indoors. In any case, our mother could use a quiet morning to herself.

We drove in the white-and-red Bel Air out Highway 87, leading north and up into the hot, ripening wheat fields in the direction of Havre, which was a hundred miles away. The Highwood Mountains, east of Great Falls, were to our right at an indistinct distance, blue and hazed and more mysterious looking than the way they looked with town as their point of reference. After an hour, we passed Fort Benton where we could see the Missouri River below the highway—the same shining river we saw out our school windows. It was smaller and calmer and headed east along the base of chalk and granite bluffs, on its way (I already knew) to its meeting with the Yellowstone and the White and the Vermilion and the Platte and finally the Mississippi at the border of Illinois. The highway went down and along a creek bottom, then up again onto a bench with more cropland,

and different blue-tinted mountains ahead of us—longer and lower than
the Highwoods, but just as hazy and timbered and foreign looking. These
were the Bear's Paws, my father announced authoritatively. They were on
the Rocky Boy Indian Reservation, which meant Indians lived there but
didn't own anything outright because they didn't need to with the government taking up the slack, plus they weren't competent to own land anyway. He'd done business out here before, he said, and we could drive onto
their land without trouble or permission.

WE DROVE UP the narrow highway through the wheat until we passed
a small dusty town with a grain elevator, then quickly came to another,
which was Box Elder—the name of the shady trees on our block. It had a
short little main street across some railroad tracks, with a bank and a post
office, a grocery, two cafés and a service station, and was surprising to be
out there in the middle of nothing. We turned east off the highway onto
a narrow dirt and gravel road that headed straight toward the mountains,
where the ranch was that my father's new company hoped to sell. Nothing more than mountain foothills and oceans of wheat lay ahead of us. No
houses or trees or people. Ripe wheat stood to the road verges, yellow and
thick and rocking in the hot dry breeze that funneled dust through our
car windows and left my lips coated. Our father said the Missouri River
was to the south of us now. We couldn't see it because it was down below
more bluffs. Lewis and Clark, who we knew about, had come all the way
up to here in 1805 and hunted buffalo precisely where we were. However,
this was the part of Montana, he said—steering with his left elbow out
the window—that resembled the Sahara through a bombardier's sights,
and wasn't a place where an Alabama native could ever be happy living.
He teased Berner and asked if she felt like she was an Alabamian—since
he was. She said she didn't and frowned at me and puckered her lips and
made a fish mouth. I told my father I didn't feel like an Alabamian either,
which seemed to amuse him. He said we were Americans, and that was

all that mattered. After that we saw a big coyote in the road with a rabbit in its mouth. It paused and looked at our car approaching, then walked into the tall wheat out of sight. We saw what our father said was a golden eagle, poised in the perfectly blue sky, being thwarted by crows wanting to drive it away. We saw three magpies pecking a snake as it hurried to get across the pavement. Our father swerved and ran over it, which made two thump-bumps under the tires and the magpies fly up.

When we'd driven several miles out this unpaved road with our dust storm behind us, the wheat abruptly ended, and dry, fenced, grazed-over grassland took up, with a few skinny cows standing motionless in the ditches as our car went by. My father slowed and honked his horn, which made the cows kick and snort and shit big streams as they heaved out of the way. "Well, pardon us," Berner said, watching them from the back seat.

After a while, we drove past a single, low unpainted wooden house built off the road, flat to the bare ground. Visible a ways farther down the road was another one, and a third one you could barely see in the shimmering, weltering distance. They were dilapidated, as if something bad had happened to them. The first house had no front door or panes in its windows, and the back portion of it had fallen in. Parts of car bodies and a metal bed frame and a standing white refrigerator were moved into the front yard. Chickens bobbed and pecked over the dry ground. Several dogs sat on the steps, observing the road. A white horse wearing a bridle was tethered to a wooden post off to the side of the house. Grasshoppers darted up into the hot air the car displaced. Someone had parked a black-painted semi-trailer in the middle of the field behind the house, and beside it was a smaller panel truck that had HAVRE CARPET painted on its side. A couple of skinny boys—one without his shirt—came to the vacant front doorway and watched us drive past. Berner waved at them and one boy waved back.

"Those boys are Indians," my father said. "This is where they're living. They're not as lucky as you two. No electric out here."

"Why would they live here?" Berner said. She looked out the rear window through the dust at the run-down house and the boys. Nothing about them indicated they were Indians. I knew all Indians didn't live in teepees and sleep on the ground and wear feathers. No Indians went to the Lewis School that I was aware of. But I knew there were Indians who stayed drunk, and people found them in alleys in winter, frozen to the asphalt. And there were Indians in the sheriff's office who only handled Indian crimes. I'd thought, though, if you went where Indians lived, they'd look different. These two boys didn't look any different from me, even though their house was ready to collapse. Where were their parents, I wondered.

"I think you could ask the same question about the Parsons family, couldn't you?" my father said, as if this was a joke. "What are *we* doing in Montana? We oughta be in Hollywood. I could be the double for Roy Rogers." He broke into a song, then. He often sang. He had a mellow speaking voice I liked hearing, but he didn't have a good singing voice. Berner usually covered her ears. This time he sang, "Home, home on the range, where the goats and pachyderms play." It was one of his jokes. I was thinking these Indian boys didn't play chess or have debates, or probably go to school at all, and would never amount to anything.

"I admire Indians," my father said, once he'd quit singing. Then we were silent.

We drove past the second falling-in house, where there was a doorless black car turned upside down with no tires, or glass in any of its windows. This house's roof had big holes through the shingles. There were tall lilacs and hollyhocks around the door like at our house, and someone had made a circular pig pen out of car radiators. The pigs' snouts and ears were visible over the top. Behind the house there was a row of white-painted bee hives that someone in the house was tending. This captured my attention. I already had read my book on bees and was making plans to convince my father to help me build a single hive for the backyard. I knew where to send off for bees in the state of Georgia. Soon, I'd heard on the radio, the Montana State Fair would come to the fairgrounds not far from our house, and I intended to visit the bee exhibit there, where bee apparatus would be on display, and demonstrations about smoking hives and bee apparel and honey harvesting were to be conducted. Keeping bees was similar to chess in my mind. Both were complicated and had rules and required skill and setting goals, and each offered hidden patterns for success that could only be understood with patience and confidence. "Bees unlock the mystery to all things human," the *Bee Sense* book—which I'd checked out of the library—had said. All these things that I wanted to learn about, I could've easily learned in Scouts if my mother had been willing. But she wasn't.

A heavy-set, pale-skinned woman wearing shorts and a bathing suit top walked to the front door and shielded her eyes from the sun as we went past.

"We have our Alabama Indians, too," my father said in a voice intended to make Berner and me think everything out here was completely ordinary in case we thought it wasn't. "We have the Chickasaw and the Choctaw and your Swamp Bulgarians. They're all related to these people out here. None of these folks have been treated fairly, of course. But they've maintained a dignity and self-respect." This was hard to see in the houses we passed, though I was impressed the Indians knew about bees, and considered there was more to them than I knew.

"Where's the ranch you're going to sell," I asked.

My father reached across the seat and patted me on my knee. "We passed that a long time ago, son. It didn't look good to me. You're observant to remember. I just wanted you children to see some real Indians while we're out here. You oughta know an Indian when you see one. You live in Montana. They're part of the landscape." I wanted to bring up the subject of the State Fair right then, since he was in a good humor, but he was distracted by the Indians and I thought I might sacrifice my opportunity to discuss the subject later.

"Nobody answered about why they live out here," Berner said. She was sweating and using her damp finger to draw a pattern in the fine road dust on her freckled arm. "They don't have to. They could live in Great Falls. It's a free country. It's not Russia or France."

It was as if our father had stopped paying attention to us then. We drove down the rutted road another mile until we came close enough to the Bear's Paw Mountains that I could make out the tree line and scattered patches of scabby snow the sun never reached all summer. It was hot where we were, but if you went up farther, it would be cold. At a certain point along the road, with the dry, wasted landscape running on ahead unchanging, we pulled off between some fenceless fence posts, turned around, and began back the way we'd come—past the broken-down houses on the left, and the Indians, back to Box Elder and onto Highway 87 toward Great Falls. It felt as if nothing had been accomplished coming out there, nothing our father was interested in or worried about or needed to see—nothing having to do with selling or buying a ranch. I had no idea why we'd gone there. My sister and I didn't discuss it once we got home.

7

WHAT HAPPENED WAS THAT BY THE FIRST WEEK of August, my father and the Great Northern man—Digby—and my father's Cree accomplices had conducted three stolen beef transactions that had all gone satisfactorily. Cows were stolen, killed and delivered. Money changed hands. The Indians went away. Everyone was put at their ease. My father believed his recalculated scheme worked well, and didn't feel precariously in the middle in any way that worried him. He was a man unable not to believe that if things were going well and smoothly, they wouldn't go well and smoothly forever. Very much like the Indians, who relied on the government, the Air Force had sheltered him from the life most other people faced. And because of what he'd done expertly in the war (mastered the Norden sight, dropped bombs on people he never saw, not gotten killed), he felt that being taken care of was justifiable, which fostered a tendency not to look into things—any things—too closely. Which, with his beef scheme, meant not remembering that middle manning stolen beef carcasses hadn't finally worked out successfully at the air base. His scheme had caused him, in fact, to lose his captain's bars and in one way or other had landed him back in civilian life long before he was ready—if he ever would've been ready after so much time away.

It's also possible that our mother, by being studious and aloof, caused him to feel she was observing him and calculating whether some new failure of his was going to be the reason she should leave him. So that despite his apparent success, his optimistic nature, his new fresh start in the civilian world, her private uncertainties accumulated, and eroded his confidence for the "feel" he believed he had for what he was doing. All he wanted was for life to stay on a steady course until school started again and our mother could go back to teaching, leaving him free to learn the farm and ranch business and be able to go on doing the things he wanted to with Digby and the Indians—since it was all for our benefit.

LIFE AT THIS TIME still felt completely normal to me. I remember in early August, my father insisted we all go down to the Liberty to see *Swiss Family Robinson* at the Saturday matinee. My father and I both loved it. But our mother insisted Berner and I read the book—which she still had from high school, and which was a great deal less optimistic and romantic than the motion picture. She had begun her class with the Sisters of Providence by early August and came home with more books, and talking about what the nuns said about Senator Kennedy. People in the South, they said, would never let him win; someone would shoot him before election day. (My father assured us that wasn't true, that the South was sadly misunderstood, but it was true that the pope in Rome would now have a say-so in American life, and that Kennedy's father was a whiskey baron.) There was more talk about the Space Needle, which our father said he wanted to see and would take us when it was finished. My sister brought her boyfriend home twice during this time, though never inside the house. I liked him. His name was Rudy Patterson. He was a year older and was a Mormon (which I looked up, and Rudy said meant polygamists, among other things), and already went to high school, which made him intensely interesting to me. He was red-headed and raw-boned and tall with big feet, and had a little pale skim of a mustache he was proud of. Once, he and I walked across the street and shot baskets against the backboard the town had installed there. He told me his plan was to leave school soon and go to California and join a band, or else the Marines. He'd already asked Berner if she wanted to go with him or possibly meet him there some time later, and she'd said no—which made Rudy say Berner was tough as nails, which she was. While we played, under the dense, sweet-smelling bonnet of elms and box elders, thick with humming cicadas, Berner had sat on our front porch steps—exactly as our mother had—squinting into the sun, hugging her knees and watching us scrimmage around. She called out, "Don't you tell him what I said. I don't want him in on my secrets." I didn't know which of us she was talking to—Rudy or me. I didn't know Berner's secrets, although I had once thought I knew everything about her because we were twins. But she must've had new secrets by then, since she no longer talked to me about private matters and treated me as if I was much younger than she was and as if her life had started in a direction leading her away from mine.

WHAT I KNOW firsthand about bad things—seriously bad things—was that late in the first week of August my father came home one evening, and though I didn't see him, I knew something unusual was going on in the house. You become sensitized to such things by the sound of a porch door slapping closed too hard, or the thump of someone's heavy boot heels hitting the floorboards, or the creak of a bedroom door opening and a voice beginning to speak, then that door quickly closing, leaving only muffled noises audible.

It was hot and dry and dusty in our house in midsummer, which affected Berner's allergies. (It was always drafty and cold in winter.) My mother kept the attic fan turned on and liked to sit in the cool bath in the early evening before she cooked dinner, when pastel light shone in through the tiny, square bathroom window. She burned a sandalwood candle on the toilet top and stayed in until the water was cold. My father had been out of the house, supposedly learning about land sales. But when he got home, he went right into the bathroom where our mother was and started talking in a forceful, animated way. The door closed on what he was saying. But I heard him say, "I've bumped into some trouble with this . . ." I didn't hear the rest. I was in my room reading about bees and listening to my radio. I felt the need to perfect my strategy for getting to the State Fair. We had never gone in the four years we'd been there. My mother saw little reason for it, since she didn't like the rides or the smells, and Berner wasn't interested.

My father stayed talking to my mother in the bathroom for a long time. It began to get dark outside, and my sister came out of her room and turned on the lights in the living room, closed the curtains and turned off the attic fan so that the house became still.

In a little while the bathroom door opened and my father said, "I can worry about all this later. Just not now." My mother said, "Of course. I guess I don't blame you." He came to the door of my room, which was open. He was wearing his black Acme boots and a white shirt with arrow-slit pockets and pearl buttons and his rattlesnake belt. He liked to dress well after being in a uniform most of his life. Learning to sell ranches had persuaded him he needed to look like a rancher even if he didn't know anything about ranches. He asked what I was doing. I told him I was learning about bees and intended to visit the State Fair, which I'd mentioned already. There would be a 4-H tent there, and boys my age would be demonstrating the fine points of beekeeping and honey harvesting. "Sounds like a large-size undertaking to me," he said. "You have to be careful you don't get stung to death. Bees gang up on you is what I've heard." He walked down to my sister's door and asked her about her activities and talked about her fish. My mother came out of the bathroom, looking serious, and wearing a green cloth bathrobe and a towel wrapped around her wet hair. She went in the kitchen dressed that way and began taking food out of the refrigerator. My father went in the kitchen after her and said, "I'll get this straightened out." She said something I didn't hear because she said it in a whisper. Then my father walked out onto the front porch, where it was dark and cooler. The street lights were on. He sat in the swing, which had a thin, popping chain, and rocked to the sound of the cicadas. I heard him saying some things to himself, which made me know he was worried. (He talked to himself often—they both did—as if some conversation couldn't be shared. There was more of such talking when things bothered them.) Once, as he sat rhythmically swinging, he laughed out loud. In a little while he walked out to the street and got in his car and drove off—I guessed—to try to get whatever was worrying him straightened out.

THE NEXT DAY was Sunday. Again, we didn't attend any church. My father kept a big family bible, which had his name written in it, in his dresser drawer. He was officially a Church of Christ member and had been saved years before in Alabama. My mother professed to be an "ethical agnostic," in spite of being Jewish. Berner said she believed everything and also nothing, which explained why she was the way she was. I believed nothing at all that I can remember, not even what belief meant, other than birds flew and fish swam—things you could demonstrate. Sunday, however, was still a day set aside. All day long no one spoke much or loudly, particularly in the morning. My father watched the TV news and later baseball, wearing Bermuda shorts and a T-shirt, which he didn't do on weekdays. My mother read a book, worked on her school plans for the fall, and wrote in her journal, which she'd kept from when she was a teenager. She usually took a long walk by herself after breakfast, up Central Avenue and across the river into town, where nothing was going on and the streets were mostly emptied. Afterward she came home and cooked lunch. I'd designated Sunday as my day for practicing chess moves and learning more of the rules, which the boys in the club had informed me were the keys to everything. If you completely internalized the complex rules, you could then play intuitively and with daring, which was how Bobby Fischer played, even when he was only seventeen—not much older than I was.

Nothing was discussed that Sunday morning about what needed to be "straightened out" the night before and that our parents had spent an hour in the bathroom discussing. I wasn't aware what time my father got home from wherever he went that night. He was simply there Sunday morning in his Bermudas, watching TV. The telephone rang several times. I answered it twice, but there was no one on the line—which wasn't that out of the ordinary. Nobody let on anything was peculiar. My mother went on her walk to town. My father watched *Meet the Press*. He was interested in the election and believed Communists were taking over Africa but that Kennedy would prevent it. Berner and I went out into the hot, sunny yard and repositioned the poles of the badminton net to give ourselves more room beside the house to play. It was a pretty, vacant morning. Hollyhocks were blooming against the side of the garage. There was nothing to do in Great Falls.

At eleven, the Zion Lutherans, kitty-corner across the street on the side of the park, began clanging their bell as usual and taking in. Cars and pickups arrived as they always did and parked along the curb opposite our house. Families with children walked up to the gray wood building and disappeared inside. I liked watching them from the front porch swing. They were always in good spirits and talked and laughed about subjects that interested them and that I assumed they agreed about. I'd once walked over on a weekday to look in the doors and see whatever there was to see. But the doors were locked and no one was there. The gray clapboard building felt like a store that had gone out of business.

It was just when the Lutherans' bell had begun ringing that an old car pulled up in front of our house and stopped. I thought the driver—a man—was one of the Lutherans and would get out and go across to the church. But he just sat in the old, crudely painted red Plymouth and smoked a cigarette as if he was waiting on something or someone to start paying attention to him. The car was from back in the '40s and was muddied up and dented, and for some reason seemed familiar—though I couldn't have said why. It had its rear side window broken out and its tires didn't match and one on the back lacked a hubcap. It had been in more than one accident and looked out of place in front of our house, parked behind our father's Bel Air, which was shiny and clean.

After the man had sat inside smoking for a while—Berner and I watched from the side yard by the badminton net holding our rackets—he looked around at our house and suddenly climbed out, which made the driver's-side door emit a bang, before he slammed it back.

At almost that same instant my father came out the front door, still in his Bermudas, and went down the concrete walk as if he'd been watching to see if the man would get out. Now that he had, something immediate needed to be done about it.

We both heard our father say, "Okay, whoa. Whoa-whoa-whoa-whoa," as the man came slowly up the walk. "You don't need to be showing up here now. This is my home," he said. "This is going to get settled." Our father laughed at the end of saying that, though nothing seemed funny.

The man just stood on the concrete walk with his chin dramatically lowered, and stared at our father. He didn't step back when our father approached saying "Whoa-whoa-whoa-whoa"; he didn't offer to shake hands; he didn't smile as if anything was funny. He was dressed as if he'd come from someplace cold, because he had on heavy maroon woolen trousers and scuffed brown shoes with no socks, and a bright red cardigan over a dirty gray sweatshirt. It was a strange outfit for August.

When he'd stepped up onto the sidewalk, it was clear things hurt in his legs. He had to navigate himself using his shoulders, and his knees pointed in. He wasn't a large man—not as tall as our father—but he was heavy, as if his bones were cumbersome and awkward to move. He had a great growth of oily black hair tied in the back to make a long ponytail, and thick black-rimmed glasses. His complexion looked orangish and roughed up with acne whelps, and he had a Band-Aid on his neck. He wore a wispy goatee and might've been fifty years old, but possibly was younger. He was a stark presence to be in our front yard, since he gave the impression of being unhappy to be there. As far away as Berner and I were standing, by the badminton net, I could smell an odor on the man—a meaty smell and a medicine smell at the same time. After he left, I smelled it on our father.

When the man declined to shake hands or to step back, our father put his hand on the man's shoulder and stepped close to turn him, and they started talking and walking back toward the Plymouth instead of toward our house. But at a certain point the man took a step sideways off the concrete onto the grass—and away from our father's grip. He looked away—not toward Berner and me—but away from our father in the other direction, as if he didn't want to look at him or us. Then he spoke—Berner and I both heard this. "This could turn out real bad for everybody, Cap," he said. "Cap" was what our father had been called in the Air Force. The man moved his eyes around and focused them on my father. He said something else then, under his breath, as if he knew Berner and I were listening and didn't want us to hear. After he'd spoken, he crossed his arms, leaned back and set one foot out in front of the other in a way I'd never seen anyone do before. It was as if he wanted to see his own words floating away from him.

Our father began nodding and put both hands in his Bermuda pockets—not saying anything, just nodding. The man began to talk very intently then, and faster. It was muffled, though I could hear the word *you* spoken emphatically, and the word *risk* and the word *brother*. Our father looked down at his rubber sandals and his bare feet and shook his head and said, "No-no-no-no," as if he was in agreement with what he was hearing, though the words seemed like he wasn't. Then he said, "That's not reasonable, I'm sorry," and "I understand. Well, all right." Tautness went out of his body at that point, as if he was relieved, or disappointed. Then the man—we later found out his name was Marvin Williams, though he was called "Mouse" and was a Cree Indian—turned away without a concluding word and walked in his painful, shoulder-navigating, knees-in way back to his Plymouth, banged open the door, cranked the motor noisily, and drove off without looking back at our father, leaving him standing on the concrete walk in his shorts and sandals, watching. The Lutherans' church bell was ringing again—a last call to worship. A man in a light gray suit was closing both front doors. He looked over at our house and waved a hand, but our father didn't see him.

LATER THAT MORNING our mother returned from her walk and cooked blinis—our favorite. During the meal our father didn't say much. He told a joke about a camel that had three humps and said moo. He said Berner and I should learn how to tell jokes, because it would make people like to have us around. Afterward, he and our mother went in their bedroom and closed the door and stayed a very long time—much longer than they'd stayed in the bathroom the previous night. Before our mother got home from her walk, our father had taken off his sandals and played badminton in the yard—us against his one. He cavorted all around, sweating his upper lip and getting out of breath, trying spiritedly to strike the shuttlecock and laughing and having a wonderful time. It was as if things couldn't be better, and the Indian's visit hadn't been about anything important. Berner asked the man's name, which was when we found out it was Marvin Williams, and that he was a Cree. He was "a businessman," our father said. He was "honest but demanding." At one point in our game, he just stood in the warm grassy yard, hands on his hips, smiling, his face red and sweaty. He took a deep breath and said he thought things would soon be better for us all. We might not necessarily be staying in Great Falls but might be experiencing a move to a more promising town he didn't name—which shocked and instantly worried me, because the start of school was just weeks away and I had made my plans for chess and raising bees and learning a great number of other things. I was happy with the direction things were going—which in retrospect was crazy, because I had no idea about the direction things were going. It was probably, I came to think, in the hours after the Indian, Williams-Mouse, stood in our yard and threatened to kill our father, and possibly kill all of us if he wasn't paid (which was what I found out he'd said in his menacing, soft voice), that our father began putting together thoughts of needing to do something extraordinary to save us, which turned out to be thoughts about robbing a bank—about which bank to rob, and when, and how he could enlist our mother so he could lessen the likelihood anyone would find out, therefore keeping them out of jail. Which didn't happen.

8

LATER, WHEN I KNEW THE WHOLE STORY, AS MUCH as I'd ever know, I found out that the Friday before the Saturday my father talked to my mother when she was in the bathtub, then drove off into the night, the Indians had delivered four butchered Hereford carcasses to Digby at the Great Northern loading dock and had gone away expecting to be paid the next day by our father. Digby had decided that because the stolen beef arrangement worked so seamlessly, he could now take receipt of even more beef, which he would supply to a friend who was the head waiter on another Great Northern train, a concession for which he, Digby, would be well paid. Our father had considered this an excellent development for everyone. But when he went on Saturday night to Digby's little bungalow in Black Eagle to collect the money—part of which was our father's for dreaming up the scheme—Digby told him two of the carcasses had arrived in a rancid state (it was summer, and too hot to transport dead meat in an unrefrigerated carpet truck) and weren't fit to serve to other Indians, much less to dining car passengers luxuriating between Seattle and Chicago. Digby said he wasn't about to pay our father for meat like that. He'd in fact already had the beeves trucked off and dumped downstream in the Missouri in case anybody—the railroad police, for instance—found him with it, uninspected, without a bill of sale or any explanation for it being in the depot's cold box.

This was an unwelcome surprise to our father, who told Digby in no uncertain terms that he ought not have taken delivery if the meat was "off." But since he *had* taken it, the meat and its cost ($400) was his—Digby's—responsibility.

What our father believed was that Digby, who was a spindly, bug-eyed, little-girlish-voiced character in a bow tie and white jacket, had become frightened of the Indians—whom he already distrusted and who distrusted him—so that his elaborate plan to buy more beef had begun all at once to seem like the bad idea it was. This realization expanded into an even greater fear of being caught and losing his high-paying dining car job. There was other illegal activity, it later came to light, that Digby was embroiled in, for which the Great Falls police would've loved to put him in jail. Dining car employees and Pullman porters were known to run strings of girls all along the main line. A girl climbed on in one town, transacted business during the ride, then climbed off the next morning.

Our father didn't for an instant believe the meat had arrived spoiled. That had never happened before and he saw no reason it ever should. But when he returned to Digby's house (after he'd counseled with my mother in her bathtub), to again demand his $400, and ready to pound it out of Digby with his fists (which was not like him, except he was desperate), Digby had already left town on the Western Star and was on his way to Chicago, where he had another separate life, leaving our father to contend with the Indians.

Our father was then in the exact predicament he might've known he could land in and ought to have taken precautions about. (For example, being present when the meat changed hands would've been such a precaution; having an amount of cash in his pocket sufficient to indemnify the sale should something go wrong would've been another.) However, all he had in his possession at that moment that could ensure the deal was whatever was left from his monthly Air Force pension, whatever little money our mother had from teaching nine months a year in Fort Shaw, and our Chevrolet. Our parents had nothing set aside for an emergency, which this had become. They had never even had a checking account. They paid for everything with cash.

The next morning—Sunday—Mouse, or Williams, arrived at our house, stood in the yard with my father, and said what he'd said about killing us, a threat our father took very seriously. Williams also stated that he and his associates had incurred greater risk by stealing four cows instead of one, and had gone to much more perilous difficulty in butchering them and transporting them, and had been laughed at by the Negro Digby when they delivered the meat and demanded they be paid $600 instead of the $400 they were originally owed. Williams further told our father that one of his associates was under surveillance by the reservation police specifically due to the cow-stealing scheme, and needed money to make a trip to Wyoming to hide for several months. For which reasons, Williams said, he and his friends were now owed $2,000, and not $600 or the $400 they'd agreed to. Where the $2,000 amount came from he didn't offer to explain.

Our father wasn't a man accustomed to being threatened. He was accustomed to getting along well with people, amusing them, being admired for his looks, his nice manners, his southern accent, and for his valiant bombardier's service in the war. Being threatened with murder exerted a big impact on him. He immediately began to brood and fester about how he could get the money, and quickly came to the extraordinary idea of finding a bank to rob. At that moment, it must've seemed better than having the Indians kill him and my mother and Berner and me, better than gathering us all three up, loading us into the Bel Air and abandoning everything in the middle of the night, never to be heard from again. Other ways of getting the money—borrowing it (he had no credit, his in-laws disliked him, he had no salary and nothing to borrow against), or of coping with the situation, such as by going to the Great Falls police or reasoning with Williams—either didn't occur to him or, he might've felt, would only lead to worse problems. Later, when it might have occurred to him to go to the police and throw himself on their mercy, he'd already decided robbing a bank was a good idea, and that was that.

WHEN MY MOTHER was in the North Dakota Women's Penitentiary in Bismarck, where she was imprisoned after her and my father's trial, she wrote about the next days and the ones preceding them in her chronicle— an account that goes into great detail about what she and my father did. She'd had aspirations to be a poet when she was in college at Walla Walla, and possibly she thought a well-written version of their story would offer a future for her when she got out of prison—which she never did. In her chronicle she is extremely critical of our father and his flaws. She doesn't excuse herself or plead she was crazy or forced into participating, or even try to explain how she was talked into it. (She does express sorrow about what happened to my sister and me.) In her writing she says she believed she was the person she'd always thought herself to be—reflective, smart, imaginative, possibly alienated and skeptical, conserving, mirthful. (She wasn't that.) These were the values that caused her never to want Berner and me to assimilate in the places my father's Air Force job took us. Those places, she felt, would dilute and corrupt what was good and important about us and render us stale and ordinary in terms specific to Mississippi, Texas, Michigan, Ohio, places she had low regard for and considered unenlightened. She uses these words in the chronicle: *dilute, conserving, alienated, stale, corrupt.* She believed she and my father should never have married—she should've seen ahead that they both would've been happier if they hadn't. This was where she wrote about marrying a college professor and having a life as a poet and other such things. She says she definitely should've left him the minute the subject of a robbery came up, since she was already considering leaving him. Except what she found out about herself—she wrote—was that while all the ways she knew herself to be (when she looked in the mirror and saw the unusual person she was) were accurate and true, she was also weak. Which she'd never thought before, but was the reason, she believed, she'd married smiling, good-looking, romantic Bev Parsons. (She was pregnant, but she could've taken care of that, something even college girls in the '40s knew how to do.) Being weak was why she hadn't long ago left Bev and taken us away. These facts now confirmed to her that she was just like anybody else, which led her inexorably (by her demented logic) to robbing a bank. Not that she believed she was a criminal. She never thought that. Her parents hadn't raised her to be capable of believing such a thing (which may have had to do with being Jewish where there were no Jews, and with preserving a feeling of specialness that didn't allow adopting other people's views and cautions, as reasonable as they might've been).

But what I thought—and I thought it when Berner and I were inside our house alone and our parents were in their cells in the Cascade County jail—was how young our parents were then. Only thirty-seven and thirty-four. And that they were not the people to rob a bank. Yet because very few people do rob banks, it only makes sense that the few who do it are destined for it, no matter what they believe about themselves or how they were raised. I find it impossible not to think this way, because the sense of tragedy would otherwise be overpowering to me.

Though it's an odd thing to believe about your parents—that all along they've been the kind of people criminals come from. It's like a miracle in reverse. I'm sure it's what my mother meant when she said she was "weak." To her, the two words—*criminal* and *weak*—may have meant the same thing.

9

B Y MONDAY MORNING SOMETHING HAD CHANGED
in the house. Large occurrences were going on—larger
than my father beginning a new job, or leaving the Air
Force, or packing up and moving to a new town. Our parents had stayed
in their room with the door closed until late the night before, and I knew
they'd argued. I made out he was determined to do something she dis-
agreed with. I heard their closet door slam a few times, and my mother
say, "This is the last time . . ." and, "You will not get him . . ." and, "This
is the craziest. . . ." Each time her voice started loud and quickly fell away
so I couldn't hear the last. Three different times my father walked out of
their bedroom and went out onto the front porch. (I heard his boots on the
boards.) He came back inside each time and their door closed, and they
began talking again. "So what choice do you see?" he said. And "You're
always timid in these things." And "That's not how you get caught, anyway." After a while they said only a few words to each other. Then that
tapered off. I left my room and went to the kitchen, where the light was
on, and drank a glass of water. A bead of orange light shone under their
door. When I climbed back in bed, Berner was there. She didn't say anything. She just lay breathing and chilled, her face to the wall that had my
college pennants on it. This was not something we'd done since we lived in

Great Falls—though we'd slept together in smaller houses when we were children. I wasn't comfortable with her in bed. But I knew she wouldn't have been there if it hadn't been important, and that she'd been listening the way I had. She smelled of cigarettes and hard candy, and all her clothes were on. We went to sleep after our parents stopped talking. Though in the morning when I woke up, both my fists were clenched and ached, and Berner was gone, and we didn't talk about it when I saw her again. It was as if it hadn't happened.

MY FATHER was generally in a good humor in the mornings. But that Monday morning he acted grave about something. My mother seemed to stay out of his way. She fixed our breakfast, and we all sat down and ate. Over his eggs, my father asked Berner and me what we thought we could do that would be useful to the Republic, which was a thing he said when he wanted to know what plans we had. I reminded him that the State Fair was starting that day, and I had my interest in the bee demonstration—which would be useful. He didn't comment on this and seemed to forget he'd asked. He didn't joke about anything or smile. His eyes were reddened. He didn't thank our mother for breakfast. He hadn't shaved, which he always did when he went to the base, and took care about. His unshaven skin had a gaunt bluish cast. What was wrong with him became the only issue at the table, but nobody asked. I saw our mother look at him irritably from behind her glasses. Her lips were tightened and hard, as if he'd behaved toward her in a way she didn't like.

It was also noticeable to me that our father wasn't wearing his new trousers or his black tooled boots or one of his arrow-pocket shirts, which was how he'd been dressing when he went to work at the farm and ranch sales company. Instead, he'd put on his old blue Air Force jumpsuit and a pair of paint-stained low-cut white tennis shoes, clothes he wore when he mowed the grass or watered. He'd scissored off the insignias when he'd taken his discharge, including the patch that said "PARSONS." He looked like someone, I thought, who didn't want to be recognized by anyone who knew him.

After breakfast there was even less talking. Berner went in her room and closed the door and played a record on her record player. My mother cleaned the kitchen, then went out on the front porch in the morning sun and drank tea and did her crossword book and read a novel for her class with the nuns. I followed our father around the house. He seemed to be going someplace, and I wanted to find out where and if I could go. He took his leather toiletries kit out of the bathroom cupboard and put various items in. He put socks and underwear into his old Air Force canvas bag while I stood in the bedroom door watching. We were a family who didn't travel unless we were moving to a new town. Staying put was a luxury, my father always said. His fondest wish was to live in one place like everybody else. A person was free to settle anywhere in our country, he believed. Where you were born meant little. That was the beauty of America, and wasn't true of those countries we'd liberated in the war, where life was confined and provincial. What I feared was that he and our mother had decided to go apart. His behavior seemed to me how things would be if that was happening. Silence. Tension. Anger. Though they'd never talked about going apart that I'd ever heard.

When I saw him zip up his blue bag (I'd seen him put his pistol in it—his big black .45 caliber he left the Air Force owning), I said:

"Where are you going?"

He looked up at me where he sat on the side of his bed. (Our parents slept in two beds.) It was hot in the house, the way it got in the morning. We didn't turn on the attic fan until afternoon. It was only nine. He smiled at me, as if he hadn't heard me, which happened sometimes. But the way he'd looked at breakfast—gaunt and sleepless—left his features, and his color came back.

"Are you a private detective on a case?" he said.

"Yes," I said, "I am." I didn't want to say, *Are you and Mother going to go apart?* I didn't want to hear that.

"I'm leaving on a business trip," he said and went on fiddling with his bag.

"Are you coming back?"

"Well, certainly," he said. "Why? Would you like to go with me?"

Our mother was suddenly beside me in the doorway, clutching her book. She set her hand on my shoulder and gripped it. She wasn't tall but could take a hard grip. "He's not going with you," she said. "I have uses for him here that'll benefit the country." She pushed me right out of the doorway and stepped into their bedroom and closed the door. I heard heated talk then, though they were whispering because they knew I was listening. "You can't . . . you can *not* under any circumstances . . ." she said. And he said, "Oh, for Christ fucking sake. We'll talk about it later." He rarely ever cursed, and neither did she. Berner did. She'd learned it from Rudy. It was shocking to hear him say that to our mother.

I thought our mother might open the door suddenly and be angry at me for listening, so I went back to my room and sat down in front of my green-and-white chess board. I felt calm behind the rows of white pieces established in their specific purposes, waiting to walk into battle at my command.

In a little while, my father went out the front door, carrying his canvas bag with the pistol inside, and got in his car. He never told me what the business was or even said good-bye. I suspected his business had nothing to do with selling farms and ranches, but with the Indian who'd been at our house. In any case, I knew it was important or he wouldn't be leaving in a rush. It felt to me that something was in our life now that had never been in it before.

10

WHAT MY FATHER DID DURING THE NEXT DAYS was drive around eastern Montana and western North Dakota (places he'd never been), searching for a bank he could rob. His plan was not to rob a bank right away but to choose a town and a bank, based on criteria he'd developed in his head, then go back to Great Falls, briefly re-enter family life, then come back and rob the chosen bank a couple of days later. This plan seemed less hasty and more thought out, more susceptible to recalculation and even abandonment—wiser, as a way to go about bank robbing. The opposite of that was how people's actions lurched off wrong and they landed in jail.

It's odd to imagine, of course: you pass a car on a lonely rural highway; you sit beside a man in a diner and share views with him; you wait behind a customer checking into a motel, a friendly man with a winning smile and twinkling hazel eyes, who's happy to fill you in on his life's story and wants you to like him—odd to think this man is cruising around with a loaded pistol, making up his mind about which bank he'll soon rob.

I think that even though my father was frightened by the Indians—and by what calamity Williams-Mouse had promised would befall us if the money wasn't forthcoming—by the time he'd driven the long way east into the vast, voided parts of Montana stretching all the way to North Dakota, had sized up banks and towns, thought about places to hide, noticed the number of state troopers and deputies he passed, determined how far from the state line a bank would be (being southern meant state borders signified something to him that they didn't mean to people in other places we'd lived)—by the time he'd done all that, the idea of a robbery had begun to seem if not reasonable, at least acceptable, and an idea that provoked surprisingly little worry. I judge this by how he acted when he got home, two days later, which was confident and ebullient, once again in high spirits—as if he'd had a large problem when he left but it had turned out to be the simplest thing in the world to solve. Which was typical of how he minimized his problems. I also judge his unburdened frame of mind by the fact that he gave some thought that I go with him to commit the robbery. Not that he reached the point at which a robbery was proposed to me. I only found it out later, in my mother's chronicle, though I heard through closed doors words actually spoken about it between them, but didn't fully understand: that in his view I could've been a persuasive accomplice. My mother (his other choice) would, he felt, be immediately recognizable because of her foreign appearance and small stature and because she was unfriendly to most people—a liability, he believed. He wanted robbing a bank to be congenial. (I'm sure wanting me to be his accomplice was part of what finally made her go herself—and do the most foreign thing she could ever do.)

I already knew from things he'd said that my father entertained longstanding thoughts about robbing a bank—although I never took any of it as serious. My mother's chronicle makes clear he never gave any specific thought to being caught—because he was too clever. He also felt that robbing a "national bank" was "a crime without any victims," since as long as a person made sure to steal less than $10,000 (he got much less than that), the federal government, he believed, would make sure none of the depositors lost their money. As I've said, he had a strong reliance on the government, going back to the New Deal days and the REA, extending through his years in the Air Force, where everything was taken care of because much was owed to him for his service. You would say now he was a life-long Democrat.

As for getting caught—once he'd seen what eastern Montana and the western Dakotas looked like (blank, empty, unsociable, poor)—he couldn't imagine anyone would ever notice him, especially if my mother wasn't there to stand out. He would be a friendly, inconspicuous man dressed unmemorably, driving an unmemorable car with a son. (He intended to steal North Dakota license plates so his Chevrolet wouldn't be noticeable either.) He knew he looked like no one who'd ever rob a bank. So he could rob one without even resorting to a mask or a disguise. He would do it quickly, then drive back into the baked, engulfing landscape and be back to Great Falls by evening. No one would be the wiser.

Which makes a kind of sense—to the right kind of person. The sheriff of Cascade County, where Great Falls is located, told the *Tribune*, later, after our parents were caught, that many people think Montana is an easy place to commit a robbery and not be caught—which is why so many robberies occurred there (something else my father didn't know). People think, the sheriff said, that once they commit the robbery they then become swallowed up by empty space, and no one notices them because there are so few people there to notice anything. The truth was, he said, a bank robber always stands out in Montana. After all, he's typically the only one who's committed that crime—which is why he's out there by himself. Whereas most everybody else knows fairly well that they haven't committed a crime. Plus, in my father's case, everyone would notice a friendly face because there were very few of those out there on the best of days.

MY MOTHER must've recognized everything clearly. When my father drove away Monday morning in his blue jumpsuit and carrying his

loaded pistol, and feeling so terrified people were going to murder us
that he had to rob a bank to get money, our mother immediately began
to act like our lives were in the grip of a great change. She instantly set
all three of us to cleaning our house—something she'd never paid much
attention to, since our houses were always rentals with plumbing and
gas seepage odors and were never clean when we arrived. She tied a red
kerchief on her head that bushed her hair out, put on an old pair of cotton
trousers she rolled the cuffs up on, found a pair of black rubber gloves
to save her fingernails, and began scrubbing the kitchen floor and the
bathroom tiles, sweeping out the closets and washing the windows, taking the dishes out of the cupboards and cleaning the shelves with Bab-O.
Berner and I were assigned to wash the floors and doors and woodwork
and closet corners and window moldings in our rooms with soap cakes
and rags, and to clean our window glass with vinegar—which turned
my hands dry and sour smelling. She told us to make a selection of our
clothes to give away to St. Vincent de Paul, and to pile these on the enclosed back porch beside my bicycle, to be taken away. I was dispatched
up the disappearing stairs to the attic—in case we'd forgotten things to
throw away up there. It was overheated and dark and smelled of mothballs and rot and was full of dust and soot, and I was conscious of rat-
tlesnakes and poisonous spiders and hornets nesting in the rafters, and
came down quickly without bringing anything with me.

When we asked why we were doing this cleaning, our mother said it
was because when our father came home from his business trip we would
possibly be leaving Great Falls and would have to turn the house back
over to Bargamian, the owner, who lived in Butte. He had our deposit,
which my mother wanted returned. (My father said Bargamian was "one
of her tribe." But our mother said he was Armenian, which was a race of
victims.)

She didn't say where we might be going. And since we'd heard our father say the same thing on Sunday morning, I believed it might be true—

and felt dread about school beginning in two weeks, and whether I'd ever be able to go there.

Several times in the next days while our father was gone, the phone rang and I would immediately answer it, thinking it was him. But again no one was there. Finally my mother answered it and said, "What is it you want? Who is this?" No one on the other end said anything, and then the line went dead.

At least four times in the next days, I happened to look out our front window and saw one of two vehicles slowly pass our house. One was the junker red Plymouth that Mouse had driven up in on Sunday. It wasn't Mouse who drove it this time, but another younger man, not necessarily an Indian. Other times it was a worse-looking car—a brown station wagon, broken down on its springs with a crumpled roof. Several people were in it, including a large woman who I thought *was* an Indian. Each time, the driver stared at our house but didn't stop. It didn't take a genius to understand that these Indians had something to do with why we might be leaving, and also why we had driven out to Box Elder in the days before (to get a closer look at things pertaining to the Indians), and why I felt dread, and possibly why our father was now finding us a new place to live.

The other remarkable thing that happened when my father was away was that Berner appeared out of her room wearing red lipstick, which my mother made humorous mention of by calling her a "femme fatale" who would soon be headed to New York or Paris to begin her famous acting career. This didn't faze Berner. She'd un-bunched her hair from the severe, middle-part, brushed-back way she'd kept it, and let it hang straight down toward her shoulders in a messy confusion I didn't like because it emphasized the flatness of her facial shape and made her freckles seem as if her face was dirty, instead of fresh, the way it always had been even with her pimples. When we were cleaning, I asked why she'd exaggerated her looks in this way. She frowned at me and said it was because "her boyfriend" (Rudy)—who we'd seen little of—had told her she needed to look more like a grown woman if he was going to be interested in her. She told me she was thinking about running away with him, but if I mentioned it to our mother she'd murder me. "It's driving me crazy to be here," she said and turned her mouth down. This shocked me, because it had never occurred to me that life with our parents could be intolerable, or that running away could be an option. I didn't think either was true for me.

The other thing that went on while Berner and I cleaned the house and our father was driving crazily around the wilds of Montana and North Dakota deciding which bank to rob, was that our mother entered a new, strange state of mind. Scrubbing and airing out the house was certainly one thing. But she also, in my hearing, made several more telephone calls to her parents in Tacoma, not asking them to let her come home, but to provide a place for Berner and me to go live. She spoke to them in the most natural, affectionate voice, as if she and they saw each other once a month instead of never in nearly sixteen years. They would accept Berner, I understood them to say, but not me. A boy was too much. It was just one more thing, however, that made Berner believe she would have to run away—facing a life with two stern, suspicious, uncomprehending old Poles she didn't know and who possibly wouldn't like her, but who, as though by accident, happened to be her grandparents.

THE SPECIFIC TRAIN of events by which our mother saw to my welfare and saw to it I didn't fall into the hands of the State of Montana, I'll get to eventually, since it's the important part for me. But for those two days, when we were scouring the house before my father came back on Wednesday night with a bank selected, my mother's state of mind remains the subject of greatest interest—even after all these years she's been gone.

Anyone might think a woman whose husband was possibly losing his mind (or at least part of it), and who was preparing to rob a bank, who'd led his family almost to ruin, who considered it a novel idea to involve his only son in the robbery, who was threatening jail and disaster and the dissolution of everything the two of them understood about life (and a woman who was already thinking of leaving the same man, anyway), you'd think this woman would be desperate for an opportunity to get away, or to involve the authorities to save herself and her children, or would find an iron resolve, would hold her ground, and let nothing go forward and thereby preserve her family by the force of her will. (My mother, as small and disaffected as she was, seemed to have a strong will, even if that turned out not to be true.) But that isn't how our mother behaved.

Once the house was as spotless as it would ever get, and once she'd made the calls to her parents and whatever anger toward our father had subsided (because he was gone), she became suddenly—*not* in soaring spirits, because she was never in soaring spirits, but—unexpectedly tranquil. Which was also not usual. It was as if she felt relieved—for the first time in recent weeks or longer. As if something important had been decided and assigned to its proper place. She laughed with us, teased Berner about becoming a famous movie star, and me becoming a college professor or a chess champion or a bee expert. She expressed views on many different things in the world—things I didn't know she was aware of and hadn't discussed with us. Senator Kennedy—who she was not impressed by. The earthquake in Morocco. The Cuban revolution—information she must've gotten from the radio, the way I had. She watched TV with us— *Douglas Edwards, Restless Gun, Trackdown* (shows I watched). She made jokes about the soap operas and other shows that were on.

Berner and I didn't talk to her much during these days. We were both participating with her in an awkward, self-conscious manner that didn't cause us to align against our father, but that respected an unexpressed division that now existed between them that had partly caused him to leave on a "business trip" without saying such things as when he'd be back. (I actually wondered several times, as my fantasy, if he'd gone away to rob a bank.) There didn't seem to be a way for me to start a conversation about this division—even with my sister—without opening all of it up. So we simply cleaned the house, ate our meals, watched the two channels on TV. I read my chess book, plotted out unworkable opening strategies, looked at beekeeping catalogs, and longed for school to start. Berner, as usual, stayed in her room, listened to her radio, tried on cosmetics, shaped and reshaped her hair, used the long cord to talk privately on the telephone to Rudy, and began (I'm sure) to plot her escape, from which she'd never come back, since very soon there would be nothing to come back to. If our mother, in that short time, expressed a change in how she herself saw the whole world, it would've been a change that had been happening for years, and had only suddenly become clear in those two days when our father was away.

I'VE ALWAYS BELIEVED that how our mother looked must've played a part in the way she changed and became tranquil while we waited for my father to come home and take life where it would go. How she looked— her size (the same height as Shirley Temple when she was fifteen), her appearance (rarely smiling, bespectacled, her studious Jewish foreignness), her visible disposition (skeptical, sharp-witted, self-defending, frequently distant)—had always seemed to be involved in everything she thought or said, as if her appearance created her whole self. This may be true of anyone. But everything about her distinguished her in any of the places our family ever lived—which wouldn't have been true in Poland or Israel or even New York or Chicago, where plenty of people looked and acted like her. Nothing about her ever made her less visible or likelier to fit in. And while I couldn't have stated it then, I took it as a given that all things about her (what she told us, what she advised, what she disliked, the things she championed) owed their existence only to that person she was—and not to what others thought of her. Not to the community. Not even to common sense. She never wrote this in her chronicle, but because of how she was, and looked, everything must've been a trial for her: driving to teach school at Fort Shaw; the moving and the houses; the unacceptable towns; my father's jokey, dumbbell Air Force associates with their stupid schemes to forge ahead of the pack; having no friends. As I said, she possessed what she for a time believed was a strong will. And that will must've never let her think anything but that, given how separate she was from all that surrounded her (except Berner and me, whom she loved), most of familiar life was worthy only of her disdain. Familiarity, fitting in—because it wasn't available—weren't worth her respect. Which is another way of explaining why she didn't want us to assimilate.

Why she felt tranquil then (maybe she only felt confirmed)—why she joked with us and teased Berner about her future as an actress, and laughed to say I would be a college professor, and watched TV with us, and talked about *The Secret Storm* and *As the World Turns*, and how true they were to life—may just have meant that given how life had cast her apart, what she'd realized was that she endured not a burden, but in fact possessed a great, untapped, years-suppressed longing for change. And that with my father going crazy, and preparing to rob a bank (which she knew about), she may have experienced not desperation or terror or greater alienation (which would've been conventional). But *freedom*. From all the forces that oppressed her. She may have concluded that this freed feeling came directly from the very qualities that isolated her, and that they weren't a torment but her strength. That would've been characteristic of her and of her skeptical state of mind. This may have made her feel better than she had in a long time. It is strange that she would. But she was strange.

Which doesn't explain why she didn't bundle Berner and me onto a train to Tacoma (or Chicago, or Atlanta, or New Orleans), and didn't let our father come home to an empty house, and have that be what brought him to his senses—if he had any. And it doesn't explain why, when my father did come home the next day, with his bank picked out and a great humming ebullience for getting going, she decided not to leave then and there, or talk him out of it, or go to the police, or draw a line in the sand, but instead became his accomplice and threw her life away when he threw his. When you think hard on why two reasonably intelligent people decide to rob a bank, and why they remained together after love had begun to evaporate and blow away, there are always reasons like these, reasons that in the light of a later day don't make any sense at all and have to be invented.

11

THE LONGER I DELAY CHARACTERIZING MY FATHER as a born criminal, the more accurate this story will be. He became one, it's true. But I'm not sure at what point in the chain of events he or anyone or the world would've known it. *Intention* to be a criminal must weigh in these things. And a case can be made that he never had clear intention before he robbed the Agricultural National Bank in Creekmore, North Dakota. Possibly he lacked the intention even immediately afterward—and didn't have it until it dawned on him what might happen to him as a result. To Bev Parsons, in the state of mind he'd descended to, there was something so necessary and also unexceptional about the undertaking that there couldn't have been any grounds for objecting—which says something not good about him, I know. And since, again, he didn't consider himself the type of person to commit an armed robbery, actually committing one didn't immediately change his opinion of himself, and possibly didn't right up to the moment detectives came to our house, walked around the living room discussing "a trip to North Dakota," and then told both our parents, almost casually, they would have to have handcuffs put on and go to jail. This may be how many criminals who're new to their work think about their actions and themselves.

* * *

BUT HOW do people act when they're about to climb in their car and drive off to rob a bank? If you'd driven past our house on Wednesday night, noticed our lights burning, seen through the windows my mother in the kitchen cooking dinner, seen the neighbors' lights on, my father fresh out of the shower, sitting on the front porch steps lacing on his shoes in the cool, humming twilight, the moon high and clear, cars moving beyond the park, his hair wet, smelling of Old Spice and talcum, rehearsing to Berner and me stories of what he'd seen on his "business trip"—the prairie like a great inland sea ("like the Gulf of Mexico"), the northern lights, no mountains, but an abundance of wild animals, the two of us sitting rapt, blissful—would you have thought that there was a man getting ready to commit an armed robbery? No, you wouldn't. Though admittedly I'm intrigued by how ordinary behavior exists so close beside its opposite.

All the signs, the warnings we think we know about disaster are mostly wrong. A child's view of them is just as likely to be as good as an adult's. And might be better. Years ago, I knew a man who hanged himself—a stockbroker with many, many woes and mental problems and a feeling of hopelessness that nothing good could reach. But in the week that led to his terrible moment, which he'd planned to the last detail—his wife all arranged to find him when she came home from a Florida vacation with her girlfriends—the people who knew him said he seemed to have moved the weight of the world off his shoulders, and to be in the most high-flying spirits. He laughed, told jokes, teased people, made plans in a way he hadn't in anyone's recent memory. They believed he'd turned a corner, had figured life out, found a path back to the old self—the person they remembered happily and were excited to have back with them. And then that: swinging from the chandelier in the foyer of the house he'd built only two years previous and claimed to love. It's a mystery how we are. A mystery.

WHEN MY FATHER got home Wednesday night at about eight he was in a buoyant humor. You would've thought he'd cinched the best business deal in the world, discovered a gold mine or an oil well or won a lottery. He still had on his Air Force jumpsuit and his grass-stained tennis shoes and hadn't shaved. He'd brought back his blue bag that had had his gun secretly in it. (I'd gone into his sock drawer during my house-cleaning assignments to satisfy myself that I'd seen what I'd seen. It wasn't there. He'd had it with him.)

For a little while after he arrived he strode around our house, talking— talking to our mother in the kitchen, talking to Berner and me, sometimes just talking to himself. He was loose-limbed and relaxed and looked into all the rooms, as if he'd noticed how clean they were. His speaking voice was confident and sounded to me more southern than usual, which was the way he talked when he felt unguarded, or when he told a joke or had a drink. The changing effects of modern life were on his mind: there was a satellite in the sky now that predicted the weather and looked like a star at night. He thought this could be a boon to aeronautical navigation. In Brazil the government had constructed a completely new city right out of the jungle and moved thousands of people there. This would solve racial problems, he thought. We could all buy a new kidney now when our old ones wore out—which was self-evidently good. He'd heard this news on a Canadian radio station in his car. It'd come in clearly because he'd been close to the border during his drive.

After his shower, as I said, he accompanied Berner and me out onto the front porch at dusk and told us what the prairie looked like—an ocean. We looked up for the satellite circling in the sky, and he said he believed he saw it, though we didn't. He talked about his growing-up years in the state of Alabama and all the funny things people said and how colorful it was compared to Montana—where people lacked a happy sense of humor and thought being hard-bit and unfriendly were virtues. He asked us both again—because he often asked this—if we felt like we were Alabamians. We both again said we didn't. He asked me where I felt like I was from. I told him Great Falls. Berner first said nowhere, then she said she was from Mars, and we all laughed. He talked for a while about having dreamed of being a pilot but only qualifying as a bombardier and how disappointed he'd been, but that disappointments were educational and sometimes reversed outcomes were better. He talked about the terrible errors people had made in learning to drop bombs, and what a heavy responsibility it was. Once or twice our mother came outside from the kitchen. He'd brought home two bottles of Schlitz beer, and they'd each drunk one—which they didn't regularly do. It made them playful, which was how our mother'd become with us while he was gone. She'd put on a pair of white pedal pushers that revealed her thin ankles, some flat cotton shoes, and a pretty green blouse—clothes we didn't know she owned. She looked like a young girl and smiled more than she normally would've and held her beer bottle by its neck and drank it in small swallows. She acted affectionately toward our father and laughed and shook her head at silly things he said. A couple of times she patted him on the shoulder and said he was a card. (As I said, she was a good listener.) Though he didn't seem any different to me. He was a man in a good humor most of the time.

Berner did tell him when we were still on the porch and cicadas had started working in the trees, that strange people had been driving past our house and there'd been phone calls where no one talked. The people who'd driven past, she believed, were Indians. My father just said, "Oh, those boys are all right. Don't worry about them. They don't understand the white man's ways. They're fine, though."

I asked him about the business he'd been prospecting after. He said that was all working out perfectly, but he needed to go back soon to settle things, and maybe I'd go with him this time. We could all go. I asked if what he'd said on Sunday was true—that we might be moving to another town. I was still fretting about school, the chess club, etc., the things I had a stake in. He smiled and said no, we wouldn't be moving. It was time for our family to settle down and Berner and I should make some friends and live like respectable citizens. He looked forward to success at

his job selling ranch property. He'd teach me the tricks of that as soon as
he learned them, though I didn't see how this squared with a new business opportunity. I thought about asking him why he'd taken his pistol
on a business trip. But I didn't because I didn't think he'd tell me the real
reasons. Thinking about it now, none of what he was saying seemed the
least bit true to me. I just knew I was supposed to believe it. Children get
as good at pretending as adults.

When we ate dinner it was after ten thirty. I was sleepy and not hungry anymore. The telephone rang two more times while we were at the
table. One time my father answered and laughed heartily and said he'd call
whoever it was later. The other time he stood and listened as if someone
was talking seriously to him. When he came back he said, "Nothing, that
was nothing. Just a follow-up."

At the table our mother asked him if he'd noticed anything different about Berner. He certainly had, he said. Her hair looked better and
he liked it. She pointed out that Berner was wearing lipstick—which she
was, again—and if we didn't watch out she'd run away to Hollywood or
France. My father said Berner could go up to the Sisters of Providence
with our mother and arrange to become a nun with a vow of chastity—
which made my mother laugh, but not Berner. I remember that night, now,
as the best, most natural time our family had that summer—or any time.
Just for a moment, I saw how life could go forward on a steadier, more
reliable course. The two of them were happy and comfortable with each
other. My father appreciated the way my mother behaved toward him. He
paid her compliments about her clothes and her appearance and her mood.
It was as if they'd discovered something that had once been there but had
gotten hidden or misunderstood or forgotten over time, and they were
charmed by it once more, and by one another. Which seems only right and
expectable for married people. They caught a glimpse of the person they
fell in love with, and who sustained life. For some, that vision must never
dim—as is true of me. But it was odd that our parents should catch their

glimpse, and have frustration, anxiety and worry pass away like clouds dispersing after a storm, refind their best selves, but for that glimpse to happen just before leading our family to ruin.

I WILL SAY THIS about our father. All during that night when we were a family, laughing, joking, eating—ignoring what was hanging over us— his features had changed again. When he'd left home two days before, he'd looked fleshy and exhausted. His features had been loose and indistinct and washed out—as if his every step was reluctant and unpracticed. But when he came back that night and strode around the house declaring on what interested him—satellites, South American politics, organ transplants, how all our lives could be better—his features looked sharpened and chiseled. In the grainy light above our supper table, he'd become intent and precise-looking. Our father had small hazel eyes—light brown disks you wouldn't pay attention to. They would've seemed weak eyes because he squinted when he smiled. And since his face was big boned, his eyes were often lost in the overall effect. However, at our dinner table his face now seemed to be *about* his eyes, as if they saw a world they hadn't before. They gleamed. When he looked at me with these eyes, I at first felt good and positive. But eventually I became uncomfortable. It was as if he was reappraising everything, as when he'd roamed around the rooms in our house two hours before and seemed to be seeing them for the first time, and was taking a new interest in them. It had made the house feel foreign to me, as if he was planning a use for it that it hadn't had. His eyes made me feel the same way.

During all these years I've thought about his eyes, and how they became so different. And since so much was about to change because of him, I've thought possibly that a long-suppressed potential in him had suddenly worked itself into visibility on his face. He was becoming who and what he was always supposed to be. He'd simply had to wear down through the other layers to who he really was. I've seen this phenomenon in the faces of other men—homeless men, men sprawled on the pavement in front of bars or in public parks or bus depots, or lined up outside the doors of missions, waiting to get in out of a long winter. In their faces—plenty of them were handsome, but ruined—I've seen the remnants of who they almost succeeded in being but failed to be, before becoming themselves. It's a theory of destiny and character I don't like or want to believe in. But it's there in me like a hard understory. I don't, in fact, ever see such a ruined man without saying silently to myself: *There's my father. My father is that man. I used to know him.*

12

THINGS YOU DID. THINGS YOU NEVER DID. THINGS you dreamed. After a long time they run together.

After Berner and I had gone to bed on the Wednesday night my father returned, I listened to my parents in the kitchen, talking, laughing, washing dishes. The noise of water running. The clatter of plates and silverware. A cabinet opening and clicking closed. Their softened voices.

"Nobody would ever think . . ." my father said, then I couldn't hear the rest.

"Do you want to make a family outing out of it?" my mother said. The water went on, then off. It was her more sarcastic voice.

"Nobody would ever think," he said again. Then my name. "Dell."

"You're not. No," she said.

"Okay." Dried plates being stacked.

"So, are you happy?" Too loud for me not to hear.

"What's happy got to do with it?"

"Everything. Absolutely."

And this was my dream: running out in my pajamas into the kitchen light, where they were standing, looking at me. My tall father—his small eyes still gleaming. My tiny mother in her white pedal pushers and pretty green blouse with green buttons. A face of grave concern. "I'm going," I say. Fists clenched. Face damp. Heart pounding. My parents begin to recede in my vision, as when you're sick and fever shrinks the world and distance lengthens. My parents grew smaller and smaller until I was in the harshly lit kitchen alone, and they were at the vanishing point, just about to disappear.

13

I SLEPT LATE ON THURSDAY, FROM HAVING BEEN UP and hearing them move around in the night. Our mother came in my room at eight—her glasses, her face soft and peering, close to my face, her small cool hand touching my bare shoulder. Her breath smelled sweet with Ipana and sour with tea. The door to my room stood open. Our father's figure passed by it. He was wearing blue jeans and a plain white shirt and his Acmes.

"Your sister's had breakfast. There's Cream of Wheat for you." Her eyes were focused on my face, as if she saw something unexpected there. "We have to go away for a day. We'll be back tomorrow. It'll be a good experience for you two to look after things." Her face was calm. She'd made her mind up on something.

Our father stopped in the doorway, his hair combed and shiny. He was shaved. My room smelled like his talcum. He was very tall in the empty door space.

"You and your sister don't answer the phone," he said. "And don't go anywhere. We'll be back tomorrow evening. This'll be good experience for you."

"Where're you going?" I gazed up at the sunlight behind him in the living room, my eyes burning from too little sleep.

"I have some more business. I mentioned it," he said. "I need your mother's opinion." He was talking softly, but I could see a vein in his forehead was prominent.

She looked at him—as if she hadn't heard this before. She was kneeling beside my bed, her fingers lightly on my chest. "That's right," she said.

"Can we go with you?" I said.

"We'll take you next time," he said.

My dream passed in my mind. I'm going. Shouting. Fists clenched.

"Look after your sister." He smiled knowingly. "She's under Colonel Parsons' jurisdiction here." He made a joke out of things if he could.

"Are you going to shoot somebody?"

"Oh my God," my mother said.

My father's large mouth, which had been smiling, fell open. He squinted—as if a glaring light had been switched on. "Why would you say that?"

"He knows," my mother said. She stood beside my bed and stared down at me, as if I was to blame for something. I didn't know anything.

"What do you think you know, Dell?" My father's smile resumed its activity across his face. He seemed understanding.

"You took your pistol last time."

He took a step forward into my room. "Oh. People carry guns out here. That's common. It's the Wild West. You don't ever shoot anybody."

My mother was looking at me steadily. Her small eyes were intent behind her spectacles, as if she was studying me for some sign. She was sweating under her blouse—I smelled it. It was already hot in the house.

"Are you afraid?" she asked.

"No," I said.

"He's not afraid," my father said, and stepped out of the doorway and looked toward the clock in the kitchen. "We need to go." He disappeared into the hall.

My mother continued to stare at me, as if I'd become a person she didn't completely know.

"Think of some wonderful place you'd like to go, why don't you?" she said. "I'll take you there. You and Berner."

The front screen slapped shut. "He's under Colonel Parsons' jurisdiction here," I heard him say. He was talking to Berner on the porch.

"Moscow," I said. I'd read in *Chess Master* that great players came from Russia. Mikhail Tal—who was famous for his sacrificing style and terrible stare. Alexander Alekhine—noted for his aggressiveness. I'd looked Moscow up in the *Merriam-Webster*, and then in the *World Book*, and finally on the globe on the dresser in my room. I didn't know what the Soviet Union was, or why it was different from Russia. Lenin, who my father said played chess, had played a part in it. And Stalin. Men he despised. He said Stalin had put Roosevelt in the grave the same as if he'd shot him.

"Moscow!" my mother said. "My poor father would have a heart attack. I was thinking of Seattle."

The Chevrolet horn honked in the street. I heard the screen door close again. Berner was coming back inside, ready to take care of me. "His pot's boiling over," I heard her say. My mother leaned forward, kissed me quickly on my forehead. "We can talk about it when I get back," she said. Then she left.

WHEN WE LIVED in Mississippi, in Biloxi—which was in 1955, when I was eleven—my father worked at the base there and stayed home on the weekends, the way he did in Great Falls. He liked Mississippi. It was close to where he'd grown up, and he liked the Gulf of Mexico. If he'd left the Air Force then and there, instead of when he did, things would've worked out better for him and for our mother. They could've gotten divorced and gone their separate ways. Children can make their adjustments if their parents love them. And ours did.

My father often took me to the movies on Saturday mornings when there was something he wanted to see or had nothing else to do. There was an air-cooled theater called the Trixy, which was on the downtown main street that ended at the Gulf. The movies started at ten and lasted straight until four, with shorts and cartoons and features running continuously, all for a single admission, which was fifty cents. We would sit through everything, eating candy and popcorn and drinking Dr Peppers, enjoying Tarzan or Jungle Jim and Johnny McShane and Hopalong Cassidy, plus the Stooges and Laurel and Hardy and newsreels and old war footage, which my father liked. We'd emerge at four out of the cool, back into the hot, salty, breathless Gulf coast afternoon, sun-blind and queasy and speechless from wasting the day with nothing to show for it.

On one such morning, we were there in the dark side-by-side, and onto the screen had come a newsreel from the 1930s, relating to the criminals Clyde Barrow and Bonnie Parker, who'd terrorized (the announcer said) several states of the Southwest, robbing and killing and making an infamous name until they were killed in an ambush on a country road in Louisiana, by a posse of deputies who shot them from the bushes and brought their careers to an end. They were only in their twenties.

Later, when my father and I walked out into the steamy, sun-shot afternoon—it was June—our eyes hurting, our heads dull, we found that someone (the Trixy's operators) had parked a long flatbed truck in front of the theater. On the truck bed was an old gray Ford four-door from the '30s, and all over it were shiny holes, and its windows were busted out, its doors and hood perforated, its tires deflated. Up beside the car wheel was a painted sign that read: ACTUAL BONNIE & CLYDE DEATH CAR—WILL PAY $10,000 IF YOU PROVE IT'S NOT. The proprietors had placed a set of wooden steps up to the car, and the theater customers were invited to pay fifty cents to climb up and inspect it, as if Bonnie and Clyde were still inside dead, and everyone should see them.

My father stood on the hot hard concrete, peering up at the car and the customers—kids and grown-ups, women and men—filing past, gawking, making jokes and machine-gun noises and laughing. He didn't intend to pay. He said the car was a fakeroo, or it would never be there. The world didn't work that way. Plus it was fresh painted, and the bullet holes didn't look real. He'd seen bullet holes on plenty of airplanes, and they were bigger, more jagged. Not that this would stop anybody from throwing their money away.

But when we'd stood on the sidewalk, looking up at the car for a few minutes, he said, "Would you become a bank robber, Dell? It'd be exciting. Wouldn't that surprise your mother?"

"I wouldn't," I said, looking speculatingly up at the gleaming holes and all the country yokels peeping in the car windows and yowling and grinning.

"Are you sure?" he said. "I could give it a try. I'd be smarter than these two, though. You don't use your noggin, you end up a piece of Swiss cheese. Your mother'd take this wrong, of course. You don't need to relate it to her." He pulled me closer to him. His shirt smelled starchy in the sunlight. We walked on then into the afternoon.

I never told my mother, and never even thought of it until long after the day my sister and I stood on the front porch and watched our parents drive away to rob a bank. I didn't put those things together then, though later I did. It was a thing he'd always wanted to do. Some people want to be bank presidents. Other people want to rob banks.

14

W HAT I KNOW OF THE ACTUAL BANK ROBBERY
itself I mostly know from my mother's chronicle, and
from issues of the *Great Falls Tribune,* which I've already said took the view that the event was a comic, cautionary tale it was
the newspaper's duty to bring before the public eye. Though I have also
constructed the robbery in my head—fascinated that it should've been our
parents who committed it, so ridiculous and inexplicable as to make the
reportable facts inadequate as an explanation.

CONCEIVABLY MANY OF US think of robbing a bank the same way we
lie in bed at night and dedicatedly plot to murder our life-long enemy;
fitting together complicated parts of a plan, adjusting the details, reach-
ing back to reconcile earlier calculations with late-occurring possibilities
for being caught. Eventually, we find ourselves facing the one unerasable
problem in logic that our cleverness can't work out all the way. After
which we conclude that though it's satisfying to think we could murder
our enemy in ambush (since it needs to be done), only a deranged or
suicidal person would carry out such a plan. That is because the world is
set against such acts. And in any case we're amateurs at the business of
scheming and plotting and murdering, and don't have the concentration

needed to defeat what the world is so set against. At which point we forget about our plan and go to sleep.

To succeed, my parents would've had to realize their car would be recognized immediately. My father's blue jumpsuit would be identified as Air Force issue—even minus its insignias. The unfaded mark of previous captain's bars would be easily noticed. My father's good looks and obliging southern accent and manners would be memorable to everyone in a North Dakota bank. The fact that he had mentioned his wish to rob a bank to several people at the base in Great Falls would be recollected (though he intended it as a joke). Our parents would've also had to realize that contrary to my father's intuition, people who rob banks don't blend into the population, but stand out because they've become something or someone different from who they were and from everybody else—even if they don't realize it. For all these reasons, discovering who robbed a bank quickly begins not to be difficult at all.

But for my parents, who drove away on Thursday morning completely innocent, with only a trivial debt owed to a small group of ineffectual Indians—something they could've ironed out successfully any number of ways—this kind of thinking didn't occur. Although most certainly it *did* occur to them, even as soon as they were driving home to Great Falls the next day—as felons; any thoughts of getting away with what they'd done rising away from them into the flat summer sky.

15

WHAT THEY DID WAS DRIVE EAST ON HIGHWAY 200, through the towns of Lewistown and Winnett, into the Musselshell drainage toward Jordan, Circle and Sidney, through the summer-hard, dry-grass table-land that stretches from the mountains to Minnesota. They were where they knew no one and nothing, other than what my father had discovered on his "business trip," which probably seemed like a great deal in his mind, and helped create the sensation they were invisible.

IN HIS TWO DAYS of incessant driving, criss-crossing the border of North Dakota, he'd come to the town of Creekmore (population 600 then), and the North Dakota Agricultural National Bank. He'd had lunch in a café across Main Street. No one talked to him or seemed to pay attention to his jumpsuit. (There was an air base in Minot, not far away.) This made him believe people would be stunned into memoryless-ness if, dressed in that way, he walked into the bank the second it opened, brandished his .45, took what was in the tellers' drawers and whatever other money was lying around loose—made no effort to go in the vault, unless it happened to be standing open with money in view, and he could steal it easily—put it all into his canvas bag and be gone. In less than three minutes he could be driving west toward the Montana border, and back into fast-closing insignificance. My mother would be waiting but would not exit the car because of being so distinctive looking. She would have the motor idling the whole time he was inside doing the robbery, and would drive them away. Yes, it was a bold plan. But my father believed it was simple enough to work, and he had used his noggin to figure it out. It would be an advantage that he'd never been in the bank before. Most bank thieves would've felt the need to "case" the scene, and by doing so would implant unconscious memories in anyone's mind who saw them later—though my father didn't think anyone would see him later. What few people there'd be in the tiny Agricultural National at that early hour would be mesmerized by the sudden appearance of his menacing .45 and pay no attention whatsoever to him or what he might look like. That was all the gun was for—a distraction. He could get away with at least five or six or even the limit of ten thousand dollars. That was using his noggin, too.

The complicated part of his plan involved avoiding detection once the robbery was finished. Wide-open spaces would be his chief ally. But to improve on that advantage, he'd driven on the previous Tuesday down to the Montana town of Wibaux, across the border and south from Creekmore. In his capacity as a land agent, he'd made inquiries at the Wibaux Bank and at an insurance office and at a bar about ranches in the area that might be for sale, and where the owners had already departed, and about how he could contact them on behalf of a customer in Great Falls. His view was that the territory was dotted with such empty places. No one paid any attention to them. No one else would be visible out there, horizon line to horizon line.

Armed with information from the town merchants, and a section map, he'd driven to several ranch sites until he found one that was clearly in disuse, where vehicles and equipment were in evidence but no one was present. He drove into the ranch yard, got out, and knocked on the door. He peered in windows to be sure no one was home. He intended to start one of the farm trucks without a key, but found the key was in the one he chose and that it started. He looked to see if a shed could be opened and if the house itself could be easily entered, and found both were possible.

His plan was that he and our mother would drive to this isolated ranch on Thursday night. They'd sleep in the car or in an outbuilding, or even in the house—without turning on any lights. They'd hide the Bel Air in one of the outbuildings. He would affix onto one of the farm trucks the North Dakota plates he'd stolen while he was in Creekmore and was carrying in his Air Force bag with his pistol and a cap (his only disguise). This ranch vehicle—a Ford truck—the two of them would drive the next morning the short distance across the North Dakota border to Creekmore. My mother would park it on the street near the front of the Agricultural Bank just at opening time. My father would exit the truck, walk in the bank, rob it, leave and get back in the truck. She would then drive back across the border to the Wibaux ranch where the Chevrolet was waiting. They would change clothes, throw the gun, the cap, the blue bag and the North Dakota plates—everything but the money—into the farm pond or into some creek, or down a well, then drive on to Great Falls, like two people who'd been on an outing but were now headed home. Berner and I would be there waiting for them.

My father elaborated this plan to my mother during their drive east on Thursday, through Lewistown, toward North Dakota. She had immediately disapproved. She knew nothing about robbing banks; but she was again a careful listener and was deliberate and believed my father's plan was too complicated and contained many opportunities to go wrong. For some reason she was committed to robbing a bank—the only truly reliable explanation for which is the simplest one: people do rob banks. If this seems illogical, then you are still judging events from the point of view of someone who's *not* robbing a bank and never would because he knows it's crazy.

What, my mother said, if the people who owned the ranch came home and found the two of them asleep in the car or in the house? (He had an answer there: they'd grown sleepy and gotten off the road to be safe. No one would prosecute them. They wouldn't have robbed a bank yet. They could go home.) But what if the old truck broke down halfway out of Creekmore? (For this he lacked an answer.) And what if someone was waiting when they got back to reclaim the Chevrolet? (He assumed that if the ranch was vacant when he found it, it would be vacant until he had no more use for it—which was his mind's habit.)

His whole idea, my mother said, had too many moving parts. Too many places where it could break down. Simpler was better. She cited the over-elaborated structure of the scheme that had landed him in the middle between the Indians and Digby. He wasn't cautious enough, wasn't prudent, had seen too many gangster movies in Podunk, Alabama. She had never seen even one, didn't know about the Bonnie and Clyde car and what he'd told me about a taste for holdups. But she was now engaged.

A better plan—so simple—was to change the plates on their Chevrolet to North Dakota ones, drive it into Creekmore at the early hour he'd proposed, park *behind* the bank, not in front in full view; go in the bank, rob it, walk out and around the building, get in the car where she'd be waiting, lie down in the back seat, or even get in the trunk, after which she'd drive away like she'd driven in. Nothing rushed. Everything would look natural. This plan took advantage of people's human habit of finding most things to be unremarkable as long as they themselves weren't involved. This would include everybody on the street at nine o'clock on Friday morning in Creekmore, North Dakota—a town where nothing but unremarkable things took place.

My mother's chronicle doesn't say anything about arguments my father put forward against her simpler plan. It was a long drive—four hundred miles. They stopped for lunch, got gas in Winnett, had all those hours together in the car, plenty of time to express their views in full. My mother only says eventually she "persuaded him" that the best idea was to stay in the town of Glendive, Montana, to make themselves visible but un-exceptional where they stayed and where they ate dinner. The next morn-ing they would get up, drive the sixty miles to Creekmore, do what they planned to do, then drive straight home to my sister and me. She does say he should've worn a mask. But he refused because no one knew him in the town, and his own face was already a mask. A handsome mask.

IN HINDSIGHT, it is a cruel irony that my mother's plan prevailed. For all its potentially unsound points, my father's plan might've worked better than hers. He'd spent some time (possibly years) devising and deliberat-ing it, whereas her self-assured plan didn't get them caught immediately but got them caught just the same. The Bel Air was remembered from the time my father had lunch in the Town Diner in Creekmore the previous Tuesday. It was also double recognized when they'd driven it into town on Friday morning, parked behind the bank, then driven out of town after the robbery. It was made mental note of by both the room clerk at the Yel-lowstone Motel in Glendive and by the sheriff of Dawson County, who noticed the Great Falls plates and the sticker from the BX store on the windshield. There was also my father's amusing Dixie accent and Sunday-dinner manners, his Air Force jumpsuit, and the service-issue .45. The bank guard even noticed the tiny, frayed pinholes on the jumpsuit shoul-ders. He'd been an Air Force staff sergeant and guessed accurately that the holes and the fabric discoloration had been left by captain's bars. My par-ents simply did not understand life in small prairie towns, where everyone notices everything. Though none of these last matters might've connected to them directly—at home by then, with us in Great Falls—without the Chevrolet being identified by people nobody thought would be noticing things or putting things together with other things they didn't even know they'd noticed but surprisingly had. As it turned out, my father wasn't all that memorable to anyone in Creekmore—until it was time to testify against him, when he became very memorable.

I have always wondered what they talked about—our mother and father—in the car together on their drive across the middle of Montana, the
pistol in the satchel, speeding toward their fate with my sister's and mine
trailing not far behind them. I've always assumed it was different from
what you'd think—as many things turn out to be. In my (you could call
it a) fantasy, they didn't argue, didn't seethe or dread or loathe. He didn't
try to persuade her to commit robbery. (He didn't have to.) She didn't
rehearse the reasons a robbery wouldn't be necessary. (That was already
settled.) He thought the money would set life up right, make him flush,
keep us all together, let us settle into Great Falls and be a normal family. (He *did* say that.) Or else he'd concluded what a failure he was, what
a paltry mess he'd made of things, and burned to accomplish something
impressive (more than selling ranches or cars or stealing cows), something
that would either put him and us all on easy street, or blow easy street to
smithereens so nothing would ever be the way it had been again. Both
or either could be true, given his mercurial, imprudent character. But it's
clear he wanted more than any $2,000 to pay off Indians, since he could've
settled that without robbing a bank. The *more*—whatever it was—was
what the robbery was about for him.

For our mother, of course, it was different. She wasn't an obvious risk
taker and had good sense. She was brought up to know things, to appreciate fine discriminations and could view an alternate future that was still
realizable even at thirty-four. But because she'd agreed to do it—go with
him, devise her simpler plan, sit in the car, wait, drive them away once
the robbery was accomplished, and was even in a good humor the night
before—it has to be accepted she did it, if not willingly, at least knowingly,
with an idea about how things could be better for her once the robbery was
over.

In her best brain, she would've seen it as a mistake; that they could've
left the house and their few possessions right where they lay, and in the
middle of the night driven away. Nothing was special about Great Falls

now that he wasn't in the Air Force. They both hated accumulation and possessed little but the Chevrolet and two children. Her brain simply must not have tracked all the way out that far. Because if her brain had, the uncertainty would've been forbidding.

My guess is—fifty years gone past now—that with her newfound sense of freedom and relief, unexpectedly encountered while Bev was roaming the Dakota badlands, trying to pick a bank to rob, Neeva came to the remarkably mistaken conclusion that robbing a bank was a risk that would facilitate things she wanted. It was a miscalculation not very different from the one that had swayed her to marry Bev Parsons in the first place—giving up on the life she could've had, to lead what might've seemed a more adventurous and unexpected one, but wasn't. With half the money from a robbery she wouldn't *have* to go back to her miscalculated life—which had become a reproach. Robbery might've seemed better than driving off into the night, and waking up in some dusty, alien Cheyenne, Wyoming, or Omaha, Nebraska, followed by more of the same she'd already had enough of. In her chronicle she wrote that on their drive to Creekmore, she'd told my father that once the robbery was behind them, without even knowing how much they'd get, but supposing it'd be enough, she'd be taking half the money and us two children and leaving. She wrote that he'd laughed and said, "Well, wait and see how you feel."

To me, it's the edging closer to the point of no return that's fascinating: all along the trip, chatting, sharing confidences, exchanging endearments—since their life was officially still intact. They weren't felons. How amazingly far normalcy extends; how you can keep it in sight as if you were on a raft sliding out to sea, the stitch of land growing smaller and smaller. Or in a balloon swept up on a column of prairie air, the ground widening and flattening, growing less and less distinct below you. You notice it, or you don't notice it. But you're already too far away, and all is lost. For reasons of our parents' disastrous choices, I believe I'm both distrustful of normal life and in equal parts desperate for it. It's hard to hold the idea of a normal life, and also the end they came to, in my mind at one time. But it's worth trying, since I repeat: otherwise very little of this story can be understood.

The last glimpse of them—before they became something else—tells me that in the Chevrolet headed east, side by side, free from their children for the first time, alone together, the two of them may have felt a last bit of the old affinity from the night before, could've tracked it all back. Like anyone's parents. A sense that one completed in the other something unique and likable and so basic as never to have been addressed or fully experienced—but once, at the beginning. Of course, had my mother not gotten pregnant, and had my father not done the right thing, it could've all been smiled away as a passing attraction, marveled at later as having been something like love, something that had been present in both of them but ended without issue.

16

THE DRIVE TO GLENDIVE TOOK THEM SIX AND A half hours. They checked into the Yellowstone Motel. My father made a point of cheerfulness to the room clerk, while trying to say nothing memorable. He left my mother in the car while he signed them in so she wouldn't be noticed and make an impression. He and she took a nap in the hot, musty beaverboard cabin with the blinds pulled. At seven, when it was still full light—though the town was emptied and bridge swallows were swarming and diving at their images in the mirror surface of the Yellowstone—he drove into town, ate his dinner alone at the Jordan Hotel, and asked for a covered plate of beef and macaroni to take back to his wife, who was sick in the room.

How they passed that night together—the last before they became felons—there's no way to know, since my mother doesn't say in any detail. There's no template for such a night. They were alone in their sweltering cabin. They'd talked out the subjects they needed to talk about or had any imagination for. Ordinary people would've waked up panicked at two A.M., slick with sweat, roused the person lying beside them, snapped on the table lamp and shouted, "No, wait! Wait! What is this we're doing? It's very well to threaten these things, hatch a plan, drive to here and fantasize it'll work out. But it's crazy! We have to go home to our children, figure this out another way." That's the way reasoning people think and speak and act when they have a reflective moment. But it's still not what our parents did. "I did not sleep well the hot night in Glendive," is what my mother wrote. "Had bad dreams of being in a boat—a ship—passing through (it must've been) the Panama Canal, or maybe Suez, getting stuck, not being able to go forward or back. B. slept soundly, as always. Woke early. Was dressed and in the chair, doing something to his pistol when my eyes opened on him."

What they did next was rise at seven thirty, leave clothes scattered around their room, eat no breakfast, hang the DO NOT DISTURB card on the cabin door, and drive away from the motel. It was supposed to look as if they were staying on, sleeping late, then going someplace where they had business, with the expectation of returning.

They drove east through the tiny town of Wibaux, near where my father had formulated his original plan—the vacant ranch, the borrowed truck—before giving in to my mother's simpler one. Beyond Wibaux, they crossed the North Dakota border—only a small metal sign announcing another state was being entered. Not far beyond the state line they turned off onto a dirt farm road, drove a mile into the barley fields to where a creek ribboned past a clump of green cottonwoods with magpies up in the limbs. My father got out in the steaming morning light and exchanged license plates—the green-and-white Peace Garden State North Dakota ones he'd stolen three days ago replacing the black-lettered Treasure State ones he intended to put back on. He changed into his blue jumpsuit and tennis shoes, which he thought rendered him invisible, and folded his good clothes under some fallen tree limbs, along with his boots. My mother stayed in the car, fearing snakes. Then the two of them drove back up onto the highway, turned east and soon after rolled into Creekmore, which was the first town beyond the border—chosen for that reason.

The Agricultural National Bank was near the western end of Main

Street in downtown Creekmore. My father was surprised the street was so
populated at 8:58. Ranch trucks and wheat-mowing machinery and grain
trucks were moving about and people were in town for shopping. It was a
town of early risers. As per their plan, he didn't drive down the main street,
but turned at the first corner where there was an insurance company, drove
a half block to the back alley he knew was there—weedy and graveled
with an automobile repair where you turned in, but no building behind
the bank itself. He drove down the gravel alley to where he could pull
in behind the bank, and where two other cars were parked—employees.
He didn't intend this to take long. He wanted everything as unremarkable as possible, which is why he decided not to disguise himself or wear
a mask—the thing my mother had advised. Even then he didn't believe
he looked like a bank robber. He had clear, even features, a fresh haircut.
He'd shaved. Nothing (but the jumpsuit) distinguished him as anything
but a clear-faced, even-featured North Dakota adult.

It was three minutes after nine when they arrived behind the bank.
Our father got immediately out wearing a brown cloth cap, and with his
loaded gun in his jumpsuit pocket. The two of them had not spoken. He
walked straight up the shadowy, half-paved side alley that separated the
bank from a jewelry store and emerged out onto the Main Street sidewalk.
The sun was much brighter and the sky bluer, higher, than he expected.
He saw spots from the sun—he reported this to our mother. For a frightening moment he didn't know which way he was supposed to turn. Plus,
there was so much more activity at street level, even more than five minutes ago. Our mother wrote that he nearly turned around and walked
back down the alley—which he still could've done. But on the spur of
the moment he decided that all this activity would be a diversion when he
walked out of the bank—which would be in no more than three minutes,
carrying a full bag of money. He wouldn't stand out and could disappear
back down the alley unnoticed.

He walked the few steps along the hot pavement to the big brass and beveled-glass bank door. He had a thought that he should've worn sun-glasses, which would've made a good disguise in addition to shading his eyes. He walked straight into the bank, but immediately paused as the door closed behind him. It was so cool inside, so shadowy and quiet and still. Outside had been bustling and hot and noisy. And he was shocked at how small the bank was. Again, he'd never gone inside on the chance someone would remember him. A single customer stood at one of three brass-barred tellers' windows, chatting through the grate—a small thin, blond woman. She was watching the teller count out bills to put into a cloth pouch to be the till for the jewelry store next door. It smelled clean—like Brasso—in the bank, he told my mother, or like the inside of a new refrigerator.

At this point our father snapped to attention, drew his .45 caliber from his pocket and stepped toward the occupied teller's window—two others were unattended. He proclaimed to the room that the bank was now being robbed. By him. He announced that the jeweler customer and the two bank officers—men in suits, staring up at him in surprise from their desks behind the metal fence enclosure where bank business was conducted—as well as the elderly uniformed bank guard seated at one of the vacant officers' desks, should all lie face down on the marble floor and do nothing except what he said. If anybody activated an alarm, made a noise, tried to get up, run, or did anything sudden or unexpected, he said he'd shoot them. (This he later denied saying.)

This moment—the moment of proclamation, the gun revealed, the stagy commands of "don't move or I'll shoot"—may have been the moment when our father most truly enjoyed and realized himself (since he'd dropped a sky full of bombs on Japan), when he felt the exhilaration to be finally doing what he'd so long wanted to do, feeling not only that he'd earned the chance, due to circumstances going unfairly against him (the Indians, the jobs, the Air Force, my mother), but also that an armed robbery was a satisfactory solution and compensation, since he wasn't really stealing from depositors but from the government, for whom he'd sacrificed much, killed thousands, been a patriot, and which had infinite resources to assure that no innocent person lost a penny, while he solved all our family's problems in one deft swoop.

It's not likely this exhilaration lasted long. With one eye on the bank officers and the guard, and paying little attention to the jeweler's clerk, who painfully kneeled down and moved out of the way by slithering like a snake over the hard floor, my father put his canvas bag up onto the marble counter under the teller's bars, and instructed the teller to empty all three cash drawers, plus what the jeweler had yet to receive but which was counted out there, into the mouth of the bag—and do it in a hurry and without talking. It was at this point, as the teller was handing the bill packets into the bag, which was big enough to hold a bowling ball, that one of the two officers, a dapper vice president named Lasse Clausen, who later testified against my father in court—raised his head off the floor, looked up at my father and said, "Where are you from, son?" (He had detected my father's Alabama accent.) "Because you don't have to do this, you know. This is the wrong way to go about things." This caused the jeweler's clerk, flat on the cold floor, to say, "And you won't get away with it. Somebody'll shoot you before you get out of town. You're not the only one with a gun around here."

Our father told our mother that when he heard these words it was a very deflating experience and caused him to feel a "great wave of resentment" toward all the people in the bank. He was tempted to shoot them, one by one, removing any chance he'd be caught, and serving them right for being unluckier than he was. The reason he didn't—he told her—was that he hadn't *planned* to shoot them. During the years when he'd possibly harbored thoughts of robbing a bank—relishing the idea—no one had gotten killed in his plan. He intended to keep to that plan—which was what a smart person did. But he could've killed them, he said—having already done so much worse in his life. It's possible he was only bragging after the fact, since killing them would've been a different thing to do personally, not like dropping bombs out of an airplane.

When the cash drawers were emptied into the bag, the young woman teller stood behind her window and looked straight at my father. She said later she looked at him the same as if she knew him. He, too, knew they'd all taken a good look at him, that they hadn't been shocked by his pistol or even by a robbery. Their bank had been robbed not long before, just not by him. They were already in the process of catching him. He was probably more shocked than they were. He said later to my mother that this was the first time the idea of being caught came seriously into his thinking. It made him want to abandon the robbery right then. Only that wasn't possible. He looked up at the big clock over the open bank vault. 9:09. The brass and silver and steel vault tunneled back temptingly into the rear wall. Thousands more dollars were there. But he'd determined he couldn't carry that much money in his bag—plus he didn't need that much. He'd been in the Agricultural National four minutes. Everyone had looked at him. Everyone had heard his mellow voice and his Dixie accent. Everyone would see him in their mind's eye for the rest of their lives when they told about being in the bank the day it was robbed. He knew all of this. He might even have liked it. He could smell sweat on himself—sweat they could smell, too. There was nothing left for him to do but take the bag of money—which held $2,500—and leave. Which he did. Without saying another word. It already felt very much like robbing a bank was the wrong thing to have done.

17

MY MOTHER HAD SHOVED OVER INTO THE DRIVER's seat after my father had parked behind the bank. She'd pushed the seat far forward so her feet would reach. She was waiting with the engine started when he came out the alley with his canvas bag. He got straight into the back seat, crouched under a blanket, and she pulled slowly away so nothing that had gone on in the bank would seem to have anything to do with a white-and-red Chevrolet Bel Air with North Dakota plates, idling out of town toward the west.

She wrote that when she pulled to the corner of Main Street, ready to turn left, she saw nothing she didn't expect to see down the block at the bank. A woman was just walking in. No alarms were going, no sheriffs or state police arriving, or people running out shouting "robbery!" They would get away with it, she thought. She'd soon be looking at a new life that didn't include our father or Great Falls, Montana.

ACCORDING TO THEIR PLAN, she drove back toward the Montana line, with my father hiding in the back, and onto the bumpy farm track through the barley fields, to the cottonwoods and the stream where they'd stopped less than an hour before. My father got out in the dust and heat, shucked off his jumpsuit and tennis shoes and, in his undershorts, stuffed the money (he already knew there was less than he'd intended to steal) into the space behind the back seat. He crammed the jumpsuit, shoes, his gun, the cap and the blanket, and the green-and-white North Dakota license plates into the blue bag, along with several dusty rocks, and put it in the stream. The bag didn't sink, only eddied off in a tuft of yellow foam and disappeared. But he believed this was as good as sinking it, since nobody would be out there to see it. He then put his jeans back on, his white shirt and boots, reattached his Montana plates. My mother drove them back up to the highway, and turned left in the direction of the border, and they put it all behind them.

In Glendive they stopped in at the Yellowstone Motel. Our father went inside their room, collected the clothing they'd left. He walked up to the motel office, spoke to the room clerk—who was not the clerk who'd checked him in the evening before. When he paid—in cash—he joked about the sky now being full of satellites and soon everybody would know everything everybody did—which later struck the room clerk as a strange thing to say. My father walked back down to the cabin, carried my mother's little suitcase to the Chevrolet, where she was waiting. He got in the driver's seat and drove them away toward Great Falls. Everything had gone according to my mother's simple plan. If they'd entertained conscious thoughts about being caught—and they should've—it's possible those thoughts might've left their minds as they drove home, rendering them relieved and happy, while they thought about Berner and me waiting for them, and for a better life to commence for all of us.

18

THREE THINGS I'VE THOUGHT ABOUT—HAVING TO do with the aftermath of their armed robbery and with our parents becoming criminals headed very soon to jail.

One was that they'd always been very different from each other. My sister and I acknowledged this over the years we were growing up. These stark differences—in personality, appearance, outlook, temperament (I've described them)—made up opposite ends of the continuum that measured out my and Berner's lives. We were both composed of these human traits that made them different—some represented in me, some in Berner—though that didn't make us any more similar. I was optimistic, but not as optimistic as our father. I was cautious, but not as adamant and skeptical as our mother could be. Berner looked like my mother but was taller, even at fifteen—five foot eight. She had a sweet side, like our father, but she guarded it and mostly acted as if it wasn't there, which I'd say was like our mother. We were both reasonably smart like our mother. But Berner was practical, which wasn't true of either of our parents. She was also moody and defeatable, as both of them could be, and at some point she tended to accept defeat and destiny, which I have never done.

But when our parents came back from robbing the North Dakota bank, and we were all once again in our house—before the police detectives came—my sister and I noticed almost immediately how our mother and father seemed *less* different from each other. They were much more in agreement, much less given to sighing or bickering with each other, or being each other's adversary or opposite—something that had never been true until they left and came back that way. I decided this newfound bond had formed even before they left, on the night they were in such high spirits—as if, as I said, it had been remembered, an old affinity rising again and holding them, so that they were less like ends of a continuum and more just two people who'd once gotten married because they liked each other.

God knows what could've been going on in their brains in the days immediately after the robbery. Stolen money was somewhere in our house. They must've felt conspicuous, and that they were now in a hostile world (whereas a day before they'd been invisible). Previous life, which they'd grown impatient with for their private reasons, must've seemed bewilderingly and abruptly out of reach—the raft having drifted out too far, the balloon ascended. The past was cruelly ended, the future jeopardized. Though this may also be what joined them: an unexpected mutual awareness of consequence. Neither of them had been richly imbued with that. Lacking an awareness of consequence might've been their greatest flaw. Though each of them had reasons to know that acts had results.

The second subject didn't come into my thinking until I'd read my mother's chronicle—decades after she'd taken her life in prison—when I learned my father wanted *me*, not her, to be his accomplice. I wanted to know then: Would he have explained to me that he intended to hold up a bank and wanted me to help him? What words would he have chosen to bring this matter up to a fifteen-year-old? Would he have come in my room where I was waking up on Thursday morning and asked to have a private talk and imparted it then? Would he have waited until we were in the car heading east through the Musselshell and brought this outlandish subject up then? Would he have told me just as we were driving into Creekmore? Or would he have never told me, just used me as camouflage, left me sitting in the car behind the bank, waiting for him to reappear, knowing nothing?

And if he *had* told me, what could I have answered? No? Would no have been possible? (In theory it would've.) Of course, I'd have said yes, or at least would've said nothing and gone with him. I was not rebellious or mouthy like my sister. I loved him and wanted to see things his way. And if I'd become his accomplice, what would've changed between us after that? Everything, most likely. Would I have grown up all in one day? Would my life have been ruined? Would we have been more like brothers than father and son? Would I be a criminal now instead of a school teacher? All possible.

Which begs another question: what would've happened if we'd been caught together—captured and put in jail; or set upon by police like Bonnie and Clyde, shot to death and laid out for pictures? "Man and son commit bank robbery. Both are killed." This is a line of thinking he didn't treat himself to, and a fate my mother saved me from.

And if the two of them hadn't gotten caught, would that have spelled the end of it for them as bank robbers? Which is the third thing I've wondered about. For our mother, definitely yes—as far as you can know such matters. She had her purpose for doing it once—at least by my reasoning: to leave her unsatisfactory life behind. If that purpose had been achieved, there's no doubt she'd have begun her new life (with Berner and me) somewhere else. She was only thirty-four. It's not far-fetched to think of her as a teacher in a small college somewhere—less alienated, probably unmarried, in basic agreement with her lot—her bank robbery left far behind.

For my father, it's much less possible to be sure. He had a taste for bank robbery, or believed he did. If the robbery had worked out, his nature—as I said—was to think it would always work out and could probably be improved on. At least one more time. He also always believed—although proof mounted that he was mistaken—that he didn't seem like the sort of man to rob a bank. This was, of course, his great misunderstanding.

19

WHEN THEY ARRIVED HOME, IT WAS AFTER seven on Friday night. They seemed tired and distracted but relieved to be home. I was excited and began to tell them how Berner and I'd passed the two days—what had happened, what we'd seen, what we thought about. The Indians had made several more trips past our house. The telephone had rung numerous times but we hadn't answered it. Berner and I had eaten leftover spaghetti and boiled eggs and made toast. We'd played chess, watched *The Untouchables,* Ernie Kovacs, the news. I'd mowed the lawn and observed the bees working on the zinnias beside the garage. We'd sat on the porch swing at night and watched the sky-glow. I'd heard noises from the State Fair, then going on not far from our house—the announcer's loudspeaker voice at the Wild West Rodeo and the chuck wagon race, the cheering crowd. A calliope. A man's amplified voice laughing.

Our parents had things on their minds and were preoccupied with each other. It was as if they were taking care not to make the other irritated. Our mother took a bath, then went in the kitchen and cooked French toast and sliced ham. Our father liked breakfast for supper and believed it was good for digestion. He went out to the street and drove the car around to the alley in back of the house—a thing he didn't often do, since he was proud of the Bel Air the way he'd been of the demonstrators he'd tried and failed to sell. He also locked it and brought the key inside instead of leaving it in the ignition as usual.

When we sat down at the dinner table, our father announced that the business deal they'd gone away to investigate was something a person would be crazy to get involved in. Oil wells, he said, profoundly—then smiled and shook his head as if it had been a pathetic idea. Our mother had pointed this out, he said. It had been wise to take her. She had a sharp business mind. He said he now intended to throw himself full-time into learning the farm and ranch sales game. It was steady. Opportunity would soon come along by which we could own land of our own. We were staying in Great Falls. Berner and I could plan on school in two weeks. He intended to make Bargamian an offer for our house. It was a "Craftsman house," and they weren't made anymore, he said. It needed painting a new color and new wallpaper, and he wished it had a front "foy-yay" and a fireplace. But it had other elegant touches—the medallion in the living room ceiling being one. He admired the house's symmetry and solid lines. The outside light was nice through the living room windows—which was true—and it was cool in summer. It reminded him of "the dog-trot" he'd grown up in in Alabama. But there'd be no more thought of moving. Which made me relieved, though it may not have affected Berner, since she'd already decided to run away with Rudy Patterson and put everything she knew of life behind her.

I had noticed my father hadn't returned home with the blue bag he'd left with the morning before and didn't mention losing. He was finicky in the military way about things he owned. When I'd looked again in his sock drawer for his pistol, it was gone again. I decided that on his business trip something must've happened that made him not bring his pistol back. I couldn't imagine what. I also noticed that after we'd eaten supper and he'd assured us we'd be staying in Great Falls, he sat down in the living room, still in his boots and white shirt and jeans, and turned on the TV to *Summer Playhouse,* and talked to my mother through the door to the kitchen, where she was washing dishes. He told her he really felt at home in Great Falls, but he was sure he'd be happy back in Alabama, too. There was a benefit to being near kinfolks. To which she answered that it was never a bad idea to stay close to where you came from. Many people lived their whole lifetimes fighting that idea. He was very lucky, she said, to be figuring this out when he was still young.

All of it was a lie, of course—what they were proclaiming, how they were acting toward each other, what they wanted us to believe, how they painted the future. They were embroidering the surface of the acts they'd committed, seeking to dress it up, give good appearance to what they'd hoped would be the result. Events, though, aren't the same as what you make up. Our parents were running ahead of disaster. But they'd come to a familiar, still place, where everything was where they'd left it—including Berner and me—where it looked the same and under other circumstances still might've been the same. They might've thought *they* were the same, able to go forward in their previous ways. Their same old problems were there. Their same desires. That there was calamitous consequence to be dealt with now, events in motion, coming to take them over and stamp their lives as finished, simply hadn't fully dawned on them. They could still make themselves think, act, talk in the old ways. They're both forgivable for that, even likable—for being charmed by one last taste of the life they'd tossed away.

20

ON SATURDAY MORNING I WOKE TO THE SOUND OF my mother speaking on the telephone. She was insisting on something and waved me away when I walked down the hall to the toilet, past where the telephone sat in its nook in the wall. My father didn't seem to be in the house. The car was gone from where he'd put it in back. A change in the weather had occurred overnight. The house was now cool and breezy, and the front and back doors were left open. Pale clouds you could see through the kitchen window hurried over from the west, and the light had turned a yellow-green. The curtains billowed, and the elms in our yard and in the park across the street sawed back and forth as if rain was coming. Our pile of cast-off clothes still lay on the back porch awaiting the St. Vincent de Paul truck. Inside, the house seemed fresh and almost calm in spite of the breezes. It felt like a morning in which something significant was expected in the afternoon.

When she left off talking, my mother announced she was walking to the Italian's on Central, where she bought our groceries. Berner was still asleep. I could go if I wanted to, which made me happy. I didn't spend enough time with my mother, in my estimation. She spent more time with Berner.

However, my mother said very little on our walk. At the Italian's she bought a *Tribune*—something I'd never seen her do, since she maintained no interest in what went on in the town. On the way, I attempted to introduce some subjects of concern to me. My Schwinn was old and had been bought used in Mississippi and didn't fit me anymore. A Raleigh was what I'd been thinking about—an English bike, with thin tires, hand brakes, gears, and a basket behind the seat. I wanted to carry my books and chess men to school when I started. I hadn't been allowed to ride to school before, but I assumed I would be now. I reminded her that I planned to construct a single-box bee hive in the backyard, and expected to do that before spring, when the bees I was ordering from Georgia would arrive. There'd be benefits from that. Pollination of the hollyhocks. Honey—which we could all share—was useful for allergies, which would be good for Berner. Plus, it would be educational, since the bees were very organized and purposeful, and I'd be able to write school reports about what I learned, as I had about the smelting process and the Salk vaccine—which Berner and I'd both had. I reminded her that the State Fair was still going on, and I hoped to visit the bee exhibit. Today was the last day. She told me, however, that my father would have to see about all that—she was busy. She reminded me that she didn't like fairs. They were dangerous. People who worked there were known to kidnap children—which I thought she was making up. Clothes were on her mind. Berner needed different undergarments. I wasn't growing up very fast, but Berner was growing up much faster—which I'd noticed and my mother said was natural. I could wear my clothes from last year one more season. I didn't feel like I was getting any of my important points across.

When we were in front of our house, the doors to the Lutherans were swung open and activity was going on inside. Under the wind-whipped trees, my mother looked up through the arch of moving limbs and observed that the air had a seam of cold in it now (which I couldn't feel). She was sorry about it. We'd see some snow on the western peaks soon. Fall would be on us before we knew it.

When we came back inside, my mother made tea and a baloney sandwich and went out on the front steps in the breezy sunlight and read the newspaper. She had the big Stromberg-Carlson going in the living room, which wasn't customary. She was on the lookout for word about their robbery, wanting to hear if news had made it as far as Great Falls—though I didn't know that. Later in the day I looked through the paper to find out the closing hours at the fair. I wouldn't have noticed anything, and I have no memory of a robbery being described. None of it had happened in my life yet.

However, I was very aware that the Indians had stopped driving past our house and staring hatefully in at us. The phone had stopped ringing. A black-and-white police car drove by two or three times that morning, and I know my mother saw it. I observed nothing to be wrong. The only thing I was conscious of was a sensation—and I couldn't have described it—of movement taking place around me. Nothing was visible at the surface of life, and it was the surface of life that I knew about. But children in families have this sensation of movement. It can signify someone is taking care of them, that things are being invisibly looked after, and nothing bad is likely to happen. Or it can mean something else. It's the sensation you have if you're brought up right—which Berner and I thought we were.

By noon, our father hadn't returned and my mother got dressed to go somewhere—which also never happened on Saturday. She put on the suit she sometimes wore to teach school—a thick green wool outfit with large pale pink plaids—nothing you'd wear in the summer. She put on stockings and black shoes with slightly high heels. Dressed and walking around inside the house, finding her purse, she looked stiff and uncomfortable. Her suit seemed to scratch at her, and her shoes made loud noises on the floor. She'd puffed up her hair in the bathroom mirror, so it looked spongy and made her features small, almost hidden, which she must've wanted. When Berner saw her, she said, "I've seen it all now," and went back in her bedroom and closed the door.

I stood in the living room and asked my mother where she was going. I was still feeling those sensations of things moving around me. The chance of rain had already come and gone, as mostly happened. The day had turned humid and bright and steely hot. My mother told me she was being picked up by her friend Mildred Remlinger—the school nurse where she taught and who she rode with every day when classes were in session, but who she never saw after the summer started. I had never met Mildred, but my mother said Mildred was encountering personal problems she needed to discuss with another woman. She wouldn't be gone long. Berner and I could eat the rest of the baloney if we got hungry. She'd cook dinner.

Eventually Mildred's car drove up in front and the horn honked. My mother went hurrying out, down the steps, and got in the car—a brown four-door Ford—which drove away. I thought the odd sensations I was feeling were being created by my mother.

After a while Berner came out of her room and we ate the baloney and some cheese. Our father still hadn't come back. Berner said we should take some of the cheese down to the river and feed the ducks and geese, which was something we did. We had little to do if we weren't in school or in the house with our parents, watching them and being watched by them. Being a child under those circumstances was mostly waiting—for them to do something, or to be older—which seemed a long way away.

The river was only three blocks from our house, in the opposite direction from the Italian's. Berner wore her sunglasses and her white lace gloves to cover her hands and her warts. On the way, she advised me that Rudy Patterson had told her Castro would soon develop an atomic bomb and the first thing he'd do was blow up Florida. That would start a world war none of us would escape from—which I didn't believe. She said Rudy had also said Mormons wore special garments that protected them from non-Mormons, and that they were forbidden to take them off.

She then told me she'd begun climbing out her bedroom window at night and meeting Rudy, who'd often steal his family's car. They'd drive up on the rimrock by the municipal airport and park where they could see the lights of town and listen to radio stations from Chicago and Texas and smoke cigarettes. This was where Rudy had digressed about Castro and how he was serious about breaking out of Great Falls. He felt older than his age, already had hair on his chest, and could pass for eighteen. What else they did in the car was what I wanted to know. "We kissed. Nothing nasty," Berner said. "I don't like his mouth too much, and that little mustache. He doesn't smell good. He smells like dirt." Then she showed me a bruise where her turtleneck covered it. "He gave me this," she said. "I clobbered him for it. Mother'd shit about it." I knew what it was. "A tongue tattoo," a boy at school had called it. He'd had one right where Berner's was. He said it'd hurt to get it. I didn't understand why you'd do a thing like that. No one had explained to me about sex at that point. I only knew what I'd heard.

For a while we stood in the weeds by the river, where grasshoppers and flies flitted and buzzed around the edge of the hissing, shining water. Cars were banging over the Central Avenue Bridge not far away. Midday was hot and still. The smelter always left a bitter, metal taste in the air, and the river itself was metal smelling, though it was cool near the surface. The tall buildings in Great Falls—the Milwaukee Road and the Great Northern depots, the Rainbow Hotel, the First National Bank, the Great Falls Drug Company—were across the river and foreign looking. A bald eagle sailed along just above the flat pavement of river toward Squaw Island and the Anaconda stack—five hundred feet tall and impressive to me—then lit in a tree on the far side and instantly became tiny. Whitefish rose for the yellow cheese balls we floated on the current. Mallards swam close and flapped and squabbled over them as they drifted back toward the bank and the reeds. I trapped a warm grasshopper between my two hands and laid it onto the river film. It circled down the stream trying its wings, trying to rise. Then it disappeared. A big Air Force refueling jet rose into the sky from the base. It banked south and went out of sight before its sound could reach us. I liked Great Falls, but it was never a town I cared much about. I imagined climbing onto the Western Star and riding away to some college—Holy Cross or Lehigh—everything in my life after that being on its way.

21

WHEN WE WALKED BACK HOME, SUN BEAT THE tops of our heads. A moist, hot wind up from the south stirred the dust on Central Avenue. Tires of passing cars girdered, and the trees were dusty and brittle-leafed. There was no cold seam in the air.

The Lutherans were inside having a wedding. Doors, front and side, were opened out and two tall silver fans were positioned to create a circulation. Two men in western hats stood in the churchyard in shirt sleeves, holding their jackets and smoking. A muddy red pickup was parked alone at the church's curb. Tin cans and silverware and a few old boots were strung to its back bumper. "Just Married—Heaven Bound" and "Poor Girl" were scrawled on the side windows in white.

Berner and I stopped and she considered the open front door through her sunglasses, as if a bride and groom might come out. We'd never been inside a church.

"Why would you ever get married?" Berner said and looked disgusted. "You pay for what you can get for free." She carefully spit down between her tennis shoes onto the grass of our front lawn. I'd never thought to ask that question, though I sometimes believed Berner knew what I thought before I thought it. She *was* growing up quicker than I was. She didn't like anything she didn't understand.

"Rudy's parents aren't even married," she said. "His real mother lives in San Francisco, which is where he's headed when he busts out of here. I'm thinking about going with him. You can't tell them or I'll strangle you." She grabbed my arm and pinched me so hard my ears hurt, even with her white gloves. She was much stronger than I was. "I mean it," she said. "You little turd."

She'd said things like that to me before. Called me a turd. A molly-hop. A peter. I didn't like it, but I thought it meant things were still close between us. It made me feel better than I'd been feeling.

"I wouldn't say anything," I said.

"Nobody'd listen, anyway," she said and sneered at me. "Mr. Chess Man. That's who you are." She went up the steps into the house.

OUR FATHER was sitting at the dining room table, applying Cat's Paw to his black cowboy boots. I'd seen him do it to his Air Force shoes a hundred times. His wooden polish kit was open on top of the *Tribune* my mother'd been reading. He'd also been paring his fingernails. The half-moon slivers were scattered on the paper.

He had taken the globe off my dresser and set it on the table in front of him. The room smelled sweet with the polish. He'd turned on KMON for the Saturday farm report. He had on his regular Saturday attire—rubber sandals and Bermudas and a red-flowered Hawaiian shirt that showed his coiled snake tattoo on his forearm. It spelled the name of the Mitchell he'd dropped bombs out of. *Old Viper.* He had another one on his shoulder: Air Force wings, which hadn't been earned by being a pilot—something he'd always been disappointed about.

He put on a big smile for me. He'd looked glum and concentrated when we came in. He didn't act like he felt well. He hadn't shaved, but his eyes were gleaming the way they had when he'd come back from his first business trip.

Berner kept on walking through the room and didn't stop. "I got hot," she said. "I'm going to sit in a cold tub, then feed my fish." No one had turned on the attic fan, but Berner did when she went down the hall. Air began moving. I heard her door close.

"I want to talk to you," my father said, carrying on with his rag and his paste polish. "Take a seat here."

I wasn't used to being completely alone with him, even though I was supposed to spend more time with him and less with my mother. Normally she was close by. He always wanted to engage in a serious discussion when he got me alone. It usually had to do with wanting me to know he loved us, and that he was always working for our welfare, and that he had a personal stake in our individual futures—about which he was never specific. It always made me feel he didn't know Berner and me very well, because we took those things for granted.

I sat beside the clutter of rags and blackened toothbrushes and the round Cat's Paw tin. The globe was turned around to show the United States. "I certainly wish I could take you to the State Fair." He stared straight at my eyes, as if he was saying something that meant something else. Or as if I was caught in a lie, and he was trying to make me understand the importance of not lying. I didn't lie at that particular time.

"Today's the last day it's on," I said. The announcement was in the paper he was cleaning his shoes on. He'd probably seen it, which was why he'd brought it up. "We could still go."

He looked out the window as a car went past, then looked at the globe. "I know that," he said. "I just don't feel top flight today."

Once in Mississippi we'd gone to a traveling county fair that set up its tents not far from where we lived. He and I went one night. I threw rubber balls at rag dolls with red pigtails, but didn't knock any over. Then I shot a rifle loaded with corks and knocked over some swimming ducks and won a packet of sweet chalky lozenges. My father left me while he went in a tent for a show I wasn't old enough to see. I stood outside on the sawdust, listening to people's voices and the music of the rides and the sound of laughter from the fun house. The sky was yellowed by the carnival lights. When my father came out with a crowd of other men, he said that had been an experience, but said nothing else. We rode the Dodge-em cars together and ate taffy, then went home. I'd never been to another fair and hadn't cared much for that one. Boys in the chess club had said the Montana Fair showcased livestock and poultry and agriculture and was useless. But I was still interested in the bees.

My father breathed out through his nose as he worked polish into his boot leather. He had a forceful smell, stronger than the Cat's Paw—an acrid odor that I believed had to do with not feeling good. He sat back, put down his cloth and rubbed his hands over his face as if his hands had water in them, then pushed them back through his hair, which released more of the odor. He squeezed his eyes closed and opened them.

"You know when I was a little boy in Alabama, I had a friend down the street from us. And one of our neighbors, this old doctor, had his office in his house, and he invited my friend in one day. This old doctor tried some foolishness with my friend that wasn't right." My father's gleamy-dark eyes focused down on the polish tin, then rose to me dramatically. "You understand what I mean?"

"Yes, sir," I said, though I didn't.

"My friend, whose name was Buddy Inkster, made him quit, of course. He went straight home and told his mother. And do you know what his mother said?" My father blinked at me and tilted his head inquiringly.

"No, sir."

"She said, 'Buddy, you tell that ole man to cut that stuff out!'"

My sister began running her bath water. Even with the fan going I was hot in my clothes. I'd begun sweating under my shirt collar. The bathroom door closed and went locked.

"Do you know what his mother was saying?" My father picked up the shoe-polish lid and carefully squeezed it back on with two fingers. It made a soft click. "*Now,* of course, if that happened, he'd—I mean the old sawbones—he'd be put in jail and people would be out after him with pitchforks and torches. You know?" I didn't know. A car honked outside on the street, its motor revved, then it roared away. My father didn't seem to hear it. "Well, she was saying that Inkster should learn to live with things and go on about his business. Do you understand that?"

"I think so." It was what I'd thought.

"Bad things can just happen to you," my father said. "And you live on through them." He was trying to make his story have an effect on me. He seemed to be saying you can miss important parts of what people do and say, but you still have to rely on yourself to understand them. What I thought he was really telling me, though—not quite using those words— was that something bad might be approaching *me,* and I needed to figure out my own ways to get through it. He wanted me to be responsible for Berner, too. Which was why he told me and not her, and only proved he didn't know Berner nearly as well as he didn't know me.

"Do you and your sister think about what you should do with your lives?" His eyes looked dry and tired. His fingertips were smudged with polish. He was wiping them off finger by finger on his flannel rag. He seemed to be addressing me from a distance now.

"Yes, sir," I said.

"So. What do you think?" he said. "About the future."

"I want to be a lawyer," I said, for no reason except that a boy in the chess club said his father was one.

"I wish you could hurry up, then," he said and appraised his finger-nails after his cleaning job on them. Black was still under their edges. "You have to find ways to make everything make sense." He smiled faintly. "Make a hierarchy. Some things are more important than others. It may not be what you expect." He turned his gaze out the front window onto SW First. Lutherans were mingling under the trees in the park across from their church. The wedding was letting out. People were fanning themselves with their hats and paper fans, and laughing. My mother was just exiting Mildred Remlinger's Ford at the curb. In her green-and-pink plaid wool suit, she looked tiny and unhappy. She didn't say anything back into the car, just closed its door and began walking up toward the front porch. Mildred's car drove away. "Here comes trouble," my father said. I expected him to say I mustn't discuss our conversation with her. He often said that, as if we had significant secrets—which I didn't think we did. But he didn't say that. Which made me understand that our conversation had been agreed to by them, though I hadn't understood what it was really about: them being caught, and what Berner and I would do after.

My father smiled at me his conspirator's smile. He stood up from the table. "She's going to have everything all figured out," he said. "You wait and see. She's a smart cookie. Smarter than I am by a long way." He went to open the door for her. Our conversation ended there. We didn't have another one like it.

22

YOU HEAR STORIES ABOUT PEOPLE WHO'VE COM-
mitted bad crimes. Suddenly they decide to confess it all,
turn themselves in to the authorities, get everything off
their conscience—the burden, the harm, the shame, the self-hatred. They
make a clean breast of things before going off to jail. As if guilt was the
worst thing in the world to them.

I'm willing to say now that guilt has less to do with it than you might
think. Rather, the intolerable problem is of everything suddenly being so
confused: the clear path back to the past being cluttered and unfollow-
able; how the person once felt being now completely changed from how
he feels today. And time itself: how the hours of the day and night advance
so oddly—first fast, then hardly passing at all. Then the future becoming
as confused and impenetrable as the past itself. What a person becomes in
such a situation is paralyzed—caught in one long, sustained, intolerable
present.

Who wouldn't want to stop that—if he could? Make the present give
way to almost any future at all. Who wouldn't admit everything just to
gain release from the terrible present? I would. Only a saint wouldn't.

* * *

ANOTHER BLACK-AND-WHITE police car cruised past our house several times that Saturday. The uniformed driver seemed to take careful notice of our house. Our father went to the front window several times and looked out. "Okay. I see you," he said more than once. He and our mother had been friendly and talkative to each other the day before. Now, though, they operated *around* each other in a way I was more used to. Our father seemed to have not enough to do. She, on the other hand, was purposeful. Not much was talked about. I attempted to interest Berner in "the positional concept" and in the "aggressive sacrifice," which I'd been reading about and demonstrated to her on my bed, with my roll-up board. She said she didn't feel good and I couldn't understand because it was about life and wasn't a game.

SINCE OUR MOTHER had come home from seeing Miss Remlinger, she'd gotten busy again in the house. She washed a load of clothes in the tub washer and hung them on the pulley line in the backyard—standing on a wood box to reach the clothespin sack. She cleaned the bathtub—which Berner always left dirty—and swept the front porch where the wind had blown grit into the cracks. She washed the dishes that had been left in the sink the night before. Our father went out in the backyard and sat in one of the lawn chairs and stared at the afternoon sky and practiced the eye exercises he'd learned in the Air Force. After a while he came in and brought the card table out of the hall closet and set it up in the living room and got down a jigsaw puzzle and sat in front of it with the pieces spread across the table top. He liked puzzles and believed they asked a special intelligence. He'd also done several paint-by-numbers pictures over the years, which he'd put briefly on display, then placed in the same closet and never looked at again.

He pulled up a dining room chair for anybody who wanted to collaborate on the puzzle, and began getting the pieces spread out and turned

over, and studying them and fitting the obvious ones together like tiny is-
lands. He asked Berner if she wanted to work on it, because it would make
her feel better. But she said no. It was the puzzle that formed a painting of
Niagara Falls, painted by Frederic E. Church. It showed the great, rushing
green water melting over low red rocks and turning white and yellow as
it fell into the white-aired chasm. We'd put it together many times, and it
naturally made me remember our mother's photograph of her parents and
her, who'd been underneath the falls in a boat. It was our father's favorite
because it was dramatic. It represented the Hudson River School of painting, the box said, which made no sense to me because the box also said
it was the Niagara River—not the Hudson. I always wondered if there
wasn't a formula for joining the pieces so you could put the whole puzzle
together in an hour or less. Figuring out the picture every time and searching for the right pieces seemed like the hardest way of doing it. Plus, I
didn't know why you'd want to do it more than once. It wasn't like chess,
which could seem the same every time you played, but the number of different moves you could make was endless.

For a while I stood beside our father and pointed out purple-and-
blue sky pieces and the parts that were clearly the river. Berner asked our
mother if she could be allowed to leave the house and go for a walk, because the fan was bothering her sinuses, but both of them said she couldn't.

Our mother spent a good period of time again on the telephone in the
hall—something my father pretended not to pay attention to. She finally
took the phone on the long cord into their bedroom and closed the door.
I could make out her buzzing voice underneath the rattle of the fan. "No,
we wouldn't be doing this under ordinary circumstances, but . . . ," I heard
her say. And ". . . No reason to think that'll last forever . . ." was something else. These bits of conversation spoken to who I didn't know made
our father, sitting in the living room piecing together Niagara Falls, seem
strange to me—as if our mother was his mother, too, and had to look after
him as well as us.

After a while I went to my room and lay on my bed. Berner came in and closed the door and announced that, in her view, our parents were crazy. She said that after our mother had finished talking on the telephone she'd come out to the kitchen, and she—Berner—had gone and looked in their room as if she could detect who our mother had been talking to. Our mother's suitcase was lying open on her twin bed, articles of her clothes already in it. She went out and asked why the suitcase was there, and our mother said we'd soon be taking a trip. She didn't say to where. Berner asked if our father would be going, and our mother had said he certainly could if he wanted to, but probably he wouldn't. Berner said this conversation made her feel sick to her stomach and want to throw up— though she didn't—and after a while it made her want to run away from home and right then get married to Rudy Patterson. I thought I wasn't going to be invited to go with them on that trip.

At four o'clock our mother went in their bedroom to take a nap. When her door was shut, my father came to my room and looked in, then went to Berner's door. He wondered if we'd like to take a drive over to the fair-grounds, since he'd read admission was half-price the last afternoon and at night there'd be fireworks. He said there wasn't any reason not to stick our noses in. He smiled in a way I thought of as mischievous and gave the impression he was putting one over on our mother.

I, of course, did want to go very much. There were important, com-plicated things to be learned. Experts would be demonstrating in a glass-sided hive where the queen bee lived and how to deal with smoke pots so you didn't get stung to death—which my father had said and worried me.

Berner said she wasn't interested. Lying on her bed, she said people in school said only smelly Indians went the last day because they were broke and always drunk. She'd seen enough Indians after the carfuls that had come past our house all week while the two of them couldn't be bothered to stay around.

Our father had put on his polished cowboy boots and a pair of pressed jeans he wore to the land-sales office—though he hadn't shaved or combed his hair the way he usually did. He was smiling, but he looked strange again, as if his facial features weren't fixed on their bones right. Standing in Berner's doorway he told her he regretted the Indians coming by, but they were pacified now. Once his uncle Cleo had invited him to drive with him down to Birmingham. But he'd had a little girlfriend named Patsy at the time. He told Uncle Cleo he couldn't go because he had a chance to see Patsy. Then the next month Uncle Cleo got killed at a train crossing where the gate didn't work, and he never saw Uncle Cleo again and always regretted not going with him.

"I don't see that was your fault," Berner said from her bed, where she was filing her fingernails. "Maybe Uncle Cleo should've been more careful." She enjoyed bickering with him and feeling superior.

"No doubt about it," our father said. "I just thought I could go to Birmingham with Uncle Cleo any ole time. And it turned out I couldn't."

Berner said something I couldn't hear because of the fan. I thought she said, "So are you going to get killed if I don't go?"

"I hope not," my father said. "I truly hope that doesn't happen." Berner had a mouth—I already said that. My father's word for her was that she had "hauteur."

"That's blackmail," she said. "I don't want to be blackmailed."

"Maybe I'm not saying it right," our father said.

Then Berner said something else I didn't make out. But I knew she'd relented by the complaining tone in her voice. I heard the floorboards squeeze in her room. She couldn't resist him when he focused in on her. Only our mother could. We loved both of them, for what it mattered. This shouldn't get lost in the telling. We always loved them.

23

WE DROVE UP THIRD STREET, ALONG THE RIVER, past where Berner and I'd walked and fed the ducks. The sky had come unsettled again and windy, moving smells around. Flat, purple-bottomed clouds slid up out of the south. Whitecaps danced on the river surface and gulls soared in the damp breeze. There'd be a thunderstorm. It had been trying to all day. Fall was starting—our mother had been right.

I was thinking, in the back seat, not about the bee demonstration, but about the tent where the State Police exhibited their weapons for citizens' inspection. Some chess club members had speculated about the bazooka and the box of hand grenades and the Thompson submachine gun that would be on display there. There'd been conjecture about what uses the police would ever put these weapons to. The thinking revolved around Indians, who were considered a criminal element, and Communists, who plotted against America. I'd looked a third time in my father's sock drawer to find out if his pistol was there. It wasn't. I fantasized he'd shot someone (possibly the man Mouse) and disposed of the gun by throwing it in the river.

Berner sat in front and acted sullen about coming with us—which I didn't appreciate. There was traffic near the fairgrounds entrance. Twice our father looked in the rearview mirror and said, "Okay, who's that following so close behind us, Dell?" This was a game. I'd look through the rear window, but there wouldn't be anything. This time, however, I noticed the same black car twice. As we drove along outside the whitewashed fairgrounds fence, I saw the tops of the rides inside—the Ferris wheel, the Zephyr (which had been described to me at school), the curved top of the roller coaster with a train of cars snaking over and shooting down, with people waving and shouting. Music and crowd noise and loudspeaker voices were jumbled in the windy air the way I'd heard them at home—including women's voices reading out bingo numbers. The wind carried the aroma of sawdust and manure and something sweeter. It excited me to want to hurry inside before the gate shut. My jaw ached from clenching it, and my toes were tingling. Traffic, though, was clogged up by old beaters and rez jalopies full of kids and by people who were clearly Indians, walking single file along the roadside toward the pedestrian entrance.

It was just at that instant—when we were next in line to turn into the big entrance gate—that I found the packet of money. In nervousness, I'd pushed my hand into the crease between the back seat cushions and into the cool space below the seat, and my left hand made contact with something I pulled out at once. It was a packet of U.S. bills bound in a white paper sleeve, on which was stamped the words AGRICULTURAL NATIONAL BANK, CREEKMORE, NORTH DAKOTA. I was astounded. I said "Oh," loud enough to make my father instantly look at me in the driver's mirror. I stared right into his eyes, which were holding me prisoner. "What'd you see?" he said. "Did you see something behind us?" His mouth was moving below his eyes, but his voice was separate. I thought he might turn around and look at me—which Berner did. She looked straight at the packet of money, then immediately faced forward. "Did you see the goddamn cops?" my father said.

"No," I said.

People were honking behind us. We'd come to a complete stop when we were supposed to be turning left into the fairgrounds. Inside the gate, cars were parking on the grass, beyond which were the rides and the midway. A deputy was signaling us to go forward. Other cars were driving out and there was another deputy waving them on. It was a confusion.

"What the hell is it, then?" My father was irritated, glaring into the rearview, and not moving ahead.

"A bee," I said. "A bee stung me." It was all I could think of to say. I stuffed the bills down the front of my jeans. Berner turned around halfway and sneered at me, as if I was doing something I wasn't supposed to. My heart began pounding. I don't know why I didn't say *I found a lot of money. What's it doing in here?* Instead, I acted as if *I'd* stolen the money, or someone had, and I shouldn't get caught with it, but that it would go away if it was out of sight.

"Goddamn cops," our father said. "Spoil everything." He glared again into the mirror, at whoever was behind us. And instead of turning in front of the deputy and driving us into the fairgrounds, he mashed the accelerator and we spurted on down Third without turning. I didn't know why he was worried about the police.

"Where're we going?" I said, the white fence hurrying past.

"We'll go next year," my father said. "It's too crowded in there. They're letting every squaw in. And it's about to rain."

"No, it's not," I said.

"I thought you liked Indians," Berner said in her haughty voice.

"I do," our father said. "Just not today."

"If not today, when, then?" She said this only to taunt him.

"When I'm good and ready," he said. And that was the end of the fair.

24

WE DROVE DOWN TO SMELTER AVENUE AND Black Eagle. My father's eyes were fastened to the rearview as if he'd seen something he needed to get away from, which I guessed was the reason we weren't going to the fair. He pushed his fingers up through his hair and rubbed the back of his neck above his shirt collar. He looked at me because I was boring a hole in him with being angry. We were driving toward the smelter stack and the refinery, which kept its lights on day and night and had gas outlets spewing yellow flames. It stank when you got close to it. Rudy had said his father smelled like the refinery all the time, which was one reason his mother had moved to San Francisco.

"Does this mean we're not going?" Berner said.

"Most of the rides were already shut down," our father answered.

"No, they were not," Berner said. "I could see in. You were driving. Or trying to."

"I didn't care about the rides," I said. Hot refinery fumes filled the inside of the car.

"P-U-stink," Berner said, and rolled up her window as we went past the maze of pipes and giant valves and bulk tanks, and men in silver hard hats moving around on catwalks and metal scaffolds, and the long flame from the vent pipes licking the gusty air. The refinery stood between Smelter Avenue and the river. We were headed for the Fifteenth Street Bridge, which would take us back across into Great Falls.

"I wanted to see the bee exhibit," I said hopelessly and felt heartsick. It was one more thing I wouldn't get to learn.

"Bees are smarter than we are," Berner announced. The found money was bulging, lopsided in my pants front. Berner looked around at me again and smirked. She always pretended to know things I didn't and belittle me.

"Bees are like the people out here in Montana, if you ask me," our father said, angling to turn onto the bridge. "They're all one way. Worker bees. Spiritless. A bunch of hobnobby Swedes and Norskies and Germans who managed not to get bombed to smithereens. They're all tight like Jews. I've sold cars to 'em." He sometimes said he'd bombed the Japs so Jews could run pawn shops. I was tempted to tell him that the organism of the hive was not the individual bee, and humans could learn a big lesson from them. But I didn't want to draw attention to myself when I had the money in my pants.

"Where're we going," Berner said.

Our father was checking behind us in the mirror. "We'll go out to the base. Watch the jets take off." We'd done this every place we ever lived. He thought it was recreational. His eyes found me to see how I would take this in instead of going to the fair, which was now a bust. His eyebrows flickered, as if this was a joke Berner wasn't included in. I didn't smile back.

"Mother's got her bag half packed up," Berner said. "Where's she going?"

We were out onto the old WPA bridge. Our father sniffed, pinched his nostrils, then sniffed again. His eyes flickered toward the mirror, not at me. "I'm just married to your mother, okay? I can't read her every thought or know every single detail about her. She loves you very much. Just like

I do." He was agitated. He added, "I've got some bothers of my own right now that would occupy a wild beast's attention. I don't get everything perfect every time, I realize."

"Where'd you go when you left?" Berner looked straight at him, her freckled face pale, as if she was getting carsick. Our father looked in the rearview yet again. I looked to see what was behind us. A black Ford was there with two men in the front seat wearing suits. They were talking to each other. One was laughing. I couldn't remember if it was the car I'd seen at the fairgrounds, but I believed it was.

"Your mother might have to take you kids on a trip," he said. "Don't let it worry you."

"Did you hear what I said to you?" Berner said.

"Yes, I did." Our father clicked on his turn blinker as we were about to depart the bridge and intended to go east toward the base. But he suddenly speeded up, drove straight off the bridge, went another block, and turned right on Seventh toward downtown, and onto a pretty shaded street of white frame houses—nicer than ours—with more substantial elms and oaks and better-tended lawns and a redbrick school. I didn't know who lived here. Possibly the chess club boys whose fathers were lawyers. I'd never been in this part of town, though Great Falls wasn't very big. It was a town, not a city.

I looked behind us. The black Ford had turned and was still there, the two men still talking. We weren't going to the base to watch jets either.

"What'd you do with your pistol?" I said.

My father's eyes shot up at me, then back at the Ford. "What do you know about that?"

"I looked in your drawer."

He sighed in a frustrated way. "You oughtn't do that. That's my private affairs." He wasn't angry. He never got angry with us. We hadn't done anything anyway.

"Why is it private? What *makes* it private?" Berner said.

"Do you children know what making sense means?" His eyes kept running up to the rearview. We'd come all the way down Seventh to the river again. Whitecaps were still lathering the water's wide surface. Across the river was the fair, the tops of the Zephyr and the Ferris wheel and the roller coaster visible under the skating clouds. Nothing had been taken down. We could've been there.

My father suddenly twisted around in the driver's seat, though he was driving, and glared at me. I clutched my hands over the lump of money in my pants. The world would crack open if he saw it—I thought so, anyway. His eyes burned into me. His features—I could only see the right side—his cheek, his chin, his mouth, one eyebrow, they all seemed to be in motion. It frightened me. He wasn't watching where he was going. I'd forgotten what he'd said.

"I asked you a question. Do you know what making sense means?"

We'd talked about this subject earlier when he was polishing his boots. The game of chess made sense. You just had to wait to see what the sense was. He wouldn't be interested in that. "Yes," I said.

He gaped back around at the street. We were passing the back of the Cascade County jail. "What'd you say?" My voice hadn't been very loud.

"Yes, sir," I said, louder. "I do."

He looked around at me again, as if he still hadn't heard me. His breath was stale. He blinked at me. He seemed changed.

"Why don't you ask *me*?" Berner said, her chin up, defiant. "I know all about it."

"Good!" He glared at her as if she was thwarting him. "I'll tell you, though, just in case." He sawed his hand across his mouth and back up through his hair. "It means you accept things. If you understand, then you accept. If you accept, you understand." He fired an angry look at Berner, then his eyes flashed to the mirror again. The black Ford was there. The two men in suits. They looked to me like school principals, or salesmen.

We were driving toward the Central Avenue Bridge through the business section of town. Bars. The Rexall. Woolworth's. A tall office building at the bottom of which was the hobby shop where I bought my chess men. The city auditorium. There wasn't much traffic. All the people were at the fair for half-price. Our house was just across the river in its little shabby neighborhood.

"I don't think what you said is right," Berner declared. She looked around at me and fattened her cheeks. She looked old, like a school teacher. She liked defying him and wanted to give herself another excuse to run away.

"Well, *you're* wrong," our father said. "You're just wrong."

"I don't understand things," Berner said, "but I accept them. And I don't accept things, but I understand them." She folded her arms tightly and stared out the window at the river moving along under the bridge we were now on. "*You* don't make sense. That's all. And you know it."

Our father smiled oddly and shook his head. "Do you two children think I'm being mean to you? Is that it?" He regarded the mirror again to find out if the black car was still behind us—if it had made the turn onto the bridge. It had.

Neither of us said anything. I didn't understand why he'd even ask that. They were never mean to us. "Because I'm not," he said. "I just want you to learn an important lesson about life. Some things you have to accept and understand—even if they don't make sense at first. You have to make them make sense. That's what grown-ups do."

"I'll choose not to grow up in that case," Berner said spitefully. Our father was talking, I realized, about the money stuffed in my pants. He was saying one thing and meaning another. He'd seen me find it—in the mirror—or seen me stuff it down, when he'd looked around at me. What he was trying to tell me to do, before we got home, was to put it back where I'd found it, accept what I couldn't understand about where it came from. The worst thing would be for me to still have it down my pants when we drove up to our house and for it to have to be explained. Putting it back was what made sense. Once it was back, everything would be fine.

"I don't see any reason for you to start crying," our father said. Berner's arms were folded tight across her belly and she was staring fiercely out her window. "Nobody's done anything bad to you, sister."

"I'm not your sister," she said angrily. "And I'm not crying."

"Well, yes you are, too. But you shouldn't be." He looked at her, then back at the street. Central Avenue was leading us home.

At a certain point in our life Berner had stopped crying altogether, as if she couldn't stand to cry and hated how it made people—me, in particular—act toward her. She got angry instead. But I could tell she was crying because she put her little finger to the corner of either eye and breathed in deeply. There was no boo-hooing or sobbing or yowling like when we were children. I hadn't cried in longer than I could remember— longer than her. Our mother never cried. Though once our father had cried when he was watching a war movie on TV.

This was the only chance I'd have—with my father concentrating on Berner—to transfer the money packet back below the seat. I hunched forward as if I was tying my shoe and wrestled the packet out of my pants and crammed the wad back into the seat crevice where it fell out of my grip and made me feel, in the next second, a hundred percent better and lighter. When I looked up at the rearview mirror, my father was staring a hole in me again.

"What're *you* doing?" he said. Berner cast an aggrieved look at me as if I'd betrayed her. Her face was stricken. She turned away and looked out at the street again.

"Tying my shoe," I said. Our street was approaching. The crown of the elms and box elders in the park rocked in the breeze, the Lutherans' low belfry barely in sight among them.

"Ask your sister why she's standing on her lip." Our father clumsily reached a hand over and patted Berner on her shoulder. She didn't look at him. "I don't have any idea. I swear to God. Maybe she'll reveal it to you. Will you tell Dell, sweetheart, why you're crying? I'm not a mean man. I don't want you to think I am."

"People cry because they're miserable." Berner spit her words.

We were making our turn at the park. "Miserable?" It always shocked him when people didn't feel exactly the way he felt about something.

I'd looked again out the back window. The Ford with the two men had followed us through the turn past the Lutherans. Our father swerved suddenly to the curb, as if he wanted to get out of the black car's way. The Ford slid slowly by. The two men looked in at us. One was talking and the other was nodding. They drove to the corner, turned on the west side of the park and carried on slowly up to Central. I realized they were the police, but had no idea why they'd be following us. The money stuffed behind the seat didn't enter my thinking.

"Who do you think those two palookas are?" our father said, watching the Ford merge out onto Central. His fists were gripping the steering wheel. His jaw muscles were knotting as if he was working up to say something else. We sat silently in front of our house. White confetti from the Lutherans' wedding blew across the pavement onto our grass.

"Maybe," my father said. He stopped and smacked his lips and smiled at Berner who was still staring away, miserable. He turned to me, but I didn't know what I was supposed to say. "I was about to say those fellas are probably Mormon missionaries. They're wearing suits and ties. Maybe they've got a book they want us to read. I should've stopped and talked to them. That could've been interesting. Don't you think?" This meant he wanted us to think the men were a joke and we shouldn't give any thought to them. "Whadda ya say, sister?" It was his Dixie talk. He thought people liked it. His eyebrows danced up, and he shot me a look that meant we were again in cahoots and Berner wasn't. It was a look I always liked.

"I wish I was a long way from here," Berner said mournfully. "I wish I was in California or Russia."

"We all wish that sometime, sweetheart," our father said. "You and your mother seem to wish it more than most. You two'll have to discuss it." He twisted around to me. I expected him to say something, but he just smiled his big white-tooth smile, as if a battle had been lost. He popped open his car door and went on talking as he got out. "We're catching things on the upward stroke here, you two. We've put up with a bunch of hooey long enough."

Berner frowned, then sneered, as if he was contemptible and pathetic, which I didn't agree with, even if we hadn't gone to the fair.

"There you go," my father said outside the car, as if I'd answered him. "That's all I need to know." He leaned into the doorway where Berner and I were inside. Wind gusted up the street, swirling confetti and bending the tree tops more. Rich rain smell flooded in. It was going to storm. "You kids, get out now," my father said. "This is where we live. There's nothing we can do about it. Home sweet home. At least for now."

25

WHEN WE CAME IN, OUR FATHER ANNOUNCED he was dead tired and went into his and our mother's room and lay across his empty bed with the ceiling light on, still in his clothes and boots, and went straight to sleep, one arm over his eyes.

As the day slowly ended the neighbors' windows lit up and it began to rain—softly, then harder—picking up wind and sheeting rain drops against the windows. Chill breeze pushed through the house, ballooning the curtains and unsettling the newspaper on the dining room table. Our mother closed the windows and drew the curtains that were already damp, and turned on table lamps and put my father's shoe-shine kit away.

She didn't have much to say and seemed business-like. She cooked supper in the kitchen and didn't speak about Miss Remlinger or the calling she'd done or ask where we'd gone with our father. I informed her, however, that we'd left with the promise of visiting the fair, but it'd been too crowded. I didn't stray into finding the money under the seat or Berner crying and wanting to go to Russia, or the two policemen following us. I felt I should put all that off until later.

Berner, as usual, went in her room when we got home and closed the door without saying anything to anyone. Her radio was tuned low to music, and I could hear her moving around, scraping metal clothes hangers in her closet and talking to her fish, which must've made her feel less lonely. I believed she was packing clothes for her getaway. I wouldn't be able to talk her out of it, and I couldn't tell our parents. It was the way we'd always done things. Twins didn't cause one another trouble. But if she ran away I thought she'd come back. Nobody would hold it against her.

I sat in my own room with the window cracked open, feeling the shush of wind as the light fell, rain slashing the house shingles and spattering inside. There was no thunder or lightning, just whipping summer rain. From time to time it would stop, and through the wall I could hear my father snoring, and my mother in the kitchen and crows up in the wet tree limbs, squawking and hopping around, resettling themselves before the rain began again. I gave thought to the fair shutting down, rain drenching the sawdust and the tents and exhibits, workers dismantling the rides, loading them on trucks, and the bee exhibit and the gun display locked up and taken away. I got down my *World Book* letter "B" and read about bees. Everything in the hive was an ideal, orderly world where the queen was honored and sacrificed for. If this didn't happen, everything fell into confusion. Bees, as I'd read before, were the key to everything human, because they responded perfectly to their environment and to other bees. This was something specific I could write a report about right at the start of school and get off on a good footing. I put a pencil in at the page and closed the volume. I'd be more relaxed when school started and my father was back to work and my mother was teaching.

After a while my father's sleepy voice began speaking in low tones. His sock feet bumped the floor. The noise of dishes and pots and pans were clattering in the kitchen. My mother spoke, also in low tones. ". . . A fish in deep water," our father said. ". . . In the best of all worlds . . . ," she said. I wondered if they would talk about the money behind the car seat, or how my father's pistol had gotten lost, or where they'd gone, or my mother's suitcase on the bed. Lying on my own bed in the soft night breeze, rain dampening the bottom of my bedspread, the line of hall light below my door, such questions swirled around. They were very close to me, then just as suddenly very far away, so that I grabbed the sides of my mattress and held it. I felt the way I felt when I'd been sick with scarlet fever, years before, and couldn't completely be awake. My mother had come in and sat by my bed and laid a cool finger on my temple. My father had stood in the doorway—tall, shadowy. "How is he?" he'd said. "Maybe we should take him." "He'll be all right," my mother said. I'd pulled the spread up to my chin and squeezed.

I listened to an owl out in the dark. I wanted to think my thoughts through again. But there was no holding back sleep. And so for a time I let it all rush away from me.

26

DO YOU WANT YOUR SUPPER?" MY MOTHER SAID softly, leaning over me. Her glasses lens caught light from somewhere behind her. Her palm was on my cheek; her fingers smelled of soap. She brushed my hair, held the helix of my ear lightly between her thumb and forefinger. I'd twisted into my sheets and couldn't move my arms. My hands were asleep. "You're very hot," she said. "Do you feel sick?" She went to the foot of my bed and touched the bedspread. "It rained in on you."

"Where's Berner?" I was thinking she was gone.

"Ate and went to bed." My mother pulled the window closed.

"Where's Dad?" Something strenuous had passed through me. My mouth was pasty-weedy, my hair stuck to my scalp. My joints ached.

"He hasn't gone anyplace."

She moved back to the doorway. Amber light was in the hall. Water was trickling behind the walls, or outside. "It rained and rained," she whispered. "Now it's stopped. I made you a sandwich."

"Thank you," I said. She passed back out the door and disappeared.

AT THE DINING ROOM TABLE, I ate the grilled cheese with a pickle and a leaf of lettuce and French dressing—things I liked. I was hungry and ate in a hurry and drank a glass of buttermilk. My father believed it was restorative. My clothes were wrinkled and damp. The house was cool and clean smelling, as if the wind had scoured it. *We* had scoured it days before. It was ten thirty at night, the wrong time to be eating supper at the table.

I heard my father's boot heels on the front porch boards. His back passed by the window. Occasionally he coughed and cleared his throat. Several cars drove past—their slanted lights fell across the curtains, which were partly open. One stopped at the curb. A strong beam of light opened and flashed around the damp yard. You couldn't see who was inside. From the dark porch, my father said, "Good evening, fellas. Welcome. We're all here, supper's on the table." He laughed loudly. The light went out, and the car idled away without anyone speaking or getting out. My father laughed again and paced some more, whistling notes that didn't make a tune.

My mother had gone back into their bedroom. From where I sat at the table I could see her. More of her clothes were in her suitcase. She was folding other clothes and laying them on top. She looked out through the door, and for some reason being seen startled me. "Come in here, Dell," she said. "I want to talk to you."

I came in my sock feet. I was heavy-bodied as if I'd eaten too much. I would've lain on her bed and gone to sleep in front of her.

"How was your sandwich?"

"Why're you packing?"

She went on folding clothes. "I thought we'd go to Seattle on the train tomorrow."

"When will we be back," I asked.

"Whenever we're ready to."

"Is Berner going?"

"Yes. She is. I explained it to her already."

"Is Dad?" I'd asked this before.

"No." She went to the closet and rehung the empty hangers that had been on the bed.

"Why not?" I said.

"He has some business to tie up. He likes being here anyway."

"What're we going to do in Seattle?"

"Well," my mother said in her business-like voice. "It's a real city. You'll meet your grandparents. They're interested to know you and your sister."

I stared hard at her the way Berner stared at me. She hadn't said why we were going, and I knew I wasn't supposed to ask.

"What about school?" My heart began speeding up. I didn't want it to be that I wouldn't be starting. That happened to boys you never saw again. My throat tightened. My eyes burned as if tears were already in them.

"Don't worry about that."

"I already have a lot of plans," I said.

"I know about them. We all have plans." She shook her head as if this was a silly conversation. She looked at me and blinked once behind her glasses. She looked tired. "You have to be flexible," she said. "People who aren't don't go far in the world. I'm trying to be flexible."

I thought I knew what that word meant, but it seemed to mean something else, too. Like "making sense." I didn't want to admit I wasn't whatever flexible meant.

Wind rose outside the house and blew water out of the leaves, clattering on the roof. Inside was perfectly still.

My mother walked to the bedroom window, cupped her hands to the glass and peered out. The window pane reflected the room and her and me and the bed with her suitcase and clothes. She was very small in front of the window. Beyond her, I could see only shapes and shadows. The garage with the pale hollyhocks and zinnias growing beside it. The empty clothesline where she'd retrieved the clean clothes. An oak sapling my father had planted and tied to a stake. His car. "What do you know about

Canada?" she said. "Hm?" This was a sound she made when she was wanting to be friendly.

Canada was beyond Niagara Falls in my father's puzzle. I'd never looked it up in the encyclopedia. It was north of us. Hot tears were in my eyes. I breathed out as far as I could and held it. "Why?" My voice was constricted.

"Oh." She leaned her forehead against the window glass. "I have the habit of only seeing things the way they're presented to me. I'd like you to turn out different. It's a weakness of mine." She tapped the pane lightly with her fingernail. It was as if she was signaling someone in the dark. She took off her glasses, breathed onto the lenses, and wiped them on her blouse sleeve. "Your sister's different," she said.

"She's a lot smarter than I am." I quickly rubbed my eyes and wiped my hand on my pants leg so as not to be noticed.

"She probably is. The poor thing." My mother turned and smiled at me in her friendly way. "Why don't you go back to bed now. We're leaving in the morning. The train goes at ten thirty." She put her finger over her mouth to signal me not to say anything. "You don't have to take anything but your toothbrush. Leave everything here. Okay?"

"Can I bring my chess men?"

"Okay," she said. "My dad plays chess. Or he used to. It'll give you two something to disagree about. Now you go."

I went out of their room. She went back to packing her suitcase. Everything else I'd have wanted to say or ask—about the police, about school and Berner running away, about why we were going—there wasn't a chance for. It was what I said already: things were happening around me. My part was to find a way to be normal. Children know normal better than anyone.

27

LATER, MY MOTHER CAME IN AGAIN AND TUCKED A dry blanket under my feet where the mattress was damp. I kept my eyes closed but could smell mothballs from the blanket. My door closed quietly, and I heard her knock on Berner's door. Berner said, "I have a stomach ache." My mother said, "You'll get used to that. I'll bring you a hot water bottle." Her door closed, and in a while my mother came back in her room and they talked some more. Berner's bedsprings squeaked. "Of course, of course," I heard my mother say. Then her footsteps went back to the kitchen where water began running.

The rain stopped altogether, and cool air again filtered through my room. I'd thought I might hear the fireworks at the fair and had re-raised the sash to hear them. But I only heard the furnace whistle at the smelter and a siren out in town. In the air was the strong scent of cows from the freight yards. I heard my father's footsteps, then their two voices, speaking. They spoke briefly, in a clipped way, followed by silence, as if they had little to say. In a while my mother—I recognized her footsteps—went back to their bedroom and closed the door. My father went back out to the front porch and sat on the swing—the screen door squeaking open and closed.

I thought of Seattle then for a time. I'd only seen a few cities—none of them large. My picture of Seattle was of the sun inching up from below a dark ocean, buildings gradually growing in silhouette as light found them. Only I remembered then that the sun came from the east. Light would fall on the buildings from the other direction. I tried to imagine the space needle, what that would look like. A great needle high in the air. Then I must've gone to sleep. The last thing I remember was that I'd been wrong about the sun coming up, and that I'd never tell anyone about it.

IN THE NIGHT when I got up to use the toilet, I found my father alone at the card table with his Niagara Falls puzzle spread out like a meal in front of him. All the lights in the front of the house were on. Niagara Falls was almost complete. Only a few pale pieces of jagged sky needed setting in. He was wearing the clothes he'd had on earlier—his white shirt, which was wrinkled, and jeans, and his boots that were scuffed on their toes. However, he'd shaved and smelled like he'd had a bath. He looked around at me and seemed happy to see me, though I intended to go straight back to bed.

He just started talking. "You know, when I was a boy. Your age . . ." He fingered a piece of puzzle and held it up for inspection, then tried it in the empty space in the sky, where it fitted down perfectly. His fingernails still had shoe polish under them. ". . . I was a pretty good athlete. Sports were crucial. Nobody had anything else to be happy about. You know what the Depression was, I'm sure."

I'd already read about Roosevelt and Hoover and the Workers' March and bread lines, in civics. I said, "Yes, sir."

"Well . . ." He carefully tried another piece of the puzzle, which didn't fit. He shook his head. "I could've been *very* capable in sports—football and baseball, too. Just nobody ever taught me anything. You know? The coaches didn't. You sank or you swam on your native ability. So . . ." He smiled like he was happy to be explaining this. "I sank." He cleared his throat and swallowed. "That's what led me to join the U.S. Army. Not directly. But eventually." He picked up a smaller puzzle piece and delicately pressed it into the empty space and made a humming noise when it fit. There were only four more pieces not in place. He turned in his chair and inspected me. I had on my blue-and-white-striped pajama bottoms and was barefoot. "Why are you awake?" he said. "Do you have big bothers?"

"No, sir," I said. Though I did. School. Leaving. Why he wasn't going with us. Why the police were following us and driving by our house. I had plenty of bothers.

"Well, that's great," he said. "That's the way it should be if you're fifteen. Isn't that what you are?" He relaxed back into the dining room chair.

"Yes, sir," I said.

He used a puzzle piece to scratch in his ear. "Your mother's holding herself out for something, I think. It's possible she always has. A future life. I don't blame her. But I'm not sorry I married her. We wouldn't have you and your sister otherwise." He looked at the puzzle piece as if it had something interesting attached to it. "She's a little resentful toward me at the moment. She'll figure it all out when you get to Seattle. She *went* to college—unlike myself."

"Why didn't you go?" I wanted to ask him why he wasn't going with us, and why she'd resent him, but I asked this instead. I'd always wanted to know.

"The subject just never came up." He looked unconcerned. "It was believed I was already smart enough. For my prospects. Which was probably right."

"Are you coming with us to Seattle?" I knew he wasn't, but I wanted to seem as if it was still possible he would.

"I'm happy here. I told you this afternoon. I'll be here when you get back. This is your mother's plan."

"Are you going to go to work again?"

He smiled broadly and went back in his ear with the puzzle piece. "If they'll have me. I'm just getting started. I do have a knack for it, I think."

He held the piece up, turning it back and forth for me to see. He'd done this trick many times for Berner and me when we were little. His eyes got round. His smile flickered at the corners as if he felt uncertain about something—which he didn't. He suddenly popped the puzzle piece in his mouth, chewed it and swallowed down in a big dramatic gulp, after which he cleared his throat, coughed exaggeratedly. "Boy," he said. "That was tasty. I like puzzles better than pennies and buttons."

"It's in your hand," I said. I touched my ear, where such things also often turned up.

"I ate it," he said. "Would you like one? I have three left." He picked up one of the last pieces.

"It's in your hand," I said again.

He put both his hands on his knees and tapped them and nodded. I was waiting for him to produce the piece. "You go to bed, colonel," he said. "You've got a busy day. We all do." He reached and grabbed my bare shoulder and pulled me to him so I could feel his big body—very warm and citrusy smelling. He clapped my back three times, then held me out at arm's length and looked serious. I was still waiting on the puzzle piece to reappear. Like a fool. "We'll work on your physique when you come back," he said. "You need some new muscles. When I see you again, that's what we'll do."

"Where's the piece of the puzzle?" I said.

He pointed to his belly with his finger. "Right down about there," he said, and poked himself and looked down. "It's not a trick *every* time. That's the magician's secret. Good night."

"Good night," I said. I went back to my room, closed the door, and went to sleep in my cold bed.

28

SUN SHONE THROUGH THE WET LEAVES INTO MY room, a webbed rectangle of light on the floor and the foot of my bed. The Lutherans' Sunday bell had waked me up. I'd been awake in the night, or else I'd dreamed a dream so vivid I thought I'd done the things I dreamed. A bat had been trapped against my window screen. I'd climbed out of bed and pushed the sash higher and tapped the screen with a pencil eraser, careful not to hurt it through the tiny squares. I saw its little grimaced human face, its gray silky skin, its pulsing wings. It stared at me as if I'd called it. I tapped the screen lightly. It looked from side to side. Then it vanished, free, the screen empty.

A car had been stopped in the alley, just past the garage, its motor running, its exhaust heavy in the air. A light snapped on inside. Two men were visible, wearing suits. The one riding was reading something to the one driving—holding a piece of white paper. They both leaned and looked at our house, through the clothesline posts. They couldn't see me. There was no light behind me. One of the men, however, pointed a finger at me, then their light was extinguished. The motor revved. Tires splashed over the wet gravel. Then the dream ended.

* * *

I HEARD Berner's voice down the hall. I lay staring at water stains in the ceiling—flaking rust outlines like states of the union. How long ago the Lutherans' bell had rung, I didn't know. A dog had howled a street behind ours. Possibly our trip to Seattle was postponed. If I stayed in my bed it might be forgotten. I didn't want to go.

I heard our mother speaking in a clipped voice to Berner. Almost immediately my door opened and my mother was there, cross-looking and intent. "I let you sleep. But we have to go now." She had the pink pillowcase with white scalloped edges off her bed. "Put what you're taking in this." She stepped in and dropped the pillowcase on my bed. "Don't take much. We'll buy what you need new where we're going." She stared at me. I was covered to my chin, sunlight dividing the floor and a section of the white wall. Our mother was again wearing the green wool suit skirt with the pink plaid, but now she had on a white blouse. She looked smaller and younger dressed this way. Her features were collected around her nose and glasses. "Your sister's dressed," she said. "Don't make me have to tell you again." She disappeared, my door left open as a warning.

I put on my clothes in a hurry. There didn't seem time to take a bath. Into the pillowcase I put my balsa-wood box of chess men, my *Chess Master* magazines, my *Chess Fundamentals*, and my *Bee Sense* book I'd checked out of the library and meant to return. I put in two volumes of the *World Book*—the "B" and the "M," which were thick ones and held more information. I put in a pair of socks, Jockey underpants, a T-shirt, and nothing else, since my father had said we'd be back. I went to the bathroom and cleaned my teeth, washed my face and under my arms ("the airman's bath," my father called it). I combed my hair and used the Wildroot my father let me share. I hadn't seen him, only heard his voice. "These children need to eat," he'd said. "They can eat on the train," my mother answered him in a testy way.

Berner was sitting in the living room, waiting, wearing her loose gray-and-blue polka-dot dress and her white tennis shoes and white socks.

Her hair was pulled back in the bushy way she usually wore it. She wasn't wearing lipstick. She was sitting on the davenport with her freckled knees pressed together and looked irritated and pale, as if she still had her stomach ache. Her green overnight case sat between her feet—a present my parents had given to her for our fifteenth birthday. It bore a stamped alligator-skin pattern, and she'd made no bones about hating it. It had been a prize at a raffle at the base. When I passed the hall door, heading to my room, she stared at me from behind her glasses with a dead-eyed expression. The Niagara Falls puzzle, all put together, still lay on the card table, lacking only the piece my father had eaten. It could never be finished and was useless.

Our father walked out of the kitchen then, dressed as he'd been in the middle of the night. He looked large and loose-limbed and in good spirits, though he hadn't shaved and was gray faced. "You're a grown-up girl now," he said to Berner. "You still don't look like you feel very well. You better stay at home with me." She was obviously about to say something contrary, but my mother's voice came out of the kitchen. "Just don't. Don't pester her. She feels fine."

My father gazed around the living room as if a lot of people were in it and were listening to him. He saw me and smiled and winked. "She's my daughter," he said loudly. "I'm not pestering her. I'm talking to her. I'll take care of your fish while you're gone," he said.

That was when the doorbell rang out through the house. My father looked at me. He was still smiling. He extended his two arms in a frustrated way I'd seen him do before to express amazement—palms up, as if rain was falling out of the ceiling. "Well, I just wonder who this'll turn out to be," he said and began walking across the living room to open the front door. "Maybe it'll be those Mormons, and they'll have the good news we've been waiting for. We'll have to just go see, won't we?"

From the kitchen, my mother said, "Who is that?" She dropped a dish onto the floor then. It broke to bits just as my father was pulling the door back to whatever news was waiting for us.

29

TIME HAS TO BE TALLIED DIFFERENTLY NOW. FOR the next day and a half—until Monday at noon—hours went past in a galloping, confused way. I remember details but few of their connectors. Leading up to then, time had been almost seamless, the durable order of family life. Even now I can sometimes think the next two days didn't happen, or that I dreamed them, or misremembered them. Though it's wrong to wish away even bad events, as if you could ever have found your way to the present by any other means.

TWO LARGE MEN were standing on the porch when our father opened the front door. Our mother walked out of the kitchen and sat down at the dining room table. Her suitcase was beside the davenport, where Berner was still sitting with her green case between her feet. I was in the hallway, holding my pink pillowcase with my chess men and my books inside. Our mother hadn't bothered to pick up the dish she'd dropped.

"Why hello there, Bev," one of the men said from outside the door. They were both wearing suits with their front buttons unbuttoned. Both were wearing snap-brim hats made for summer wear. They were heavy-bodied, bigger than my father, but not taller. They were the men who'd been behind us in the black Ford and who'd been in the alley behind our house when I thought I'd been dreaming. The larger and older of the two had a big fleshy-soft reddish face with heavy brows and a fat neck that went up into his chin. He wore glasses. He'd been the one riding, and who had pointed me out. They were the police.

Our father cast a look around behind him toward our mother. He smiled as if the police knowing his name and knowing we lived here was comical.

"What's all the commotion about, boys?" our father said in an exaggerated way. The two men had moved into the doorway. They were too large to get in side-by-side and had each turned a little.

"Not any commotion, Bev," the big policeman said and inched farther in, taking a look past our father at whatever else was inside our living room. His mouth seemed to be about to smile but not quite. The other man was younger and slenderer but still big with a broad face and slitted blue eyes. I'd been told this look meant a person was of Finnish extraction. He was looking inside, too. "Who else you got in here, Bev?" the older policeman said. My father took a step back and held his arms away from his sides and looked around the room himself.

"Us chickens." He seemed relaxed about what was happening.

"Happen to have a pistol on you, do you?" The big policeman extended his large hand and touched my father's shoulder. Both men were inside our living room now. It felt filled up, all the space gone. Six people. There had never been six people in it before. I could hear the older policeman breathing.

"I sure do not." My father looked down the front of himself as if this was where a pistol would be. "I don't own a pistol." His voice had more of his southern accent in it now.

"Not in the house somewhere?" The policeman's gaze was casting around. His lenses magnified his pale blue eyes.

"No, sir. Not in this house." My father shook his head.

"Have you been out visiting in North Dakota recently, Bev?" The big policeman didn't act very serious, as if this was an ordinary conversation. He stepped by my father toward me, where I was in the hallway door. He leaned past and looked down the hall to the bathroom and our parents' bedroom. The taller, younger policeman stared at my father as if that was his job.

"How're you, son?" The big policeman put his big hand on my shoulder. He smelled like a cigar and like leather. He was wearing rubber overshoes that had mud on them. Little mud cleats had already come off on our clean floor.

"Fine," I said. A gold badge was attached to his trouser belt under his coat. His belly was tight under his white shirt. He had a tiny gold triangle pin on his lapel.

"You going on a trip?" he said in a friendly way.

I looked at our mother. "We're going to Seattle. On the train today. To see their grandparents," she said.

"I haven't been to North Dakota," my father said.

The big policeman kept his hand on my shoulder. He took an appraising look into the kitchen where the broken dish lay on the linoleum. "Is that your Chevy around back?"

"Yes, it is," my father said. "I haven't owned it very long."

"But you've owned it a couple of days, haven't you?" the policeman said. I didn't want to move with his hand on me.

"Oh, yes," my father said. He grinned at my mother like this was an amusing question. His features were alive on his face, his eyes darting, his mouth seeming to move before he spoke. He had a little pill of spit in the corners of his lips. He licked one away and made his jaw muscles jump. Both his hands were swinging at his sides as if he was about to do something unexpected.

"Maybe you children could go sit in your rooms," our mother said.

Berner immediately stood, picked up her overnight case, and started toward the hall. But the big policeman raised his hand and said, "Better stay in here, I guess." He pulled me toward him so I felt his pistol under his coat. Berner stopped and looked at our mother. Her mouth made a wrinkled line, which meant she was irritated.

"Do as you're told," my mother said. Berner walked stiffly back to the davenport and sat on it with her case on her knees.

The big policeman walked to the piano and leaned to get a close look at my father's discharge and the picture of President Roosevelt and the metronome.

"You still have your Air Force flight suit?" The policeman pushed his glasses down to the tip of his nose and drew closer to the discharge as if it interested him.

"Gracious no," my father said. "I've got a better wardrobe. I'm in the farm and ranch business now." I had no idea why he would lie about that.

"What's your name, young lady?" the big policeman said. He looked around at Berner. The other policeman kept his eyes on my father.

"Berner Parsons," Berner said. It sounded wrong to hear her say it inside our house.

"Did you go on a trip to North Dakota recently, Berner," the policeman asked.

"No." She shook her head.

"Don't talk to him," my mother said, suddenly very angry. Though she stayed in her place at the table. "She's a child."

"You sure don't have to talk to me." The policeman smiled at my father in a way that made his red policeman's cheeks fatten and his eyebrows rise. He pushed his glasses back up on his nose and put his thumbs under his belt and hitched at his trousers, revealing white socks above his muddy overshoes. He gave out a sigh. "Maybe we can go outside, Bev, and talk a little more. Bishop can entertain everybody till we're back." He nodded to the other policeman, who moved away from the door.

"Okay," our father said. His southern accent was very distinct. He was still swinging his arms back and forth and looking side to side as if everyone was watching him. It wasn't a good way to see him be. He looked hopeless. I've always remembered that.

The policeman, Bishop, reached behind and pushed open the screen door. Sunlight had broken through the trees and warmed the air outside. Last night's rain was sparkling on our lawn. Lutherans were walking to church. Our father moved toward the door with the big-bellied policeman guiding him, his hand in the small of our father's back. "What're we going to talk about?" our father said as he stepped out onto the porch. He ran his hand through his hair and looked down where his boots were going.

"Well, we'll dream up something," the big policeman said, following him.

"You don't have to say anything," our mother shouted.

"I know I don't," our father said.

The other policeman, Bishop, closed the glass front door. I couldn't see anything else that went on outside, and then we were all four alone together in our house.

3 0

I T COULD'VE BEEN FIVE MINUTES, BUT IT COULD'VE been fifteen, that we were in the house with the policeman, Bishop. The Lutherans' bell rang several more times. They'd shut their doors and commenced their service.

Sun was on the roof, and it had become hot and still in the living room. Normally, we would've switched on the attic fan, but none of us moved. I set my pillowcase down and sat on the piano bench. My mother kept her eyes on me, as if there was something I needed to be thinking. I didn't know what. I wondered what it was my father didn't have to talk about. I assumed the police would leave soon and we would talk about it. We'd missed our train now.

The young policeman stood with his back to the front door, his hands in his coat pockets. He was chewing gum, and at a certain point took off his hat and rubbed his forehead with a white handkerchief out of his pocket. He had short, almost white-blond hair and looked younger with his hat off. I thought he was thirty, although I didn't know about people's ages. His hair and his broad face and his slitted eyes didn't fit together, but seemed natural for a policeman. He looked like the kind of boy Berner might like. His eyes had a wildness that was like Rudy's.

"Do you go to school?" he said to me. My mother kept staring at me but didn't speak. I didn't know what she wanted me to do or not do. Berner was squirming in her clothes. She put her green case down and sighed a deep sigh to indicate she was impatient.

"Yes," I said.

He wiped his eyes with his handkerchief, folded it and put it inside his coat, then returned his hat to his head. The hat made him look too young to wear a hat.

"Meriwether Lewis," I said.

"You're in junior high?" He seemed surprised. "You don't look big enough." I looked at my mother. I didn't know what was going on in her head. "I went there fifteen years ago," Bishop said. "I got some kids now." He looked at my mother and let his eyes stay on her. "Are you very well acquainted in Great Falls?" He said this to her. My mother let her eyes move to him, then down to her hands folded on the table top. She suddenly directed her gaze to the front window where she could possibly see my father and the other policeman. "Are you these children's natural parents?" Bishop said, when she didn't answer the first question. He leaned against the door jamb, his eyes on my mother as if she was strange-looking to him—which she must've been.

"Is that any business of yours?" she said.

"No," Bishop said. "I wouldn't say so." He pulled on the lobe of his left ear and smiled. My mother let her eyes shift toward the window again.

The policeman laughed in the front yard, as if he and our father were enjoying a joke. I could hear them through the glass door. It made me think everything was all right now. The policeman said, "Oh, that's understandable, Bev. It's our job."

"You two don't seem like bank robbers," Bishop said. "You look like people who'd work in a grocery store."

I couldn't get breath in my lungs for a moment then. My mouth went open to speak. But words didn't come out. I closed my mouth and tried to breathe a complete breath. I didn't want to look at Berner.

"That's not any of your business either," my mother said.

"Now there's where you're wrong," Bishop said.

Someone was speaking on the other side of the front door. Heavy footsteps bumped the porch boards. My mother stayed where she was at the dining room table. My heart had begun slamming in my chest. I wanted her to announce that no one here was a bank robber. Instead, she just stared at me. "You two don't go anywhere. Just stay in this house," she said to both Berner and me. "Do you understand? Don't leave here with anybody unless it's Miss Remlinger. Is that clear?" Her hands shifted from her left holding her right, to her right holding her left.

The front door opened—it seemed sudden—and the big policeman came striding right in. He had his straw snap-brim in his hand. His head was nearly bald and round and had red blotches on it. I could see our father outside on the lawn with his hands behind his back. He was grinning toward the front door and shaking his head and shouting something. I thought he was shouting at me, but I couldn't understand him.

"Aren't we going to Seattle?" Berner said. She was still sitting on the couch in her polka-dot dress. She couldn't see out the door.

"Just do what I say," our mother said.

"I'm going to have to ask you to stand up now, Mrs. Parsons," the big policeman said. Calling her "Mrs. Parsons" was unexpected and shocking.

There was a lot of movement in the room then, a lot of commotion—shoes and chairs scraping the floor, material rubbing against material, breathing and leather squeezing together. Bishop produced a pair of silver handcuffs, and he and the bald policeman moved around the dining room table and put their hands on my mother's shoulders. "Come on and stand up for me, Neeva," the big policeman said. He set his hat on the table. Our mother didn't stand up or move, but became rigid and did not speak—though her lips were parted. The two policemen on either side raised her by her arms and turned them back and pulled her hands together behind her. She didn't resist, but her hands had been trembling, and she kept blinking behind her glasses, then looking upward. The big policeman took the handcuffs and clicked them carefully onto my mother's wrists. "Don't make 'em too tight for the ladies." He smiled when he said it.

Our father had gone on talking where he was, outside by himself. "This could be a lot worse now," I heard him say. Some of the Lutherans had come out of their church building and were watching. One man in a cowboy hat said something that I couldn't hear. "All right, all right," my father shouted out. "The fair's left town. The fair's left town."

"I have two children here," our mother said to the policemen, who'd begun moving her awkwardly around the dining room table, her hands behind her. Because she was small, her arms didn't reach easily around to her back. It is not simple to describe what I saw. The big policeman's cigar odor was all inside the room, as if he'd been smoking. He was breathing stiffly. My mother's feet didn't move willingly, but she didn't struggle or say anything other than to say she had two children. Her eyes became fixed in front of her—not on me—as if what she was doing was difficult to perform.

"Oh, yes, I know you do," the big policeman said, moving her forward almost daintily. "I know that."

"Tell us where you're going," Berner said. She looked calm, but she was in shock the way I was. We had no idea what to say or do. "We'll be here when you come back," she said. The police were leading our mother through the front door. Our father was on the sidewalk, talking like a crazy man. My sister and I watched it all. It's not an occurrence that you could imagine happening.

I stood up from the piano bench then. Standing seemed to be what I should do. My heart was still pounding, but I felt calm at the same time, as if there was nothing around me.

"Remember what I said." Our mother was talking, but not looking around. They were on the porch, and she was staring at her feet, taking care going down the front steps, both policemen holding her arms so she seemed even smaller. "Don't go anywhere until Mildred comes to get you."

The big bulky policeman turned back at the bottom step and said, "Get me my hat, sonny." His hat was still on the dining room table.

I went across the room, picked up the little straw hat—it was amazingly light and smelled like sweat and cigars. I walked onto the porch and handed it to him. He flipped it up onto his bald head with the hand that wasn't holding my mother's arm.

"Somebody'll come look after you kids," he said.

Our mother's face flashed around at me. Berner had come to the door. In my memory's eye, our mother's face was surrounded by darkness. "You leave them strictly alone," she said in an angry voice. "I've made arrangements for them." She was addressing me.

"It's a juvenile matter," the big policeman said and took a harsher grip of her arm. "You're not involved in it now."

"They're my children." She glared at him.

"You might've considered that," he said. "They belong to the State of Montana today."

The two of them moved my mother along down the concrete walk where my father was, hands trussed behind him, laughing and gawking. Bits of white confetti were stuck to the concrete walk from yesterday.

"Do I get to see a lawyer?" my father said. He seemed in high spirits. "I don't think I know one."

The policeman, Bishop, began leading him toward the police car and getting the back door open. "You won't need one, Bev," he said.

"You know you don't have to do this, I don't gauge." My father was looking around back toward me. I don't *gauge*, he said. I'd never heard him say that before.

"You're wrong there," Bishop said.

As she was being put into the back seat of the police car, our mother's glasses slipped off one side of her face and ear. The big policeman, who had her arm, delicately replaced them so they were where they belonged. She looked around at me again from the open car door. "Just stay in the house, Dell," she called out. "Don't leave with anybody but Mildred. Run if you have to."

"I won't," I said. I thought she had tears in her eyes.

Our father was on the far side of the car, in the street. He was being forced down inside the door. He suddenly looked up over the car roof. His wild eyes found me, and he shouted out, "I told you. Nothing distinctive about these monkeys." The policeman Bishop set his hand more firmly on top of our father's head and pushed him hard down into the back seat, where our mother already was. Our father said something else, but I couldn't understand it. Bishop slammed the door. More people were watching from the steps of the church where they'd come out to see. It was a spectacle, the worst possible thing that could happen, happening in the worst possible way.

Bishop came around to the driver's side of the police car. The older, bulky policeman got into the passenger's side. My mother's face was there in the rear side window. She was speaking angrily—it looked like—to our father on the seat beside her. She didn't see me. The police car clanked down into gear and pulled off slowly toward the corner of the park. I stood on the front porch and watched it all take place. *Let* it take place. *Let* my parents be arrested and driven off as if it was all right with me. Sun was shining in separate streams through the elm leaves. Air was heavy and warm. Faint diesel aroma drifted from the freight yards. Out on Central, the police siren whooped once, the motor revved and sped up. Other cars in the street pulled out of the way. Then I went back inside rather than stand and watch and be a spectacle to our neighbors, who I didn't know. I couldn't really think what else to do. I couldn't just stand there. Then that part of this was at an end.

31

YOU'D THINK THAT TO WATCH YOUR PARENTS BE handcuffed, called bank robbers to their faces and driven away to jail, and for you to be left behind might make you lose your mind. It might make you run the rooms of your house in a frenzy and wail and abandon yourself to despair, and for nothing to be right again. And for someone that might be true. But you don't know how you'll act in such a situation until it happens. I can tell you most of that is not what took place, though, of course, life was changed forever.

WHEN I CAME BACK in the house, Berner had gone in her room and shut the door. I stood alone in the middle of the living room and looked around, my heart beating fast and my feet full of bees. I surveyed the pictures on the wall—the ones that had come with the house and our few. The picture of President Roosevelt and my father's discharge. There was my pillowcase with my belongings; my mother's suitcase; Berner's alligator overnight bag. I let my gaze inventory my mother's small shelf of books, the Niagara Falls jigsaw on the card table, the scratched piano and the few pieces of Montgomery Ward furniture we'd brought to Great Falls when I was eleven. None of it amounted to anything. The stained Persian carpet on the floor. The television. My father's record player. The wallpaper with its repeated pattern of a sailing vessel. The stained ceiling with the fruity light fixture and the medallion my father admired. I was in charge of it—for the moment, at least. I needed to assess things properly. Be calm and orderly.

I actually didn't think of our parents at that moment—on their way across the river to jail. I didn't wonder about the bank they'd supposedly robbed. On the one hand, it didn't seem possible they hadn't robbed one, since they'd been arrested for it and hadn't said they were innocent. I lacked a developed idea about bank robbery and people who did it. Bonnie and Clyde didn't seem like our parents. The Rosenbergs, who I knew about, were entirely different. Truly, when I thought about our parents in those first hours, it wasn't about whether they'd robbed a bank or hadn't; it was more that they'd gone behind a wall, or a boundary, and Berner and I were left on the other side. I wanted them to come back. Their life was still our real life, the big life. We still lived in between them. But they would have to come back across the wall for life to go on. For some reason, it seemed doubtful that they would. Possibly I was still in shock.

What I almost immediately thought of was the money under the car seat. I felt a panic that someone—the police—was going to find it. The Agricultural National Bank, which was printed on the sleeve around the bills, meant nothing to me. The big policeman had mentioned North Dakota, but my father had denied going there. He'd bought the Chevrolet not long ago—so the money could've been there all along and had nothing to do with him or any bank robbery. Still, I made the connection. Possibly there were other packets in the car. These needed to be removed—although I had no idea where to put them in case the police came back and looked through the house, which I knew they did when something had been stolen.

I went out the kitchen door and across the yard. I crawled in the warm back seat of the Bel Air, which wasn't locked, and delved down between the cushions until I felt the packet, cool and tightly wrapped. I ran my hand all around up to the elbow, feeling the bolts and the molding of the

chassis and dust and grime. I found an unopened package of clove gum
and a button, and an empty envelope from a St. Patrick's hospital—all
of which I left there. I didn't find another money packet there or under
the front seat or in the glove box, and decided there weren't any. I stuffed
the one I found into my pants' front the way I did before and crawled out
and hurried back across the yard to the house, where I hoped the police
wouldn't be waiting. Once inside, I put the bills (I didn't think of counting
them, though the top one was a twenty) under the silverware tray in the
kitchen drawer—which made the tray sit too high for the drawer to close.
Though after I'd done that I took the packet out and tore off the wrapper
and took the wrapper to the toilet and flushed it down. That was the correct thing to do. My parents would think it was a wise idea. I returned the
packet to the drawer, made two stacks of the bills and put them side by
side, which let the drawer close in a way no one would notice.

After that I simply went back in my room. (There was no noise from
Berner's room, and I didn't want to talk to her.) I closed my door and
pulled the shade. I turned off the overhead light and lay down with my
clothes on—the way I'd done the day before. I lay still and watched my
chest rise and fall, felt my heart beat inside it, observed my breathing and
tried to regulate it by taking deep inhalations. That was how our mother
had told me it was possible to go to sleep if you woke up at night with a
teeming brain, which she said she often did. If I went to sleep, I believed it
was possible that when I woke up, all these events would be over with. Or
it might've been a dream, and I would wake up on the train to Seattle, and
be with Berner and my mother headed to a new life where there would be
another school and I'd know people. It was twelve thirty, noon. My Baby
Ben was ten minutes slow. The Lutherans' bell was ringing again. The dog
a street away began howling. Outside was bright sunshine, but in my room
was shadows and cool. Birds were singing. Somewhere I heard something
dripping, dripping. As expected, I had no trouble going to sleep. I slept for
a long time.

32

A VOICE WAS ALIVE IN THE HOUSE WHEN I WOKE up. I assumed it was the police—talking to Berner, beginning to search for the money. My heart had quieted. But it immediately began pounding. The kitchen drawer would be the first place to look.

I opened my bedroom door abruptly, intending to startle whoever was there, possibly make them run away. But it was Berner, in the hallway speaking into the telephone receiver, standing by the little receptacle outside our parents' bedroom. She was wearing her pajamas with blue elephants. She was barefoot, looping then unlooping the phone cord around her thumb, pushing a finger into her thick hair and smiling at something she was hearing. Her voice was deeper. She'd put on makeup again and lipstick. "Oh, yes," she was saying. "I don't know. That's a good idea." Her voice sounded like my mother's. I didn't know who she was talking to, but I assumed it was Rudy Patterson. He was the only person I knew she knew, and she had told me what they did.

I was relieved it wasn't the police. I had a strong feeling, however, they'd soon be back. The older detective had said so. I went to the front window and looked out. Our street and the park were empty in the dappled sunlight. The Lutheran church was locked up. Shade fell across our lawn in a pretty way. In the park, the fat young deaf boy from up the street who I'd seen before was throwing a stick for a black Labrador dog. It ran, picked up the stick, then brought it back and dropped it at the boy's feet. He petted the dog's head and said something to it. No police cars were there. Occasionally the boy would turn almost secretly and look at our house.

I walked to the kitchen window and looked out to where our father's car was. But it was gone. The space it had occupied beside the garage was like a box of air the Chevrolet had been in a moment before, then vanished from. I instantly opened the silverware drawer and expected to find nothing. But there were the two stacks of twenties under the plastic tray, which let me know I wasn't dreaming and these goings-on were really happening.

I picked up the pieces of the broken dish my mother had dropped earlier and put them in the trash under the sink. They were all large pieces and didn't require a broom. In a little while Berner came in the kitchen. She seemed—in her elephant pajamas—unfazed, as if being in the house this way was better, and she'd been waiting for this time and intended to make the most of it.

"They pulled his car away. A big wrecker truck came," she said and looked out the front window. "Nice big ole doggy." She watched the boy throwing his stick in the park. I wanted to move the money. I didn't want to have anything to do with it. "I don't think anybody's coming," Berner said. She scratched her behind below her pajama-bottom waist, while she stared out at the boy with his dog. Her hair was bushy and disheveled from sleeping on it. "That means we can do whatever we want to."

"Why?" I said.

Her lips made a mean smile, and she squinted at me and breathed out the way she did when she was acting superior. "I'll do whatever I want," she said. "Whatever you do will be what you want." She pointed her finger at her ear and made a circle, then pointed it at me. "You're loony," she said. She often said that.

"What're you going to do?"

"I don't know." She opened the refrigerator door, looked inside and closed it back. "It won't be nothing. I've done nothing enough. Rudy wants to get married."

"You can't," I said. I knew you couldn't do that. We were fifteen. She'd already told me she didn't want to get married. She'd said it yesterday.

"Some places they'll let you. We'll go to Salt Lake City, Utah. It's better than here. Though he's not in the church now."

I was disgusted to hear this. It made everything about me and everything I thought feel flimsy. Standing in our kitchen in her pajamas, talking about getting married to Rudy, she cast a shadow on me and whatever I thought—as if my fate had to be like hers, and you could tear my plans apart like wet tissue and watch them disappear.

Only, I didn't feel that way about myself and my plans. I could feel my own outline now. I would be myself no matter what else happened. My heart went calm then, which I thought was a positive sign. If I'd really felt all was lost and my life was over because I was tied to my sister, I don't know what I would've done. Except I'd have had very little chance of going on from that moment.

"I won't be getting married right off the bat," Berner said. She turned and peered out the window again. Suddenly she whipped around with a big distorted smile. "Mother told me I have to take care of you." Tears all at once sprang from her eyes. It's possible I was starting to cry, too. We both had reasons to. But she cut hers off. "I hate their goddamn guts," she said.

"You don't have to run away," I said. It was an awful feeling we had.

"Yes, I do," she said. "I . . ." I wanted to put my arms around her. It seemed like the most natural thing to do if I was going to be in control of everything. The telephone started ringing in the hall—loud, jangling miserable rings that destroyed the quiet in the house. And that's how the moment passed—Berner and me almost holding on to each other, the phone ringing, and nothing else taking notice of us.

33

WHAT WAS LEFT OF SUNDAY IS A PART THAT'S not very clear. I remember everything feeling free inside the house and the house feeling comfortable with just the two of us in it. We ate some food out of the refrigerator—cold spaghetti and an apple. We ate looking out the front window at the park in the late afternoon shade. Cars drove by. One or two slowed and people inside leaned into the windows and looked at Berner and me standing there. One person waved and we both waved back. I didn't understand what anybody could possibly know about us. It was forward thinking of our mother to discourage us from assimilating, since if anybody—someone from the chess club—had come to gawk at us, I'd have been humiliated. And worse, because I hadn't done anything personally to feel humiliated about except have parents.

Before it got dark, Berner and I took a walk around the block, against our mother's instruction that we not leave the house. We did it because we could. No one noticed us. All the neighbors' houses were silent and shut up looking on Sunday afternoon. The neighborhood seemed nicer than I'd always thought it was.

We came back and sat on the front steps and watched the sky turn purple and the moon come up and a few lights prickle on in our neighbors' windows. I noticed a paper kite that had been caught high up in the tree limbs in the park. I wondered how you'd get it down. We expected any moment for a car to drive up and strangers to tell us we had to go with them someplace. But no one came.

We didn't talk much about our parents. We both assumed, as we sat on the steps watching bats flit around the darkening trees in front of the humped moon, and pale stars showed up in the eastern sky, that they'd done what they were accused of doing. It had been too dramatic not to be true. They had gone away overnight—which they'd never done before. The pistol had disappeared. There was the money, and the Indians calling us and driving by. I may even have briefly wanted it to be true—whether I could've said so or not—as if by robbing a bank our father had supplied himself with something he'd been lacking. What it meant about our mother was a more difficult question. It could also be true that Berner and I, for that afternoon, may have lost the part of our minds that makes you fully aware of what's happening to you when it's happening. Why else would we have become calm, and taken a walk? Why else would I have thought my father was more substantial because he'd robbed a bank and broken our lives apart? It doesn't make much sense. Neither one of us thought to ask *why* had they robbed a bank, *why* had that ever seemed like a good idea. To us, it had just become a fact of life.

WHEN WE FINALLY WENT IN, it was full dark. Mosquitoes were in the air. Moths fluttered at the windows, and the cicadas were humming. Sunday night traffic on Central had all but stopped. We locked the doors and pulled the curtains and turned off the porch light. No matter what Berner thought, I believed someone would come and get us—the police or the juvenile officials, and that the police would search the house. We decided we'd let no one in—as if we were the man and the wife who lived there.

I went to the kitchen and got the money and told Berner where it'd come from. I didn't know if she'd seen it the day before, but she said she hadn't. She said she thought it was money our parents had stolen and we should hide it or else put it down the toilet. We counted it out at the dining room table and it was five hundred dollars. Berner then changed her mind and said we should divide it and each decide what to do with our half. We'd be accused anyway, because we had it, so we should keep it. She said there might even be more hidden in the house, and we should find it before the police came. We went in our parents' bedroom and looked in our mother's purse, inside their drawers and under their mattresses, in their clothes closet, inside their shoes, and up on the closet shelves where there were older shoes and sweaters and my father's Air Force hat. We found no more packets of money, though our mother had thirty dollars folded in her change purse. We also found what she had called her "Jewish book," which I'd seen but didn't know anything about. It was small and had what she'd said was Hebrew writing in it and was in her bottom dresser drawer with some baby pictures of us and a View-Master with a Taj Mahal card and her eyeglass prescriptions and some artists' pencils and her poems and her journal, which we still wouldn't have dared to read. The book had a name I couldn't pronounce when she'd said it and began with an "H." I'd never asked more about it. It occurred to me there was no place in a house a person could hide anything where no one would find it, and that the police were professional at finding things. Our house had no cellar, and again I was unwilling to go in the attic on account of it being hot and the home of snakes and hornets. We couldn't guess where more money was, and we eventually stopped looking.

In our father's monogrammed "P" leather jewelry case, however—which smelled like him—I found his high school ring, bulky and gold with a square blue stone and engraved with a tiny "D" for Demopolis, and two tiny rearing horses on each side, for the Mustangs. He'd said Demopolis meant "where the people lived" in Greek, and he liked it because it signified everyone there was equal. I put the ring on—it only fit my thumb—and decided I'd wear it, since now I wasn't likely to have one of my own. His gold captain's bars were in there and his wristwatch, and his blue-and-white Parsons name tag, and his metal dog tags and a paper box containing his war ribbons. Farther back in the closet was his heavy Air Force uniform, cleaned and pressed and ready to put on, though without the ribbons and bars. I put the jacket on. It was much too large for me and too hot to wear in the house. I'd had it on other times, and it was important feeling and I liked it. No money was in the pockets. When our father had put it on in the mornings and left the house for the base, he'd always been in a good humor. That had only been a few months ago. That time was gone now, no matter how not long ago it was.

Berner took out a pair of our mother's dark wool trousers she only wore in the winter, and held these up for display in front of the door mirror as if they were funny. They were too small for her to put on, though she tried. So she found a pair of flat black cloth shoes our mother had sent away for and squeezed her large bony foot inside and clopped around their bedroom with them half on, heels slapping, saying our mother lacked a sense of style, which wasn't true. She had a style of her own. We must've known our parents wouldn't be back. We wouldn't have put on their clothes and laughed and imitated them if life had a chance to be normal again.

Just after nine o'clock, a knock sounded at the front door. Of course, we thought it was the police and turned off the light in the bedroom. I crawled down the hall on my hands and knees—in my father's tunic—then crawled around to the kitchen. No one could see me through the front door glass. I got to the kitchen window and looked over the sill into the dark front yard, where the moon hung above the canopy of leaves and limbs, and the empty basketball backboard across the street cast shadows in the street lights. Rudy Patterson was standing on the front walk, tall and long armed and looking up at the sky, smoking a cigarette and holding a paper sack, waiting to be let in. He was talking to someone I couldn't see. I thought he might be singing. The porch light wasn't turned on.

I knew he was coming to take Berner away with him—that it was all

planned. I'd be left in the house alone to face whatever happened and fend
for myself. They were on their way to Salt Lake or San Francisco. That's
what she'd decided. I didn't know what to do, but I didn't intend to let him
in. I wanted the door locked and to stay in the house with Berner. I didn't
think it would be better for her to run away. The same was true for me.

She had come to the hallway door and looked around the corner, as if
she didn't care who saw her. "Who's that?" she said.

I said, "It's Rudy. He can't come in. Mother said no one could come in."

"I forgot about him," she said and moved out of the hallway. "I told
him to come. He can come in. Don't be stupid. He and I are in love." She
went straight to the front door and let Rudy Patterson into our house.

NO MATTER HOW I'd felt when I saw Rudy standing out on the moonlit
walk, when he came in our house he—at least for a time—changed everything. He was not the sort of boy you'd expect to have a good effect.
But when he came in the door, time stopped and our lives stopped with it.
Everything outside disappeared, as if the future and the past had come to
their ends at once and it was just the three of us.

Rudy was immediately loud when he got inside. He walked around
our living room, smoking his cigarette and inspecting things. The same
things I'd taken a tally of earlier that day. The piano. The pictures on the
wall. My father's discharge. My mother's suitcase and my pillowcase with
my possessions inside. He seemed older and bigger than the last time I saw
him, when we'd shot baskets in the park and Berner sat and watched us.
He was only sixteen and had wild, curly red hair and long, red-freckled
arms and big hands with hair already on the backs, and his little mustache that Berner didn't like. He had veins in his biceps below his T-shirt
sleeves, and scratched, scuffed-up knuckles, as if he'd been crawling on
rocks or possibly fighting. He wore dirty tight black dungarees with a
wide belt and a brass buckle and a little scabbard knife on the side and
thick black ankle boots—the kind men wore at the air base or where his

father worked at the refinery. He bore little resemblance to the boy my sister had been friendly with in the summer and who I'd liked because he was nice to me. Something unusual had happened to him since the last time I saw him. I had no idea what.

But I still liked him and saw now, how my sister might decide to run away with him. He seemed mysterious and dangerous. I considered it might be a good idea to run away with them myself, and not face tomorrow and all it would probably contain.

As he was roaming the room, Rudy carried on talking. He'd never been inside our house. Possibly it made him nervous and act in an exaggerated way. He'd been drinking, too. In his paper sack he had three bottles of Pabst beer, plus a cellophane bag of peanuts in-the-hull, which he ate and left the hulls on our father's Niagara Falls puzzle. He also had a half pint of Evan Williams whiskey in his back pocket, which he referred to as "the pete." He made a considerable presence in our house, which was already in a strange state.

Rudy knew about our parents being in jail and us being alone. It was Rudy Berner had been talking to when I woke up, and she had told him. He said his own father and stepmother didn't get along at all and that Mormons were crazy, anyway. He didn't believe what they believed. Mormons had invented a secret language, he said, that they only spoke to each other. They planned to enslave Catholics and Jews, and Negroes were to be sent to Africa or else executed. Washington, D.C., would be burned to the ground. If you left the Mormon Church, they hunted you down and brought you back in chains. He took "the pete" out, pulled a drink off of it, smacked his lips, then shockingly handed it to Berner, who pulled a drink, then handed it to me and I pulled one. I swallowed mine down all at once and had to clench my teeth to keep from choking. It made my throat constrict and burn all the way to my stomach, and hurt more there. Berner took another drink. She'd done it before. She didn't scowl, and afterward she patted her lips with her fingers as if she'd liked it. Rudy then gave her a cigarette, which he lighted and she smoked and held away from herself between her thumb and middle finger. This was in the living room of our house! Twelve hours ago our parents had been there. Their rules had governed our behavior and determined everything we did. Now they were gone, and so were their rules. It was a dizzying feeling. I felt I had a rough idea, then, about what the rest of my life would be.

Berner sat down in one of the living room chairs and just watched Rudy. His behavior was a kind of performance. He walked around the room saying his parents had threatened him with becoming a ward of the state, and that was the most terrible thing that could happen. It meant you were sent to a big orphanage in Miles City and strangers could adopt you and make you their private property. At his age nobody would adopt him, so he'd be a prisoner left in the foul company of mean ranch boys whose parents had died or had abandoned them, or filthy Indian kids whose parents were perverted. Your life was ruined even if you survived it. This eventuality, I thought, was what our mother was fearful of and why she'd been definite about Berner and me not leaving with anyone but Miss Remlinger.

The living room soon smelled like Rudy's cigarettes and whiskey and beer. It had been clean not long before. We would have to clean it up again tomorrow. I went and turned on the attic fan, which began its clatter-racket and drew some smoke away. All the doors and windows were locked shut from when I'd locked them earlier.

I still was wearing my father's Air Force tunic, and Rudy said he'd like to try it on. I took it off, and he put it on, and it fit him better than it fit me. It also had an instant effect on him. He walked around our living room some more with his cigarette and his beer, but as if he was an officer, and our house was a staging area for a war he would soon be fighting.

"I'm ready to shoot down a lot of Commies now," he said in a made-up official voice as he strutted about. Berner said she was, too. He was drunk, of course. I thought he looked a little silly. Part of his large presence had already begun to fade—though I still liked him. Possibly I was a little drunk myself.

"Do you have any music we can play?" Rudy said, admiring himself in the smoky glass mirror that hung over the davenport and had been in the house when we got there.

"He's got some records," Berner said, referring to our father.

"I'd like to hear one," Rudy said. He set his hands on his hips like pictures of General Patton I'd seen in the *World Book*.

Berner went to the phonograph and got out one of our father's 78s from the cabinet and put it on the turntable—things I'd only seen him do.

Right away, Glenn Miller's band started playing one of our father's favorites. "The Little Brown Jug." Our father had great respect for Glenn Miller, because he'd died in the service of his country.

Rudy instantly started dancing around by himself. He swooped and slid across the living room, smiling and dipping his knees and raising and lowering his arms and turning circles—his beer in one hand, his cigarette in the other.

"You have to dance with me." He said this to me. He danced over, put his arms around me and pulled me up where I was sitting on the piano bench. He danced me backward, twirled me around, fluttered his fingers, pushed me and pulled me, stepped on my feet with his big black boots, smiling and smelling like whiskey and cigarettes, his scuffed hands now and then clutching my shoulder and the middle of my back. I'd never danced before. I didn't think I was really dancing now. Our mother and father had danced in my memory, but not recently. Their size difference didn't make that easy. My mother liked Russian ballet and hated "middle-brow ballroom tastes," which was what my father was accomplished at.

Berner was frowning at me with her cigarette in her mouth while Rudy and I were whirling around. I enjoyed it. "Quit dancing with your boyfriend," she said, "and dance with your girlfriend."

"I've given Dell-boy his big thrill now," Rudy said, out of breath but smiling wildly. He turned loose of me and began dancing the same way with Berner, who couldn't dance any better than I could. My head was spinning and I felt a little sick to my stomach. I sat down in the chair where Berner'd been sitting, while they danced around in front of me.

After "The Little Brown Jug," the next song was "Stardust," which was one my father regularly played. Berner and Rudy danced stiffly at arm's length at first. He maintained a serious expression as if he was concentrating on his footwork. Berner seemed bored. Then they moved in closer, and it was clear they'd been that close before. Berner's face appeared over Rudy's shoulder and she had her eyes closed. They were almost the same height and in many ways looked alike—more alike than she and I did. They both had freckles and large bones. Berner's white tennis shoes slipped around on the rug in clumsy step with Rudy's boots, both of them holding their cigarettes, Rudy holding his beer. I took another drink out of the Evan Williams bottle, which was on the floor, and again suffered the stomach burning, but the aftermath wasn't as bad and instantly calmed me, though I hadn't realized I wasn't calm. I sat back in the green armchair and watched Berner and Rudy dance together—Rudy in my father's Air Force tunic, Berner clinging on his neck. I had the feeling someone was almost certainly about to bash in the front door and find us smoking and drinking and carrying on in these ways we shouldn't be. But I didn't care. I was happy. I was happy Berner was happy. It was always hard to please her. Just for that moment it was as if I was watching our parents dance, and everything was back the way it was supposed to be.

AFTER THEY'D DANCED to another Glenn Miller song, Rudy's face got red. He was sweating with my father's tunic on. He suddenly quit dancing, skinned off the coat and threw it on a chair, and resumed walking around saying he wouldn't be staying long. Berner stood in the middle of the floor watching him. He said he had a plan to get some money that night, but it'd be best if he didn't tell us how. (It was stealing, I assumed.) He said he could go to Deer Lodge prison if he got caught in a crime, because he was seventeen. People were watching him, whereas in California there were so many people he wouldn't stand out the way he did in Great Falls, which he said was a "hell hole," and he hated it.

He asked Berner if anything was in the house to eat. All he'd had were his peanuts he'd "lifted" from the Italian's, and the beer and the whiskey he'd bought from an Indian with money out of his father's wallet. Berner said there were frozen steaks in the ice box—steaks our father had brought from the base. She could cook one. He said that would be wonderful.

Rudy and I sat for a time then in the dining room under the overhead light and with the front curtains closed so no one outside could see us. Our family had sat there two days ago. Rudy smoked and alternated his beer and his whiskey. Berner put a frozen steak straight into a frying pan to cook it on the Westinghouse—which was what our father called it. I'd never seen her cook anything and didn't believe she knew how. I didn't know how. Rudy had picked up a book of our mother's off the shelf in the living room—her Arthur Rimbaud poems—from which he read a line or two. "In spicy and drenched lands—at the service of the most monstrous exploitation, industrial and sultry. . . ." I've remembered that. Rudy still seemed friendly and mysterious to me. His tangled red hair and veiny arms worked in favor of him seeming out of the ordinary. I didn't think he was smarter than I was. He didn't play chess—that I knew about. He didn't know anything about other places on the globe—which I did. He had no plans to go to college, but was planning to run away. I was fairly sure he'd never read *Time* or *Life* or *National Geographic*. Which didn't mean he lacked his own intelligence—including wearing a knife on his belt and steel-toe boots and drinking and smoking and having schemes to get his own money and knowing about Mormons, and whatever he and Berner did in his father's car up by the municipal airport. That amounted to something.

At the table Rudy said he looked forward to winter in a new climate—which would be California, where his real mother lived. He said his father'd told him he—Rudy—probably should never even have been born, or at least should've been born to someone else who had a lot of patience. He put his cigarette into his beer bottle and lit another one (there were no ashtrays in our house), and predicted he'd end up in jail. He didn't seem to remember that our parents were in jail at that minute and we might be feeling raw about it. He said the whole time he'd lived in Great Falls he'd made no friends, and something was wrong with a town where you didn't make friends. This had been Berner's and my experience, also, but I'd believed it had to do with our mother's fear of fitting in. He looked hard across the table at me, then suddenly did remember the terrible situation Berner and I were facing, and said we hadn't done anything that he knew of to deserve our predicament. Which was nothing I'd thought anyway. I felt already that if our parents had robbed a bank—no matter what reasons they had for it—the fault was theirs. That was clear enough. Rudy didn't mention joining the Marines or marrying Berner—which had been talked about before.

Berner came from the kitchen with Rudy's steak on a white plate she set down in front of him. A knife and fork were laid across it. It was just the steak. Nothing else. It looked hard as a shingle and was curled up at the burned edges where it was fat. It didn't look good to eat. Berner set her hands on her waist, pushed her hip to the side and frowned at the steak as if she disliked how it looked. "I never cooked anything but soup before," she said. She pulled a chair out and sat across from Rudy and kept frowning at the steak. Even with the attic fan running, the house was hot. Moisture was standing on Berner's upper lip. Rudy was also sweating. The burnt-steak odor moved in the air around us.

"This looks great," Rudy said. He still had his cigarette in his mouth. I thought he was going to eat and smoke at the same time. He cut right into the steak, but wasn't able to cut very far. We both sat watching him. He put his table knife down, took his little red-handled scabbard knife out of its sheath and cut right into the steak with ease.

"It's perfect," he said and ate a chunk that I could see was still frozen inside. He chewed vigorously, laying his cigarette on the edge of his plate. Smoke funneled out his nose as he was chewing. He drank a swig of his beer. Then he cut another piece, but turned in his chair before he ate it and looked around the room behind him, where we'd been dancing and drinking whiskey. My father's tunic was on the chair, the jigsaw puzzle of Niagara Falls was on the card table top littered with peanut hulls. My pillowcase with my belongings and my mother's suitcase from the morning were where they'd been all day, ever since the police came. Rudy seemed to want to check that everything was the same.

He turned back to his steak with Berner and me watching him and cut his piece in half. His boots scuffed the floor, as if eating involved effort. He took another drag on his cigarette, raised his chin, delivered a French inhale, then forked the small wedge of steak into his mouth and chewed, smiling as he did it. "I believe"—he cleared his throat and swallowed—"that we could do just as good by ourselves out on the tramp. That's my view." I didn't know what his mind was on about. I didn't know what "on the tramp" was.

"Where do your parents think you are, right now," Berner said. "Do they think you ran away?"

"Probably," Rudy said, chewing forcefully. "If somebody fished me out of the Missouri River, they wouldn't even come down to see my body." These words seemed to excite him, and he got up from his chair, his hunting knife in one fist and his cigarette in the other, and executed three or four thrusts in the air over the table. Each time he stabbed the empty air he went, "Ah! Ah! Ah!" and his eyes squinted as if he was striking someone he hated. It wasn't very impressive.

He sat back down, cut another piece of his steak and ate it, breathing audibly. He looked at me and grinned. He had a warm smile. "Do you want some of this, Dell? It's really good." He pushed his plate toward me, the knife and fork still on it. He kept his hunting knife in front of him in case he might need to stab some things again.

"I'm not hungry," I said. Though I was.

He turned to reinsert his knife into its little sheath without wiping the meat grease off. "I've had my fill-up now," he said. He'd had two pieces and a half. He wiped the back of his hand across his mouth, then stubbed his cigarette on the sole of his boot, licked the stub and put it in his shirt pocket. He coughed to cover up a belch. "I could go right to sleep," he said. He covered his mouth again. "I gotta go get some money, though."

"Where're you going to get that?" Berner said. She hadn't said much. We'd been watching Rudy like he was an animal in a cage.

"If I told you, you'd be my accomplices, and you'd go to jail." He stood up and walked back into the living room, patting his belly as if he'd eaten a three-course meal instead of a piece of frozen steak. He put a fresh cigarette to his lips and lit it from a paper matchbook out of the same pocket. He seemed to be looking around for something. He reminded me of my father when he came back from his business trip. Berner and I were still sitting at the table, watching him like spectators. Probably Rudy had a decent heart and had suffered because his parents didn't love him. He wouldn't have hurt anybody. But he seemed undependable and erratic. His mouth, when he wasn't smiling, sank in toward his little teeth and made him look deceitful, like somebody we shouldn't know, even if we weren't his accomplices. Rudy was a person I could imagine being a ward of the state, being imprisoned in some empty, windswept landscape where there'd be barbed wire and terrible things would happen to him, and escape would be impossible. I still had on my father's class ring. Two rearing gold mustangs. I wished it could be magic and make my father appear and take control of things that were happening to Berner and me. Of course, he was the cause of all of it.

"Do you want to stay here tonight, or not?" Berner said in a brazen voice—which was an outlandish thing. Not a thing you could say.

"That's not a good idea," I said.

"I don't think it is either." Rudy was still inspecting things in the living room, not giving Berner's invitation any credit. He was for sure looking for something he could sell at some pawn shop out by the base. But there wasn't anything in our house to sell. My father's tunic. The Glenn Miller records. The metronome, which he wouldn't have recognized. He could've been looking for the money we had. Only he wouldn't have known about it. "Somebody might come looking for me. It wouldn't be good if I was here." He frowned at me as if we agreed, and put his thumbs under his belt.

"You're here now," Berner said, irritably. "What's the difference?"

"The difference is nobody's come." He was again studying my father's Air Force discharge, framed beside President Roosevelt—which the policeman had also done. If he wanted them, he could take them. I just wanted him to leave before somebody did come.

"My old man hates Roosevelt," Rudy said. He pronounced it "Roo" to rhyme with "zoo." He looked around at me as if he wanted my opinion. "He sold the country down a muddy river, he thinks. His wife's a Commie and feels sorry for everybody, especially niggers." I hadn't heard that word spoken much. A boy at school whose father was a doctor said it. Our father had never said it. He didn't hate people, and neither did we.

"Are you staying here or are you going?" Berner said sharply. She stood up at the table and picked up Rudy's plate.

"I'm on the night shift tonight," he said, as if he wanted to be casual about things. I thought he might take down the picture of President Roosevelt and carry it away. He walked over to the table at the end of the couch, picked up his paper sack of remaining beers and walked to the front door. A car passed our house and sounded its horn. It was after eleven. Somebody shouted out in the warm summer night. "Yoo-hoo-hoo. Jailbirds.

You jailbirds. Jailbirds. Yoo-hoo-hoo." The car honked again. Someone laughed. Then the car accelerated and noisily whooshed away.

"We'll never see you again. Is that it?" Berner frowned, holding Rudy's plate. "That'd be all right with me."

"I'll be back and you know it," Rudy said. He wanted to seem like a grown man to us. Like I said, his red hair and his cigarettes and his scuffed-up arms and knuckles worked in his favor. "You and me'll get out of here for good. I'm a man of my word."

"You're not a man," Berner said. "You're sixteen."

"I won't be next week. You won't have to wait long to know all about that." Rudy lost his big smile. He stood holding the glass doorknob, as if he was apologizing, and we were passing judgment on him. Which we were. "You just have to be patient." He pulled the door back.

Berner said, "This is where it's got me so far." She turned and walked into the kitchen.

"Don't let anybody else in here, Dell," Rudy said, ignoring her. "They'll come get you if they can."

"My mother already told us that," I said.

Rudy removed his cigarette from his mouth, cleared his throat, blew smoke into the room, took a quick, almost surprised look around at whatever he'd decided not to take. Then he stepped out the door and closed it hard. Berner had already begun washing dishes in the sink. I expected this would be the last I'd see of Rudy Patterson, and I was glad. He hadn't helped anything. And although there was no way I could know it, that is what turned out to be true.

34

T HAT NIGHT, SUNDAY NIGHT, BERNER AND I straightened the house, washed the dishes, emptied the butts and peanut hulls and beer bottles, and the mud from when the police had been there—all that had made the house feel crappy. We put away the Niagara Falls puzzle and the card table and placed my globe back on my dresser, hung our father's Air Force jacket back in the closet and put our mother's suitcase and Berner's back where they belonged, and my pillowcase in my room.

We didn't talk very much. Berner concluded she'd never see Rudy again, that people like him luckily exited your life—at least in her experience (which was nothing). He didn't love her, and she wasn't in love with him for that matter. I said I liked him well enough, but she'd be better off not running away and staying here until our parents came back. I was trying to assert myself as the man in the house, taking charge of things no one could control.

MY ROOM had grown chilly with the sun gone from the roof. I turned off the attic fan and lay in the broken moonlight and concentrated on my parents. I wanted to make my heart be calm. It'd been beating hard all that day, as if I'd been running around and around a track.

Our parents were changing again in my thinking, sliding together, not as if they'd found their love again, but as if they were only one person and had relinquished their distinguishing details. This wasn't true; they were whoever they were. And if the day had been shocking and confusing to me, it had been much worse for them. Still, feeling this way—that they were less distinct in my mind—was a relief. As I said, I may have lost part of my mind for that day. Losing your mind is probably never what you think it'll be.

What we were supposed to do the next morning, or all the next day, I wasn't sure. If someone came, we would just stay in the house. If Mildred Remlinger came, she'd tell us what we were expected to do. Several times when I was in bed, the telephone rang. Berner went out once to answer it, in case it was Rudy calling. But I could tell no one was there when she said hello. Then she didn't answer it again.

At some point I went nearly to sleep—my heart still strangely pounding. Then I was aware Berner had come in the room and gotten into my bed—the second time in one week. As I said, we hadn't slept in the same bed since we'd lived in Great Falls. But I'd missed her when our parents had moved her to her own room, and I was happy she'd come back. I'd have never climbed in bed with her. She'd have thrown a tantrum or made fun of me. But I was very glad not to be alone.

She'd been crying and smelled like her tears and like cigarettes. She wasn't wearing any clothes, which was a shock. Her skin was cold, and she squeezed close to me in my pajamas. Crying had made her colder. She took my hand and held it against her belly. "Warm me up," she said. "I can't sleep." She snuffed her nose and sighed. "I drank that whiskey. It keeps you up." She pushed close to me. I smelled soap on her, and Vicks and toothpaste and smoke in her hair. She pushed her bumpy face into my neck, her cheeks were damp and cool, and her nose was stoppered up.

"I was asleep," I lied.

"Go back, then," she said. "I won't bother you." A train whistle sounded in the night. My arms were folded. She gripped my hand.

"I'm going to run away by myself," she whispered, close to my ear. She cleared her throat and swallowed and sucked back her nose. "I'm crazy," she said. "I don't care what I do."

She didn't say anything for a while. I lay beside her, breathing. Then she kissed me, suddenly, hard on my neck, underneath my ear and shoved in closer to me. I didn't mind her kissing me. It made me feel safe. She let go of my hand and moved hers, which was rough and bony. "I wanted to do it tonight with Rudy," she said. "But I'll do it with you."

"All right," I said. I wanted to. I didn't care.

"It won't last that long. We did it already, in his car. You should know about it, anyway."

"I don't know about it at all," I said.

"Then you're perfect. It won't even matter. You'll forget about it."

"All right," I said.

"I promise you," she whispered. "It's not even important."

And that's enough to tell. It doesn't bear repeating. It meant little, what we did, except to us, and only for the time. Later in the night Berner woke and sat up and looked at me and said (because I was awake), "You're not Rudy."

"No," I said. "I'm Dell."

"Well, then," she said. "I just wanted to say good-bye."

"Good-bye," I said. "Where are you going?"

She smiled at me—my sister—then she went to sleep again with my arms around her in case she was cold or scared.

35

IT WAS STRANGE TO WAKE UP IN THE HOUSE WITH OUR parents not in it. We'd waked up without them there not that long before—when they'd gone away to rob the bank—but this time, Monday, everything was different. They were in jail—we assumed they were—and we had no idea what would happen to the two of us.

I slept all the way to eight—until my room was steamy from sunlight and I woke up sweaty. The hall fan was going again. Berner wasn't in my bed. The sheets beside me were cold as if she hadn't been there for some time. Through the walls traffic hummed on Central. An airplane took off up the hill at the airport. It occurred to me Berner had left, and I would have to make my way through the day alone.

She was in the kitchen, however, when I got dressed. She had re-cooked the steak from last night and eaten part of it and left a square on a plate for me—which I ate with cold milk. The house still smelled like beer and cigarettes. I thought we should take the garbage out before it got hotter.

Berner had dressed in her Bermuda shorts, which she hardly ever wore and that showed her hairless freckled legs and long feet. She had on tennis shoes and a sailor blouse and had taken a shower. She'd brushed her

hair back and held it with a red rubber band. There was no talking about
what had happened in the night. She didn't seem unhappy about it, and
neither was I. We weren't the same people we had been, and that was good
in my view.

"We have to go to see them," Berner said, washing her plate and mine
in the sink, staring out the window at the side yard—the badminton net,
the neighbor's house, one pole of the clothesline. "If we don't, they'll get
taken someplace, and we'll never see them." With her wet fingers she
picked up a newspaper off the counter and dropped it on the table where I
sat. "Somebody left us a nice present inside the porch screen."

It was the day's *Tribune*, folded to display pictures of our parents—
two separate ones, side by side—taken in jail. They were each holding a
white card that said "Cascade County Jail," with a number underneath it.
Our father's black hair was disheveled, though he was smiling. Our mother's mouth was tense and turned down in a way I'd never seen her look.
She was wearing her glasses and her eyes were close together and were
opened wide and staring out, as if she was gazing at a terrible scene. The
headline read "N.D. Bank Robbers." Whoever left the paper had straight-
pinned a handwritten note to the top of the page that said: "Thought you'd
like to see this. I'm sure you're very proud."

I was surprised anybody would leave this for us. It made my hands
tremble when I saw it. Our parents had robbed the Agricultural National
Bank in Creekmore, North Dakota, last Friday morning, the story said.
A gun had been involved. The sum of $2,500 was taken. Our parents had
fled to Great Falls and been arrested in a rental house on the west side of
town. Our father, whose name was put in quotation marks ("Beverly," as
was our mother's, "Neeva"), was described as an "Alabama native" who
was discharged from the Air Force and had been watched for some time
by the Great Falls police on suspicion of committing crimes that involved
Indians from the Rocky Boy reservation. Our mother was described as
being from "Washington State" and as teaching school in Fort Shaw. She

had no prior arrests, but an investigation of her citizenship was under way. They were to be extradited to North Dakota in the coming week. No mention was made of any children.

Berner was letting water drain out of the sink. "They're just liars. Like everybody else," she said.

I couldn't remember anything they'd lied about. Then I thought of the gun. It was a terrible surprise to read this in the newspaper—almost as bad as to know about it. "Extradited" was a word I knew from TV. It meant they wouldn't come back. The packet of money was probably what they'd stolen, and we shouldn't keep it.

"If we go to the jail, they'll grab us," Berner said matter-of-factly. She walked to the front window that looked out on the street and the park. Morning light was sharp and bright on the top of a car parked in front of the Lutherans. Fluffy clouds ran along above the trees against the perfect sky. "We still have to go, of course. Even if they are liars."

"Yes," I said. "I want to." I didn't want to get handed over to the juvenile authorities, but there wasn't any choice. We couldn't *not* go to see them. "What'll we do after we see them?" I wanted Berner to be assured we'd get away.

"We'll go have lunch at the Rainbow Hotel," she said, "and invite all our friends and have a big party."

Berner never told jokes—something our father said was like our mother. She didn't have a funny bone was what he said. But saying we'd go to the Rainbow Hotel and invite our friends made me think maybe she'd been telling jokes all the time, and no one knew it. Nothing about Berner was simple. She turned at the window, folded her arms and looked at me, staring hard at my forehead the way she did when she wanted me to know I wasn't very smart. Then she smiled. "I don't know what we're going to do," she said. "Whatever children do whose parents are in jail. Wait for something bad to happen."

"I hope nothing does," I said.

"You don't have to go looking for it," Berner said. "It finds you where you're hiding."

It's possible some people are born knowing things. Berner had figured out already that everything that had happened in the last day and night had happened to us—not just to our parents. I should've known that. I was so much younger than she was, even though our ages were the same. Over the years, I would never know the world as well as she did—which is good in many ways. But, in many other ways, it's not at all.

36

THE JAIL WAS IN THE REAR OF THE CASCADE COUNTY
Courthouse, on Second Avenue North. We'd driven past
it two days before with our father. I'd ridden my bicycle
by it on the way to the hobby shop. It was a large, three-story stone building with a wide lawn and concrete front steps, a flagpole, and the number
1903 chiseled into the stones above the entrance. Old oak trees shaded the
grass. On the high roof was a statue of a woman holding a scale—which
I knew had to do with justice. When you passed the courthouse you'd
sometimes see sheriff's cars, and deputies escorting people wearing handcuffs into and out of the building.

Berner and I made a complete tour around the block before we went
in. We wanted to determine if we could see cell windows from the street,
which we couldn't. When we walked into the echoing lobby, right in front
of us was a sign that said JAIL IN BASEMENT—NO SMOKING. No one else
was in the lobby. We went down a flight of shadowy steps to a metal door
that had JAIL painted on it in red. This door we went through, and beyond
it was a hall that ended at a lighted office behind a glass window. A deputy
in a uniform sat at a desk behind the window, reading a magazine. Behind
him—this was unexpected—you could see right to a barred door beyond
which was a concrete corridor where jail cells lined one side. Opposite the

cells was a long wall with barred windows at the top that let in pale light that looked cool and pleasant, although it was obviously a bad place to be. Our parents would be in there.

When Berner and I had walked from our house across the Central Avenue Bridge, past the Milwaukee Road depot, into the downtown and over to the jail, the morning had been bright and warm with the same high fluffy western clouds that flattened over the mountains, heading east to the plains. The river had smelled sweet in the heated morning breeze. Once again, people were canoeing on it, the last of the summer. We'd brought two paper sacks with toiletries we'd decided our parents would need in jail. My father's safety razor. A bar of soap. A tube of toothpaste and a toothbrush, a tube of Barbasol, the bottle of Wildroot, a comb and a hairbrush. Berner had brought things for our mother.

As we crossed the Missouri there was plenty of Monday morning traffic. Twice I thought a car passed that had some boy I knew from school inside it. Berner and I wouldn't have stood out—two kids walking across the bridge, carrying paper sacks. Invisible people. Again, though, if I'd thought someone recognized me and had an idea I was going to the jail to visit my parents who were locked up, it would've been too much for me. I might've jumped in the river and drowned myself.

The deputy behind the glass was a big smiling man with carefully parted short black hair, who seemed glad to see us. Berner told him—through the speak-hole—who we were and that we thought our parents were locked up in there, and we'd like to visit them. This made the deputy smile even more broadly. He left his desk and came around through a metal door beside his window and into the room where we were—it was just the end of the hall and had plastic chairs bolted to the floor, which was painted brown. It smelled like piney disinfectant, plus something sweet like bubblegum. The jail was a place you smelled more than anything else.

The deputy said he needed to see what was in our "pokes," which was a word my father sometimes used. We showed him our sacks. He laughed and said it was nice of us to bring these articles, but our parents didn't need them and jail rules forbid gifts. He'd keep them and we could take them back home. He was a heavy, moon-faced man who filled out his brown uniform. He had a severe dipping limp that made him have to reach and touch his leg above his knee at every step. Each time he did it his leg made a soft, metal click sound. I assumed his leg was wood. A wound from the war. I knew about that. He could only be a sheriff if he agreed to be the jailer. I believed we might see Bishop and the other, red-faced policeman who'd arrested our parents, that they'd recognize us and talk to us. But they weren't in sight, which made the experience of being there even stranger.

Once the jailer—who didn't tell us his name—had taken our sacks and made us pull out our pockets and show inside our shoes, he went back in his office and came out with a big metal key. With another smaller key, he unlocked the door he'd come out of and that had CELL BLOCK written on it and led us back through. Beyond the metal door the floor was painted pale yellow and felt much harder and colder through my shoes than our floor at home. My shoe soles seemed to stick to it. This was how anyone locked up inside felt—that jail existed for the opposite reason from why your home existed.

While we were walking to the jail, Berner and I had talked about what we would say to our parents. But once we were inside, and the barred door behind the deputy's desk was unlocked using the big metal key, we didn't talk. Berner cleared her throat several times and licked her lips. She was wishing, I thought, that she hadn't come.

Beyond the first barred door was a space just big enough for the three of us to stand in, then another barred door, which made breaking out impossible. Inside, it smelled like the same piney disinfectant but with food odors and maybe urine, like the boys' room in school. The door-opening noise echoed off the concrete. A black hose lay coiled below a faucet on the long wall, and the floor, which wasn't painted there, was damp and shiny.

No one was visible down the row of cells. A man's voice—not my father's—was speaking on a telephone somewhere. Outside the high barred windows across from the cells, a basketball was being dribbled and feet were scuffling. Someone—a man—laughed, and the ball bounced off a metal backboard just like in the park where Rudy and I had played earlier in the summer. Except for the watery green light filtering from outside, the only light came from bulbs high in the concrete ceiling and protected by wire baskets that barely let any light reach the floor. It was like a shadowy cave to be there. I thought it was exhilarating, although the feeling was lessened by our parents being inside.

"Not many guests with us, today," the crippled deputy said as he let us through the second barred door and locked it back. He wasn't wearing a pistol. "They check out early on Monday. They've had enough of our hospitality. We generally see them again, though." He was cheerful. A tiny red transistor radio had been propped up on his desk, and I could hear Elvis Presley singing at a low volume. "We're paying special attention to your mom in here," the deputy said. "Your dad, of course, he's a real pistol." He began leading us down the concrete corridor, which shone in the green light and shadows. The first cells we passed were empty and dark. "We don't expect to have your folks in here with us too long," he said, his leg clicking and being hauled along. He was wearing a hearing aid that filled his left ear. "They're off to North Dakota Wednesday or Thursday."

Then unexpectedly we were in front of an occupied cell, and there our father was, seated in the partial dark on a metal cot with a bare mattress that had its white ticking falling out in wads on the concrete. Something made me think he'd cut it open himself.

"You two kids shouldn't be here," our father said loudly, as if he knew we were coming. He stood up off his cot. I couldn't see him very well—his face, especially—though I saw him lick his lips as if they were dry. His eyes were wider open than usual. Berner had kept on walking and hadn't seen him. But when she heard his voice she said, "Oh, I'm sorry," and stopped and she saw him, too.

"I just trusted the government too much. That's my big problem," he said, as if he'd been saying this before to someone else. He didn't move closer to the bars. I didn't know what he meant. His face contained a worried, exhausted expression, and he looked thinner, though it had only been a day since we were all at home. His eyes were reddened and darting around the way they did when he was trying to find someone to please. His voice sounded more southern than it had. "I never gave a thought to killing anyone, if there was ever a consideration about that," he said. "Though I could've." He looked at us, then sat back down on his cot and lightly jammed his fists together between his knees, as if he was exhibiting patience. He was dressed as he'd been when the police came. Jeans and his white shirt. His snakeskin belt had been taken away and so had his boots. He was just in his dirty sock feet. His hair wasn't combed and he hadn't shaved and his skin looked gray—exactly like his picture in the newspaper.

A feeling of calm came over me then. Not what you'd expect. I felt safe with him where he was. I intended to ask him about the money. Where it came from.

"We brought you toilet articles, but they won't let us give them to you," Berner said in an awkward, higher-pitched voice than usual. She had her hands behind her. She didn't want to touch the bars.

"I already have a toilet in here." Our father looked to the side of where he sat, at a lid-less commode, which was foul looking and smelling. He rubbed one wrist, then rubbed his other one and licked his lips again as if he didn't know he was doing it. He rubbed his cheeks with his palms and squeezed his eyes shut, then opened them.

"When are they going to let you out?" I said. I was thinking Berner had said they were liars and could now remember other things. North Dakota. His blue flight suit.

"What is it, son?" He smiled a weak smile up at me.

"When are they going to let you come home?" I said loudly.

"Probably someday," he said. He didn't seem interested in it. He rubbed his hand through his hair the way he'd done Saturday in the car. "Don't get all bothered around about this. Aren't you about ready to go to school?"

"Yes, we are," I said. It was if he was under the impression he'd been in jail longer than he had. He'd known before when our school was starting.

"Did you and Berner play chess together?" He hadn't spoken to her yet.

"Where's Mother?" she said abruptly. We'd thought they'd be in the same jail cell. Then she said, "Did you rob a bank?"

"She's somewhere in here." Our father motioned his thumb toward his cell wall, as if our mother was behind it. "She's not speaking to me," he said. "I don't blame her." He shook his head. "I didn't hold up my end very well. I hope this isn't anything that seems ordinary to you two." He didn't answer Berner's question about robbing a bank. I wanted him to, because I remembered him saying, years before, "I could give it a try."

"It doesn't," Berner said.

He smiled at us out of the shadowy light. You'd think if you visited your father in jail you'd have many things to say to him. Berner had planned to ask if they needed anything, and if we should call someone, and who that would be. His family? A lawyer? Our mother's school? Almost all the ways I expected to feel weren't the ways I felt. Jail put a stop to everything—which was what it was intended to do.

"We oughta step on down and see your mother now," the deputy said behind us. His radio was still playing at the end of the row of cells. He saw we didn't have more to say and didn't want to embarrass anyone. Someone had begun talking outside the high barred windows. The basketball bounced once and stopped. "There's that satellite wa-a-a-y, way up there," a man's voice said. "Who said?" someone answered. Then the ball bounced again.

"Jail's not a place for you children to come," our father said again, looking up at us in a way that seemed worried. A vein in his forehead was visible.

"That's right," the deputy put in. "But they love you."

"I know they do. I love them," he said, as if we weren't there.

"Do you want us to call someone?" Berner said.

My father shook his head. "Let's wait on that," he said. "I'm talking to a lawyer. We have to go to North Dakota pretty soon."

Berner didn't say anything and neither did I. I still had his high school ring on my thumb. I put that hand behind me, so we wouldn't talk about it.

"I wish I had some ways to make you children happy now." Our father clasped his hands together and squeezed them. "What good can I do in here?"

"They know that, Bev," the deputy said. I should've asked about the money right then, but I forgot.

A telephone rang, its shrill noise echoed down the row of cells. Berner and I stood there a few more seconds. We didn't know what else we were supposed to say. We were just supposed to come.

The deputy put a hand on my arm and his other one on Berner's and moved us away from where we were standing. He knew how everything worked.

"Good-bye," Berner said.

"All right," my father said. He did not stand up.

"Good-bye," I said.

"All right, Dell. Son," he said. He didn't answer about the bank.

37

OUR MOTHER'S CELL WAS AT THE FAR END OF THE row of unlit cells and wasn't different from our father's, except a white metal sign had been hung on the bars with a thin metal chain. This sign said SUICIDE, painted in red block letters. On the walk down, the deputy told us there were no special facilities for "the girls." The best the county could offer was some privacy.

Our mother was seated on a cot like the one in our father's cell, but it wasn't torn open with wads falling out. She was beside another woman, talking quietly. Another cot was there. The commode wasn't stained and filthy like my father's.

"Here's your children to visit you, Neeva," the deputy said in an optimistic voice. He urged us forward, then stood back against the wall so we could be almost alone with her. "Go ahead," he said. "She's glad to see you."

"Oh, dear," my mother said and stood up right away. She had her glasses in her hand. She fitted them on as she came to the bars. She looked small. Her skin was blotched. The tip of her nose was red. She was wearing white tennis shoes without laces and a loose dark-green dress buttoned up the front with white buttons and no belt. She didn't seem to have any breasts underneath. Behind her glasses her eyes were wide and peering.

She smiled at us, as if we looked strange to her. My eyes naturally went to the SUICIDE sign. It had to do with the other woman, is what I believed. "How did you know to come here?" she said. "I said to wait for Mildred."

"We didn't know where else to go. We just came," Berner said. "We saw Dad. He didn't say much."

Our mother put her hands out through the bars. I hadn't said hello yet, but I held her right one and Berner held her left. She squeezed both our hands. She seemed even more tired than when she'd talked to me in my room the night before last. I noticed she'd taken off her wedding ring, which startled me. The other woman was wearing the same green dress and tennis shoes. She was tall and heavy-set. Even with her sitting down you could see that. She got up off the cot where she'd been sitting and lay down on the other one and turned her face to the wall. She groaned when she got settled.

"We brought you some toilet articles, but they won't let you have them," Berner said. "We thought you'd be together with Dad."

"Okay," our mother said, still holding our hands and looking at us, smiling. She wasn't talking very loud. "I feel very light in here. Isn't that strange?"

"Yes, ma'am," I said. Her voice sounded normal, as if she could've come right out and walked around and talked to us. It was a greater shock seeing her—more than it had been to see our father, who didn't seem out of place in jail. I felt unincluded, though, and not light about things. I wondered where her wedding ring was, but didn't want to ask.

"When are you going to get out?" Berner said authoritatively. She was crying and trying not to cry.

"I must've had a little let-down," our mother said. "My friend and I were just talking about that." She looked around to the big woman with her face turned to the wall and breathing deeply, one foot on top of the other. "I tried to call you two," she said. "I only had one call they'd let me make. You didn't answer. I guess you were out someplace." She blinked at us behind her spectacles. A sweat smell came off of her. It was the smell she always had. The starchy-clean smell of her jail dress was also in the air.

"What's supposed to happen to us now?" Berner said, tears draining onto her cheeks, her mouth pressed closed, her chin quivering. Outside the jail, cars were moving on the street. A car horn sounded. Outside was so close to where we were. I didn't want Berner to be crying. It wasn't helping anything.

"Where are we going?" I said. I was thinking about Miss Remlinger, who was coming to our house to get us.

"You'll see. It'll be a surprise. It'll be wonderful." Our mother smiled through the bars and nodded. "I'm saving you two. Mildred's coming. I'm surprised she hasn't already."

A young man in a tan suit and carrying a briefcase entered through the two sets of barred doors, let in by another deputy. He came in our direction but stopped at our father's cell. One of my father's hands extended out, and the man grabbed it and shook it. My father laughed and said, "O-kay, o-kay." Seeing this man talking to my father made me realize my parents had less to do with each other now. This may have been why my mother felt light. Something had left her. A weight.

"Don't you think you children should go home?" our mother said through the bars. A beam of late-morning sunlight penetrated down into her cell. She let go of our hands and smiled. We hadn't been there two minutes. We hadn't said anything that made any difference. I don't know what we expected.

"Don't you love us?" Berner said, fighting her tears. I looked at Berner and took her hand. She seemed desperate about everything.

"Of course I do," our mother said. "That oughtn't worry you. You can rely on that." She reached one small hand up to touch Berner's face, but Berner didn't move closer. Our mother left her hand there in the air for a moment.

"Are you going to commit suicide?" I said. The red sign was right there. I couldn't ignore it. I'd never said that word before saying it to my mother.

"Of course not." She shook her head. She looked up at the windows behind us. This was a lie. She did do it in the North Dakota State Penitentiary and probably had already made mention of it in the jail that day. "I told you," she said. "I had some weak feelings before."

The man in the tan suit, who'd been speaking to our father, said, "Well, all right. You just sit tight here. I'll have a word with your better half now." His briefcase snapped shut. He'd been exhibiting some papers and having our father sign them.

"She's got a federal case against me." My father's voice echoed down the line of cells.

"I'll bet she does. A lot of people do." The young man laughed and began walking toward us, his boots hitting sharp knocks on the concrete.

The deputy stepped close to Berner and me from behind and said, "This is your parents' lawyer now, kids. We better let him get a word with your mom in private. Come back and see them later. I'll let you in."

Berner looked at the man approaching and instantly stopped crying. Our mother smiled at the two of us. Tears were in her eyes. I saw that.

"I've decided I'm going to write something." She nodded at me as if this was news I'd like.

"What is it?" I asked. The deputy put his hand on my shoulder. He was pulling me away.

"I'm not sure what it'll be yet," she said. "It'll be a tragic-comedy, whatever it is. You'll have to tell me what you think. You're a smart boy."

"Did you rob a bank?" Berner said. Our mother didn't acknowledge this. The deputy moved Berner and me away from her cell so she could have her words with the lawyer. She wouldn't be there much longer. I never saw her again, though I didn't know I wouldn't at the time. I would've said more than I did say if I'd known that. I was sorry Berner asked her about the bank, since it had embarrassed her.

*   *   *

ON OUR WAY OUT, we again passed the cell where our father was. He was
lying on his busted cot in his sock feet, holding a sheaf of papers, reading.
We must've crossed his light because he turned, half sat up and gaped at
us. "Okay?" he said and flapped the papers toward us. "Did you get to see
your mother?" The deputy kept us moving along.

I said, "Yes, sir," as we passed his cell door.

"That's good then. I know it made her happy," he said. "Did you tell
her you loved her?"

I hadn't said that, but I should've.

"We did," Berner said.

"There you go," he said.

That was all we had time to say. I've thought many times, since I never
saw him again either, that it was better than saying what was true.

38

I T'S A GOOD MEASURE OF HOW INSIGNIFICANT WE WERE, and of the kind of place Great Falls was, that no one came to see about us, or to get us and transport us to someplace safe. No juvenile authorities. No police. No guardians to take responsibility for our welfare. No one ever searched the house while I was there. And when no one does that—notices you—then people and things quickly get forgotten and drift away. Which is what we did. My father was wrong about many things; but about Great Falls he wasn't. People there didn't want to know us. They were willing to let us disappear if we would.

Berner and I walked home that Monday by a different route. We felt different now—possibly we each felt freer in our own way. We walked up to Central past the post office and down toward the river, along by the bars and pawn shops, a bowling alley, the Rexall, and the hobby shop where I'd bought my chess men and my bee magazines. The street was bustling and noisy with traffic. But, again, I didn't feel anyone staring at us. School hadn't started. We weren't out of place. A boy and his sister walking back across the bridge in the sunny breeze, the river sweet and rank on a late morning in August—no one would think: These are those kids whose parents went to jail. They need to be looked after and protected.

We stopped at the railing in the middle of the bridge and watched pelicans glide and soar above the river's current. Swans floated at the near bank where a skim of yellow dust rocked on the surface. We watched two people paddle a canoe downstream toward the smelter stack and the Fifteenth Street Bridge. On the walk Berner had worn her sunglasses and been silent—no talk about our mother and father. At the railing, with the Missouri sliding beneath us, her hair rose and fell in the puff of dry breeze, her hands gripping the iron barrier, as if the bridge might become a train and pull away. She seemed young, too young to run away and be on her own. We were fifteen. But our ages really didn't matter. These were the true facts we were facing, and age doesn't figure into that.

It's odd, though, what makes you think about the truth. It's so rarely involved in the events of your life. I quit thinking about the truth for a time then. Its finer points seemed impossible to find among the facts. If there was a hidden design, living almost never shed light on it. Much easier to think about chess—the true character of the men always staying the way they were intended, a higher power moving everything around. I wondered, for just that moment, if we—Berner and I—were like that: small, fixed figures being ordered around by forces greater than ourselves. I decided we weren't. Whether we liked it or even knew it, we were accountable only to ourselves now, not to some greater design. If our characters were truly fixed, they would have to be revealed later.

It's been my habit of mind, over these years, to understand that every situation in which human beings are involved can be turned on its head. Everything someone assures me to be true might not be. Every pillar of belief the world rests on may or may not be about to explode. Most things don't stay the way they are very long. Knowing this, however, has not made me cynical. Cynical means believing that good isn't possible; and I know for a fact that good is. I simply take nothing for granted and try to be ready for the change that's soon to come.

And by then I was well on my way to knowing how to subordinate one thing to another—a lesson the game of chess teaches you, and does so almost immediately. The events that made all the difference to our parents' lives were becoming secondary to the events carrying me onward from that August day. Learning this unsimple fact has been what this telling has been about up to now—that and seeing our parents more clearly. I believe that's why I felt freed when Berner and I stood on the bridge that day, why my heart was beating hard with exhilaration. That may have been the elusive truth and why I let my father's ring drop into the river and didn't afterward think much about it.

Best to leave us on the bridge that morning, better than to think of me at home, watching from the porch as Berner not long after, walked away down our shady street and out of my life, toward wherever hers would take her. To concentrate on Berner leaving would make all this seem to be about loss—which isn't how I think about it to this very day. I think of it as being about progress, and the future, which aren't always easy to see when you're so close to both of them.

Part
Two

39

WHAT HAPPENED WAS, MILDRED REMLINGER drove up to our house in her battered old brown Ford, came straight up the walk, up the steps and knocked on the front door, behind which I was waiting alone. She came right inside and told me to pack my bag—which, of course, I didn't have. I had only the pillowcase still containing my few possessions. She asked where my sister Berner was. I told her she'd left the day before. Mildred looked around the living room and said this would have to be Berner's choice now, wherever she was, because we didn't have time to go and look for her. Juvenile officials representing the State of Montana would be coming there soon, looking for Berner and me to take us into custody. It was a miracle, she said, they hadn't come already.

Then with me in the car seat beside her, Mildred drove us out of Great Falls that late morning of August 30, 1960, and straight north up the 87 highway in the direction our father had taken Berner and me not so long before, when we saw the Indian houses and the trailer where the beef was killed, and where he may have gained a first inkling he and our mother were headed for trouble.

Mildred didn't much speak at first, as Great Falls settled into the landscape behind us. She must've felt I understood exactly what was happening to me, or else that there was no way to explain it, and we should be quiet and I should cause no one any trouble.

Up on the benchland north and west of the Highwoods, it was nothing but hot yellow wheat and grasshoppers and snakes crossing the highway and the high blue sky, and the Bear's Paw Mountains out ahead, blue and hazy but with bright snow on their peaks. Havre, Montana, was the town farther north. Our father had delivered someone a new Dodge there earlier in the summer, and ridden the Intermountain back to Great Falls. He'd described it as a "desolate place, down in a big hole. The back of beyond," where, he said, he'd encountered the flagship of the Polish navy—which was another of his corny jokes. I couldn't imagine why Mildred would be driving us there. On the map Havre was nearly as far north as you could go in Montana, and as far north in the whole country. Canada was just above it. But I was still acting on the trust that adults often do strange things that in the end are revealed as right, after which someone takes care of you. It's a crazy idea and should've seemed crazy to me then, given all that had happened in our family. But I felt I was doing what our mother had planned for me, and for Berner, too. Given my character, that was all I needed to think.

IN HAVRE—which did lie at the bottom of a long hill, with the Great Northern yards, a narrow brown river, and a line of rimrock running along the northern side of the highway—Mildred looked at me across the car seat and told me I was too thin and peakèd and was possibly anemic, and I should eat something because I might not run into food the rest of that day. Mildred was a large square-hipped, authoritative woman, with short black curly hair, snapping small dark eyes, red lipstick, a fleshy neck, and powder on her face that masked a bad complexion, though not very well. She and her car both smelled like cigarettes and chewing gum, and her ashtray was full of lipstick butts and matches and spearmint wrappers, though she hadn't smoked while we were driving. My mother had said

Mildred had been afflicted with marriage problems and now lived alone. It was hard for me to see how a man would marry her (though I'd sometimes felt that way about our mother). She was large and wasn't pretty at all, and was bossy. Mildred wore a green silky dress with little red triangles printed on it and large red beads, and stiff hosiery with heavy black shoes, and seemed uncomfortable dressed that way. In the window behind her on a wire hanger were her white nurse's costume and cap, which seemed a much more natural thing for her to wear.

In Havre, we drove down the hill to First—which was the main street—and found a sandwich shop across from a bank and the GN depot. We sat at the counter inside, and I ate cold meat loaf and a soft roll with butter and a pickle and lemonade, and felt better. Mildred smoked while I ate and watched me and cleared her throat a lot and talked about having grown up on a beet farm in Michigan and her parents being Seventh Day-ers, and her brother going to Harvard (which I'd heard of), and about how she'd run away with an Air Force boy and "landed" in Montana. The boy eventually transferred, and she'd stayed on in Great Falls, studied nursing, and married another time before figuring out it wasn't for her—which was when she'd taken Remlinger back as her name. She said she was forty-three, though I'd thought she was sixty or more. At a certain point she turned on her stool and pinched my earlobe and asked if I thought I had a fever or was coming down with something. I didn't, although I felt anxious about where we were going. She said I should go to sleep in the back seat after lunch, and this was what let me know we weren't just going to Havre that day but were traveling farther on.

FROM HAVRE, we drove north, across a wooden railroad viaduct over the tracks and the muddy river and along a narrow highway that angled up the rimrock grade high enough to let me look back to the town, low and dismal and bleak in the baking sunlight. I was farther north than I'd ever been and felt barren and isolated, becoming unreachable. Wherever

Berner was, I thought, was better than this. But I couldn't make myself ask anything because I realized the answer might've been something I wouldn't like, after which I wouldn't know what to say or do about my life, and would've had to face the fact that I'd made a mistake staying and not going with my sister (although she hadn't asked me).

The land north of Havre was the same as we'd been driving through: dry, unchanging cropland—a sea of golden wheat melting up into the hot unblemished blue sky crossed only by electrical wires. There were very few houses or buildings to signify people lived up there or needed electricity. Low green hills lay far out ahead in the shimmering distance. It was improbable we were going there, since I speculated those hills would be in Canada, which was all that lay ahead of us from my memory of the globe in my room.

Mildred again didn't talk much—just drove. She did smoke one cigarette, but didn't like it and tossed it out the vent. Buzzards hung in the sky, curving and motionless. I believed that if a person were to be lost where we were, buzzards would be the only way you'd be found, but you wouldn't survive.

At a certain point, Mildred took in a deep breath and let it out as if she'd decided something she'd been keeping silent about. She licked her lips and pinched at her nose and cleared her dry throat again.

"I should tell you *some* things now, Dell," she said, steering with two hands, her stocking feet on the pedals, her black shoes off and pushed aside. She was staring firmly ahead. We'd only passed two cars since Havre. There didn't seem to be a place visible where we were going. "I'm taking you up to Saskatchewan to live for a little while with my brother, Arthur." She said this abruptly, as if it wasn't an enjoyable thing to say. "It won't have to be this way completely forever. But right now it does. I'm sorry." She licked her lips again. "It's what your mother wants. You oughtn't fault yourself for it. I'm disappointed your sister broke away. You two could've made a good team."

She looked over at me and faintly smiled, her short hair flittering in the hot window breeze. Her teeth weren't particularly straight and she didn't smile a lot. I felt as if Berner was actually there beside me and Mildred was addressing us both.

"I don't want to do that." I said this with absolute certainty. Mildred's brother. Canada. I felt sure I didn't have to do any of that. I had a say-so.

Mildred drove on for a time without speaking, letting the highway plunder on beneath us. Possibly she was thinking, but probably she was just waiting. Finally she said, "Well, if I have to take you back, they'll arrest me for kidnapping you and put me in jail. Then the one human being who can help you—and who's not a confirmed criminal, and who's willing to do your poor mother a last favor'll be out of reach. They're looking for you to put you in an orphanage. You better think on that. I'm trying to save you here. I'd have saved your sister if she'd been smarter."

My throat had already begun tightening, and this tightness screwed right down into my chest and made a pain, and I suddenly couldn't bring in enough air, even though we were going sixty, and hot wheat fragrance was blasting in the windows. I felt an urge just to shoulder open my door and fling myself out onto the rushing pavement. Which was nothing like me. I wasn't violent and didn't do things suddenly. But the black road seemed to be my life shooting away from me at a terrible speed, with no one to stop it. I thought if I could pick myself up and start walking I could get home, even find Berner, wherever she'd gone. My fingers found the door handle, squeezed it, ready to give a pull. Berner had said she hated our parents for lying. But I'd refused to hate them and remained the loyal one who stayed and did what our mother wanted. Which made me the one bad things were happening to now. I couldn't have said what I was expecting, or what my mother's plan for me was. She'd explained everything to Mildred and not to me. But I wasn't expecting this. I felt like I'd been tricked and abandoned, and that my loyalty wasn't respected, and I was here now with this odd woman, where only the buzzards would find me if I took control over

my life. Being young was the worst thing. I knew why Berner had strived
to be older and had run away. It was to save herself.

The airlessness in my chest ached the way it does when you drink
too-cold water and feel paralyzed. But crying would be the signal of even
greater defeat. Mildred would think I was pitiful. I squeezed my eyes tight
shut, clutched the warm door handle, then released it and let hot air from
outside overcome my tears. I don't now think it was so much what Mildred had said—that I was being driven to Canada to be put in the care of
strangers—as much as it was the accumulation of all that had passed in my
life in the last week's time, and that I'd tried to take control of but failed.
Mildred was only trying to help me, and help my mother. How I felt on
hearing what I'd heard was more than anything a kind of grief.

"I don't blame you," Mildred said finally. She must've known I was
crying. "It doesn't give any comfort to know nothing's your fault. You
might like it better if it was." She adjusted her big legs in her seat, raised
her chin and sat forward as if she saw something up the road. I'd stopped
crying. "We're crossing the international border to Canada up here," she
said, settling back in her seat. "I'll tell 'em you're my nephew. I'm taking
you to Medicine Hat to buy you school clothes. If you want to tell 'em I'm
kidnapping you, that'll be the time." She pruned her lips. "We'd like to
stay out of jail if we can, though."

Ahead, where the highway was only a pencil line into the distance,
two dark low bumps became visible on the horizon, backed by blue sky in
which there was not a cloud floating. I wouldn't have seen the bumps if I
hadn't looked where Mildred was looking. It was Canada there. Indistinguishable. Same sky. Same daylight. Same air. But different. How was it
possible I was going to it?

Mildred was scrapping around in her big red patent leather purse on
the floor and continuing to drive. The dark bumps quickly materialized
into two low, square shapes that were buildings—side by side on a rise of
prairie. A car sat beside each one. It had to be where the border started. I

didn't know what happened there. Possibly someone could take me into custody, put me in handcuffs, and send me to an orphanage or back home where there was nothing but an empty house.

"What are you thinking about," Mildred asked.

I peered ahead at the sky above Canada. No one had ever asked me what I was thinking straight out. It hadn't mattered in our family what Berner and I were thinking—though we always were. *What have I got to lose?* were the words I said silently, which *was* what I was thinking, though only because they were words I'd heard other people say—in the chess club. I wouldn't have said them to Mildred. But I was shocked that what I was thinking felt true. What I said was, "How do you know what's really happening to you?" It was just what I made up to say.

"Oh, you never do." Mildred had her paper driver's license in the hand she held the steering wheel with. We were already approaching what were two wooden cabins established side by side. The highway split where it passed them. "There are two different kinds of people in the world," Mildred said, "well, really, there're lots of kinds. But at least two are the people who understand you don't *ever* know; then there're the ones who think you always do. I'm in the former group. It's safer."

A bulky man in a blue uniform stepped outside the wooden hut on the right, which we were approaching. He was fitting a policeman's hat down onto his head and waving us forward. A red flag I didn't recognize—but that had a little English flag up in its left corner—fluttered on a pole beside the hut. A sign under the flagpole said YOU ARE ENTERING CANADA. PORT OF WILLOW CREEK, SASKATCHEWAN.

The other cabin beside it was the American one. The Stars and Stripes flew over it—though I suspected not the fifty-star one that included Hawaii. A border was two things at once. Going in and going out. I was going out, which felt significant. A smaller hatless man, in a different blue uniform and wearing a badge and a side pistol, stepped out of the American cabin into the breeze. He watched Mildred pull ahead. Possibly he knew about me and was preparing to come arrest us both. I looked straight forward, sat still. For some reason I couldn't have explained, I wanted us to get across, and felt exhilarated and afraid we might be prevented. Of the two types of people Mildred had mentioned, I must've been in the first group also. Otherwise why would I ever be where I was, with everything I'd ever understood disappearing behind me? It wasn't what I expected to feel. I had waked up in my bed alone, had watched my sister walk away out of my life, possibly forever. My parents were in jail. I had no one to look after me or out for me. *What have I got to lose?* was probably the correct question to be asking. The answer seemed to be *very little*.

40

THE HIGHWAY UP INTO CANADA LAY ACROSS MORE endless cropland, indistinguishable to my eye from below the border, but with more houses and barns and windmills and evidence of people. The green hills that I'd first seen from north of Havre were, Mildred said, the Cypress Hills. They were like the Alps, she said, set out on the prairie by themselves—an anomaly from when there were glaciers on the plains. They had their own isolated forest and animal life. The people who lived there didn't like strangers. The towns we passed through, however—Govenlock, Consul, Ravencrag, Robsart—looked like any ordinary towns in Montana. Though I thought if you grew up in a place with such a strange name—including Saskatchewan (a name I'd rarely heard before)—then you'd always feel strange about yourself. Nothing later in life could be as completely normal as it had been for me living in Great Falls.

Driving north in the low, late-day sun, Mildred recited to me what she knew about Canada that she felt might prove useful. Canada was owned by England and contained provinces, not states of a union—though there was practically no difference, except Canada only had ten. People mostly spoke English, but in a different way she couldn't describe, but I'd be aware of it and could learn it. She said they had their own Thanksgiving, but theirs wasn't on Thursday and wasn't in November. Canada had fought beside America in the same world war my father had fought in and had gotten involved in it even before we did, due to Canada's obedience to the Queen of England, and in fact had an air force as good as ours. She said Canada wasn't an old country like ours and still had a pioneer feel, and nobody there really thought of it as a country, and in fact in some parts people spoke French, and the capital was back east, and nobody respected it the way we did Washington, D.C. She said Canada had dollars for money, but theirs were different colored and were sometimes mysteriously worth more than ours. She said Canada also had its own Indians and treated them better than we treated ours, and Canada was bigger than America, though it was mostly empty and inhospitable and covered with ice much of the time.

I rode along thinking about these things and how they could become true just by passing two huts marooned in the middle of nowhere. I felt better than I had earlier in the day when I didn't know where I was going. It was as if a crisis had passed or been escaped. What I experienced was relief. I only wished my sister, Berner, had stayed to see it with me.

More wheat fields ran past, and the afternoon air was sweet and cool. I made out individual dust torrents where farmers were operating combines in the distance. Grain trucks sat out on the cut-over ground, waiting to haul the wheat away. Tiny distant figures moved around the trucks as the harvesters emptied loads and the trucks moved off. Once we were out of the hills, there were no landmarks. No mountains or rivers—like the Highwoods or the Bear's Paw, or the Missouri—that told you where you were. There were even fewer trees. A single low white house with a windbreak and a barn and a tractor could be seen at a distance, then later another one. The course of the sun would be what told you where you were—that and whatever you personally knew about: a road, a fence line, the regular direction the wind came from. There was no feeling, once the hills disappeared behind us, of a findable middle point from which other points could draw a reference. A person could easily get lost or go crazy here, since the middle was everywhere and everything at once.

Mildred told me some things about her brother, Arthur Remlinger. He was American, was thirty-eight years old, and had lived in Canada for several years by his own choosing. He was the only one in her family to go to college, and had hoped to become a lawyer, but for various reasons hadn't finished his studies and had become disenchanted with America. He lived north of where we were, in the small town of Fort Royal, Saskatchewan, where he ran a hotel. It was just a coincidence, she said, that she and he lived across the border from each other. She saw him infrequently, which she didn't consider important. She loved him. The reason her brother was agreeing to take charge of me, she said, was because I was American and had no place to go, and it was a favor to her. He would find things for me to do. He had no children of his own and would be interested in me—and in Berner, too, if she hadn't run away. He was an unusual man, as I would see. He was cultivated and intelligent. I'd learn many things being around him and would like him.

Mildred decided on another cigarette and expelled smoke from her large nostrils so it rushed out the window. She'd been driving for hours—just to get me away from where I was imperiled. She could only have been exhausted. I tried to picture where we were going—Fort Royal, Saskatchewan. It sounded foreign, and threatening because it was foreign. I could only feature the same prairie all around us, where there was no place for me.

"How long am I going to stay with your brother?" I only said this to make myself say something.

Mildred sat up straighter and gripped the wheel in both fists. "I don't know," she said. "We'll have to see. Don't spend time thinking old gloomy, though." Her cigarette was in the side of her mouth, and she was talking with the other side. "Your life's going be a lot of exciting ways before you're dead. So just pay attention to the present. Don't rule parts out, and

be sure you've always got something you don't mind losing. That's important." This advice was not very different from what our father had said to
Berner and me the day we didn't go to the State Fair. I understood it was
what adults thought, though it was the opposite of the way our mother saw
things. She'd always ruled out a great deal and understood the world only
in her own terms. Mildred fattened her cheeks and fanned herself with her
hand, which meant she was hot inside her green silky dress. "Does that
make sense to you?" She reached across the seat and knocked her soft
fist against my knee the way you'd knock on a door. "Does it? Knock,
knock?"

"I guess it does," I said. Though it didn't really seem to matter what I
agreed with. That was the final time Mildred and I talked about my future.

41

CHARLEY QUARTERS CLIMBED DOWN OFF HIS TRUCK fender, holding a small metal can I later learned had beer and ice cubes in it. He'd been waiting for us in the town of Maple Creek, Saskatchewan—to drive me and Berner the rest of the way to where Mildred's brother lived. He was her brother's all-around man, Mildred said, and she didn't like him. He was Métis, and was unsavory. Once the hand-off of me was over, she was going to drive back to Great Falls through Lethbridge, Alberta, so as to not attract attention at the border where we'd crossed before. The American border policeman had watched us when we drove through. He would wonder why she came back alone.

Charley Quarters set his can on the truck hood and came back to Mildred's window and leaned in on his elbows. He looked across at me with an unfriendly grin on his wide lips. I just stared up at the mare's tails in the west—the sky behind them purple and gold and bright green, turning blue in the high reaches. I tried not to seem afraid, which I was.

Mildred pushed him back with her palm. He had a strange, sour-sweet odor on him I could feel in my nose—from his clothes and possibly his hair. He was small and chesty and dense looking and muscular, with an over-sized head. He wore dirty brown canvas trousers, black rubber boots the trousers were tucked into, and a tattered purple flannel shirt with its elbows out and a pocket torn off. His black greasy hair was clamped in the back with a woman's rhinestone barrette, and he had slitted blue eyes and big ears. His teeth, when he smiled his unlikable smile, were large and yellow and all in evidence. He looked like a dwarf. I'd seen a picture in my *World Book* (left behind in Great Falls). But he was taller than a dwarf, though his legs bowed out. He seemed cocky and rough, which I'd heard some dwarfs were.

He reached into Mildred's car and plucked one of her Tareyton cigarettes out of her pack on the dashboard and put it behind his ear.

"I thought we had two packages in the cargo." He leered at me again, as if he knew I wouldn't like being talked about as a cargo. He spoke in spurts.

Mildred said sharply, "You just take care of this one. Or I'll come up there and find you."

Charley kept grinning, and she had to push him back again. I wondered if this clipped way of talking was the way Canadians talked. "Does it have to eat?" Charley said.

"No," Mildred said. "Just get him up there and get him put to bed."

Two large men in bib overalls and straw farm hats stepped out the door of the hotel across the street. The town was empty and the street shadowy at sundown. The sign over the front door of the hotel said THE COMMERCIAL. Low lights were on inside when the door opened. The two men stood on the sidewalk and talked while they watched us. One of them laughed at something, then they walked to separate pickups, backed away from the curb, and drove slowly in opposite directions. They were Canadians, too.

"Is there something wrong with him?" Charley said, smiling as if I amused him.

"He's just fine." Mildred reached and clutched my arm and looked at me. "He's like the rest of us, aren't you?"

"Is he an orphan?" Charley Quarters said, looking in the back seat at Mildred's white uniform hung in the window. He reached a hand in and touched it.

I stared straight out the windshield at four tall grain elevators, half in shadows, silhouetted against the lighted sky. Swallows swerved in the twilight. A single lit bulb dangled where the funnel pipe hung in the nearest elevator, a pile of grain illuminated on the ground beneath it. I hadn't connected this word with orphanage up until then.

Mildred stared right into Charley's leering face. "He's got a mother and a father, unlike you. They love him. That's enough for you to hear about."

"Love him to death," Charley said, and stood up straight, backed away into the street, and looked at the sky—blue in the west, dark in the east. The mare's tails were already faded and there were faint stars. This was the man I was leaving with. In all likelihood I'd be left alone and forgotten.

"Now what I'll do," Mildred said this to me then, "is write you in care of my brother. I'll find out what I can about your folks and send that to you. Remember what I said about not ruling parts out. You'll be fine. I promise." She unexpectedly leaned toward me and pulled my face to her mouth, gripped my neck, and kissed me right on my jawbone. She squeezed me hard when I didn't kiss her back. Cigarettes and the fruity odor inside Mildred's purse, and cake makeup, and the spearmint she chewed was what she smelled like. Her spongy shoulders were shoved against my ear. "You've had a time," she whispered. "Just 'cause *their* life got ruined doesn't mean yours does. This'll be a start for you. Your sister's already made hers."

"I didn't want a start," I said, my throat suddenly constricted again—with anger at her just for saying that.

"We don't always get to choose our starts." She reached and levered my door open, pushed it back and shoved me in that direction. "Now, go on. We're putting off the inevitable here. This is an adventure. Don't be afraid. You'll be fine. I said so."

I didn't feel right saying anything more to her, even if I could've. My pillowcase with my possessions packed to go to Seattle was on the back seat floor. I hauled it over, climbed out onto the pavement, and closed the car door. Whatever Mildred had agreed with my mother to do, she'd done now. But what I wanted to do was climb back in the car with her and have her drive us as far away as we could go. Only that wasn't in my mother's plan when she could still plan things for me. So I did what I was told to—as much for my mother as any other reason. I stayed a good son to the end of it.

42

"SO DID YOU HEAR ALL ABOUT ME?" CHARLEY QUAR-ters said. We were rattling along through the dark in his old International Harvester. I could only see the bright gravel roadbed in the headlights with the dusty shoulder shooting by, thick wheat planted to the verges. It was cold with the sun off. The night air was sweet as bread. We passed an empty school bus rocking along. Our headlights swept its rows of empty student seats. Far away in the fields, cutting was going on after dark. Dim moving truck lights, the swirl-up of dust. Stars completely filled the sky.

I said I hadn't heard anything about him.

"It doesn't matter," he said. A lever-action rifle was barrel-down on the seat between us, close to his leg. His truck stank of beer and gasoline and the same strong sour-sweet stinging odor I didn't recognize. There was an animal carcass in the bed of the truck, but I couldn't tell what it was. "Here's what's going to happen," Charley said. "I'm going to be re-sponsible for you up here. But you'll look after yourself unless I need you. You have work every day. You sleep in the Overflow House by my trailer. You eat in the hotel. A.R. owns it. You get there and back on your own. Though some days I'll take you in the Rolls here. And you don't cause me any trouble."

Charley had the seat pushed far back so his feet barely touched the pedals, one hand on the wheel, and he was smoking Mildred's cigarette he'd previously put behind his ear. He was drinking another beer out of a regular can. A deer stood at the edge of the highway, chest-high in the wheat, its green eyes gleaming into the headlights. Charley sawed the wheel toward it, but it moved effortlessly back. "God *damn* that," Charley shouted. "I coulda got that one." He leered at me, as if he was trying to scare me, and it amused him. "How old do you guess I am?" he said, cigarette clenched in his teeth.

"I don't know," I said. I hadn't answered anything about having duties. I hadn't expected to have any. I had no idea what I'd see once the sun was up.

"Don't you give a shit?"

"No," I said.

"Fifty! But I look younger." He talked in this clipped way. "You think I'm Indian. I know that already."

"I don't know," I said.

"May-tee," he said. "You don't know what the fuck that is, do you?"

"No," I said. Mildred had mentioned Métis, but I didn't know about it or even how you spelled it.

"It's the bloodline of the ancient kings." Charley elevated his blunt chin and let the smoke out the sides of his mouth as he talked. "Cuthbert Grant—all the way back. The line of martyrs." He snorted in the cold air. "Indians are entirely different. A lot of mental illness there. Too much drinking and inbreeding. They don't accept us. They want to kill Métis if they get the chance."

He suddenly stood on the brake. I got my hands to the dashboard just in time. Though I pitched out of my seat onto my knees and my heart started pounding. We were stopped in the bright alley of gravel between the wheat fields. "I need to. You need to?" Charley said. He had the engine killed before I could answer and was out the door, spraddling his legs in front of the truck, in the bright lights. He had his penis already out where I could see him and was pissing a hard stream down onto the dirt, concentrating fiercely. I wanted to. I hadn't had the nerve to say so to Mildred, though she was a nurse and would've seen such things. But I didn't believe I could do it in front of Charley, on the highway. I could've with my father. I was a town boy. So I just sat in the ticking truck, the headlights illuminating Charley and the widening circle of urine on the ground, road dust shifting through the open door, bringing in the lemony piss odor. "What happened to you?" he called out from the road. He made a little gasping sound before he quit. "Did you get kicked out down there? You commit a crime?"

I hated to be staring at him and to see his private part. I said, "No." I didn't want to say, *My parents got put in jail in Great Falls. My mother didn't want me to be in an orphanage. She wants me to be here in Canada.*

Charley spit into the urine circle, then sucked back, clearing his nose. "Secrets are good," he said, zipping up. "Up here's a good place to hide." Mosquitoes and gnats were filtering out of the wheat into the headlamp heat. Some came in the open truck with me. Then a sudden, quick flicking flash of wing fell in through the light, twisted upward, and was gone again. A hawk or an owl, drawn to the insects. It made my heart pound harder. Charley didn't see it. "You know anything about A.R.?" He was still out in the road, talking, staring into the darkness above the cone of headlight. I believed he meant Mildred's brother.

"Mildred said he was her brother." I didn't think he could hear me.

He scuffed his black rubber boots around on the gravel. "You'll think he's strange." He didn't seem to be doing anything now. "What do you want to be called?"

"Dell," I said.

"How many years have you got, Dell?"

I knew what that had to mean. "Fifteen," I said. "Almost sixteen."

Charley came back to the doorway and climbed up into the driver's seat, his animal odor accompanying him. "Are you lonely?" He started the truck with a roar. The headlights dimmed then brightened.

"I miss my parents," I said, "and my sister."

"So where'd *she* go? Some orphanage?" Charley closed his door and rolled up his window. Mosquitoes were whining around us.

"She ran away," I said.

"Good for her." He was silent, his hands on the steering wheel. "You don't know anything about anything, do you?"

"No," I said.

"What do you want *me* to tell you?"

"Why would anybody take me up here?" Again, what I said was only what I was thinking, as I had with Mildred.

Whatever had intruded into the headlights a moment before fell through again in full view. An owl—a curved, white face, wings extended, thorny feet grasping, its eyes intent on something beyond the light's edge. Then it was gone. I'd never seen an owl; I'd only heard them from my room at night in Great Falls. But I knew what it was. Again, Charley didn't seem to notice.

"A.R.'s peculiar. He's American," Charley said. "He's been up here a long time. Maybe *he's* lonely for company. I don't know. Let me feel your hand."

His tough, hard hand, which was shockingly big, found mine and captured it and squeezed it four or five or six quick successive squeezes. His hand was thick and short-fingered and blunt-nailed and grainy like his canvas pants. I tried to pull my hand back, but he held on, squeezing even tighter. "Did that old nursy try to fuck you," he said, as if he was about to laugh.

I couldn't look at him. I said, "No."

"She wanted to. I could tell that. She wanted to fuck me, too. We could've both done that. You don't want to let anybody do you that way, though. You wait on some nice girl. I got shown things too early. And here

I am." Struggling, I got my hand free and pushed it under my leg where he couldn't get it. He scared me. "Okay, there are you, Dell." He revved the truck, which made a racket. The headlights brightened down the road. Insects swarmed up. "You don't have any interest in Hitler, I guess, do you?"

"No," I said. All I knew about Hitler was what my father had related. "Schicklegruber," he'd called him. "Little Adolf, the wallpaper installer." My father hated him.

Charley pulled the truck down into gear. "He interests me," Charley said. "He had his struggles. I'm misunderstood most of the time, too." He held two stubby fingers up under his nose, his eyes suddenly wild. He turned toward me, gawking. "Look-it this, see? He looks like this, eh? Got his little cute mustache. Nein, nein, nein! Achtung! Achtung!"

My father had said Hitler was dead, his wife with him. Suicides.

"He was a good artist, you know," Charley said, revving the truck again. "I fancy myself a poet. But we don't have to talk about all that now." He mashed the accelerator, and we lurched away into the dark. It was Canada where I was now. It was my mother's plan.

43

LIFE-CHANGING EVENTS OFTEN DON'T SEEM WHAT they are.

Voices woke me. A man laughing, then the mutter of a second voice, then the sprung-metal bang of a car hood being shut. Then more laughing. "I just wish a woman would tell me one thing I didn't already know," a voice that sounded like Charley Quarters said. These voices were somewhere outside the room I'd been asleep in, a room I remembered entering, but didn't recognize. The cool smell of earth and something tangy and metallic and sour thickened the air. A thin gray cotton cloth with a white border was tacked over a window beside my bed—which was only a metal folding cot—softening what had to be morning light. I didn't know morning light *where,* or how long we'd driven the night before, or if *here* was my destination.

I sat up. The room was small and low ceilinged and green shadowed, as if water danced behind the curtain. I was tight-headed. My back and legs ached. I was wearing my Jockeys; my clothes and shoes and socks were heaped on the linoleum floor at the end of the cot. My memory was broken in pieces: a truck's headlights crossing a small white building; a door opening in; a flashlight beam jittering over a room with a cot in it; Charley Quarters urinating on the brightly lit gravel, staring intently down; an owl's plush face like in a dream; a mention of Hitler and Filipino girls; me—fighting to be awake, but failing.

I pulled aside the cloth and looked out the dusty window. One of its panes was cracked across, the glaze crumbled on the sill. Outside was a lilac bush, and behind it a patch of grass with dew still sparkling. Beyond that, a narrow asphalt street, pocked and heaved up, a concrete sidewalk humped and weedy, a square of perfectly blue sky, like a barrier.

An old white trailer on rubber wheels sat across the broken street—a rectangular flat-top trailer a person would live in. A TV antenna tilted on its side on the roof. Beside the trailer was an open-mouthed Quonset with a wind sock on top. Beyond that, a tall, wooden grain elevator with a steepled roof. The elevator bore faded lettering, high up on its bin. It said SASKATCHEWAN POOL and under that, PARTREAU.

Charley Quarters' dented International pickup sat outside the trailer. Charley stood in front of it, speaking to a man holding a straw hat, with a tan jacket over his arm, and wearing a pale blue shirt. Charley was still dressed in his black rubber boots, his pants legs stuffed in, and the same flannel shirt. All around, the trailer's yard was strewn with rusted metal implements, tires and empty barrels, bicycles, animal cages, an ancient motorcycle, and a green Studebaker car up on wood blocks—its windows out. Pieces of scrap metal had been bolted or welded together to make odd shapes and set off in the weeds by themselves. A bicycle wheel joined to a swather blade. A hay baler equipped with a steering wheel and a mirror. A sundial made of a wheel rim. Shining pinwheels and flashing whirligigs had been stuck up on wood sticks in the clutter, fracturing the sunlight. A makeshift wooden flagpole with the same flag as the border was leaned against the trailer's side.

Charley turned, his short powerful arms gesturing spiritedly first at the trailer, then at the window I was looking out of. I thought he was discussing me, and that the man in the blue shirt listening must've been Arthur Remlinger. Mildred's brother. I heard Charley shout, as if he wanted others to hear him, "Nothing's foolproof around me." He reared back and laughed. The other man looked at the building where I was, set a hand on his hip and said something and nodded. Charley turned and started across the grass toward me.

I quick got my T-shirt and pants on. I didn't want to be in my Jockeys if Charley was coming to get me. I pushed my shoes on without socks. I looked for a door to get outside. There was another, empty cot in the room. All around in the shadows were piled cardboard boxes, barely allowing room for the cots. There was no lamp. I heard Charley's voice already outside, "Who would you wish yourself on? I ask you that. . . ." I didn't know who he was talking to.

I hurried through a low door into a kitchen room—tiny, airless, jumbled. More boxes were stacked there, a cast-iron stove, an old TV with a cracked screen, and what looked like a stuffed dog or a coyote placed on top of an oak ice box with corroded latches. I shoved my shirttail in my pants and went through a door out into a tiny dirt-floor vestibule room with its own windowed door, then right into the brash sunlight. Which stunned me, struck my eyes, and made me shut them, just as Charley rounded the corner of the house. Green, then silver, then red spots swam in my vision. My scalp tightened on my skull. I didn't know what was about to happen. But I thought it was important. I was far away from Great Falls.

"Okay. Here he is," Charley called out loudly. I forced my eyes to open. The white stucco building where I'd been sleeping was the one in my dream that the car lights had swung past. It sat flat to the ground, scabs of stucco rotted off, laths and interior plaster showing through. I zipped my pants. My shoes were untied. I shielded my eyes, my face twisted. "A.R.'s here." Charley exhibited his large square teeth, grinning as if this was unpleasant for me and he enjoyed it. "Come up here now. He wants to see you." He turned around and I came after him through the weeds, and we crossed the crumbling street toward the trailer and the Quonset, where the man in the blue shirt was speaking into the window of a shiny maroon Buick three-holer I hadn't seen before.

I took my chance for a look around. It was a town, but not like one I'd seen—even when our father had driven Berner and me out to the Indian reservation in Box Elder and we'd viewed their homes. A few gray wooden houses were scattered along the remains of several town streets. There was likewise evidence of where other houses had been—empty brick foundation squares, falling-in wood outbuildings, a standing chimney, and open ground where something had existed but was gone. The five or six still-standing houses looked vacant—their outer doors hanging open on hinges, their yards weeded in. Some had no roofs, others had their roofs boarded and rough-patched, their chimneys crumbled and porches sagging. No electrical wires ran to anything except the white trailer and the Quonset and the house I'd just been sleeping in, and to one other house where the roof had a hole that rain could fall in. A large woman wearing a loose gray dress stood on the back steps there, watching us across the distance. A looping clothesline was strung up in the backyard. White sheets and women's underwear bloomed in the dry breeze.

Off toward what looked like a paved highway, two big flapping grain trucks rumbled past a dilapidated row of flat-top business buildings across from the elevator. These buildings looked abandoned, their windows out and doors missing. No people were in evidence. At the edge of the town, which became visible as I walked across to the Quonset, a border of box elders and Lombardy poplars (I recognized these from Montana) had been planted to block the wind, but had died. Beyond these and the town's edge were cut grain fields dotted with straw bales, and in the near distance, a bladeless windmill, and a black oil pumper patiently delving. Farther on, the land stretched away not flat but rolling, without mountains or hills, and almost no other trees as far as I could see. Only the horizon broke the line of sight a great ways off.

"Okay, here he is." Charley was still shouting. I followed him across the weed lot toward the trailer and the Quonset where the new-looking Buick sat. The Quonset, I could see, housed an old cloth-top Jeep back in its shadows, and a flat single-axle trailer loaded with what looked like geese but were wood decoys, and a pile of shovels. "I woke the little baby up," Charley carried on. "He's used to soft treatment down in the States. He won't survive up here." He looked around for me. Charley was even stranger in the daylight—his knobby head larger, his shoulders unnaturally narrow, his legs bandied out at the knees where his boots stopped, his black hair still clutched back with his rhinestone barrette. He was a disturbing sight out in the open.

I put my hands in my pockets to keep from shading my eyes. They ached. Grasshoppers popped in the choke weeds and crawled across the ground at my feet, rattling like snakes—which made me tense. Tiny brown birds flitted among the flashing pinwheels and whirligigs and metal sculptures. The sun baked my hair and my shoulders and stung my eyes, though the hairs on my arms were cold and prickly. I'd begun to perspire in my hairline.

The man holding his tan jacket and a straw hat, who'd been talking through the window of the Buick—a woman was visible in the passenger's side, laughing at something she'd just heard—this man stood up and began walking toward where I was.

"I had to pry him outa the bed," Charley said still loudly—for the man's benefit. "This is Mr. Remlinger. You can call him 'sir.'"

I shielded my eyes again. Sun shone behind the man's head. I was nervous. This was the man who was responsible for me. Arthur Remlinger.

"We've been waiting on you," the man said. I looked up to see his face. He was tall and handsome and had fine blond hair parted carefully on the right side, the opposite side I parted mine on. He wasn't smiling, but he seemed interested. I didn't say anything. "Tell us your name, why don't you?"

"Dell Parsons," I said. My name sounded strange being spoken there.

The man looked at Charley Quarters and smiled. "Does 'Dell' stand for something else? It's unusual."

"No, sir," I said.

"Go on, speak out," Charley Quarters said.

"Weren't there supposed to be two of you?" The man stepped closer to me as if he needed to see me better. A pair of metal-rim spectacles hung from a string around his neck. His large hands were bony and manicured. He seemed amused.

"The other one ran off before she got here," Charley said.

"Well, too bad," Arthur Remlinger said. "You look tired. Are you all worn out?" He fanned his face with his straw hat.

"Yes, sir," I said. He hadn't said his own name. Arthur Remlinger wasn't a name that went with the way he looked. It seemed like an older man's name.

"And people are hunting for you, is that our story?" His eyes moved to Charley, then back to me. He wanted me to talk more, but I didn't feel comfortable talking.

"I don't know," I said. Warm breeze spun the silver whirligigs in the weedy yard. They made soft clicking sounds, fluttering.

"He doesn't enjoy talking," Charley said. He turned and looked at the devices spinning. They seemed to make him happy.

"Well. If the RCMP come out here," Arthur Remlinger said, "you just say you're my nephew from back east. They don't know where Toronto is. Would you like me to give you a Canadian name?"

"No, sir," I said.

He smiled, then the smile vanished off his face as if he was uncertain about something that had to do with me. He had a dent in his chin that showed when he smiled. His complexion was smooth and pale. He was unusual looking. "There aren't any of those anyway," he said, and began turning his hat around in his fingers, as if he was appraising me. His gaze rose above my shoulder toward the stucco shack where I'd slept. "Are you accommodated in your little house. Over there?" He spoke that way—as if each word was chosen specifically.

I was sweating down my cheek. I looked around at the terrible shack. A plank shed sat in the weeds beyond it. I knew this was a privy. A large white dog stood outside, facing the door, wagging its tail. A silver whirligig had been placed by the side of it, which meant Charley used the privy. My father always told jokes and stories about privies. They stank and you used the phone book for your paper and never had privacy. I'd never thought I'd have to use one. I didn't want to go back in the stucco shack. "I don't know," I said. "I'd . . ."

"You can move things around inside just as you please. Some of those boxes are mine," Arthur Remlinger said, still turning his hat. "You won't be easy for somebody to find there, if that's our goal. No one'll bother you." He rubbed his ear, which was large, with the heel of his hand. He seemed uncomfortable now. "Fort Royal's where I live down that hardtop four miles." He turned and looked toward the highway. "Which is east. We'll find you something to do at the hotel. Have you been alone before?"

"No, sir," I said.

"I'd imagined not," he said. "I assume you've worked though."

"No, sir," I said. I didn't know what Arthur Remlinger knew about me, but I believed he must've known most everything—though possibly not that I liked to play chess and was interested in bees, or had never worked because my mother didn't want me to for her own reasons.

"Do you feel strange here?" He looked as if something had just occurred to him. His brows furrowed. I'd never met anyone like him. Mildred had said he was thirty-eight, but his face was a young man's handsome face. At the same time he seemed older, given how he was dressed. He wasn't consistent, the way I was used to people being.

"Yes, sir," I said.

He turned his straw hat around inch by inch with his long fingers, on one of which was a gold ring. "Well," he said, "some things are regrettable

that happen to us, Dell. We can't do anything about them." He looked over
my shoulder again at the stucco house. "When I got here . . ." He stopped as
he looked at the house, then began again. "I lived in your little house there.
I'd stand out in the grass and stare at the sky and fantasize I saw brightly
colored birds and I was in Africa and the clouds were mountains." His blue
shirt, which looked to me like a nice shirt, was sweated through in places on
the front. He kept his pretty beige jacket over his arm.

"He's American, like you are! So he's strange," Charley suddenly said
and laughed. He was referring to Arthur Remlinger. He'd been watching
the brown birds flit around his pinwheel garden, but also listening without
seeming to. He started walking away toward the trailer, which had a wood
crate under its door for a step, his rubber boots kicking the weeds, sending grasshoppers and the small birds arcing up. "You two are birds of a
feather," he said.

"What do you enjoy doing, Dell?" Arthur Remlinger's blue eyes had
almost no color. He cocked his head and put one hand awkwardly in his
trouser pockets as if we were going to have a conversation now. He seemed
to want to speak to me, but not to know what to say. Mildred had said he
was unusual, which he certainly was.

"I like to read," I said.

He pursed his lips and blinked at me. This seemed to interest him.
"Are you planning to attend a good college then when you're older?"

"Yes, sir," I said.

He was wearing soft suede boots one of his pants legs was tucked into.
They looked like expensive boots to me. He was dressed in an expensive
way, which made him even more out of place being here. He rubbed one
boot toe on the dusty ground, then turned and looked back at the car. The
woman inside was watching us. She waved but I didn't wave back. "You
and Florence'll probably get on," Arthur Remlinger said. "She's a painter.
She's a devotee of the American Nighthawk school. She's very artistic."
He nodded. This seemed to amuse him. "I have one of her paintings on

the wall in my rooms. I'll show it to you when I see you again." He cast his gaze all around where we were—the hot weeds, the Quonset, the broken-down house trailer, the remnants of the town nobody lived in. "They'd definitely burn what's left of this place down where I'm from," he said.

"Why?" I said.

This seemed to almost make him laugh, because the dent suddenly appeared in his smooth chin. But he didn't. "Oh, it would horrify them," he said. Then he smiled. "No more possibilities for success. Americans all fear that. They have an improper fit with history down below."

"How long do I have to stay here?" I said. This was the most important thing I wanted to find out, so I should say it. No one had taken up the subject of my going back to Great Falls. Arthur Remlinger hadn't mentioned my parents—as if he didn't know about them, or they weren't important.

"Well," he said, "stay as long as you want to." He situated his straw hat up onto his head. He was ready to go. The hat had a leather cord strung from the brim that he pulled under his chin. It made him look entirely different—slightly silly. "You might like it here. You could learn something."

"I probably won't like it," I said, which seemed rude and not grateful, but true.

"Then I guess you'll find a way to leave," he said. "It'll give you some purpose." He turned and began walking away back toward the Buick. "Dell, I'm awfully glad you're here. I'll be seeing you soon." He said this without turning. "Charley'll tell you about your work."

"All right," I said. I wasn't sure he'd heard me, so I said it again. "All right."

That was all there was to meeting Arthur Remlinger. As I said, life-changing events can seem not what they are.

44

IN OUR MOTHER'S "CHRONICLE OF A CRIME COMMIT-
ted by a Weak Person," she wrote as if Berner and I were present and could read her thoughts the instant she wrote them,
and were her confidants who would benefit from what she was thinking.
Her chronicle represents to me her truest voice, the one we children never
heard, but the voice in which she would've expressed herself if she ever
fully could've—without the limits she'd imposed on life. The same must
be true with all parents and their children. You only know a part of each
other. Our mother didn't live a long time in the North Dakota prison. And
anyone can tell—true sounding or not—that she was beginning to break
apart when she wrote this.

Darlings,

*You two have crossed over a national boundary now, which is
not like going down the street, you know. It's a new start, though of
course there's no such thing as a whole new start.* [She and Mildred
had obviously discussed this.] *It's just the old start put under a
new lamp. I know all about that. But you'll have a chance together
in Canada and won't be blemished more by your father and me. No
one will care where you came from or what we did. You won't stand*

*out. I've never been there, but it seems so much like the U.S. Which
is good.*

*I can remember Niagara Falls—looking across them when I
was a girl, with my parents. You've seen that photograph. Whatever
it is that separates people, the falls insisted on it (to me they did,
anyway). We don't discriminate carefully enough, you know, between
things that seem alike but are different. You should always do that.
Oh, well. You're going to have thousands of mornings to think about
all this. No one will tell you how to feel. You already imagine the
world as its opposite, Dell. You told me so. That's your strength.
And, Berner, you have a taste for the unique, so you'll do fine. My
father crossed many borders after Poland, before he got to Tacoma,
Washington. He always drew authority from the present. Most
definitely.*

*I've discovered a brand-new coldness in me now. It's not bad to
find a cold place in your heart. Artists do this. Maybe it has other
names. . . . Strength? Intelligence? I rejected it before—for your
father's sake. Or attempted to. I'm just trying to be helpful to you
from here, but am at a disadvantage. I'm sure you understand. . . .*

I've read this "letter" many times. Each time I've realized that she
never expected to see either Berner or me again. She knew very well this
was the end of the family for all of us. It's more than sad.

45

LONELINESS, I'VE READ, IS LIKE BEING IN A LONG line, waiting to reach the front where it's promised something good will happen. Only the line never moves, and other people are always coming in ahead of you, and the front, the place where you want to be, is always farther and farther away until you no longer believe it has anything to offer you.

The days that followed my first meeting with Arthur Remlinger—August 31, 1960—must not, then, have been lonely days. Were it not that they ended in calamity, they might've been seen as full and rich for a boy in my situation—abandoned, everything familiar gone away, no prospects other than the ones I found in front of me.

My work duties at the beginning—before the Sports arrived and the goose shooting began—were all conducted in Fort Royal, Saskatchewan, in the Leonard Hotel, the hotel Arthur Remlinger owned. He himself lived in an apartment on the top third floor, with windows that faced the prairie and from which you could see (what I imagined were) hundreds of miles north and west. I was expected to walk to my work each day, or to pedal one of Charley's falling-apart J. C. Higgins two-wheelers down the highway, where big grain trucks had strewn a golden carpet of wheat chaff along the roadside, beyond which the Canadian Pacific tracks ran parallel, serving the elevators from Leader to Swift Current. On occasional days, Charley would take me in his truck—often with the Swedish woman, Mrs. Gedins, the other Partreau resident, silent and staring out the window—and deliver me to the Leonard, where my work was swamping bedrooms and bathrooms, which paid me three Canadian dollars a day, plus my meals. Mrs. Gedins worked in the kitchen, preparing the food for the hotel dining room. I had half my afternoons to myself and could either pedal the highway back to Partreau, where there was nothing to do, or else stay and be fed early supper with the harvesters and railroaders in the poorly lit dining room and get back after dusk. I was specifically forbidden by Charley to hitchhike the highway. Canadians, he said, didn't believe in hitchhiking and would assume I was a criminal or else an Indian and would possibly try to run over me. And hitchhiking would make me stand out and attract suspicion and draw the notice of the Mounties, which no one wanted. It was as if Charley himself had something hidden that couldn't stand a close inspection.

Although I'd never done swamping work, except to help clean our house when our mother required it, I found I could do it. Charley showed me tricks for getting into and out of rooms quickly so I could finish the ones I was assigned—sixteen, plus the two shared bathrooms for each floor used by the roomers, who were oil-rig roughnecks and railroad-gang boys and drummers and custom harvesters from the Maritimes who moved across the prairies each fall. Many of these roomers were young, little older than I was. Many were lonely and homesick, and some were violent and liked to drink and fight. But none ever paid attention to how they'd left a room they'd slept in, or a bathroom where they cleaned themselves and used the toilet. Their tiny bedrooms smelled putrid with their odors—their sweat and filth, and their food and whiskey and the gumbo mud and bottled liniment and tobacco. Down the halls the bathrooms were rank and humid and soapy, and stained from private uses the men also never bothered to clean—as they would've in their mothers' homes.

Sometimes I would push open a bedroom door with my bucket and mop
and broom and rags and astringents, and there would be one of the boys
alone in a room with several beds in it, smoking or staring out the window or reading a bible or a magazine. Or there would be one of the Filipino girls sitting on the bedside alone, and once or twice with no clothes
on, and more than once in the bed with one of the roughnecks or some
salesman, or with another girl sleeping into the long morning. Each time
I said nothing and carefully closed the door and skipped the room that
day. The Filipino girls, of course, were not Filipinos, Charley explained
to me. They were Blackfoot or Gros Ventre girls Arthur Remlinger had
had driven in by taxi from Swift Current or over from Medicine Hat, and
who worked in the bar at night and enlivened the atmosphere and made
the Leonard more attractive to the customers, since women were not otherwise allowed. Often when I arrived in the morning for work, I would
see the Swift Current taxi parked in the alley beside the hotel, its driver
sleeping in the front seat or reading a book, waiting for the girls to come
out the side door, for the ride home. Charley told me one of the Filipinos
was actually a Hutterite girl with a baby and no husband. But I never saw
such a girl in the Leonard and doubted Hutterite girls would stoop to that,
or that their parents would permit it.

And I don't mean by this to say that I instantly, perfectly fitted myself
into the life in Fort Royal. It was far from that. I knew that my parents
were in jail, and that my sister had run away, and I was in all likelihood
abandoned among strangers. But it was easier—easier than you would
think—to turn my attention away from all that and to live in the present,
as Mildred had said, as if each day were its own small existence.

The little town of Fort Royal was a lively place in the early autumn
and benefited considerably by comparison to Partreau, where I was made
to live, four miles away—a strange, vacant, ghostly residence except for
Charley in his trailer and Mrs. Gedins, who rarely acknowledged me.
Fort Royal was a small, bustling prairie community on the railroad line

and the 32 highway between Leader and Swift Current. It must've been little different from the town where my father robbed the bank in North Dakota.

The Leonard dominated the west end of Main Street and was wood-constructed and three stories and perfectly square and painted white, with a flat roof and rows of empty unadorned windows, and offered a small featureless street entrance opening into a dark reception, a windowless dining room, and a shadowy windowless bar achieved through a narrow corridor to the back. The Leonard had a sign on its roof—which a person couldn't see from town, but that I could see from down the highway when I rode to work and back. Red neon spelled out LEONARD HOTEL in squat square letters, and beside it was the neon outline of a butler offering a round tray with a martini glass. (I didn't yet know what a martini was.) It was a strange sight to see from out on the prairie. But I liked seeing it as I came and went. It referred to a world away from where it was, and I was, and yet was there in front of me every day, like a mirage or a dream.

The Leonard, in truth, would not have seemed to be a hotel—compared to the Rainbow in Great Falls, or to fine hotels I've since seen. It had little to do with the town. Few town residents ever came there, except for drinkers and ne'er-do-wells and the bad-tempered farmers who Arthur Remlinger leased goose-shooting ground from, and who drank in the bar for free. The Leonard endured the blight of disapproval in Fort Royal, which had at one time been a temperance town. Gambling and girls were available, and most decent people had never been inside.

My duties were always over by two. If I stayed to eat supper at six, that is when I would often see Arthur Remlinger—always well attired, with his lady friend, Florence La Blanc, talking and joking and making himself congenial for the paying customers. I'd been told by Charley that I wasn't expected to make conversation with Arthur Remlinger—in spite of our first meeting having been agreeable. I wasn't supposed to ask questions or be conspicuous or even friendly, as if Arthur Remlinger existed in a rare state no one could share. I was a visitor there and was to understand I had no special status or privileges. Occasionally I'd pass Arthur Remlinger in the little reception or going up the stairs where I was sweeping or performing my swamping duties with my bucket and mop, or in the kitchen when I was eating. "All right. There you are, Dell," he'd say, as if I'd been hiding from him. "Are you managing in your billet where you are?" (Or words like that; I already knew what a billet was from my father.) "Yes, sir," I'd say. "Let us know if you're not," he'd say. "I'm managing all right," I'd say. "Fine then, fine," Arthur Remlinger would say and continue on his way. I would not see him, then, for several days.

Though in truth it was a mystery to me why, if he was willing to take charge of me and my welfare, Arthur Remlinger seemed to have no wish to know me—which was significant to a boy my age. He'd seemed good-natured but peculiar when I first met him—as if something had been distracting him. But he seemed even more peculiar now, which I assumed to be how it was to know new people.

On days I stayed in town, whiling hours until I'd get to eat again— following which I'd pedal back tired to Partreau before the dark highway turned treacherous with grain trucks and farm boys beered up for the evening—I often walked about the town of Fort Royal, taking a look at what it contained. I did this both because it was new for me to be alone and not looked after; and also because the little that was there made what I saw more striking, and I'd decided the way not to be forlorn and plagued by morbid thoughts was to investigate and take an interest in things the way someone would whose job was to write about it for the *World Book*. But, too—which is at the deepest heart of those lonely prairie towns—I took my tours because there was nothing else to do, and choosing to be an investigator conferred a small freedom I'd never known up to then, having lived only with my sister and my parents. And finally, I did it because it was Canada where I was, and I knew nothing about that—how it was different from America, and how it was alike. Both things I wanted to know.

I walked the hard pavement down Main Street in my new dungarees and secondhand Thom McAns, feeling that no one noticed me. I didn't know Fort Royal's population, or why a town was there or why anyone lived there, or even why it was called Fort Royal—except possibly because an army outpost might've been there in the pioneer time. Its businesses ran on both sides of Main, which was the highway, and there seemed to me just enough of everything to make a town. Grain trucks and farm trucks and tractors passed through the middle every day. There was a barber shop, a combined Chinese laundry and café, a pool hall, a post office with a picture of the Queen on the wall inside, a community hall, two small doctors' offices, a Sons of Norway, a Woolworth's, a drugstore, a movie house, six churches (including a Moravian, a Catholic and a Bethel Lutheran), a closed library, an abattoir and an Esso. There was a co-op department store where Charley had bought my pants and underwear and shoes and a coat. There was the Royal Bank, a fire station, a jeweler, a tractor repair and a smaller hotel, the Queen of Snows, with its own licensed bar. There was no school for students, but there'd been one—its square, white frame presence sat across from a tiny, treeless park, furnished with a war monument with men's names carved in, and a flag and a flagpole. There were ten neat squared-off, unpaved streets of modest white houses where the town residents lived. These had clean lawns, often with a single spruce tree planted and a garden plot, the last petunias blooming in box beds, sometimes the English flag on a pole surrounded by white-painted rocks, or a Catholics' crèche I identified from Montana. There was also a fenced-in dirt baseball diamond, an ice rink for curling and hockey when the winter came down, a weedy tennis court with no net, and a cemetery, south toward where the fields took up and the town stopped.

On my tours I looked studiously into the jewelry shop window—at the Bulovas and Longines and Elgins, and the tiny diamond engagements and the bracelets and silver services and hearing aids and trays of bright ear bobs. I entered the shadowy drugstore and purchased a small clock for my early wake-ups and breathed the scents of the ladies' perfumes and sweet soap and the soda fountain water and the sharp odors of chemicals from the back rooms and the customers' counter. On one afternoon, I stopped in the Chevy agency and inspected the new model they had—a shiny red Impala hardtop my father would've valued highly. I sat for a time in its driver's seat and imagined myself driving fast over the open prairie, just as I'd done when he'd brought a new DeSoto home and parked it in front, and life for Berner and me had been uneventful. A salesman in a yellow bow tie came over and stood by the door, and informed me I could drive the Chevy home if I wanted to, then he laughed and asked me where I was from. I told him I was American, I was visiting my uncle at the Leonard, that my father sold cars in "the States" (a new expression to me). But he didn't seem interested after that and walked away.

On another day, I walked to the shut-down library and looked in through its thick glass door, down the aisles of empty shelving, the toppled-over chairs, the librarian's tall desk turned sideways to the door in the gloom. I read the marquee at the movie house, which operated only on weekends and only showed "horse operas." I explored down the dirt alleys behind town to the switch yard, watched the grain and tanker cars shunting east and west—as I'd also done before in Great Falls—the same gaunt rail riders eyeing me as if they knew me as they slid past in the box-car doors. I walked past the abattoir, where "killing day" was Tuesday—a handwritten sign said—and a doomed cow stood in the back corral wait-ing. I passed the Massey-Harris repair where men were back in the dark bay, soldering farm equipment with torches and masks. The cemetery was beyond the town limit, but I didn't walk to there. I'd never been in a cem-etery but didn't think it could be different in Canada.

It is, of course, very different to walk through a town when you're a member of a family that's waiting at home a short distance away—as opposed to being someone who no one's waiting for or thinking about or wondering what you might be doing or if you're all right. I did these tours many more times than once that early September, while the weather changed, as it suddenly does there, and the summer I'd lived through disappeared, and the prospect of winter arose for me and everyone. Very few people spoke to me, although no one seemed specifically *not* to speak to me. Almost everyone I passed on the street looked me in my eyes and registered me as *seen*, certifying, I believed, that a private memory had been made and I should know that. And even if nothing in Fort Royal seemed distinctive to me, *I* was someone distinctive among people who all knew one another and relied on knowing it. (This was the crucial element my father had failed to understand, and why he'd been caught after he'd robbed the bank in North Dakota.) You could say I performed my tours the way anyone would who was a stranger to a place. But it was a place odd for being in a separate country, and yet didn't feel or appear so different from what I already knew. If anything, the similarity to America made its foreignness profound, and also attractive to me, so that in the end I liked it.

One woman with her daughter passed me by where I was standing at the drugstore window, doing nothing more than looking wondrously in at the colored vessels and beakers and powders and mortars and pestles and brass scales on display—all items the Rexall in Great Falls had lacked and that made the Fort Royal store seem more serious. The woman turned and came back up the sidewalk and said to me, "Can I help you with something?" She was dressed in a red-and-white flowered dress with a white patent leather belt and matching white patent leather shoes. She didn't have an accent—I was acute to this because of what Mildred had told me. She was only being friendly, possibly had seen me before, knew I was not from there. I'd never been addressed this way—as a total stranger. Everything about me had always been known to the adults in my life.

"No," I said. "Thank you." I was aware that while she didn't sound different to me, I possibly sounded different from people she was used to hearing. Possibly I looked different, too—though I didn't think I did.

"Are you here visiting?" She smiled but seemed doubtful about me. Her daughter—who was my age and had blond ringlet curls and small, pretty blue eyes that were slightly bulgy—stood beside her, looking at me steadily.

"I'm here visiting my uncle," I said.

"Who is he, now?" Her blue eyes that matched her daughter's were shining expectantly.

"Mr. Arthur Remlinger," I said. "He owns the Leonard."

The woman's brows thickened and she seemed to grow concerned. Her posture stiffened, as if I was someone different because of the sound of Arthur Remlinger's name. "Is he going to put you into school in Leader?" she asked, as if it worried her.

"No," I said. "I live in Montana with my parents. I'll go back down there soon. I go to school there." I felt good to be able to say that any of these things were still true.

"We went to the fair in Great Falls, once," she said. "It was nice but it was very crowded." She smiled more broadly, put her arm around her daughter's shoulder, which made her smile, too. "We're LDS. If you'd ever like to attend."

"Thank you," I said. I knew LDS meant Mormons, because of things my father had said, and because of Rudy, who said they talked to angels and didn't like black people. I thought the woman would say something else to me, ask me something about myself. But she didn't. The two of them just walked along down the street and left me in front of the drug-store.

ON THE AFTERNOONS I didn't stay on in Fort Royal and conduct my investigations and keep myself occupied, I rode the Higgins back out to

Partreau with a small lunch box of cold food in my basket. This I would eat in my dilapidated house before the daylight died off. It was miserable to eat alone in either of the two cold, lightless rooms of my shack, since both were cluttered to the ceiling with the dank-smelling cardboard boxes and the dry accumulation of years of being the Overflow House for goose hunters who came in the fall and would soon be there again. There was almost no room for me, only the iron cot I slept on and the one that had been reserved for Berner, and the "kitchen room," with the bumpy red linoleum and a single fluorescent ceiling ring and a two-burner hot plate where I boiled tar-smelling pump water in a pan to make my bath at night. Everything in the house smelled of old smoke and long-spoiled food and the privy, and other stinging human odors I couldn't find a source for and try to clean, but could taste in my mouth and smell on my skin and clothes when I left for work each day and that made me self-conscious. In the mornings I cleaned my teeth at the outside pump and washed my face with a Palmolive bar I'd bought at the drugstore. Though as the weather grew colder, the wind stung my arms and cheeks and made my muscles tense and ache until I was done. If Berner had been there, I knew she would've been despondent and run away again—and I'd have gone with her.

But bringing food back and waiting until dark to eat it under the deathly ceiling ring would send me straight to my cot where I would lie miserably, trying to read one of my chess magazines in the awful light, or wishing I could watch a show on the busted television, while I listened to pigeons under the roof tins and the wind working the planks of the elevator across the highway, and the few cars and trucks that traveled the road at night, and sometimes Charley Quarters driving in late from the hotel bar, standing in the weeds in front of his trailer, talking to himself. (I'd by then looked up Métis in my *World Book* "M" volume and found out it meant half-breed between Indian and French.)

All of that would begin to conspire against me each night and swirl me up in abject thoughts of my parents and Berner, and of the certainty that

I'd have been in better hands with the juvenile authorities who would at least have put me in a school, even if it had bars on its windows, but where I would have people to talk to, even if they were tough ranch boys and perverted Indians—instead of being here, where if I got sick as I sometimes did in the fall, no one would look after me or take me to the doctor. I was being left behind while everything else advanced beyond me. There'd been no mention—because no one talked to me except Charley, who I didn't like and who never paid attention to me, and because I wasn't invited to talk to anyone and therefore knew nothing of my future—there'd been no mention that I would return to anything I'd known before or ever see my parents, or that they might come and find me. Therefore it seemed to me, cast off in the dark there in Partreau, that I was not exactly who I'd been before: a well-rounded boy on his way possibly to college, with a family behind him and a sister. I was now smaller in the world's view and insignificant, and possibly invisible. All of which made me feel closer to death than life. Which is not how fifteen-year-old boys should feel. I felt that by being where I was, I was no longer fortunate and was likely not going to be, although I'd always trusted that I was. My shack in Partreau was in fact what misfortune looked like. If I could've cried on those nights, I would've. But there was no one to cry to, and in any case I hated to cry and didn't want to be a coward.

And yet, if I didn't sink myself this way each day—becoming bitter, abandoned-feeling, corrupting the whole day following—if I simply pedaled back the four miles to Partreau and ate my cold lunch box by five rather than after dark, leaving time to assign myself an interest in things at hand, taking notice of what was present around me in Partreau (again, the way Mildred had advised—not to rule things out), *then* I could undertake a better view of my situation and feel I might sustain myself and endure.

Since, after all, it wasn't in my interest to be cast off. Even if I was visited each night by a vacant feeling of not knowing what or where I

was in the world, or how things were, and how they might go for me—
everything had already been worse! This was the truth Berner had understood and why she'd gone away and would likely never be back. Because
she saw that anything was better than being the two left-behind children
of bank robbers. Charley Quarters had told me you crossed borders to escape things and possibly to hide, and Canada in his view was a good place
for that (though the border had hardly been an event I noticed). But it also
meant you became someone different in the process—which was happening to me, and I needed to accept it.

AND SO ON those long, cooling high-sky afternoons, when a person could
see the moon in daylight, and before or after I ate my evening meal (a
busted dinette table had been thrown away in the thistles, and I brought
a broken chair from inside my shack and set these up outside the window
by the lilac bush, where I could see to the north)—on those days I would
make a second tour, around Partreau. This investigation seemed to me of
a different nature. If my walks in Fort Royal were in pursuit of that town's
difference from life I'd known, and to render myself reconciled to the new,
then my inspections around Partreau, only four miles distant, were of a
museum dedicated to the defeat of civilization—one that had been swept
away to flourish elsewhere, or possibly never.

There were only eight crumbling streets, lying north and south,
and six going west and east. There were actually eighteen empty, desti-
tute houses, with windows out and doors off, and curtains flagging in the
breeze, each house with its number, each street a sign—though only a few
names remained up on their posts and identifiable. South Ontario Street.
South Alberta Street (where my shack was). South Manitoba Street, where
a tiny empty post office and Mrs. Gedins' house stood. And South Labrador Street, which ran the margin between the town and the cut-over wheat
fields, along a three-sided, squared-off row of dead Russian olives and
Lombardy poplars and caraganas and chokecherries, where prairie grouse

perched in the branches watching the highway, and magpies squabbled in the underbrush for insects.

There had once been more than fifty houses, I calculated by walking each block and counting spaces and foundation squares. Back in the cluttered weeds and dooryards were rusted, burnt-out car relics and toppled appliance bodies and refuse pits full of cabinets and broken mirrors and patent medicine bottles and metal bed frames and tricycles and ironing boards and kitchen utensils and bassinets and bedpans and alarm clocks all half-buried and left behind. To the back of town, south and square to the fields and olive rows, stood the remains of an orchard, possibly apples, that had failed. The dried trunks were stacked husk on husk, as if someone had meant to burn them or save them for firewood, then had forgotten. Also, there I discovered the dismantled, rusted remnants of a carnival—red, mesh-hooded chairs of the Tilt-a-Whirl, the wire capsule of the Bullet, three Dodge-em cars and a Ferris wheel seat, all scattered and wrecked, with spools of heavy gear chain and pulleys, deep in the weeds with a wooden ticket booth toppled over and once painted bright green and red, with coils of yellow tickets still inside. There was no cemetery that I could see.

I took brief interest in two white bee hive boxes sitting solemnly in the volunteer wheatgrass outside the tree line where the sun caught their sides. These, I assumed, were Charley's and that he had tended them once. But the hives, which sat on bricks and lacked their important flat tops, were empty of bees. Their wood panels were loosed from their joinings; rot had taken over from below. Their thin paint was weathered and cracked, their beeswax frames (which I knew a good deal about by then) lay in the weeds beside a pair of rotted work gloves. Grasshoppers buzzed around them in the dust.

Farther—a hundred yards out in the field and beyond a dried pond bed—I investigated the lone pumping station, its motor humming in the breezy afternoon, exuding a stinging gassy odor as it sawed up and down, the hard, rounded earth saturated and black with oil that had been pumped and spilled. A pair of large, white-faced gauges attached to the motor mechanism measured what I didn't know. One day, from the distance of my shack, I watched a lone man drive through town in a pickup and out to the pumper site. He climbed out and fashioned around, consulting the gauges, inspecting various moving parts, and writing things on a pad of paper. Then he drove away in the direction of Leader and never (to my knowledge) came back.

Other days I simply walked up to the little commercial row, the businesses that had once thrived along the highway, facing across the hardtop to the pool elevator and the CP tracks. From my bed, I'd often heard freight cars late at night, the big diesels gathering and surging, the wheel springs squeaking, the brakes and sleepers crying out. It was much the way I'd experienced it in my bedroom in Great Falls. No trains stopped at Partreau. The elevator was long emptied. Though sometimes I'd be jolted awake and would step outside in the chill moonlit dark, barefoot, in my Jockeys, hoping I could view the northern lights, which my father had talked about but that I'd never seen in Great Falls—and never saw in Partreau. The blocky shadows of the grain cars and tanker cars and gondolas swayed and bumped along, sparks cracking off the brakes, lights dimmed and yellow in the caboose. Often a man stood on the rear platform—the way I'd seen photographs of politicians giving forceful speeches to great crowds—staring back at the closing silence behind him, the red tail-light not quite illuminating his face, unaware anyone was watching.

But when I inspected the little commercial frontages—an empty, pocket-size bank, a Masons' building of quarried stone from 1909, the Atlas shoe store with shoes scattered inside, a shadowy pool hall, a gas station with rusted, glass-top pumps, an insurance office, a beauty parlor with two silver hair dryers pushed over and broken apart, the floors littered with bricks and broken furnishings and merchandise racks, the light dead and cold, the busted back doors letting the damaging elements in, all the establishments emptied of human uses—I found I always thought of the life that had gone on there, not of life cast aside. And not, as opposed to what I'd first thought, like a museum at all. I had more positive views. Which made me feel that although I hadn't been taught to assimilate, a person perhaps assimilated without knowing it. I was doing it now. You did it alone, and not with others or for them. And assimilating possibly wasn't so hard and risky and didn't need to be permanent. This state of mind conferred another freedom on me and was like starting life over, or as I've already said, becoming someone else—but someone who was not stalled but moving, which was the nature of things in the world. I could like it or hate it, but the world would change around me no matter how I felt.

46

AS THE SUMMER WEATHER CHANGED INTO FALL, my daily duties changed as well. The wind thickened and came to us more from the north, pushing dust up from the fields. Larger, bulkier clouds ran in fast, and gray rain swept across the prairie toward the east. I began to see more of Charley Quarters. He drove me in more regularly with Mrs. Gedins. And after midday, he'd take me in his truck out over the long section roads and involve me in his doings, which mostly pertained to shooting coyotes—first glassing them at a great distance, then driving the switchbacks to intercept them where he'd gauge they'd cross the road. It also involved pouring water down gopher holes to roust them, and running his various traps for rabbits and foxes and badgers and muskrats and occasionally a small deer, sometimes a lynx or an owl or a hawk or a goose—all of which he'd shoot or dispatch with his knife. He'd throw the often still-twitching, blinking carcass into his truck bed, to be skinned and dried and stretched and in some instances tanned and preserved in his Quonset, then driven up to Kindersley and sold at Brechtmann's, where I wasn't permitted to go. He told me he sometimes saw moose on the prairie, resting in the shelter belts or the swales, and that their antlers were valuable, but these animals were no longer plentiful. He referred to this work as his "rough taxidermy." He told me trapping was how the Métis had maintained their independent life, but that game was disappearing and provincial laws were passed against the ancient practices. It was now necessary to work for the likes of Arthur Remlinger, who he seemed to dislike and dismiss, but who was a given in his life that would never change.

I was made to come along and learn to drive the truck—which Charley referred to as the half-ton—because as the days grew colder and the migrations of wild geese and ducks and cranes poured in from the north (Lac La Ronge and Reindeer were places he often mentioned), and stopped over in the wheat and on the flats and pothole ponds below the South Saskatchewan a few miles north of Fort Royal, I was expected to do my part. Which meant to learn about shooting (though I was not allowed to shoot), and to accompany Charley to the fields to spot the evening geese in order to know where they'd be "using" the next day, and to dig goose pits, and to go the following morning before light to set decoys and situate the Sports in their pits so that when darkness lifted and first light found the decoys, the Sports would be able to shoot the geese as they flew in great droves up off the river to the fields to feed.

My most important job would be to sit in the truck cab with binoculars, a thousand yards away from the decoys, as the red sun inched above the horizon, while Charley hunkered in his pit with the Sports—usually four of them in four pits. He would call the geese using just his human voice as his device—a strange, unnatural *ark-ike* sound he made in his throat and was proud of, and which attracted the geese to the decoys so that shooting them was easy. (He said I would never learn this, since only Métis could know it.) From the truck, with my binoculars, I could view as many as three pit setups and could watch the shot geese fall, and keep count of them as well as the cripples, to be certain the limit of five per shooter wasn't exceeded. After the shooting, when the ground was littered with dead and dying geese, and the sun was high so the birds no longer decoyed, Charley and I would take the Sports back to the Leonard in the

truck, and return with the Jeep and the flatbed trailer and collect the decoys and the carcasses and drive them in to the Quonset. There on the
cleaning log, we chopped off their wings and feet and heads with hatchets,
stripped their feathers using the plucker machine Charley had built, gutted them, wrapped them in butcher paper, and took them to the shooters
who were leaving that day, or else stored them in Charley's freeze box for
whenever the Sports were ready for home—which was usually America.

This was wholly a new life to me, who'd seen only Air Force bases
and the towns attached to them, and schools and rented houses with my
parents and sister, and who'd never had friends or fitted in, or had duties
or adventures, and who'd never spent a day alone on the prairie. And even
though I'd never worked—as I admitted to Arthur Remlinger and been
self-conscious about—I found I didn't mind work and could be serious
and persistent about doing it well—both in the Leonard and in the goose
fields. My duties were admittedly small, but I felt they were respectable.
In the Leonard, I often observed the behavior of adults when they were
alone or believed no one could see them—which seemed worth knowing.
And in the fields I was acquiring special knowledge no other boys my age,
or who'd had my life, could hope to gain—which had always been my
goal. Though most important, each day when I was set to my daily duties, my mind would leave behind the subjects that habitually preoccupied
it—my parents and their sad fate and their crime, and my sister. And my
own future. So that at the end of the day, when I got in my bed, tired and
often muscle-sore, my mind for a while would be empty, and I could go
straightaway to sleep. Though, of course, later I would wake alone in the
dark, and those same thoughts would be there to meet me again.

CHARLEY QUARTERS himself was in every way the strangest creature
I'd ever imagined to meet in life. I didn't like him, as I said, or trust him
and always felt apprehension in his presence. I never forgot him clutching
my hand in the dark truck the first night. And I was aware he observed me

when I was out of my shack, eating my brought-home supper at my dinette table, and doing my walks around, accommodating myself and finding ways to get along alone. Sometimes when we were together in the truck, bouncing out across the sea of wheat fields, I would notice he was wearing lipstick. Once he smelled of sweet perfume. On another occasion he wore dark eye makeup, and his black hair was sometimes blacker than other times, and occasionally black color smudged his forehead. I made no mention of this, of course, and pretended I hadn't noticed. Though I was sure Arthur Remlinger knew about it and possibly didn't care. They were both, I felt, as strange as strange could be. I was also always aware that because we jointly used the privy behind my house—which contained two sawn employment holes side by side, a bag of lime and a stack of old Saskatchewan *Commonwealths*—that Charley might suddenly appear when I was inside. There was no latch or lock, so that I had to pull the door closed using a nail and a length of baling twine I'd installed, which I could hold on to tightly when I was "on the throne"—which was also my father's expression. This nervousness made me naturally wary, so that I found I visited the privy only when Charley was away from his trailer—or late at night when I would be afraid of snakes—and always tried to use the guests' bathroom upstairs in the Leonard.

In truth, however, these worries about Charley (whose actual name, I learned, was Charley Quentin) never came to anything. Mostly he acted distracted when I was around, as if things were on his mind that deviled him and weren't susceptible to fixing. I never knew or asked what they were. He would often say he didn't sleep and never had. When I would sometimes look out my window in the middle of the night—the coyotes' singing frequently woke me—a light was always lit in his trailer, and I pictured him inside it just lying awake, listening to his wind chime. He once said he'd had a "bad bowel infection" when he was a boy and that often came back to plague him and kept him from a complete life. I would sometimes see him outside his trailer feeding the birds that flew around his sculptures and silver whirligig devices; he was always adjusting their little plastic propellers to better face the wind. Sometimes he would bring out a set of iron barbells he kept in his Quonset and do lifts and squats and curls in the weeds. And still other times he brought out a bag of wooden golf clubs and a peach basket of balls. He would set the balls up onto tufts of grass and stiffly strike each one out toward the highway and the train tracks, skipping them off the hardtop, or clattering them against the sides of the elevator, or just sailing them out of sight into the fields. He must've had an infinite supply of balls, since I never saw him retrieve one.

Mostly, however, he was charged grudgingly to teach me what to do when the Sports were there. It was clearly a plan devised by Arthur Remlinger to keep me occupied until he could think what else to do with me. But I was interested in learning, since I wasn't learning anything more than that by then and felt morose about it. I'd asked Charley about attending school—if I'd be allowed to, since a yellow school bus swayed through Partreau every morning, going west, with LEADER SCHOOL UNIT NO. 2 painted on its side, just like any American school bus. Every afternoon it rumbled back toward Fort Royal, the students' faces in the windows. It often passed me as I sawed my old bike along the road shoulder back and forth to work. No one inside gestured or waved or changed expression when they saw me, though once I saw the pretty, blond bulgy-eyed LDS girl whose mother had spoken to me in the street. She didn't seem to recognize me. And even though I'd gradually begun to feel better about myself, more accommodated to where I was (as Remlinger had said), each time the bus ground past I felt a renewed sensation of being left behind, and that conceivably I would never sit down in another school room, or be educated or well rounded as I'd hoped I'd be; and that possibly (which was in some ways the worst part) I'd overestimated school's importance in the grand scheme of things.

When I'd asked Charley about school, he'd ignored me. I'd learned from Mrs. Gedins—one of the few words she'd spoken to me—that a

Catholic school for wayward girls was situated down the highway toward
Leader, in the town of Birdtail, Saskatchewan, only a few miles distant. I
thought possibly I could go there on my bicycle and attend on Saturdays,
since she said school went on all week. But when I mentioned this school
to Charley, he said that only Canadian children went to Canadian schools,
and I shouldn't want to be Canadian for any reason anyway. This was on
one of the last warm blue-sky days, when a long, milky cloud line of what
could've been the first winter storm hung over Alberta, which was only
fifty miles away. Charley and I were sitting in two of his folding aluminum lawn chairs on a rock outcrop, watching below where a great flight
of geese had settled across a barley field above the banks of the South Saskatchewan. More and more birds tilted in, landed, and took their positions
to eat. The season for shooting them was only a week off. We were there
to estimate the geese's tendencies, to determine the fields they were using,
note how many birds were present, where water was standing or dried up,
and where pits might be set in for the best shooting. Even though I was uncomfortable around him, I was willing to be influenced by Charley and by
what he knew and could impart to me, since I knew nothing about hunting
or hunters or shooting geese for sport.

Charley had untied his black hair and wore a singlet undergarment
that showed his short knotty-muscled arms and made his hands and
chesty torso appear larger and more powerful. He had tattoos on both
forearms—one that showed a woman's smiling face with lush movie star
hair like Charley's, and had the words *Ma Mère* written underneath it.
The other was a blue buffalo's head with staring red eyes, the meaning
of which wasn't apparent. Charley had his old worn lever-rifle across his
knees where we sat, a cigarette clenched in his teeth, and was training his
binoculars on the long raft of geese strewn out in the distance above the
shining river, and also on a pair of coyotes who were observing the geese
from a hilltop and slowly moving closer to them.

"Canadians are hollowed out," he said, after proclaiming I shouldn't want to be one—something I hadn't contemplated. I only wanted to go to school and not be left behind. I thought Canadian schools would teach the same subjects as American schools. The children on the bus all looked like me. They spoke English, had parents, and wore the same clothes. "Americans on the other hand are all full," Charley said, ". . . of deceit and treachery and destruction." He kept his binoculars fastened to his eyes, his cigarette curling smoke into the warm air. "You're the son of bank robbers, aren't you?"

I was sorry he knew about that. Arthur Remlinger had obviously told him. But there was no denying it. I didn't think what he said about Americans was correct, however, even with my parents being bank robbers.

"Yes," I said reluctantly.

"I don't think that's so bad." He lowered his binoculars and widened his eyes at me, which made his head with its oversized cheekbones and heavy brows and large lower jaw look grotesque. He was wearing pink lipstick that day, but no eye makeup. One of Charley's dark blue eyes—his left one—had a permanent blood blotch in the white. I wasn't sure if he saw out of that eye or not. "My parents lived in a dirt-floor house in Lac La Biche, Alberta, and both died of TB," he said. "Bank robbing would've been a big step up for them."

"I think it's bad," I said, referring to my parents being robbers, not his parents dying. What had happened to my parents seemed like a long time ago, though it had only been a few weeks since Berner and I had visited them in jail in Great Falls.

Charley coughed down into his hand and spit out something substantial, which he scrutinized and flung away. "Something goes into me when I go down below," he said. "Then something goes out of me when I come back up here. Not that I can go down there anymore." He'd told me he'd traveled in America extensively in his past—Las Vegas, California, Texas. But things had happened—he didn't say what—so he couldn't go back. "It's all played out up here. They all think they're being cheated by the

goverment. But they're not," he said. "This place is waitin' to blow away."
I believed he only meant where we were then, not all of Canada, which he
probably knew nothing about. He set his binoculars on the ground beside
his chair. The air, two hundred yards below us, was thick with black-and-
white geese and their sharp cries, conniving and flapping and sporting
with and against one another, flying up and setting down. "You want to be
gone from here in six weeks, that's for sure," he said. "It'll turn into Sibe-
ria. North's the wrong direction to go, as far as I'm concerned."

"Why does Mr. Remlinger never talk to me?" I said, because that was
what I wanted to know.

Charley lifted his rifle off his knees and carefully shouldered it, still
seated in his lawn chair. I believed he was just sighting—which he often
did. "I don't get in his business," he said.

He rested back against the stretched nylon strips to steady himself
and settled the muzzle on one of the two coyotes we'd been watching. It
was a hundred yards away, trotting down a bald rise where barley didn't
grow, in the direction of a second rise around which it could go unnoticed
and draw closer to the geese. The other coyote stood farther away, beside
a pile of stones heaped up from when the field had been cleared. This second coyote was motionless, silently watching the first. I didn't speak then.

Charley lowered his rifle, gazed across the distance, took a deep breath
and let it out, bit into the butt of his cigarette, re-sighted the rifle, pushed
confidently back in his chair, cocked the hammer, breathed in again, then
out through his nose, spit his cigarette to the side, breathed in once more,
then squeezed off one deafening shot. I was sitting right beside him.

The bullet struck behind the first coyote. Even at the distance we were,
I saw the puff of dust and chaff kick up. The second coyote instantly began
running, its long back legs kicking around toward its front. It looked
back and seemed able to run forward and sideways at once. The raft of
geese below us made one enormous, piercing, frightened squealing sound
that consumed the air. They all immediately but not quickly rose off the

stubble ground in a great upheaval—a thousand geese or possibly more
(uncountable, really) beginning to flap their wings and shout and rise and
move away in one clamorous occurrence.

The coyote Charley had shot at stopped to watch the geese rise and
circle over and around itself. It turned its head in our direction—two indistinct dots, with Charley's truck a hundred yards behind us. It hadn't put
these facts together—the dots, the sound of a shot, the kicked-up dust, the
unplanned rise of the geese. It looked back up at the great swirling column
in the air around it, then scratched its left back foot behind its left ear,
cocked its head to gain a better angle on the itch, shook itself, looked back
at us, then trotted away in the direction the first coyote had gone—no
doubt, I thought, toward where other geese were.

"I'll see that devil dog again, wait 'n find out," Charley said, as if missing the coyote hadn't mattered and was just practice. He ejected the spent
cartridge, reached around where his cigarette lay smoking on the ground.
"The world's got his number—in the person of me," he said. "He thinks
he's safe. His death and my death are playmates. That's funny. I know it,
and he doesn't."

"What about Mr. Remlinger," I said.

"I don't get in his business. I said that already." Charley stuck his cigarette back between his lips and looked annoyed. "He's strange. We're all
wasted on somebody, eh?"

I didn't understand what that meant and didn't ask again. As I said,
Charley Quarters made me uncomfortable. He seemed to be involved in
life too much through death. I thought it meant he didn't care about very
much. If I gave him the opportunity to show me more about it, or tell me
(which I intended never to do), he would've. Then that was all I would've
learned.

47

O N THE DAYS WHEN CHARLEY DID NOT TAKE ME onto the prairie to learn about geese, and when I didn't stay in Fort Royal and could be alone in my shack without constant despairing, I actually began to experience the illusion of being someone who had an almost happy life and hadn't been given up on, and who still carried on an existence that, as my father would've said, made sense.

Time, in truth, didn't seem to pass. I might've been alone in Partreau for a month, or six months or even longer, and it would've seemed the same, the first day or the hundredth, so that a small, impermanent world became created for me. I knew eventually I'd go somewhere else—to a school, even to a Canadian school, or possibly to a foster home, or by some means back below the border to whatever was waiting for me. And that this present life and its daily patterns and routines and persons wouldn't last forever or even for much longer. But I didn't think as much about that as someone might imagine I would. It was a frame of mind, as I said, my father would've approved.

The occurrence that substituted for the passage of time, day to day, was the weather. Weather means more than time on the prairie, and it measures the changes in oneself that are invisibly occurring. The summer days, which had been hot and dry and windy with deep blue skies since I left Great Falls, disappeared, and autumn clouds bore in. First mackerel clouds, then marble clouds, then whiskery mare's tails with new cold slicing in behind. The sun sank southward and shone at a new angle through the dead trees around Partreau and brightly onto the white exterior walls of the Leonard. Suddenly it rained for days at a time. And after each rain—driving wind-charged sheets from the low gray clouds—the air became colder and heavier and penetrated the red-and-black plaid jacket that Charley had bought for me at the co-op and that smelled like sweat, though it was new. There were few warm days left. Woolly worms appeared in the grass. Yellow and brown spiders built nests and webs for flies in the rotted window casements of my shack. Box elder bugs were in my sheets. Harmless black and green snakes flattened out in the sun on the sidewalk chunks. Two cats emerged from the elevator across the highway, and mice moved in behind my walls. The brittle yellow grasshoppers were no longer buzzing in the weeds.

Inside the heavy school bus that passed me each day, the children had on their coats and caps and gloves. Geese and ducks and cranes had begun to fill the skies, wavering long silver skeins of them in the low sunlight, morning and evening, their distant shouts filling the air even at night. When I woke up—always early—frost came halfway up my windows, and the weeds and thistles around my shack door were stiff and sparkling in the sunlight. At night, coyotes ventured closer into town, hunting for the mice and the cats and for roosting pigeons in the broken-down houses and refuse holes. The dog I'd seen on my first day and that belonged to Mrs. Gedins, barked often at night. Once in my room, under my coarse sheet and blanket, I heard it growl and paw my door and whimper. Then many coyotes yipped and yipped, and I thought I might not see the dog again. (My mother hadn't liked dogs, and we had never had one.) But he was there in the morning, standing in the empty street, the night's trace of snow twinkling on the ground, the coyotes gone.

Why the change of weather and light produced a change in me and made me more accepting—more than the awareness of time passing—I can't say. But it has been my experience in all these years since those days in Saskatchewan. Possibly being a town boy (in town, time matters so much) and being suddenly set down in an empty place I didn't know, among people I knew little about, left me more subject to the elemental forces that mimicked the experience I was undergoing and made it more tolerable. Against these forces—an earth rotating, a sun lowering its angle in the sky, winds filling with rain and the geese arriving—time is just a made-up thing, and recedes in importance, and should.

DURING THESE EARLY COLD DAYS I would sometimes see Arthur Remlinger in his three-hole Buick, driving at great speed down the highway, headed west—toward where, I had no idea. Someplace specific, I assumed. Florence's head would frequently be visible in the passenger's seat. Possibly they were on their way to Medicine Hat—a town whose name fascinated me. Other times I'd see his car beside Charley's trailer, the two of them conferring—often intensely. After four weeks, I'd still had no important contact with Arthur Remlinger—which, as I said, was not what I'd expected. Not that I'd have wanted him to be my best friend. He was too old to be that. But that he might want to know more about me, and that I could learn things pertaining to him; why he lived in Fort Royal, and about going to college, and interesting things that had happened to him—all facts I knew about my parents and was the way, I believed, you learned things in the world. Mildred had assured me I would like him and would learn things from him. But his name—which seemed stranger being his name than Mildred's—was most all of what I knew; that, and how he dressed and talked in the little he'd spoken to me, and that he was American, from Michigan.

As a result, I'd begun to experience misgivings about Arthur Remlinger, an uncomfortable sensation of waiting that involved both of us.

Mildred had also told me I should begin to notice things in the present when I arrived to Canada. But once you do that you can believe you conceive patterns in daily events, and your imagination can run away with you, so that you make up what's not there. What I'd begun to associate with this partial personage of Arthur Remlinger (which was all I knew) was that there must be an "enterprise" attached to him, a significance that was hidden from view and wished to stay hidden, and that made him not predictable or ordinary—which is what Charley and Mildred had both told me I would notice. I'm certain, after the experience of my parents being put in jail, that I was also given to look for what might not be good, where from most appearances there was nothing bad to be found.

There *are* people like that in the world—people with something wrong with them that can be disguised but won't be denied, and which dominates them. Of adults, I'd only known my two parents by then. They were in no way exceptional or significant, were barely distinguishable as the small two people they were. And they had things wrong with them. Anyone but their son might have seen it from the very beginning. After I detected it about them, and had time to decide what was true, I never didn't see the possibility of something being wrong again wherever I looked. It is a function in myself of what I call reverse-thinking, which I've never been entirely free of since I was young, when there was so much cause to believe in it.

On one occasion, when Mrs. Gedins was busy in the hotel kitchen, I was given a key and sent to the third floor to clean Arthur Remlinger's rooms—make his bed, clean his toilet, remove his towels and washcloths, wipe the surfaces where dust had sifted out of the old tin ceiling and been blown in under the window sashes.

His rooms were only three, and surprisingly small for a man who had many belongings and left nothing neat or arranged when he wasn't there. I made no effort not to examine whatever my eye fell on, and looked further than I should've, since I believed I'd likely never know Arthur Remlinger better than I knew him then. Knowing so little and wanting to know more had caused me misgivings in the ways I've said. And misgivings can be a source of curiosity as well as suspicion.

The dark beaded-board walls of Arthur Remlinger's bedroom and his small sitting room and bathroom were shadowy with the venetian blinds closed and only table lamps lit, and were hung with a variety of unusual things. A large yellowed map of the United States with white pins pressed in at various locations—Detroit, Cleveland, Ohio, Omaha, Nebraska, and Seattle, Washington. No indication was given for what these might relate to. There was an oil painting framed and hung beside the bedroom window, showing—I recognized it—the grain elevator in Partreau, with the prairie stretching off to the north. Remlinger had said this had been painted by Florence in the American Nighthawk fashion—which I hadn't understood and couldn't look up because I'd left my "N" *World Book* volume in Great Falls. Elsewhere on the wall was a framed photograph of four tall boys, young and confident, smiling, hands on their hips, wearing heavy wool suits and wide ties, posed in front of a brick building that had the word *Emerson* above its wide doors. There was another picture of a thin, fresh-faced, smiling young man with a shock of blond hair (Arthur Remlinger, taken years before—his pale eyes were unmistakable). He was standing with one long arm draped over the shoulders of a slender woman in blousy trousers, who was also smiling—both of them beside what my father called a "ball-cap Ford coupé," from the '40s. There was a picture anybody would've recognized as a family, standing in a straight line, taken many years before. A large woman with dark hair tied severely back, wearing a shapeless, rough, light-colored dress, was frowning beside a tall big-headed man with heavy brows and deep-set eyes and enormous hands, who was also frowning. An older dark-haired girl with a brazen smile stood beside a tall, skinny boy who I felt was also Arthur Remlinger, and who was wearing a boy's wool four-button suit with too-short trousers and boots. The girl must've been Mildred but was unrecognizable. They were posed with a great sand dune behind them. At the side in the picture was a lake or possibly an ocean.

In the corner of the musty room was a standing clothes rack with belts and suspenders and bow ties hung on its brass hooks. A closet was stuffed with clothes—heavy suits, tweed jackets, starched shirts, the floor cluttered with large, expensive-looking shoes, some with pale hosiery stuffed inside them. There were women's clothes as well—a nightgown and slippers and some dresses I assumed were Florence's. In the bathroom beside Remlinger's silver monogrammed brush and combs and witch hazel bottle and shaving articles, were jars of cold cream and a hanging rubber water bottle and a shower cap and a blue decorated dish with bobby pins in it.

On the wall, above the ornamented wooden double bed, were shelves of books—thick blue ones on chemistry and physics and Latin, and leather-bound novels by Kipling and Conrad and Tolstoy, and several volumes with just names on their spines: Napoleon, Caesar, U. S. Grant, Marcus Aurelius. There were also thinner books with titles that said *Free Riders*, and *Captive Passengers*, and *The Fundamental Right*, and *Union Bigwigs*, and *Masters of Deceit*, by J. Edgar Hoover, whose name I knew from TV.

In the shadowy corners of both rooms were tennis and badminton rackets leaned against the wall. There was a record player and a wooden box on the floor beside it containing, I discovered, records by Wagner and Debussy and Mozart. A marble chess board had been placed on top of the record-player cabinet, the chess pieces made of white and black ivory and intricately carved and weighted if you picked them up (which I did). This made me think I could mention playing chess when I saw Arthur Remlinger, and that if I ever knew him better we could play and I could learn new strategies.

In his tiny parlor there was a heavy, round-arm couch with coarse covering, and two facing straight-back chairs with a low table in between, on which was a half-empty bottle of brandy and two tiny glasses—as if Arthur Remlinger and Florence La Blanc would sit facing each other, drinking and listening to music and talking about books. Opposite the tennis and badminton rackets was a tall wooden perch set beside the shaded window, with a thin brass chain wound around the bar and tied in a knot. There was no sign of a bird.

On the wall behind the perch, practically invisible in shadows, was a framed brass plaque engraved with the words "Whatsoever thy findeth to do, do it with thy might, for there is no work, no device, nor knowledge nor wisdom in the grave whither thou goest." This had no bearing on anything I understood. On a wooden hook beside the plaque was a leather holster with a rig-up of complicated straps and buckles I recognized from gangster movies to be a shoulder holster. Inside it was a short-barreled silver pistol with white grips.

I, of course, immediately drew the pistol out. (I'd already locked the door closed.) It was unexpectedly heavy to be so small. I looked through the slit behind the cylinder and made out it was loaded with at least five brass-bottom bullets. It was a Smith and Wesson. I didn't know the caliber. I held the muzzle to my nose in a way I'd also seen in the movies. It smelled like hard metal and the spicy oil used to clean it. The little barrel was slick and shiny. I sighted it out the window at the CP yard, at the rails full of grain cars sitting in the sun. Then I stepped quickly back for fear of being seen. The pistol, I felt, directly pertained to the significance and enterprise I attributed to Arthur Remlinger—more, I felt, than anything else in his rooms did. My father had had his pistol—which I never believed he'd lost, and now believed had been used in a robbery. I didn't see how by itself it allotted him significance or made him exceptional. The Air Force had given it to him free, after all. But regarding Arthur Remlinger, I did feel this way, and I again experienced the misgiving I'd been feeling—that he was an unknown and unpredictable person. It was a sensation familiar in my mind to feelings about my parents and their robbery and its terrible effect on Berner and me. I couldn't have said more about what I thought. But the pistol seemed a very definite and dangerous thing. Though Arthur Remlinger didn't seem to me to be a man who would own a pistol. He seemed too cultivated—which was clearly my error. I wiped the little handles on my shirt to take my finger smudges off and put the pistol back in its holster. I hadn't cleaned anything in the rooms the way I'd been told to and would have to come back later. But I had the sudden fear of being found out. So that I unlocked the door to the hall, looked out and saw nothing, then quickly went back down the stairs to my other duties.

48

AS COLDER WEATHER CAME ON, AND THE SPORTS began arriving at the beginning of October (when Americans were permitted to shoot), Charley said he wanted me to devote all my time to "the goose work." I'd been in my Partreau shack for a month, although as I said, time didn't seem to pass or mean much to me—not the way it had two months ago, when school was only weeks away, and the long, slow passage of days was what I wished I could command and defeat the way Mikhail Tal mastered a chess problem.

I adjusted to my little two-room house better than at first. It was necessary to use the privy—which I did only after assuring myself Charley wasn't watching me, and then would never stay long. But there was electricity to operate my hot plate and the ceiling ring and to provide some heat. I could no longer wash my face at the pump due to the chill wind. But I brought my water in at night using a bucket, and bathed by employing a tin saucepan I scavenged from a refuse pit, and scoured myself with a washrag and the Palmolive bar I kept in a tobacco tin to keep the mice and rats from finding it.

I'd dragged one of the two cots out from the back room into the kitchen—my only other room. The back room sat on the north side of the shack, and the new cold wind worked in through the stucco and the laths and whistled through the cracked panes, so that that room, which was lightless, became unwelcoming at night. In the kitchen there was an old iron J. C. Wehrle stove with split seams, and I fed this with rotted boards and pieces of broken-off dead timber and caragana twigs gathered on my tours. I washed my clothes and sheets and kitchen utensils at the pump stand and swept the floor with a broom I'd found, and considered myself to have made a good adaptation to circumstances whose duration and direction I didn't know. I wanted to get my hair cut at the barber shop in Fort Royal—I sometimes saw myself in the bathroom mirrors at the Leonard and knew I was thinner and my hair was too long. But there was no mirror in my shack, and I had little thought at night for how I looked. I only remembered the haircut when I was in bed, and that I should clip my fingernails the way my father did. But then I would forget the next day.

Several of the cardboard boxes lining the walls in the kitchen I carried into the cold north room and stacked against the window and along the wall to block the cracks and splits opening to the outside. At the drugstore in Fort Royal I bought a purple candle with lavender aroma that I burned at night, because I knew from my mother that lavender promoted sleep and because the shack—cold or warm—smelled of smoke and rot and stale tobacco and human smells from decades of lives lived there. The shack would soon fall down like the rest of Partreau. I knew if I left and came back in a year there would likely be little sign of it.

In the evenings, when I'd finished my meal and my walk and could tolerate being alone (I never felt my situation was truly tolerable), I would sit on my cot and unfold my chess cloth on my covers, set up my four wobbly ranks of plastic men and plot moves and campaigns against idealized but unspecified opponents. I'd never actually played with anyone but Berner. Arthur Remlinger was who I thought about. My strategies usually entailed brash frontal assaults. I would defeat my opponents with sacrificial attacks in the manner of the same Mikhail Tal, who'd become my hero. The endgame would always be reached with lightning speed due to scant opposition. Other times, I would attempt slow, deceptive feints and retreats (which I didn't like much), making shrewd comments and observations about what my opponent and I were each doing and what he seemed to be planning—while never divulging my scheme for victory. I did this while listening to the old Zenith, whose light glowed dimly behind its numbers and out of which on the cold, cloudless nights emerged distant voices it seemed to me the wind must've blown around the world without respect for borders. Des Moines. Kansas City. WLS in Chicago. KMOX in St. Louis. A scratchy Negro's voice from Texas. Reverend Armstrong's voice shouting after God. Men's voices in what I believed was Spanish. Others I decided were French. And, of course, there were the clear stations from Calgary and Saskatoon, bearing news—the Canadian Bill of Rights, Tommy Douglas's Co-operative Commonwealth Federation. And place-names—North Battlefield, Esterhazy, Assiniboia—towns I knew nothing about but knew weren't American. I wondered if I might dial in a station from North Dakota, which wasn't so far away, and hear about my parents being put on trial. I never found such a station, although sometimes when I lay on my cot in the dark, with the Wehrle ticking, I pretended the American voices I heard were talking to me, and knew about me, and had advice for me if I could only stay awake long enough. This and my lavender candle was the way I went to sleep on many nights.

On other evenings, I pulled open one or another of the cardboard boxes I hadn't moved into the north room, and diverted myself with the evidence of all that had happened in the house in the years before I came to be in it. On the prairie, history and memory seemed as alien as the passage of time—as if the citizens of Partreau had disappeared not into the past but into another vivid present—which explained why there was no dignified cemetery, and so much was left behind.

Arthur Remlinger had remarked to me that he'd lived in my shack in his early days, and many of the boxed possessions were his. In the softened, stale-smelling boxes I found related evidence of what I'd seen in his rooms. In one box marked in pencil with "AR" were thin books and cracked, yellowed magazines bound in cotton twine, from the 1940s. One magazine was called *The Free Thinkers*. Another was *The Deciding Factor*. There were two books I'd already seen in the apartment—*Captive Passengers* and *World Analysis*. I had no idea what they were or were about. When I pulled out *The Free Thinkers*, its cover referred to an article inside by an "A. R. Remlinger," with the title "Anarcho-syndicalism, Immunities and Privileges." I read the first page of this. It pertained to something called the "Danbury Hatters lesson," and the "Protestant work ethic," and went into detail about how workers were not "maximizing their individual freedom." The back page informed the reader that A. R. Remlinger was "a young Harvard man from the middle west" who was putting his "gold-plated education" to the service of human rights for all men. It was likely Arthur Remlinger had written articles in the other magazines, but I had no interest in opening them.

Other boxes didn't bear the "AR" initials, and in these I found life insurance policies and stacks of canceled checks and a Saskatchewan driver's license for a woman named Esther Magnusson, and collections of yellow pencil stubs bound with rubber bands, and stacks of old pamphlets and a "Milky Way for Britain" war bond brochure, much of it corrupted and nested in by mice. Some of the pamphlets had to do with the "Social Reform Gospel," and something called the "Royal Templars of Temperance." There were membership booklets about "Home-makers Clubs," and bulletins about "Wheat and Women" and the "Grain Growers Guide." One booklet had to do with "The Canadian League" and stated on its first page that foreign immigrants weren't shouldering their burden, and soldiers returning from the front should have "first choice of the best jobs." Inserted in the pages was a black-and-white newspaper picture showing a cross set ablaze and people in white hoods and robes whose faces were covered, standing, facing it. "Moose Jaw, 1927" was written under it in faded ink.

Another box contained rusted metal film canisters with reels of film inside, but no indication of what the film would show. An American flag was folded on top of the canisters in the fashion my father had demonstrated for Berner and me—"the tricorn." There were shoe boxes of letters—many addressed to Mr. Y. Leyton in Mossbank, Saskatchewan, and postmarked 1939 and 1940. These were tied with baling twine in tight stacks, some with red American three-cent stamps that bore a picture I recognized as George Washington. I considered it allowable for me to read at least one of these letters, since no one had sent a letter to me in Canada, and reading someone else's might make me appreciate the presence of others, which my existence in Partreau had all but extinguished. The letter read:

Dear Son,

We're in Duluth, having driven here with your father from the Cities where it was very nice, indeed (very modern). Much warmer there than in ole ice-box Prince Albert, that's for certain. I don't know how anyone lives there—and the wind. My goodness. You know plenty, of course, about that. I'm trying to forget most of the Canadian I learned as a child in school—for my sins. Jaqueleen was just saying it's a pity there has to be a frontier between the two. But I'm not so sure. Someone must think they know best all about it. Tennessee is where I'd happily die.

I know (or have heard) that you are thinking about the RCN, which is very brave (if you like water). I wish you'd think longer on it. Okay? We have little to gain from a big fight now. The worst could happen. Which of course you are not thinking about. Just a thought from your mum.

I have a postcard which I'll send. It shows our "Prince Charming" on his famous train trip to Sask back in '19 (twenty years ago! Heavens!). You won't remember. But your dad and your Gram and me stood you up by the tracks in Regina in your little worsted

suit, and you waved a little Canadian flag. I believe that's why you're
so patriotic. There's surely no reason to be otherwise. Take care now.
Look for my postcard, which won't fit into the env. without ruining it.
Your dad sends his best to you—which is more than I ever see.
    Love 'n kisses.
    Your Mum

I dug deeper in the box for the postcard showing "Prince Charming"
and who he would've been. But near the bottom were only more bound
stacks—of Christmas cards and dry newspaper cuttings with pictures
of smiling, crew-cut men in hockey uniforms. At the very bottom were
several loose picture cards of completely naked women posing beside or-
nate pedestals with floral arrangements and tables containing books. The
women were hefty and smiling as happily as if they were wearing clothes.
I'd never seen pictures like these, although I knew from things boys had
said in school that they existed. You could buy them from machines at the
State Fair. I spent quite a while going carefully over each one and finally
put three into my *World Book* "B" volume, since I knew I'd want to look at
them again. I did want to look at them again, and did look at them. I kept
them for years.

Also at the bottom of the box, I found a pair of wire-rim eyeglasses
and a plain gold ring. The ring was inside a yellow Bayer aspirin tin that
had two worn-smooth aspirins and a charm-bracelet replica of the Eiffel
Tower also inside it. I knew a ring was inside before I saw it. Don't ask me
how I knew. *It's probably a wedding ring,* I all but said to myself. I understood, of course, that it represented an outcome lost in someone's past and
wasn't good.

Most of the boxes I didn't go through thoroughly. One had Regina
newspapers. Another held muddy clothes and shoes the mice had ma-
rauded. Another was documents and receipts and totalings for wheat
crops and elevator fees and the purchase of a new Waterloo Boy trac-

tor. Another contained stacks of unopened printed matter about the 1948 Saskatchewan election, and pertaining to the CCF and "Social Credit." I tried to imagine how many people's or families' lives were jumbled together here, in my house. Many, many—I thought—as if they had all hoped to come back later from their present and reclaim it, but never had. Or had died. Or had just elected to put that life behind them for a crack at a better one somewhere else.

I wondered, however, what Arthur Remlinger had meant when he'd told me Americans could never let a place like Partreau stand. They would burn it as a reproach to progress. But as I heaved the boxes back up against the drafty wall of my kitchen, I decided he was probably correct. My parents, people without real possessions, without permanence, who never owned a house, who carried little with them, and whose few holdings (except for Berner and me) had by then been taken and thrown in the town dump in Great Falls—my parents were people Arthur Remlinger had been referring to, who would've cared nothing for Partreau even if they didn't burn it. They were people running from the past, who didn't look back at much if they could help it, and whose whole life always lay somewhere in the offing.

49

I WAS NOW LEARNING MANY THINGS AT ONCE: HOW TO site goose pits where the morning sun didn't find them too early but would still be high enough on a rise of land that the Sports could see out and be ready when the flights came off the river. I learned to set out the heavy wooden decoys to the right and left of the pits, and to leave a landing space where the geese could look to settle—thinking all was the same as the night before—yet not so far apart as to draw attention to the guns or the white faces of the shooters who were often too eager. Charley said Americans were usually fat or old or both and couldn't stand the cold, crumbly Regina gumbo in the pits and so were always standing up and climbing out at the wrong moments. Ducks, Charley said—Goldeneyes and pintails and canvasbacks—always swept in first, screaming in on the pits like ghosts out of the dark, low and tilting and pinging. Shooting them, though, spooked the geese, who had good hearing, so that this was discouraged. I myself would need to be careful repositioning decoys, since the Sports shot at whatever they thought they saw or heard. People had been killed. Charley himself had been shot with #2 load and had scars. He permitted loading the guns only on his signal—though there were still "sky busters," who were the dangerous ones. I was responsible to report to him any Sport who seemed drunk—though all of them would've been drinking late in the bar the night before, and I could expect to smell liquor. I had also to report anyone who appeared sick or had trouble walking or moving around or was careless handling his shotgun. Charley would verify the licenses and authorize when shooting started and ended—once the sun was high and the geese could see the ground. And as I already said, I would stay in the truck and glass the birds that fell and crippled off, and keep my tally, since the wardens were always about and would be watching with even more powerful binoculars—dividing the falling geese by the number of hunters and coming to check when the tallies didn't match. Following which they'd be passing out citations, confiscating guns, seeing who was drunk, fining Charley, but fining Arthur Remlinger the most, and forcing him to pay large sums to avoid closer notice being paid to his in-town operation—the Filipino girls, the gambling den off the side of the dining room, and whatever else he might be up to that the town disapproved of. Arthur Remlinger held the license for the "guide service," though he himself did no guiding and knew nothing about shooting or geese, and cared nothing. He was the proprietor, did the booking, kept the accounts, put up the Sports in the hotel, and collected their money—part of which he paid to Charley, who remitted a small portion to me. Though it was understood the Sports would hand around tips each day when the shooting was finished, often in U.S. currency, and everybody would be satisfied.

ON ONE OF THE LAST warm early October days, after Charley and I had spent the morning scouting and digging pits in fields the geese habitually used, I rode my old bicycle down the highway away from Partreau in the direction of the town of Leader, twenty miles west. I was intent to find the school for wayward girls Mrs. Gedins had talked about. Birdtail was six miles down the hardtop, and I meant to inquire there if I might enroll as a student at some point in the future—possibly winter, when my goose duties were over and I might be on my own. I didn't understand

what a wayward girl was. I thought it might mean a girl who was passing
through on her way to someplace else—which I was doing. I also didn't
believe there could be a school only for girls. At least a few boys would
have to be permitted, I felt—even in Canada. Mrs. Gedins had told me the
school was run by nuns. And from my mother's experience with the Sisters
of Providence, I believed nuns were openhearted, generous women who
would see a chance to help me, which was their mission and why they'd
give up marriage and a normal life. It shouldn't matter that I was American. I would not divulge that my mother was Jewish or that she and my
father were in jail in North Dakota. Life had begun to demand lies in order
to be workable. And I was willing to tell one, or many more than one, if it
meant I could go to school and not fall further behind.

It was also the case that I'd begun to believe it would be nice to be
around girls. Berner, of course, was a girl. But most of our lives we had
treated each other as being the same thing because we were twins. That
same thing was neither male nor female, but something in between that
included us both. Though, of course, that hadn't lasted. On two occasions,
Charley had taken me to the chop-suey restaurant on Main Street. Both
times I'd seen the Chinese owner's children, seated at a shadowy rear table
doing their schoolwork. I'd paid special attention to the pretty round-faced
daughter who I felt might be my age. Each time she'd noticed me, but
hardly allowed it to show. Several times since then, when I was taking my
walks around Partreau, or marshaling my chess men alone in my shack,
I'd entertained a fantastical thought that we could be friends. She could
visit me. We could walk around the empty town together, then play chess.
(I felt sure she would know how to play better than I did.) I even fantasized I could help her with homework. There was never anything more in
my thoughts than that. I never knew her name or even spoke to her. Our
friendship existed only in my mind. These real things could never happen,
and didn't. Being alone made it possible to know this sad fact of life, and
yet to imagine that it and much else could be different.

The highway and prairie west of Partreau were no different from the hardtop going east to Fort Royal. Though on my bicycle, it felt new—like a terrain I shared with no one. It was only bare, rolling crop-ground with straw bales scattered to the edge of sight, and black dots, which were oil pumpers, and above it the sparkling skeins of new geese in the sky, and gray-white smoke along the horizon where a farmer was burning ditches.

When I arrived at the Birdtail sign, there was no evidence of a town. The Canadian Pacific passed along beside the highway, as it did in Partreau and Fort Royal. But there was no crossing from when a town had been there, or a caragana break or a windmill or an elevator or foundation squares to mark where houses had stood. Mrs. Gedins, I didn't believe, would go to the trouble to lie to me. I sat and looked at the sky and all around where there was no school, then decided to ride another mile to the opposite Birdtail sign, if there was one. And when I arrived at it, there was another sign beside it that said "Sisters of the Holy Name School." An arrow pointed south up a gravel road that met the highway from out of the fields. A Christian cross was painted above the school's name. At the crest of the hill where the road went up, was an abandoned house, and beyond it the road disappeared off into the blue sky. A school could be any distance. Ten miles. With Charley I'd driven the truck miles and miles over the prairie and seen no sign of where humans lived or ever had lived. Yet for me school was still my important goal. I could ride until a school building was at least in sight and see what I thought of it.

With difficulty I guided my front wheel up the sandy tire track. Charley's old Higgins wobbled and wiggled over the stones and gravels, and pedaling uphill wasn't easy. Though as soon as I topped the rise where the vacant house sat, giving a view to miles around, the school or what had to be the school lay straight down the road in plain view at the bottom of the hill's other side—a large, square redbrick building, with four stories, sitting by itself on a low place on the prairie—not very different from the way Great Falls High School would've looked if it had been set down there. But I knew the instant I saw the building what "wayward" meant. It meant what Berner and I would've been if juvenile authorities had come and taken us. Orphans. Only orphans would be in a place like this.

The wide square of ground the school sat on had been rescued from pasture land beside a narrow dry creek. Wheat grew on the bench above it. Spindly trees were planted on the lawn and there were figures—the wayward girls, I believed—dotting the grass. The sharp October sun—tingly on my sweaty neck—made the school appear barren and still. I almost turned and coasted back to the highway. It would never be a place with big oak trees and a football field and boys my age to accept me—the way I'd almost had it in Great Falls. This would never be what I wanted. It was Canada.

Still, I'd come that far. So I just let the bike coast down the bumpy hill. I guessed it was one o'clock. Two hawks circled slowly high in the sky. As I began to pedal where the road became flat at the level of the school, some of the girls sitting on the grass, talking in ones and twos, and several who were walking the perimeter of the lawn, noticed me. Very few people, I thought, would ride a bicycle all the way to here, since there was nothing to do but go back.

A tall nun in a black gown with a white head covering stood on the school steps, supervising the yard. It was after lunch. She was talking to one of the girls, who was laughing. The nun saw me and began watching me across the distance of the lawn.

Where the school ground bordered the road, a tall barred gate stood by itself with no fence attached—which was strange, since anybody could leave or go that wanted to. Not like what I thought an orphanage was. The road entered the grounds farther on. I could see where cars were parked along the side of the building. The gate's barred doors were chained and padlocked, and up above them, connecting the brick gateposts, a metal banner with a gold figure of Christ, his arms outstretched, welcomed people through the gate in case it ever opened.

I sat on my bicycle, sweating, though a chill wind ran along the road I'd just coasted down. I would have to struggle into it when I rode back. I didn't see a boy anywhere inside the gate or even working on the lawn. There would have to be a boy somewhere, I thought. There weren't places where no boys were wanted or needed.

Two of the girls inside the yard had walked to where I was sitting on my bike outside the gate, just looking in. One was tall and skinny and had a bad complexion and a hard, wrinkled mouth that made her look grown up. The other was ordinary sized, with plain brown hair and a square, not-pretty face, and had one arm that was smaller, though not shorter, than her other one. She had a nice smile, I was glad to see, and she trained it on me through the fence bars. They were both dressed in the same shapeless light blue dresses and white tennis shoes and green ankle socks. HOLY NAME was stitched in white where a breast pocket would've been. They were like the clothes my mother had worn in jail the last day I saw her.

"What do you think you're here to do?" the tall, older-looking girl said in a hard, unfriendly way as if she wanted me to leave. Her long body loosened up when she spoke. She cocked her hip, as if she expected me to say something smart back, like Berner would've done.

"I just came out to see the school," I said and felt conspicuous being there. I was not in America. I had no business coming to a school I knew nothing about. I thought I should probably ride away.

"You're not allowed in here," the nice girl with the skinny arm said. She smiled at me again, though I could tell it wasn't friendly. It was sarcastic. One of her side-front teeth was gone and a space was dark inside her mouth, which ruined her nice smile. Both girls had bitten-down fingernails and scratches on their arms and measly bumps around their mouths, and hair on their legs, like mine. It wouldn't ever be possible to be friends with them.

Far behind the two girls the tall nun was coming down the front steps from where she'd been standing. Her robes billowed around her ankles in the breeze. Other girls in the yard stood and looked at the three of us at the gate, as if a disturbance was taking place. The nun swung her arms as she came toward us, her long legs striding out. I wanted to leave before I had to have words with her and she called the authorities. Both girls looked around but didn't seem to care about her. They smiled at each other in a mean, pleased way they'd practiced.

"Do you have some kinda girlfriend?" the older girl said. She put her hands through the bars and waggled her fingers at me. I moved back away from her. The Chinese girl in Fort Royal wouldn't waggle her fingers at me.

"No," I said.

"What's your name?" the smaller girl with the skinny arm said.

I gripped the handlebar and set my foot on the pedal, ready to push off. "Dell," I said.

"You shoo away! You shoo!" the nun had begun shouting as she came in her long strides over the lawn, a beaded harness around her waist, a big cross swinging side to side, her scrubbed-white face and mouth and eyes and cheeks and forehead tightly enclosed in starched white material. "Shoo away, boy," she shouted.

The two girls looked around at her again and exchanged cruel looks.

"You man, get away. What do you think you're doing here?" the nun was shouting. It was as if she thought something awful was about to happen or already had.

"That old whore," the older girl said and seemed natural saying it.

"We hate her. If she died, we'd like it," the smaller girl said. She had tiny, narrow, dark eyes, and when she said that, she widened them as if she was shocked by herself.

"Dell's a monkey's name where I come from. Shaunavon, Saskatchewan," the older girl said, unbothered by the nun who was quickly approaching. The girl suddenly reached her long arm farther through the gap in the bars and fastened a terrible grip on my wrist, which I tried to get away from but couldn't. She began pulling me, while the other girl laughed. I was tipping sideways, my right leg and just my shoe heel holding me up, but beginning to fall.

"Don't touch them," the nun was shouting. I wasn't touching anybody.

"He's afraid of us," the smaller girl said and started walking away, leaving the older girl imprisoning me through the bars. She was staring at me, torturing me and liking it. She dug her little stunted fingernails into my wrist skin, as if she wanted to tear it.

"Turn him loose, Marjorie," the nun shouted, almost to the gate. "He'll injure you." She couldn't move easily because of her heavy skirts.

I was being pulled off my bicycle and up against the bars of the gate. "Stop," I said. "You don't need to do this."

"But I just want to." Marjorie was pulling me against the bars to do something to me. Beat me up, I thought. She was much stronger than Berner and she was bigger. Her face was calm, but her large blue eyes were trained hard on me, and her jaw muscles were clenched as if she was straining. She was younger than I was. Fourteen, I thought, for some reason. "I want to make a man out of you," she said. "Or make a mess."

Then the nun arrived and immediately grabbed Marjorie's shoulder and pulled her back, though Marjorie kept holding on to me. The nun took hold of the girl's chin and turned her head to the side away from the gate. "Wrong, wrong, wrong," she said angrily through her pale, stiffened lips. Her black robes made everything difficult for her. The nun's eyes worked to me, through the bars. "Why are you here?" she said. Her face was getting red. "You don't belong here. Get away." She was also very young. Her face was smooth and clear, even though she was angry. She wasn't much older than Marjorie or me.

A bell had begun to ring at the school. I was all the way off my old bike but hadn't yet fallen. Marjorie still had her burning grip on my arm and no expression on her face. With my left hand I pried in under her tough fingers—where gouges were opening in my skin. I forced one finger up and then another one. I didn't want to hurt her. Then I was loose.

I stumbled backward away from her into my bicycle and fell on the gravel and knocked the breath out of myself.

"Who *are* you?" The nun was glaring down at me through the bars. Her face was scrubbed and shiny and furious. She now had a strong grip on Marjorie's shoulders. Marjorie had begun smiling at me on the ground, as if I'd done something funny. "What's your name?" the nun said.

I didn't want to say anything about myself. I began to get up and raise my bicycle off the gravel.

"His name's Dell," Marjorie said. "It's a monkey's name."

"Why are you here?" the nun said, still holding Marjorie's shoulders.

"I just wanted to go to school." I felt ridiculous kneeling on the ground, reduced in size by being here.

"It's not *for* you." She had an accent different from anybody else's I'd ever heard. She spoke fast and spit her words at me. Her dark flat eyes were furious—furious against me. "Where are you living?"

"In Partreau," I said. "I work in Fort Royal." All the girls in the school yard were walking toward the front steps, organizing themselves into a line to go inside. Another nun—short and heavy-set—was now at the top of the steps, her hands folded in front of her. Marjorie was still smiling at me through the bars as if I was pathetic.

"I wanted to kiss you," she said to me dreamily. "You didn't want to kiss me, though, did you?"

"Go back inside," the nun said, and turned loose of Marjorie's shoulders and shoved her away. Marjorie threw her head back and turned dramatically and laughed out loud and began walking to catch up with her friend.

"I'm sorry," I said.

"I don't want to see you ever here again," the young nun said through the gate. She shook her head at me and pushed her face forward and glared to make sure I understood. "If you come out to here, I will call the constables. They take you away. Do you remember that?"

"Yes," I said. "I'm sorry." I wanted to say something else but had no idea what it could be. I didn't know what desperate was, but I felt desperate. The young nun was already walking away, her heavy black gown swaying in the sunlight. I had my bicycle up on its wheels, and got it turned in the gravel. I climbed on and began my ride back up the hill into the wind toward the highway and Partreau.

50

FLORENCE LA BLANC DROVE OUT TO PARTREAU IN her little pink Metropolitan and left a bulky manila envelope leaned against the door of my shack. It had been sent from America with the words *Pass On to Dell Parsons* scrawled on the bottom, in handwriting I didn't recognize. It was just days after I'd gone on my bike to the wayward girls' school, and the week I was to move from Partreau to Fort Royal because more Sports were arriving. Charley had been told to install one of the Sports onto the other cot in my shack, and it wasn't thought (by Florence, I learned) "good" for me to sleep alone in a room with a grown stranger. Charley had smirked about this and said the old drunk goose shooters could "get lovey" after midnight. There was a tiny "monk's mop closet" on the third floor of the Leonard, down the hallway from Remlinger's rooms. I was given this room to sleep in and the use of the downstairs bathroom with the roughnecks and railroaders, and a white enamel pot for the middle of the night. Charley would collect me in his truck for my goose duties. It was beginning to be colder and windier, and I was happy to quit pedaling to town and sleeping in my drafty cabin and seeing no one. This way, I would be more available, once the goose cleaning was finished, to run errands for the Sports for tips and to hang around the bar at night. If I was busy and had less time by myself, I once again didn't think about my parents and school and Berner—all of which were important to me, but left me feeling sad as a result.

I'd had little contact with Florence La Blanc. Charley had told me she owned a greeting card store in The Hat and was a widow and once had been a local beauty who'd been free with her charms when her husband was defending Hong Kong in 1941. She looked after her elderly mother. But she was also an artist and enjoyed drinking in the hotel and playing cards in the gambling room, where she was not supposed to be let in. Everyone liked her. Her arrangement with Arthur Remlinger suited her because he had money and good manners and was handsome, in spite of being private and an American and younger than she was. She went back to The Hat when she got tired of him.

Periodically, when I was in my shack, I would look out and see Florence with her painter's easel established at various locations in Partreau—once near the back of town, facing the caraganas through which the oil pumper and the white bee hives were visible. Another time, she stood out on my street painting Charley's trailer and his Quonset. I was strictly forbidden to intrude on Arthur Remlinger's privacy. But there'd been no mention about Florence, who'd acted friendly to me at a distance, and I felt I was at liberty to talk to her. Again, no one came to Partreau. I talked to very few people on any given day. I thought she wouldn't mind. So, when I saw her seated on her wood stool in a brown smock and a soft black cloth hat, painting in the street that ran in front of the empty Partreau post office, I walked over through the weeds and clutter where houses had stood, to see what a person did to paint a true picture—not just paint-by-numbers, which I knew didn't constitute genuine painting or art.

When she saw me coming—it was the afternoon she'd left the manila envelope—Florence held up her long paintbrush and waved it back and forth like a metronome. I took this to be a signal that she recognized me—though she kept her eyes on her painting, as if it was important to keep it in view.

"I left you a mysterious parcel," she said, not looking at me. "You're much taller than a month ago. Is that possible?" Florence glanced around at me, smiling. She wasn't a large woman and had a pretty, frank, widely smiling mouth and a hoarse voice that suggested she enjoyed herself. I could imagine her laughing. Occasionally she and Arthur Remlinger danced in the bar to the jukebox music—I'd observed this. She'd held him stiffly at arm's length in one of his fine suits, looking grave and performing an awkward box step that made the other customers in the bar laugh and her, too. As I said, she also liked to play cards in what she called "the gambling pit," in the room next to the bar, where I rarely went. Her short frizzy blond hair had gray streaked through it, and she "carried some weight in her pocket," as my father said about some women. She must've been in her forties, and I could see how she'd been prettier when she was young and thin and reckless and her husband was fighting in the war. Her cheeks had tiny veins in them, which I knew was a sign of a hard life, and her sparkly eyes narrowed when she smiled so they were almost invisible. She didn't match being Arthur Remlinger's lady friend in my view, but she was somebody I thought I would like. I was happy she'd noticed me weeks before.

I stood to the side and behind Florence, so I could see straight on to what she was doing. I'd only seen the painting of the grain elevator in Arthur Remlinger's rooms, and hadn't known what "the Nighthawk school" was, or as yet anything about Edward Hopper or how a person could make a design that would be recognizable out of just tubes of paint. I believed you probably had to perform eye exercises like my father did so you could see things very accurately.

Florence was painting in the middle of Manitoba Street. Her picture was nothing more than the view straight past the vacant post office and a pair of broken-in houses to the backs of the commercial row where I walked and that had been alive when Partreau was a whole town. The sky above the buildings had not been painted in yet and was only empty canvas. The elevator and the wheat fields that rose and widened beyond the train tracks toward the horizon were also still to come. I couldn't see why this would be a subject for a painting, since it was right there for anybody to see any time, and wasn't beautiful—nothing like Niagara Falls in the Frederic Church picture, or the flower arrangements my father painted with his numbers kit. But I liked it, which I should've said to be courteous. What I did say—and wished I'd chosen something better—was, "Why are you painting that?"

Wind pushed the dry weeds back and forth. The day was growing gray as the line of a front was closing out the blue sky to the east. Charley's whirly devices were spinning wildly. Swaying ribbons of geese were hurrying in from the north, catching the last of the sun. It didn't seem to be a good day for painting.

"Oh," Florence said, "I just paint things I like, you know? Things that wouldn't get to be pretty otherwise." She was holding her wooden palette with her left thumb stuck through. Knots of different colored paint had been squeezed onto it. She'd mix two or three with her brush tip, and put paint right onto the canvas. What she was painting was exactly what I saw—which I guessed was the American Nighthawk style and seemed a miracle but peculiar. I also didn't understand what she meant by the post office being pretty in her painting. Since it looked like the post office I could see, it wasn't pretty at all. "I was never really a painter," Florence said. "My sister Dinah-Lor *was* a painter. Before she succumbed to a broken heart. My father was also a painter—in the primitive tradition, since what he *really* was, was an ice cutter in Souris, Manitoba. Maybe that's why I'm painting out here on South Manitoba Street." She turned her plump, round face toward me. Her narrow eyes were brown and sparkling, her short-fingered hands strong and red from being in the chilly wind. "You don't know where in the world Manitoba even is, do you, Dell? Or what?" She was enjoying herself the way I thought she probably always did.

"I know *what* it is," I said. It was a province. I was pleased she knew

my name. But I didn't know any more about Canada than what Mildred
and Charley had told me. I was thinking about her saying I was taller. I
would've been happy to be taller, but I didn't think a month was a long
enough time for that to happen. What I'd mostly felt since I'd been there
was smaller.

"You probably aren't even aware of what Saskatchewan means," Florence said, looking over her palette at her painting.

"I'm not," I said.

"Well. I'm happy to tell you it means 'the quickly flowing river,'
of which there's not many where we are here now. It's in the Cree language, which I don't personally speak. You just need a map and a history
book. You'll see that Manitoba, where I was born, isn't even very far from
here—in Sputnik terms." She said Sputnik different from how I'd heard
on the radio. She said the long "u" to rhyme with "root," the way Rudy
had said Roosevelt. Spootnik. She went on darkening the white front of
the wrecked post office to match what I could see was its actual deterio-
rated condition. "Otherwise," she said, "I enjoy doing things outside. And
I'm bored, of course. I used to always drive past this little town coming
over from The Hat to see Arthur. In our early romantic days. People were
still living in one or two of the houses at that time. It somehow just called
out to me." She furrowed her brows at her painting. "Has that happened to
you yet in your life? You hear a word forever, then all of a sudden it makes
a whole different sense? That happens to me all the time."

It had happened to me. It had happened to me with the word *criminal*.
It had always meant one thing. Bonnie and Clyde. Al Capone. The Rosenbergs. Now it meant my parents. I wasn't going to say that, though. I just
said, "Yes. It has."

"So. Do you like us up here?" Florence glanced at me for a third time
to be certain I was noticing her carefully applying paint to the post office.
It pleased her, I thought, to be observed painting. "Canadians always want
everybody to like it here. And *us*—especially to like us." She made a care-

ful little brush jab at the post office door, then turned her head sideways and looked at it that way. "But. Then when you *do* like us, we're suspicious it might be for the wrong reasons. America must be a lot different. I have a feeling nobody much cares down there. I don't know a lot about it. Doing things for the right reasons is the key to Canada."

"I like it," I said. Though I hadn't thought about Canada in those specific terms. I assumed I didn't like it, because I was there against my will—and no one would like that. But I wasn't sure I wanted to leave now, since I had no place to go.

"Well . . ." Florence hunched her shoulders, leaned forward on her stool, holding her palette away from her, and with her short, red-nailed thumb lightly smudged the door of the post office so it looked more like the actual gray door I could see. "That's good," she said, concentrating. "It's no fun to be miserable, I guess." She leaned back on her stool and stared at what she'd done. "Life's passed along to us empty. We have to make up the happiness part." She wiped her thumb straight onto her brown smock, which she'd done many times before, then sat up straight on her stool to admire her work. "Is it nice down where you live? Or where you did before? I've never been to the States. Never had the time."

"I liked my school." I *would've* liked it, I thought.

"That's nice then," Florence said.

"Do you know why Mr. Remlinger has me up here?" I asked. I hadn't expected to say that. But I was relieved to talk to someone who seemed to like me.

Florence looked around the side of her easel at the empty street leading to the highway, where the second two-a-day Greyhound was just going by. She looked back at her painting, her brush twitching between her thumb and her index finger. Strands of blond hair went up the pale back of her neck and under her soft hat. She had a mole there that I thought her comb would always catch on. "Well." She was talking as she studied her painting. "Are you worried because he hasn't paid any attention to you?"

"Sometimes." I wished I'd just said yes, since it was true.

"Well, don't let that bother you," Florence said, dipping her brush into a tin can on the pavement at her feet. "People like Arthur don't naturally connect to the world. You can tell that. He probably hasn't even noticed he's ignoring you. He's very smart. He went to Harvard. He may feel it's important for you to get adjusted to being by yourself. On the other hand, people are never going to do just what you want them to. He's doing you a favor. Maybe you're a novelty to him." She gave me a mischievous grin and looked up at the clouds. "And I do always loathe a marble sky." She made a line of X's in the air, using her brush, as if she could paint the sky over. Then she put her brush back in the tin can and left it.

The oil pumper was humming away out in the windy wheat field, not far off, its lever arm smoothly sinking and rising—the only unnatural noise in the air. I'd almost stopped hearing it at night, though I went to sleep listening for it.

I stood behind her and didn't say anything. Florence leaned and set her palette down on the pavement and opened her wooden painter's box, which had shiny brass fittings and contained clean brushes and silver tubes of paint, several small knives, some white rags and dark bottles of liquid, plus a deck of red-backed playing cards, a package of Export 'A's and a small silver flask. High in the sky, inching toward the east, a speck of an airplane appeared out ahead of the moving clouds, the sun against its wings. My father once had sat me in a Scorpion F-89 fighter at the National Guard base, and let me put on the pilot's helmet and move the controls and make believe I could fly it. I wondered what a person would see from an airplane here. The world curving away? The Rocky Mountains and the Missouri River? The Cypress Hills, the Saskatchewan River and Fort Royal and Partreau and Great Falls and everything in between? All in one clear view.

"Arthur told me about the difficulties. Your poor parents and whatnot," Florence said. She took out one of the dark bottles. Then she dumped the liquid from her tin can right onto Manitoba Street, unscrewed the bottle cap, and poured clear fluid into the can. "You'll have an interesting life story to tell. Pretty girls'll like you. We like men with dark pasts. My father was put in jail in Manitoba once. But he didn't rob anything, I guess."

She stuck her brush in the can and waggled it and looked back at her painting in which the post office was the only part that was finished. "On the second other hand, of course," Florence said, busy with her cleaning up, "maybe Arthur sees himself in you. A purer version. I wouldn't think so. But men do that. On the fourth hand, people do things and say things and don't *ever* know why. Then what they do affects people's lives, and later on they say they knew all about it but they didn't. That's probably why your mother sent you up here. She didn't know what else to do. So. Here you are. That shouldn't discourage you. I'm a mother. It happens. How old are you, dear?"

"Fifteen," I said.

"And you have a sister who ran away?"

"Yes, ma'am," I said.

"And what's her name?"

"Berner," I said.

"I see." She set her tin can with the brush in it back on the ground, picked up a knife and a cloth out of her painter's box, and set to scraping the knots of paint off her palette and wiping the paint on the cloth. None of this conversation was like a conversation I'd ever had. Berner's conversations, wherever she was, were probably like this one, I thought—about why things were the way they were and what you can do about them. Conversations with adults other than a person's parents had more of an outcome.

"How do you know Mr. Remlinger?" I asked.

Florence leaned her scraped palette against the leg of the tripod her canvas sat on, and squeezed her brush tip gently into the white cotton cloth. She knelt on the pavement to perform these acts. I stayed standing beside her. "If I can think back that far." She smiled up at me. Her cloth hat—which was soft black velvet—had been pushed by the wind back off her forehead. The unfinished painting, still on the easel, was also being disturbed. "I . . . met Arthur in the bar of the Bessborough Hotel in Saskatoon, in nineteen fifty. I had a French painter boyfriend at that time. A watercolorist. Jean-Paul or Jean-Claude. We'd been to the football, which I always enjoy. But he got furious at me—for something I said—and departed. And Arthur was right there in the bar. He was blond and handsome and refined and well dressed and smart and slightly eccentric for a younger man, but also something of a gentleman and slightly secretive. He had an interesting dramatic quality. And he seemed angry and bored and out of place—a bit of a confusion—which is always attractive to women. He lived down here for some reason and didn't have any idea what to do about himself. I didn't quite have my car fare back to The Hat. I could've ridden the red bus to Swift Current and switched. But he had a nice car—an Oldsmobile. He didn't own the hotel then. He only worked there. And that was that. What did I say? Nineteen-fifty? He was twenty-something. I was a bit older. And thinner. My mother was still working at Lepke's. I had one child still at home—who's now in Winnipeg. That's my life story in living color." She smiled up at me again, and went back to arranging the painting articles in her box, her red fingernails moving among the contents. I tried to gain a clearer picture of Arthur Remlinger from what she'd said and fit it to the man I'd only barely met. But I couldn't. He didn't seem distinct to me, even then.

"I'm moving into Fort Royal soon," I said, not wanting to say nothing, since I'd asked a question and she'd answered it.

"Which was *my* brilliant suggestion," Florence said, still on her knees. "Arthur thinks you're fine out here—in your little wickiup. It's interesting to live all alone out here, I realize. Very romantic. But it won't be a fit place when the hunters come. I can't really look out for you, but I can try to be aware of you. Your mother would thank me."

That was true. I believed my mother knew something like this would happen—that a person would notice me and see that I was worth something and not leave me to be lost. I didn't think people who were worth something could get lost forever, even if you couldn't explain everything about yourself, why you were where you were, etc. "Why's Mr. Remlinger here," I said.

Florence stood up stiffly—she wasn't very tall and wasn't slender like my mother. She brushed off her brown corduroy trousers and shook herself all over and patted her arms and the top of her floppy hat, as if she'd gotten cold. I had on my plaid jacket. It *was* colder now. "It must be Canada out here." She grinned. "We don't always go *to* places," she said, "sometimes we just end up there. That's what Arthur did. He ended up. 'I don't go to America, I leave Paris.' That's what the great artist Duchamp said, who would've thought my painting was a very funny thing." She looked at her painting of the post office and the empty street leading away—the scene in front of us. "I like it, though," she said. "I don't like 'em all." She took a step back and regarded her painting out the side of her eyes, then straight on.

"I like it," I said. I thought if I moved to Fort Royal I would see Florence more, and the events in my life could develop in a more positive way that would include Arthur Remlinger, who I wished I knew better.

"I know this is very strange for you up here, dear," Florence said. "But you just go with the Flo. Okay? That was my thing I said to my children. They got tired of hearing it. But it's still true." She motioned toward her Metropolitan. "If you help me carry my artistic things to my little car, I'll drive you into town and you can get supper. Charley can bring you back. You're a short-timer out here now. You can move in tomorrow." She picked up her painter's box. I took her canvas off her easel, picked up her tin can and her wooden stool and the easel, and we went on to her car. It was my last day in Partreau.

51

THERE WERE THREE ITEMS OF IMPORTANCE IN THE thick manila envelope—addressed to Mr. A. Remlinger, Esquire, from his sister, Mildred, but intended for me. One was a letter from my sister, Berner, delivered to our empty house and found there by Mildred, who checked our mailbox for days after we'd all gone. There was a short note enclosed in the envelope from Mildred herself, which said:

> Dear Dell,
>   Enclosed of regrettable interest. I will drive to their trial in N.D.
> But only so you will know what has happened. They know your
> mother had nothing to do with anything. But she was in it anyway.
>   Your old friend,
>   Mildred R.

Along with Mildred's message was an entire copy of the *Great Falls Tribune* from September 10th, which made the envelope thick. On the front page was another story about my and Berner's parents. This one said that "an Alabama man" and his wife, who was (again) "a native of Washington State," had been driven on September 8th, from the Cascade County jail to the Golden Valley County, North Dakota, jail in Beach, North Dakota, after the waiving of their rights. They had been charged with the armed robbery of the Creekmore, North Dakota, Agricultural Bank, in August, following which they had been apprehended by Great Falls detectives, in their home on First Avenue Southwest. The female, Geneva "Neva" (misspelled) Rachel Parsons, had been employed as a fifth-grade teacher by the Fort Shaw, Montana, school board. The male, "Sydney Beverly Parsons," was unemployed at the time of his capture and was retired from the United States Air Force, where he was a decorated veteran of World War Two and had served as a bombardier. The couple's two children—an unnamed boy and girl—were missing and presumed to be with unidentified relatives. Efforts were under way to return the juveniles to Montana authorities. A "not guilty" plea had been entered for the couple in their first court hearing in Golden Valley County. An attorney had been retained for them. The Great Falls crime rate for the year—the story said—had so far seen a 4 percent rise over 1959.

Printed above the story were the same photographs Berner and I had had left for us by our neighbor, the morning after our parents' arrest, and that made them look like hardened desperadoes. There was also another picture—I took interest in this—showing our parents being led by uniformed officers down a set of steep concrete steps toward a black panel truck with a star on its side. They were in handcuffs—our father was wearing a gaudy, striped, loose-fitting convict suit and looking at the ground where he was stepping so as not to fall. Our mother was wearing the beltless, shapeless dress she'd worn when Berner and I visited her and that made her look extremely small. She was staring straight into the camera, her soft face thin and focused and angry—as if she knew who would see her picture and wanted them to know she hated them (which would not have included Berner and me).

I possess this newspaper still today. I've reread the story and studied the pictures countless times—to remember them. But seated in my cold, drafty, stale-smelling shack, on the side of my cot beside the window, when I saw the second photo and read the story that made our parents sound like any life-long luckless criminals the world would barely notice, then forget (as if this story was all there was to their lives), I felt an odd sensation in my chest, like a pain without an ache. This sensation grew down into my belly the way hunger does, and stayed so that I thought for a while it might stay for a long time, just be there to plague my life in still another way. Of course, my parents looked like themselves, in spite of their prison clothes: my father tall, though thinner, but handsome (he'd shaved and combed his hair for his trip); my mother, impatient, purposeful and intense. Yet they also failed to look exactly familiar to me. Nothing that had happened had been in any way normal. Whatever changes had occurred in them and to them defied any idea I had of familiar. They looked like two people I knew, who I was again seeing across a distance, some unspannable divide, much greater than the border that separated us by then. I could say that their intimate familiarity as my parents, and their ordinary, generalized humanness had become joined, and one quality had neutralized the other and rendered the two of them neither completely familiar nor completely haphazard and indifferent to me. Passing carefully down those concrete steps toward the Black Maria that would rumble them away to North Dakota and their future, they had become something of a mystery to me, one I shared (I'm sure) with the other innocent children of criminals. Knowing this didn't make me love them less. But I thought I'd never see them again when I saw this picture. So that who they'd become in such a short amount of time were two people who were completely lost to me. All they seemed to have was each other, but they didn't really have that anymore either.

There was also a satisfaction of a kind to all of this, which may be a surprise to know, but must've made my acheless pain finally go away. I'd worried and worried about our parents' fate over the last month—had waked up worrying. I'd lost weight, grown older and more sober. I sometimes dreamed that they'd come to rescue me in their car, with Berner, but couldn't find me and had driven away. In other words, I'd all but said good-bye to my childhood on the strength of their terrible fall. But now I knew their fate (more or less), and with that could begin to recognize something of my own—which was not a bad thing. Though I was very glad Berner didn't have to see their picture or read the story. Wherever she was, I hoped Mildred hadn't also sent a manila envelope to her. As it turned out she had not.

52

Dear Dell-boy,

    I am sending you this letter in GF because I don't think you are
there but don't know where else to send it. Maybe somebody will give
it to you. Mother's funny friend, Mildred somebody, maybe. I hope
you are not reading this in the juvenile jail someplace—a terrible
outcome if you are. I wonder if you have seen our pathetic parents and
what has happened to them these days. I wonder what happened to my
fish? I love you to bits, you know! In spite of all. I still have your half
of the money you gave me. I thought about you going to their jail cell
alone after I flew the coop. Sorry. Sorry. Sorry.

    Where are you? I am living in a house with other people. A girl
who is also a runaway and who is nice. A handsome boy who left
the U.S. Navy without permission because he didn't like a fight.
Two other men and a woman are not always here but take care of us
just fine and don't ask very much attention in return. This house is
on a long street called California Street (naturally). Since I'm in
San Francisco. I forgot to say. I have not seen that unfaithful rascal
Rudy Red-Daddy. We made a pack to meet in San Francisco on a
Saturday, in a park called Washington Sq. I have not seen him or

his mother. If you see him tell him to take care of himself. I don't love
him. He could also write to me.

    It is strange to write letters to each other like grown-ups isn't it?
I wish you would come here if you are able to. I would still boss you
around. But you could play chess here. People in the Washington
Park Sq. also play. You could learn things and be the champion. I
have learned that other people (kids) can have problems with their
parents too. Not about going off and robbing a bank—not that bad—
and maybe committing suicide. But other things. Have you gotten a
letter from them? Naturally I haven't. I wonder what they think of me
at this point. Do they know I ran away? It's beautiful here and not
cold yet and things feel like they are happening. I like being on my
own. I've told people about our parents, but no one believes it. Maybe
I will quit believing it, too, or quit telling it. I wish I could see you,
even though when I left I thought I never would again. I now think we
will. I am still on the same earth as you, although I'm glad I'm not in
GF, which is a crap town and always will be.

    Someday I will tell you how I came to get here. I made it without
being killed and without being taken too much advantage of or
starving to death. Gotta skee-daddle.

    Love,

    Berner Parsons

P.S. I thought of some new things. You can write to me at this
address, and should. I am glad for the passage of time, so you don't
have to hurry.

    If you saw me you wouldn't recognize it. I have my two ears
pierced. I shave my legs and under my pits and have cut my wire mop
short and cute. I don't mind my old freckles. I have some breasts now.
The man, Uncle Bob is what we call him, asked me if I was Jewish. I
said of course. My complexion has unfortunately blossomed out. I had

a job two times as a babysitter if you can believe that for me. I can
remember being a baby myself. You still are one, where I'm concerned.
I will give you the robbed money you gave me when I see you.

It is too bad we have the parents we have and haven't been
luckier. Our life is ruined now, although there is a lot of it left to fill
up. Sometimes I miss them. I did—do—have one dream. I killed
someone in it, I don't know who, but then forgot all about it. Then it
just rises up—the killing I did—and I know I did it and other people
do too. It's terrible since I didn't really do it but still have the dream. I
wake up later feeling like I've been crying and running a race. Do you
have that? Since we are twins I believe we feel the same and see things
the same (the world?). I hope it's true. I remember one of mother's
poems. I say it out loud to the Navy boy. "Had I once a lovely youth,
heroic, fabulous, to be written on sheets of gold, good luck to spare.
Through what crime—" I can't remember it all now. Sorry. It was
French. She always thought it was about her, I guess.

Love ya again,
Berner Rachel Parsons, your twin

53

THE TIME THAT BEGAN FOR ME IN FORT ROYAL, IN the Leonard Hotel, was in every way different from my lonely weeks in Partreau, and superior to them and felt—though it didn't last long and ended in disaster—like a life I was actually living, instead of life at a standstill, the partial life of a person lost on an empty prairie who somehow makes it to shelter but stays lost, and for whom nothing could be right again.

More Sports began arriving. Five or six of them at a time—their big American cars with colorful American license plates parked in the dirt lot out behind, full of their hunting gear that couldn't fit in the tiny rooms. From my little radiator-warm closet down the hall from Remlinger, I'd hear the men's voices up through the floorboards and the pipes, talking to each other in low tones far into the night. I would lie silently in my narrow bed, trying to make out the things they said. Since they were mostly Americans, I felt they might say things I would recognize, and provide me with understandings that would be useful. I don't know what I thought those things could be. I never heard much—people's names spoken—Herman, Winifred, Sonny; complaints about insults or injuries one person or other had suffered. Someone laughing.

At night in the Leonard bar, after Charley and I had gone for our sundown scouting and determined where new pits should be dug (two Ukrainian boys were hired to dig them after dark and cover the clump piles with wheat straw), I usually came back and ate my supper in the hotel kitchen, then passed the early evening beside the jukebox in the smoky, noisy barroom, or standing behind the card players in the gambling pit, or talking to the Filipino girls who served drinks in the shadowy bar light and danced with the Sports and sometimes with each other, and who often (as I've said) disappeared with one man or another and then weren't seen the rest of the night. I no longer swamped rooms, so I rarely saw them climbing into their waiting taxi back to Swift Current.

The Americans in the bar were mostly large, loud-talking men dressed in rough hunting attire. They laughed and smoked and drank rye whiskey and beer and enjoyed themselves. Many of them thought that being in Canada was highly comical, and made jokes about having Thanksgiving in October and the strange ways Canadians talked (I'd never much detected it, though I tried) and how Canadians hated Americans but all wished they lived there and could be rich. They talked about the election campaign "down below," how they expected Nixon to overpower Kennedy, and how important it was to fight the Communists. They talked about the football teams where they were from. (Some were from Missouri, others from Nevada, others from Chicago.) They made jokes about their wives and told stories about their children's achievements, and their jobs back home, and about noteworthy events that had happened on other hunting expeditions and how many ducks and geese and other animals they'd killed. Sometimes they talked to me—if they noticed me, or if they'd earlier in the day sent me on an errand to the drugstore or the hardware for some piece of equipment they lacked. They wanted to know if I was Canadian, or if I was "Mr. Remlinger's son," or the boy of some other hunter who was there. I told them I was visiting from Montana, that my parents had gotten sick, but I'd be going home again soon and back to school—which often made them shout out and laugh and clap me on the back and say I was "lucky" to be skipping school and would never want to go back after being a "hunting guide" and lead-ing a life of adventure most boys only dreamed of. They seemed to think Canada, although comical, was mysterious and romantic, and where they lived was boring and corny, yet they still wanted to live there.

At the end of these evenings—it was before eight o'clock, when Char-ley would pass through, having checked the goose pits, and was telling the Sports to go to bed, since we were rising at four—I would climb the stairs back to my room and lie in bed, reading my *Chess Master* magazine, and later on would listen to the hunters thumping up to their rooms, laughing and coughing and hocking and clinking glasses and bottles and using the bathroom and making their private noises and yawning, and boots hitting the floor until their doors closed and they'd be snoring. It was then I could hear single men's voices out on the cold main street of Fort Royal, and car doors closing, and a dog barking, and the switchers working the grain cars behind the hotel, and the air brakes of trucks pausing at the traffic light, then their big engines grinding back to life and heading toward Alberta or Regina—two places I knew nothing about. My window was under the eave, and the red Leonard sign tinted the black air in my room, whereas in my shack there had been only moonlight and my candle and the sky full of stars and the glow in Charley's trailer. I lacked a radio now. So to set my mind off toward sleep I inventoried the experiences of the day and the thoughts that had accompanied them. I considered, as always, my parents, and whether it was hard for them to be good in jail, and what they would think about me now, and how I would've conducted myself had I been present at their trial, and what we would've said, and whether I would've told them about Berner, and if I would've said I loved them where others would hear. (I would've.) I also considered the hunters' gruff American voices and the achievements of their children, and their wives waiting at the kitchen door, and all their adventures, none of which caused me envy or resentment. I had no achievements so far, or anyone waiting for me, or even a home I could go back to. I just had my days' duties and my meals and my room with my few possessions. Yet I surprisingly went to sleep almost always relieved to feel the way I did. Mildred had told me I was not to think bad of myself, since what had happened had been through no fault of mine. Florence had told me our lives were passed on to us empty and our task was to make up being happy. And my own mother—who'd never been where I was now, and knew nothing about Canada except as a view across a river, and who did not even know the people she'd handed me over to—even *she* had felt it was better for me to be here than in some juvenile prison in Montana. And she undoubtedly loved me.

Berner had written that our lives were ruined but had far still to go. And I couldn't have made it up that I was truly happy. But I was satisfied not to haul my water in a pail, not to bathe myself using the pump and the hot plate and a bar of soap, not to sleep in the cold, drafty, acrid shack and see no one I knew, and not to share the privy with Charley Quarters. It's possible, I felt, that I was experiencing improvement, which for a time I hadn't believed I ever would. So that it was possible to think—and this was important to me—that at least some part of my human makeup was inclined to believe life could be better.

The only time I'd met Arthur Remlinger and truly had a word with him, he'd asked me—half joking—if I would like to change my name. I'd told him no, as anyone would've—especially me, wanting to cling to who I was and what I knew about myself when those points were in dispute. But in my room under the eave, I felt Arthur Remlinger possibly knew something I hadn't known. Which was: that if anyone's mission in the world was to gain experience, it might be necessary, as I'd already thought, to become someone different—even if I didn't know who, and even if I'd believed, and our mother had taught us, that we were always a faithful version of who we were when we began life. My father, of course, might've said that this first person—the person I'd started to be—had stopped making sense and needed to give way to someone who would do better. He had probably thought that about himself by then. Though for him it was too late.

54

I T WAS FOLLOWING MY ADJUSTMENT TO FORT ROYAL—
a town with a genuine life and a consideration for itself—that
I moved more into the sphere of Arthur Remlinger, which
Florence had indicated to me would occur and I was extremely eager to
have happen and couldn't have said why it hadn't happened already. In
my weeks of living in Partreau, Arthur Remlinger had seemed like a different person each time I made contact with him—which naturally confused me and made me feel even more alone than I would've otherwise.
One time, he would be friendly and enthusiastic, as if he'd been waiting
to tell me something—but never did. Another time, he'd be reserved and
awkward and seem to want to get away from me. And still other times
he was stiff and superior acting—always costumed in his expensive (and
what I thought of as) eastern clothes. To me, he was the most inconsistent
person I'd ever met in life. Though it made him fascinating, and made me
want him to like me, having never been around strange people, except
our mother, and having never found anyone precisely interesting before,
except Berner, who more than anything else was like me.

Once, on what became one of our automotive outings—after I'd
moved into the Leonard and begun to see him more, and during which
times Remlinger would navigate his Buick at battering speeds over the

bumpy highway, declaring on this and that subject that occupied him (Adlai Stevenson, whom he loathed, the deterioration of our natural rights by the forces of syndicalism, his own acute powers of observation, which, he said, should've permitted him a life as a famous lawyer)—the Buick all at once crested a dusty rise at a speed of almost ninety. And there on the pavement ahead were six colorful pheasants, wandering carelessly out of the grain to peck at gravels and wheat seeds blown off the trucks en route to the elevator in Leader. I expected him to brake or swerve. I'd been holding the sides of my seat already. But both my hands flew to the dashboard, my feet stood up hard on the car floor, my knees locked in anticipation of the big Buick drifting or skidding or swerving off into the stubble or taking flight and tumbling whatever distance ninety miles an hour would propel us, after which we'd be dead. But Arthur failed to consider the brakes. Nothing in his features even changed. He drove straight through the pheasants—one struck the windshield, two catapulted into the air, a fourth and fifth were transformed into feathers on the highway, a sixth was untouched, barely noticing the car passing. "You see a lot of those birds out here," he said. He didn't look at the mirror. I was astonished.

Later, when we'd cruised through the small town of Leader, Saskatchewan, and parked and gone inside the Modern Café for a sandwich, Arthur fixed me, across the table, with his clear blue eyes, his thin lips together, almost smiling, as if he might be speaking words silently before he said them, but then didn't smile. He was wearing his brown leather jacket with the fur collar—like the bomber jacket my father had brought back from the war—though Remlinger's was nicer. He had his green silk handkerchief tucked in his collar as a napkin. His reading glasses dangled on their string against his chest. His blond hair was carefully combed. His bony, manicured fingers with thin hairs on top maneuvered his fork and knife as if his food was of the greatest interest to him. There'd been no reason given for why he'd ignored me for these weeks. Now no reason was going to be given, I assumed, for why he'd stopped. It was just how things were.

"How long have you been here now, Dell?" Arthur Remlinger said and suddenly beamed at me as if I was someone he realized he liked.

"Five weeks," I said.

"And are you enjoying your work? Getting something out of it?" He spoke in his precise way that involved his mouth moving animatedly, as if each word had a space between itself and the next word, and he enjoyed hearing each one. His voice was unexpectedly nasal coming from such a handsome, refined-seeming man. These were things about him that made him seem old-fashioned, though he wasn't old.

"Yes, sir," I said.

He tried his fork on the surface of the fried pork chop he'd ordered. "Mildred told me you might be a little unsteady." He cut down into a small fatty edge and put that in his mouth, the tines of his fork turned down in a way I hadn't seen anyone eat. He was left-handed—like Berner. "It's perfectly all right if you are," he said. "I'm unsteady myself. And I'm easily led—or I once was. We're all unsteady out here. It's not natural being here. You and I are alike in that."

"I'm not unsteady." I resented Mildred telling him such a thing, and resented her for knowing it. I didn't want to be that way.

"Well." He looked pleased, which suited his fine features. "You've never been alone before, and you've had an unlikable experience."

There were several people in the café, farmers and townspeople, and two police officers in heavy brown coats with brass buttons, eating at the lunch counter. They noticed us. They knew who Arthur Remlinger was, just as the Mormon woman in the street in Fort Royal had. He was very recognizable.

I wasn't supposed to ask questions but was supposed to wait to be told things. But I wanted to know why he'd driven his car through the pheasants and killed them. It'd been so shocking. My father would never have done that, though I thought Charley Quarters would. It hadn't seemed to linger in Remlinger's mind. "It's not a simple chore to live up here," he said, calmly chewing his fatty meat. "I've never liked it. Canadians are isolated and in-grown. Not enough stimulation." A lock of his blond hair fell across his forehead. He moved it back with his thumb. "The writer Tolstoy—you've heard of him"—I'd seen his name on the book shelf—"he paid for peasants to come out here in the last century. I presume, to get rid of them. Some of those people are still here—their ancestors are, anyway. There was a brief civilization. People put on plays and pageants and light operas. There were debating societies, and famous Irish tenors came from Toronto to sing." His blond eyebrows jumped. He smiled and looked around at the other people in the café and at the policemen. There was a murmur of voices and the noise of silverware on plates that he seemed to like. "Now"—he went on cutting and eating and talking—"we're returning to the Bronze Age. Which isn't all bad." He wiped his lips with his silk handkerchief, fixed his gaze on me again, then turned his head at an angle to indicate he had a question. I saw he had a tiny purple birthmark on his neck in the shape of a leaf. "Do you think you have a clear mind, Dell?"

I didn't understand what that meant. Possibly a clear mind was the opposite of unsteady. I wanted to have one. "Yes, sir," I said. I'd ordered a hamburger and had begun to eat it.

He nodded and moved his tongue around behind his lips, then cleared his throat. "Living out here produces a fantasy of great certainty." He smiled again, but the smile slowly faded as he looked at me. "People do crazy things out of despair when their certainty fades. You're not inclined to do that, I guess. You're not in despair, are you?"

"No, sir." The word made me think of my mother in her jail cell— smiling and helpless. She'd been in despair.

Arthur took a sip of his coffee, holding the cup around its rim—not by its little curved handle—blowing on the surface before he sipped. "That's settled then. Despair's out." He smiled again.

I'd been inside Arthur Remlinger's rooms—seen photographs of him. Seen his books. His chess board. His pistol. He seemed approachable now—a moment when he could be my friend, which was what I'd wanted. I'd never considered asking a person why they were on the earth where they were. It hadn't been a topic in our family, who'd always moved on someone else's authority. But I wanted to know that about him even more than I wanted to know about the pheasants, since he seemed more out of place here than even I was, and since I'd become accommodated in spite of everything. We weren't very much alike, I didn't think.

"Why did you ever come out here if you don't like it?" I asked.

Remlinger sniffed, took his handkerchief out of his collar and pinched his fine nose with it. He cleared his throat the way his sister, Mildred, had. It was their only resemblance. "Well, a better question would be . . ." He turned and looked out the café window beside us onto the street where his Buick was parked beside the policemen's Dodge. MODERN had been lettered in reverse on the inside with gold paint. It had begun to snow. Wind pushed a gale of tiny, swarming flakes up the street like fog, swirling a funnel around the cars and trucks that were passing, their headlights turned on at noon. Arthur seemed to forget what he wanted to say—the better question. He was flicking his gold ring with his thumbnail. His mind had attached itself to some other thought.

He took a package of cigarettes out of his jacket—Export 'A's, the same ones Florence smoked. He lit one and blew smoke against the cold plate glass, where it swam against the snowy background. He was feeling a need to say something, to be personable and to act as if he was interested in me and my question. Though what could've been more unnatural to him? A fifteen-year-old boy who was completely unknown to him. Possibly it seemed good to him I was American. Possibly he saw himself in me, the way Florence said. But what could it have mattered to a man like him?

The way Remlinger smoked his cigarette—holding it between the fingers of his left hand in a V, his eyes averted—made him look older, his skin less smooth. His profile was more angular than when he looked straight at me. His neck with the birthmark was thinner. Some vacancy had taken over for a moment. The corners of his thin lips flickered upward beside the V. "You're the young son of bank robbers and desperadoes," he said and blew smoke onto the glass away from me. "You don't want your life just to be about that, and only that, isn't that right?"

"Yes, sir." Berner had said that no one ever believed her about our parents, and she was going to quit believing it herself.

"You want your *self* to be about other things." He was speaking very precisely again. "*More,* ideally."

"Yes, sir," I said.

He licked his lips and raised his chin as if something had just changed again in his thinking. "Do you ever read biographies?"

"Yes, sir," I said. Though I'd only read the thumbnail ones in the *World Book.* Einstein. Gandhi. Madame Curie. I'd made school reports about them. But he meant real biographies, the thick ones on his book shelf I wasn't supposed to know about. Napoleon. U. S. Grant. Marcus Aurelius. I wanted to read those, and someday felt I would.

"My thought is," Remlinger said, "people who hold a lot inside and have to hold a lot inside should be interested in what great generals do. They always understand what fate's about." He seemed pleased and spoke more confidently. "They know plans work out very, very rarely, and failure's the rule. They know what it is to be unimaginably bored. And they know all about death." He stared at me inquisitively across the table. The space knitted between his eyebrows. He seemed to want this to be the answer to my question about why he was here. He was like my father. They each wanted me to be their audience, to hear the things they needed to express. He wasn't going to answer my question now.

Remlinger took his wallet out of his jacket and laid a paper bill on the table top to pay. The bill was red, nothing like American money. He was suddenly eager to go—to get back in the Buick and drive at great speeds over the prairie, hitting whatever he wanted to hit.

"I don't like America much," he said, standing. "We don't hear a lot about it, up here." Two people at the counter looked around at him, tall and blond and handsome and peculiar. One of the policemen also turned and looked. Remlinger didn't notice. "It's strange to be so close to it," he said. "I think that all the time." He meant to America. "A hundred twenty miles. Does it seem very different to you? Up here?"

"No, sir," I said. "It seems the same." It did.

"Well. That's good then," he said. "You've adapted already. I suppose that's why I'm where I am. I've adapted. Though I'd love to travel abroad someday. To Italy. I love maps. Do you like maps?"

"Yes, sir," I said.

"Well. It's not as if there's a race we have to win, is there?"

"No, sir," I said.

He didn't say more than that. The idea that he would travel abroad seemed strange. As unusual and out of place as he was, he also seemed to belong there. It was still my childish view that people belonged where I found them. We left the café. I was never there again.

55

I CAN'T MAKE WHAT FOLLOWS NEXT SEEM REASON-
able or logical, based on what anyone would believe they knew
about the world. However, as Arthur Remlinger said, I was
the son of bank robbers and desperadoes, which was his way of reminding
me that no matter the evidence of your life, or who you believe you are, or
what you're willing to take credit for or draw your vital strength and pride
from—anything at all can follow anything at all.

IT WAS THE CASE that Charley Quarters soon related to me significant
assertions about Arthur Remlinger—about crimes he'd committed and a
desperate flight from authority, about his tendency to violent moods and
volatile dispositions that served little notice. Charley was dismissive of
him, and felt no loyalty to conceal this information. Remlinger was not a
man who prized loyalties, he said, or respected much in the world. Knowing the truth about such a person could never be a bad thing for what it
might save you from.

It was also the case (I couldn't have formed these words then and
knew them only in some uncreated part of myself) that Arthur Remlinger
looked on me as he did on everyone—from an inner existence that was
only his and bore almost no resemblance to mine. Mine simply wasn't a

fact to him. Whereas his existence was the most immediate and paid for—its primary quality being that it embodied an absence, one he was aware of and badly wanted to fill. (It was obvious from the moment you came near him.) He encountered it over and over, to the point that it was, in his view, the central problem of being himself; and was, in mine, what made him compelling and so inconsistent—this unsuccessful striving to fill an absence. What he wanted (I concluded this later, since he wanted something or I wouldn't have been there) was proof—from me or by me—that he'd succeeded in filling his absence. He wanted confirmation he'd done it and deserved not to be punished more for the grave errors he'd committed. When he ignored me those weeks I was in Partreau, trying not to believe I'd be alone forever, it was because he wasn't sure I'd be dependable to give him what he wanted—not until I'd accommodated myself to my own bad circumstances, put my own tragedies enough behind me to entertain his. He needed me to be his "special son"—though only for a moment, since he knew what bad things were coming to him. He needed me to do what sons do for their fathers: bear witness that they're substantial, that they're not hollow, not ringing absences. That they count for something when little else seems to.

I was only fifteen then, and used to believing what people told me—sometimes more than I believed what was in my heart. If I'd been older, if I'd been seventeen and just that much more experienced, if I'd had more than uncreated ideas about the world, I might've known that the feelings I was experiencing—being drawn to Remlinger, allowing my feelings for my parents to go below the waves of my thinking—that these feelings signified bad things coming to me as well. But I was too young and too far outside the boundaries of the little I knew. I'd felt something like these sensations at the time my parents planned and committed their robbery—when we'd cleaned the house, and Berner and I had waited for them to come back, and later when I'd been ready to get on the train to Seattle and forget about high school. But I didn't connect those feelings to my feelings now, or recognize they meant the same thing. I lacked skills for that kind of connecting. Though why do we ever let ourselves be drawn to people no one else would see as good or wholesome, but only as dangerous and unpredictable? I've thought over and over, in the years since then, how purely unfortunate it was to have become enmeshed with Arthur Remlinger so soon after my parents were put in prison. Still, it's something any person needs to do—to recognize the feeling when something around you isn't good, when there are threats—to remember that you've felt this sensation before, and that it means you're out on some empty expanse all by yourself and you're exposed, and caution needs to be exerted.

WHAT I DID, of course, instead of exhibiting caution, was let myself be "taken up" by Arthur Remlinger, and by Florence La Blanc, as if being taken up by them was the most natural and logical consequence of my mother sending me away after the calamity of her own bad fortune. It went on for only a brief time. But I entered into it thoroughly, as a child can— since, again, part of me was still a child.

5 6

I N THE EARLY DAYS OF OCTOBER, AFTER I WAS SET-
tled into my tiny closet room in the Leonard, I saw a great deal
of Arthur Remlinger—as if I'd suddenly become his favorite
boy, and he couldn't have enough of me. I still performed the duties I'd
been assigned, and enjoyed them. I scouted geese with Charley in the evenings, rose at four and transported the Sports out to the dark wheat fields,
situated the decoys, made loose talk with the shooters, then took up my
position to glass the falling geese.

However, when I wasn't occupied with these duties, Arthur Remlinger
made a claim for my hours. I was happy about it, since I hadn't connected
the feelings I mentioned before and had no caution (or not enough), and
had decided I liked him and found him interesting—a man I felt I could
emulate at a later time. As Florence had said, he was educated, had good
manners, dressed well, was experienced, was an American, and seemed to
like me. And as I said, I'd decided my mother had intended I'd be taken
up by strangers and had approved of it as a way to start my life in a new
direction.

Remlinger instructed me to use his first name and not to call him "sir"
—which was new to me. He took me to the chop-suey restaurant and
taught me to use chopsticks and drink tea. I caught glimpses of the owner's

daughter, but I'd stopped thinking about her or harboring hopes we'd be friends. Other nights I would eat supper in the Leonard dining room with Arthur and Florence. She brought flowers for the table and offered me forward to the other customers as if I was their relation and we had a history together and Arthur was responsible for me. In this sense he did treat me like his son, as if I actually lived in Fort Royal, in the Leonard, and it was an entirely understandable situation that a boy would do that.

On these occasions, Arthur, dressed in one or another of his handsome tweed suits and polished shoes and a bright tie, spoke more about his highly developed skills as an observer, which he believed suited him for many other walks of life than operating a backwater hotel. He said I should enlarge my own capacities so my future would be assured. He awkwardly produced a small paper notebook with blue-lined pages, which he seemed to have intended for me, and instructed me to keep my thoughts and observations in it, but never to show what I wrote to anyone. If I read it back on a regular basis, he said, I could find out how much was transpiring in the world—"a great deal"—when it might've seemed nothing was. In that way, I could appraise and improve the ongoing course of my life. He did this himself, he said.

During this time, he took me on several more driving expeditions—once to Swift Current to pay a debt, another all the way to Medicine Hat to retrieve Florence when her car had broken down. Another time he drove me bouncing out across the prairie back roads to a clay bluff above the Saskatchewan River, where a hand-pull ferry inched across the stream below. With the heater running in the Buick we watched down the river to where thousands of geese were floating and gabbling on the glistening water and had spread out across the curving banks. White gulls circled in the turbulent air above them. Remlinger's blond hair was always barbered and neatly combed and sheened and impressive, his glasses dangled around his neck, and he smelled of bay rum. In the car, he smoked and talked about Harvard and what a perfect existence it had been. (I had only a dim

idea about Harvard and did not even know it was in Boston.) He talked
more about his wish for foreign travel—he was also interested in Ireland
and Germany—and sometimes about the four-thousand-mile border to
America, which he called "the frontier to the States." The frontier, he said,
was not a natural or logical dividing point, and didn't exist in nature, and
should be done away with. Instead it was made to represent erroneous dis-
tinctions preserved for venal interests. He was a vigilant proponent of all
things in life being natural and inherent. He quoted Rousseau—that God
makes all things good, but man had meddled with them and made them
evil. He detested what he called "tyrannical government" and churches
and all political parties—particularly the Democrats, which had been my
father's favorite (and mine) due to his affection for President Roosevelt,
who Remlinger called "the man in the chair," or "the crippled man," and
who, he believed, had seduced the country and betrayed it to the Jews and
the unions. His blue eyes sparkled when he talked on these subjects. They
seemed to make him angry, then angrier. He particularly detested the
labor unions, which he called "the false messiahs." These were the issues
he'd written his articles about in the pamphlets and magazines stored in
the cardboard boxes in my shack: *The Deciding Factor, The Free Thinkers.* I
mostly didn't talk when I was with him, only listened, since he asked little
or nothing about me—my sister's name once, where I'd been born, again
if I planned to attend college, and how I'd accommodated to my new billet.
I didn't talk about my parents or say that my mother was Jewish. I suppose in the States today, he would be called a radical or a Libertarian, and
would be more familiar than he was then on the prairies of Saskatchewan.

However, none of this talking seemed to make him happy, as if talking and talking was also a burden he was bearing. He talked on and on in
his nasal voice with his mouth moving animatedly, his eyes blinking and
primarily turned away from me, as if I wasn't there. Sometimes he was enthusiastic, other times angry—which I felt was his way of accommodating
himself to the absence he contained. All of which is to say I sympathized

with him (in spite of his bad feelings for Jews) and liked the time I spent with him, though I rarely took part or understood much. He was exotic, as exotic as the place where we were. I had never known anyone who was that, just as I'd never been accustomed to think anyone was interesting.

During these days I slept well in my bed and felt optimistic about being in Fort Royal. I had little feeling of belonging and little to take part in outside my duties. But I supplied my own sensation of belonging and normality—because that was (and is) my character. I got my hair cut and paid for it with the Canadian money I made in tips. I bathed in the shared bathtub and could see what I looked like in the mirror when I wanted to. I set up my chess men on the dresser top and plotted strategies I'd employ if Remlinger and I ever played. I felt at home in the Leonard and associated with the Sports and the commercial travelers and the oil riggers who stayed after the harvest crews had passed on. I casually fraternized with one of the Filipino girls whose name was Betty Arcenault. She teased me and laughed and told me I reminded her of her younger brother, who was small like I was. I said that I had a taller sister living in California. (Again, I mentioned nothing about my parents.) She hoped to go to California in the future, she said, which was why she rode out from Swift Current to be a "hostess" in the Leonard each night. She was sallow and thin and had dyed yellow hair and smoked cigarettes and barely smiled because of her teeth. She was one of the girls I'd opened a door on and found sitting on the side of a shadowy bed, with a boy asleep beside her. I never considered doing anything with her myself, never had a clear enough picture of what I would do. My only experience of that sort had been with Berner, and I didn't remember much about it.

I found I didn't think about Partreau anymore. I rode to it every morning with Charley Quarters and cleaned geese on the cleaning log in the brittle cold outside the Quonset, across from my shack. But it was as if I'd never been inside there, never walked along the streets or stood beyond the caragana rows and stared toward what I believed was south

and wondered if I'd see my parents again. Time closes over events if you
don't know much about time. And as I said, time meant little to me there.

DURING THESE DAYS, Florence La Blanc told me she'd been thinking
about a plan for my future. This was at the dining room table, with a white
linen tablecloth and folded napkins and silverware she'd brought from
Medicine Hat and supplied along with the flowers, to create, she said, an
illusion of civilization on the prairie, and because it was Thanksgiving
—my first in Canada. If I was in school, as I should be, she said, I'd have
the day off. Of course, it didn't feel like Thanksgiving to me, since it was
Monday. But Florence had baked a turkey and dressing and had mashed
potatoes and pumpkin pie and brought them in her car, and announced
we had to celebrate our shared holiday together.

There were few diners by then—a salesman and an occasional couple
traveling east. The riggers and the railroaders and the Sports all ate in
the bar. Remlinger sat and stared away at the large painting on the dining
room wall, a tiny bright overhead light pointing down on it. The painting
showed a brown bear wearing a red fez, dancing inside a circle of shouting
men. The men's eyes were wild and excited, their mouths agape and red,
clamoring, their short arms in the air.

Florence told me, her red cheeks bright, that she'd been thinking on
me and my "plight." In her view I should remain in Fort Royal in Arthur's care through the fall. I should learn to groom myself better and
gain strength, and take more frequent haircuts. Then, before Christmas I
should take the bus to Winnipeg and move in with her son Roland, who
had a young wife and whose child had died of polio. She'd already spoken
to him about me, and he was agreeable to it. He would put me into the St.
Paul's Catholic High School, where few questions would be asked because
his wife taught there. If there was a question, she said—smiling at me,
her eyes squinted and shining—they would say I was a refugee whose
American parents had abandoned him and gone to prison, and I'd made

a courageous journey to Canada on my own, and responsible Canadians were now looking after me because I had no other relatives. Canada officials, she said, would never send me back to Montana; and Montana would never be the wiser or care. In any case, she said, it would only be three years until I was eighteen, and these years would pass quickly, and then I could choose a life for myself like any other person. We had that to be thankful for. She never for a moment seemed to consider I would reside with either of my parents again. Though it occurred to me that after three years, if either of my parents were to be released I could find them, and they would certainly want me back. I make this all sound unexceptional now, but it was very strange for my future to be talked about this way and to be in this helpless position in life.

Remlinger shifted his blue eyes to me as Florence carried on with her plan. He was wearing a handsome black jacket and a purple ascot and as always looked exceptional in the midst of the other roomers in his hotel. He blinked at me and smiled. His thin lips tightened, the dent appeared in his chin. He looked back at the painting of the bear and the clamoring men, as if something had been measured in me, a determination made, after which he'd gone back to thinking about the natural order of the universe, and how man ruined everything God had made perfectly. I didn't like being looked at this way. I didn't know what was being measured, or how truthful the measurement could be. This was a part of the sensation I felt, yet had no words for—that something not good was approaching me. I said that I believed Arthur wanted something from me or I wouldn't have been there—more than an audience, or a witness. What he may also have wanted was to transfer a bad feeling onto me, or else to prove, by my existence, that he was in error ever to feel it in the first place.

Florence, however, was happy to go on discussing my future and I was happy to think I would have one. She said I should consider becoming a Canadian, and she would give me a book about it. This would fix everything. Canada was better than America, she said, and everyone knew that—except Americans. Canada had everything America ever had, but no one was mad about it. You could be normal in Canada, and Canada would love to have me. She said Arthur had become a Canadian some years before. (He shook his head, touched his blond hair with his fingers and stayed looking away.) I didn't know this, since Charley had said he was American from Michigan, like me. But it instantly made me feel different about him. Not bad, only different, as if some part of his oddness had lifted off and left him less interesting than when I'd believed he was an American. In a way he seemed less significant. Which may finally be the only real difference between one place on the earth and another: how you think about the people, and the difference it makes to you to think that way.

57

I WROTE A LETTER TO MY SISTER, BERNER, DURING these days. I wrote sitting in my tiny room on my bed, with the square window facing the town, using thin blue paper I'd purchased in the drugstore, and a mechanical pencil I'd found in one of the cardboard boxes in Partreau. I wanted it to be commonplace that Berner and I wrote letters to each other across the great space that separated us, and that where I was at that time wasn't unusual on the grand scale of things.

In my letter I told her that I was in Canada, and even though that might seem a long way away from everything, it wasn't. I had driven to it in a day's time from Great Falls. I told her I was thinking of becoming a Canadian, which would not be a big change. I would soon be going to school in Winnipeg and having a fine new life. I said that people I had met were interesting. (This word looked very strange in my handwriting.) They had given me a job that had real duties and unique aspects—which I liked and had adjusted to well. I was learning things and liked that. I didn't mention our parents, as if I didn't know anything about them, and we could write letters to each other without bringing them in. I also didn't mention Arthur Remlinger or Florence La Blanc because I didn't know how to describe them or their positions in my life. I didn't say I didn't know where Winnipeg was. I didn't mention that Florence had referred to my current life as a "plight." And I didn't mention the strange feelings I had. I was only partially aware of them and thought they would worry her. I told her I loved her and was glad she was happy, and to say hello to Rudy if she saw him in the park. I would come to see her in San Francisco and be her brother again the first time I had the chance and could take the bus from Winnipeg. I signed the letter and folded it up in its blue envelope, made a plan to go to the post office and send it to the address I had in San Francisco. Then I laid the letter on the wooden dresser top, stood and looked out my window onto the town roofs and the earth stretching like an ocean to the horizon. I thought about what a long, long way away Berner was, and how I hadn't written anything of any importance, or personal, or about her. She would have a difficult time knowing about me from what I'd said, which was because my situation was not an easy one to describe and might worry anyone. It was not like being at home and going off to school every day, or taking the train to Seattle. It would be better, I thought, to write from Winnipeg when everything was settled, and I was in St. Paul's School and there would be more to tell that she could take an interest in and be able to understand.

I took the letter and put it in my pillowcase, which I still had from the morning we were all leaving—Berner, our mother, and me. I thought I would read it later, like the comments and observations Remlinger had told me to write in my little blue-lined notebook, so as to know what life had been like when I was living it. I never wrote in that notebook, and when I left Fort Royal I left it behind.

58

CHARLEY QUARTERS TOLD ME THAT THE WHOLE story of Arthur Remlinger would be the strangest one I'd ever hear, but I should hear it because boys my age needed to hear the raw truth (unlike what most people preferred), which would help me set strict limits for myself. Good limits would keep me where I belonged in the world. He'd known the raw truth, he said, but had failed to set his limits well enough. Where he was now, living alone in a debased trailer in Partreau, was because of that. Charley always spoke this way—referring to dark events pertaining to himself that he wouldn't relate in detail, but were understood to be shameful and wretched if a person wanted to be wholesome, which I did. Charley was disreputable and violent and possibly perverted, and I didn't like him, as I've already said. But he had an intelligence. He had boasted to me that he'd tried to be admitted to college but been rejected for being Métis, and for being too smart. I wondered if underneath he hadn't at least at one time been a boy like me, and if possibly some of that good boy survived somewhere—such as in his willingness to instruct me about limits and the raw truth.

We were cleaning geese that had been shot that morning—the big feathered pile of them dumped out on the ground beside the railroad tie we used as our cleaning log, just inside the wide-open, arched door of the

Quonset. Some of the geese were still swimming their feet, some had their bloody beaks open and working, while we employed our hatchets to strike off their heads and other parts before opening them up with knives and gutting them, then pushing them through Charley's homemade plucker machine to remove their feathers. It was the day I went into his trailer for the first and only time.

Inside the trailer, I will say, was not like anything I'd ever seen. In some senses it was like my shack for being cramped and airless and rank smelling. But it also contained the entire accumulation of Charley's life—or as well as I could make out. It was one overheated rectangular room, its windows papered up with cardboard and sealed with masking tape. A black-iron Delmar stove caked with pitch sat in the corner, its chimney pipe cut up through the low ceiling. A filthy blue couch piled with blankets was his bed. There was a terrible jumble of chairs and broken cardboard suitcases, and stacks of dried animal hides Charley was keeping to sell, plus his golfing sticks, a guitar, a small TV that wasn't plugged in, several spilled-open boxes of birdseed the rats had plundered and cans of food heaped in a corner—kernel corn and tinned fish and Co-Op tea and Vienna sausages and tubes of saltines—and dirty plates and utensils, and Charley's cosmetics box and a tiny framed mirror and more of his silver whirligigs, their propellers busted and needing fixing, his kindling box and a table fan, a pickle jar with yellow liquid in it, and a pair of boxing gloves hung on the wall. There was an old refrigerator and a standing chest with its drawers pulled out and veneer scabbing off. On top were the books Charley read. *The Red River Rebellion* was one. *CCF and the Métis* and *The Life of Louis Riel* were two others. There were stacks of loose papers on which were written what I thought were Charley's poems, which I didn't look closely at. There were framed pictures on the wall. Hitler. Stalin. Rocky Marciano. A man walking a tightrope holding a long pole, high above a river. Eleanor Roosevelt. Benito Mussolini with his jaw jutted out, and beside that, Mussolini strung to a lamppost upside down, his shirt fallen off his belly, with his girlfriend strung up beside him. There was a picture of Charley as a boy, bare-chested, bowlegged, set to throw a javelin, and a picture of an elderly woman looking sternly into the camera, then another of Charley in an army uniform wearing a Hitler mustache, with his arm raised in a Nazi salute. I didn't recognize all of these at the time. Though I knew Mussolini because I'd seen old newspaper pictures of him, both alive and dead—things my father had saved from the war.

The stated purpose to my going inside was to bring Charley his curved sharpening stone for his hatchet so he could more easily chop through the goose necks and feet and wings. But I thought he wanted me to see how a life without set limits could look. There was a rotten-egg stink inside, mixed with something sweet and chemical and food related, which were his tanning solvents and also Charley himself—worse inside for being hot and trapped. The smell was almost visible and feel-able—like a wall— even with the trailer's metal door left open and cold wind entering for the two minutes I was inside. I wanted to get away from it. Sometimes I caught a whiff of it on Charley if I came close to him or the air shifted my way. It seemed to come off his greasy clothes and his dyed hair. It was a feature you'd think no one would ever get used to and that I'd steel myself against it. Though it was a feature I did get used to, so that each time I came around Charley, I was aware of myself smelling him, and would keep smelling him, unnoticed, as if there was an attraction to his smell. It ignited in me, and for a while after that, the need to smell the thing I shouldn't, taste the taste I knew would disgust me, open my eyes to things others would avert their gaze from—in other words to forget about limits. These attractions, of course, cease when you get older and have done it enough. But they are part of growing up, like learning a flame will burn you, or that water can be too deep, or that you can fall from a high place and not live to tell about it.

* * *

CHARLEY MAINTAINED a bad opinion about Arthur Remlinger—
though he had always kept it to himself. Nonetheless he told me that
Remlinger was a dangerous, deceptive, ruthless, chaotic, shameless individual who a person like me needed to be cautious and even fearful of
because he was also intelligent and could be flattering and lead a person
to peril, which Charley implied had happened to him, though he as usual
didn't specify how. We were working on the goose carcasses. He took his
eyes off the railroad tie where we were doing the cleaning and looked out
at the empty town of Partreau, as if something had occurred to him about
it. He drew a cloud of cigarette smoke down into his lungs, held it, then
expelled it in a torrent through his large nostrils. "People" were on their
way up here now, he said. "He knows about them. He's trying to plan out
his strategy to save himself." *He* meant Remlinger. I should've noticed
his odder than usual behavior, he said. This is what I needed to be cautious about and not get close to, since his odd behavior could result in dire
events I wouldn't want any part of and would need to set limits against.
It was all ridiculous, he said. But that was how very bad things often
came about in the world. (I already knew, of course, from my own life—
whether I could've said it or not—that the implausible often became as
plausible as the sun coming up.)

When Remlinger was a college boy, Charley said, he'd held unpopu-
lar views—some of the ones I knew about. He detested the government.
He hated political parties. He hated labor unions and the Catholic Church,
and other things. He hadn't been liked by his classmates. He'd written
pamphlets for isolationist, war-opposing (some said), pro-German magazines that made his professors suspicious and wish he'd go back home
to Michigan. His father—when Arthur was young—had been unjustly
fired from his job as a machine operator, and the union had not protected
him due to his Adventist pacifist beliefs. This had created a terrible family crisis and left a stain on young Arthur, which resulted in his adopting
radical ideas while he was still in high school. His family did not share his

views. They'd put their bad luck behind them and moved to a rural setting and begun beet farming. They didn't understand their son—Artie, he was called—good-looking and articulate, intelligent, destined for a successful life as a lawyer or possibly a politician, and who'd gotten into Harvard on his brilliance. (Charley said the word *Harvard* as if he knew it very well and had been there. Remlinger, he said, had told all of this to him years before.)

Each summer Arthur came home from college and was able to find a job in an automobile factory in Detroit, where he would live in a poverty flat while he saved his money to pay his expenses when the school year began again. His family saw little of him during these times, but thought his willingness to work for his college bills was a promising sign for his future.

But during the summer of his third year—it was 1943—when he was working at his good-paying push-broom job at the Chevrolet factory, Arthur fell into an argument with a union steward who oversaw the work and made sure employees were enrolled—including the ones with summer jobs. Heated words were exchanged about Arthur not joining the union. The steward, Arthur said, knew he was the writer of inflammatory antiunion tracts. (The unions paid attention to such things and had ties to Harvard.) The outcome of the dispute was that Arthur was fired and told he should never expect to find work in the city and should move away.

This also brought on another calamity, since losing his job meant Arthur would lack the money to pay his college fees. His family had nothing to give him. He was as good as broke and couldn't pay his rent and was facing the sudden end to his college aspirations. He went to the officials at Harvard and pleaded with them for a scholarship. But because his opinions were known and disapproved of, he was turned away. The doors of Harvard were closed to him, he told Charley, and the remainder of his young life was thrown into turmoil.

An upheaval overtook him at this point. "A mental breakdown,"

Arthur had called it. He became despondent, alienated from his family, would only occasionally talk to his sister, Mildred, who asked him no questions—including how he was supporting himself. In despair, Arthur had begun to find consolation elsewhere and from other people. Those people were in Chicago and upstate New York, and shared his, by now, even more violent antiunion, antichurch, isolationist views. They considered themselves supporters of the right-to-work philosophy and had been involved in confrontations with unions over many decades. Arthur moved himself out of Detroit and went to live with a family in Elmira, New York, and worked on their dairy farm while he regained his mental stability. These farmers were violent people themselves—inspired by hatreds and resentments for wrongs committed against them by unions and by the government. Arthur became more deeply involved in their ideas. And in not very long he was sharing their resentments and their need for vengeance, and became familiar with many dangerous plots and schemes—in particular one to set a bomb in a union hall back in Detroit, a bomb meant to do no one harm, but to emphasize the right-to-work philosophy as being the right one.

Arthur, still in an agitated state of mind about not being allowed to go back to college, let himself be convinced *he* should place the bomb—in a trash can behind the union building. He told Charley he should've been in a mental hospital and would've been if his family could have been in touch with him. His sister was a nurse. Only that hadn't happened.

Instead, Arthur drove from Elmira to Detroit, with the dynamite in the trunk of a borrowed car. He delivered the bomb to its intended location, set a crude clock timer, and drove away. But before the bomb could go off—at ten P.M.—the union's vice president, a Mr. Vincent, returned to the union hall to retrieve his hat, which he'd misplaced. As he was going in by the back door, Arthur's bomb exploded, and Mr. Vincent was terribly burned. And in a week's time he died.

A great manhunt immediately began for the bomber, who no one had seen but who was presumed to be a member of violent groups that did all they could to stifle the unions in America.

Arthur was mortified to learn he had killed someone—which he'd never intended to do—and also terrified he'd be caught and thrown in jail. It was believed the criminal was from Detroit, but no one suspected twenty-three-year-old Arthur Remlinger. His name was known by the police, who supported the unions, but he was never mentioned. By the time the search for the bomber was under way, Arthur was already back on the farm in Elmira—and had if not publicly renounced his views (he never would completely), had come to his senses enough to know he was now a hunted criminal whose life was spoiled.

His choices were either to give himself up and take responsibility for what he'd done, and go to jail; or else, he told Charley, to go as far away as he could imagine going—since he wasn't charged with the crime and wasn't suspected—and try to believe no one would ever find him and that he could outlive his crime with the passage of time.

Charley looked at me beside him to see if I was listening. I had stopped cleaning geese to pay close attention—the story was so shocking to me. Charley put a new cigarette between his lips. The blood in the white of his left eye shifted and seemed to swim and shine. He wasn't wearing lipstick—which he didn't do around the Sports. But his pocked cheeks contained evidence of rouge that had been smudged in the goose pits, and his eyes still had black around them. He was wearing a black welder's apron with blood down the front, and he had blood on his arms and hands, and smelled like geese insides. He would've been a shocking sight to anyone. It had been blowing bits of hard snow all around where we were working in the Quonset door. Flakes were dissolving in Charley's hair, making his black hair dye run. My own hands and cheeks were chafed and stinging. Feathers from our cleaning work had blown into the stiff weeds and around Charley's whirligigs. Mrs. Gedins' white dog had arrived to nose into the gut box and lick its sides. We burned its contents in the oil drum each day, then Charley would scatter the feet and wings and heads for the coyotes and magpies he liked to shoot.

Charley raised his thick eyebrows and his fleshy forehead raveled up. "You can hear him talk like that, can't you? You know? His 'mental breakdown.' 'Mortified.' His 'college aspirations.' Up above everything and everybody?" Charley's lips curled distastefully. " 'Course that's when he come running up here. Nineteen forty-five. Just when the war got over. He thought—or the people who saw after him and still see after him, thought—that here was the most unreachable place on earth. They've found out that isn't exactly right." Charley's big front teeth came uncovered behind his lips. He jigged his cigarette around in his mouth on the tip of his wide tongue, as if this part pleased him. "He has to face his fate now, eh? The other fate was just his first fate. And 'course, he's scared to death." Charley looked down at a stiffening goose body on the railroad tie in front of him. He raised his new-honed hatchet and smacked it on the goose's neck, then swept the head off onto the ground for the dog.

EFFORTS WERE BEGUN by elements among the right-to-work plotters to find a place for Arthur to hide. No one was looking for him. But Arthur thought they eventually would be and couldn't face the chance of being found. The interests also didn't feel he'd hold up well, that he was erratic and a threat, and could bring everyone down. Arthur had admitted he didn't know why someone hadn't killed him right then and buried him on the farm in Elmira. "Which I would've done and not thought about it," Charley said.

Instead, Arthur told him, the owner of the Leonard, a small, devious, turbulent man named Herschel Box, who Charley had worked for as a boy, was approached to hide Arthur away in Saskatchewan. Box was an Austrian immigrant, an older man, who shared the dangerous inclinations of the Elmira and Chicago plotters and had volunteered for many disruptive assignments below the border—a house burning in Spokane where a person had been maimed, a ransacking, a beating. Box agreed to take Remlinger because he had a German name, and because Arthur had attended Harvard and Box considered him intelligent.

Arthur rode the train from Ottawa to Regina in the fall of 1945 and was picked up by Box and driven out to the little shack in Partreau—there were still people living in town, just the way he'd told me—and there he'd begun a new life in Canada.

Arthur had worked the way I worked, riding a bicycle to town, swamping and running errands for the Sports who Box put up in the hotel and charged fees for shooting. However, he didn't go in the goose fields or clean birds or dig pits the way I did. Box believed he wasn't strong enough for rough activity and made him be the room clerk and later the auditor and the night manager, until Box moved away back to Halifax, where he had a daughter and an abandoned wife. Arthur was left the run of the Leonard alone. He told Charley he remitted receipts to Box every week for three years, until Box died and surprisingly willed the Leonard to him, who he'd become fond of, wanted to protect, and had treated like a son. "Not a usual son," Charley said. "Not one I'd want."

Arthur, however, was never satisfied to be where he was—living in Box's cramped rooms overlooking the prairie, with Box's green parrot, Samson, occupying a perch in the sitting room, and completely cut off from any life he'd been familiar with, longing to go back to Harvard, constantly fearing strangers were coming to punish him for his "irreparable act" and his "views." His views were just dreamed up, he said, along with his writings, to make himself stand out to his teachers. He felt he should've been able to outlive all that and go on to be a lawyer. "A man had gotten blown to smithereens over it, of course," Charley said. But that didn't seem to matter.

Charley said Arthur had begun to experience dark angers and to suffer depressions about his life unfairly becoming about only one thing—his short career as a murderer; and that there was more to him than that, but no way to change anything or make it good. He'd matured since those early days, he felt. But his maturity wasn't being allowed to matter. It would've been better, Charley said, if he'd been arrested and taken to jail and paid his price, and could be free now and living in America where he belonged, instead of marooned in a wasted little prairie town where people were suspicious of him and disliked him as an "oddment" (Charley's word, the same as our father's). The townspeople passed rumors back and forth that he was an eccentric millionaire, or a homosexual, or an outcast who disappeared into America to do someone's bidding (which wasn't true); or that foreign interests protected him (which *was*), or that he was a criminal taking refuge from a mysterious crime. ("Rumors all have some basis, okay?" Charley said.) Though, nobody in Fort Royal cared enough to follow through to the truth. Rumor was better. The town had never accepted old Box—because he offered up lewd young Indian girls, and gambling went on, and noisy drinking, and farm husbands went to the hotel secretly and caroused, and strangers came and went in the night. But they tolerated it because they didn't want a fuss, and because a town like Fort Royal liked to ignore what it didn't approve. Once Box left back to the Maritimes, which nobody understood was part of Canada, Charley said ("nobody ever went there"), the town followed suit and tolerated Arthur, who wanted no part of the town to begin with.

Still he felt "ossified," Charley said Arthur told him—a word I didn't know and that made Charley smirk—"vexed and unaccepted" by people he never wanted acceptance from. It made him hate himself and feel desolate and helpless—and fierce regret—that he'd been so young and so panicked back in 1945 as to come all the way out here, and now be completely changed but unable to leave due to the "ossifying" fear of being caught. Going back and facing justice would be too much, Arthur said. He didn't understand how he could do that, the way he didn't understand why he couldn't go back to college—his ticket to propriety his professors had seen their chance to dispossess him of. He was a misfit everywhere and longed to go even farther away. (The "foreign travel" he'd mentioned to me. Italy. Germany. Ireland.) He was almost thirty-nine, though he looked ten years younger with his fine blond hair and unlined skin and clear eyes and good looks. It was as if time had stopped for him, and he'd ceased aging and become only one thing: Arthur Remlinger, in a perpetual present. He told Charley he'd often considered suicide and was a victim of seething night-rages, a chaos-mind that flamed up with no warning (the pheasants he'd bashed through) and that belied his true nature. He'd begun to dress himself up (which he'd never done when he was young), buying dandyish suits from a shop in Boston and having them sent out—giving them to Florence to tailor and mend and launder in Medicine Hat. He sometimes, Charley said—though I'd never observed this—referred to himself as an attorney (as "counselor"), and other times as an important writer. Charley said Arthur influenced everything around him (never positively), but wasn't a person who left an impression. Which is what I realized I had experienced as inconsistency. He knew this, and suffered by knowing it and wished to change everything, but couldn't.

Charley said he himself would've left long ago and never set eyes on Remlinger again, except that the old devil-kraut, Box, had left Arthur aware of some private knowledge about Charley—things from his past that (like Arthur, like my parents and myself) he couldn't stand to have revealed. Charley said he was "indentured" as long as Remlinger wished him to be—as servant, employee, forced confidant, joke butt, factotum and secret antagonist. It had been fifteen years—the same number of years I'd been alive.

"HE'S GETTING HIS HANDS on you now, I can tell," Charley said. He'd gathered up a pile of naked, pucker-skinned geese carcasses and begun carrying them back into the shadowy Quonset. "He has a purpose for you in his survival strategy. Unless I'm wrong. And I'm not wrong."

His freezer box sat among his stretched, drying animal skins and cans of salts and piles of decoys to be repaired, and his motorcycle and digging implements, and where it smelled like the solvents and tanning chemicals.

"I don't admire him," I said, bringing the geese I'd cleaned and feathered-out myself, to drop in the freezer with his. Though I had almost admired him.

"A person who wants his well-deserved punishment to be over with is a desperate man," Charley said, his wide back to me, so I could see the shine of his barrette in the shadows. "You don't know that," he said gruffly. "You know less than anything."

It was densely cold where we were in Charley's Quonset, everything stiff and painful to touch. "What should I know?" I asked. "What use would he have for me?"

Charley Quarters turned, his arms full of gray featherless geese bodies, and smiled the heartless way he had the first night we'd been in the truck on the dark road north of Maple Creek, when he'd grabbed my hand and squeezed it, and I wanted to jump out and run away. "I told you. Men are coming up here right now. He understands his situation. He understands himself better than I understand him. But he's weak. I don't blame him." Charley pushed up the heavy freeze-box lid with his elbow. Down inside were whitely frozen geese, hard as ingots. He dropped his armload, thumping on top of the others, and stepped back. I did the same and turned quickly toward the lighted Quonset door. I didn't like being alone and close to him. I didn't know what he might suddenly do.

THE MEN—two of them, Charley said, as he drove me back into Fort Royal in the truck—were from Detroit, in America, the scene of Remlinger's crime, fifteen years previous. Arthur had informed him about them late in the summer, when the interests that were in touch told him to prepare himself. (They still considered him erratic, Arthur admitted.) The police case had long ago been given up. But there were people who stayed aware of it and kept their eyes and ears open. And unexpectedly

Arthur Remlinger's name had become audible. "A fluke, pure and simple," Arthur said. There was no suspicion to link him to the crime or to think he might be a person to officially talk to. It would need to be a private matter. The murdered man's family and the union associates had all gotten old and had never believed Arthur was capable of murder in the first place. But when it was found out where he was—a tiny, faraway Saskatchewan town, living alone and unexplained in a hotel—and that he'd had associations with the old dead Herschel Box, a name known in their circles, then things were put together with other things known about him (the row with the union steward years before, the pamphlets, being a troublemaker at Harvard), and it began to seem plausible this Remlinger, an American who'd oddly become Canadian, might be a person to go see in the flesh. If someone could see him when he didn't know he was being seen—enter his life unnoticed—then his likelihood to be a criminal could be judged. After which—assuming he was considered guilty, or at least an accomplice—discussions could begin over what to do about him. "He must've thought I lived and breathed his fucked-up life," Charley said, driving.

Arthur said it was felt he had nothing to feel concerned about—two men sent to *look* at him. He should do nothing outside the ordinary—run away or admit anything, or act in an incriminating manner that would give these men reason to suspect he *did* blow up the union hall. (Which he *had* done, Charley said, "because nobody would make that up.")

It was thought that the two men who were on their way—driving across the middle west in a black Chrysler New Yorker, turning north and across the border to Canada—were without much dedication to their mission. Their names were known. Crosley—the young son-in-law of the murdered Vincent; and an older, retired officer, Jepps—not a family member but brought along to maintain sound sense. These two had little thought Remlinger was the man they were looking for. They were making the trip all the way to Saskatchewan as much as an adventure as a manhunt. They might do some goose shooting if it could be arranged and all else failed. Neither had they given much practical consideration to what they might do if Arthur Remlinger turned out to be the criminal, and they were faced with him—in a foreign country where they knew nothing but the language, and were forced to do *something:* demand he come back to Detroit (and do what?); go all the way back themselves and convince the police to be interested again (on what evidence?); kidnap Arthur, a full Canadian citizen, and transport him across an international border. (How, and then do what with him? Shoot him? They had pistols; this was known—which became their fatal mistake.) These were average, uncomplicated working men—more like the Sports who congregated in the bar at night than men driven by justice or vengeance. Likely, Remlinger was told, they were already thinking about arriving at the Leonard, seeing nothing was out of the ordinary about him (even though there was), and turning the Chrysler back toward Detroit. Two thousand miles.

The problem was, Charley said—which was why I needed to be careful and would be an idiot not to be—Arthur had turned bitter and moody and sinister feeling and even more chaos-minded at the idea of strangers showing up and knowing who he was and what he'd done, and having the intention to haul him back across the border to face everything he'd failed at. His father was still alive. His future was squandered. His past bad judgments were waiting. Arthur did not possess a calm state of mind, Charley said. He lacked the mental ability not to incriminate himself. Incrimination had become his whole life. These were the changes to his behavior that should've been apparent to me, but weren't.

He'd been up here all the years, Charley said, expecting someone to come and find him—suffering and waiting. A life lived in a wind-deviled, empty-vista'd town—alienated, remote, family-less; only Box, then Charley, then Florence, as companions. And now me. How had he been able to stay? I wondered this later on. The towering weather, the endless calendar, the featureless days, the unfamiliar made permanent. Impossible, any person would think. It was the "better question" Remlinger hadn't answered when we were in the Modern Café. He'd adapted, as he told me.

But it had turned him the way he was. Eccentric. Impatient. Regretful. Slightly deranged. Violent with frustration. Living a fragment of a life he couldn't give up. (He *would've* given it up if he'd had the nerve or the imagination to travel to an even more foreign place where he could again hide.) Charley, by way of dismissing him, said Arthur still saw himself as the smart, naive young student who'd never meant to kill anybody, and who'd suffered because he had—by accident and stupidity— but who wanted his punishment to be over, since his punishment had become his life.

"*You*," Charley said. We were passing the Fort Royal town limits sign, the low buildings, plus the Leonard—an enlarging dot on the prairie—the dusty main street uncongested now that the cold had started (pickup trucks left idling at the curb, the flags at the post office and the bank rattling in the wind, bundled Fort Royal residents keeping nearer the sides of buildings than the street). "*You* can't blab any of this. Not to A.R. And not to Flo. I'll skin you out raw." What he'd told me (he said again) was a warning so I would set my limits and "protect" myself from what happened if "certain events" worked out different from how they were supposed to. Charley had obviously given thought to these events but didn't describe them, so I didn't try to imagine them.

What I *was* thinking though, as we drove down Main Street, was about the two Americans on their way out from Detroit. My father said that in Detroit everyone had a good-paying job and security. It was the American melting pot. The power center. Coat of many colors. It draws the whole world to itself, he said. "Detroit makes, the world takes." Etc. These men driving out were from there and were coming to find out true things and champion them. I had never been in Detroit, but I had an interest in it from being born in Oscoda, not so far north of there. A person can have these views and ideas, but have no real experience with them whatsoever.

"Why would I be involved?" I said. I'd become bolder by then and had gotten over being shocked. We were pulling to a stop at the Leonard's small front door, over which LOBBY was painted in black. Wind buffeted the truck windows. I stared at Charley's peculiar, knobby, still-rouged profile. A dwarf's face, but a larger, strenuous body.

"If you're lucky, you won't be," he said. His big meaty lips made a hard pooched-out shape, like a kiss, that meant he was thinking. "If you were smart, you'd take the money you've been hoarding and get on the bus. Get off someplace near the border and slip across and never let yourself be seen again. If you stay here, you're just a point of reference for him, part of his strategy. He doesn't care a nickel what happens to you. He's just trying to prove something."

"They'd catch me and send me back to the juvenile home," I said.

"I'd have done better in the home," Charley said. "You always think you know the worst thing. But it's never the very worst thing."

He meant I'd do better to go back to Great Falls, walk into the police station and admit I was the missing Dell Parsons, and let it all focus down on me: be put in a locked room with bars for windows, staring through at a frozen landscape waiting for nothing to happen until I was eighteen. That had seemed like the worst to my mother. It still seemed the worst to me. I didn't have an answer back to Charley. I almost never did. He only knew about himself. But I knew, for me, what was worst—no matter what happened with Arthur Remlinger. And no matter what happened to me as a point of reference, which I understood to mean that I would just be part of a whim, and be forgotten when it was over.

Charley didn't want me to say anything else. He didn't listen to me more than he had to. I climbed out of his old truck onto the gritty, windy Fort Royal street and closed his door. "Most losers are self-made men," he said as it shut. "Don't forget that." I didn't say anything. He drove away, then, leaving me there to my future.

59

I WAS IN THE LITTLE LOBBY OF THE LEONARD—THE same afternoon Charley had told me about Remlinger earlier in the morning—when the two Americans arrived. The Leonard didn't have a legitimate lobby—just a square, dim entry room at the bottom of the center stairs, where a front desk was set up with a bell and a lamp and a row of key hooks on the wall. I'd eaten lunch and was on my way to go to sleep. I'd been up at four and would have to scout geese in the evening. Charley had made me think the Americans would be arriving soon, and I had it in mind to see them, had pictured what they'd look like, and had tried to pass through the lobby as often as possible. But I hadn't thought they'd be arriving that day.

They were registering in with Mrs. Gedins, who'd been doing her kitchen duties and heard the bell. She barely spoke to the men. Though when each of them pronounced his name—Raymond Jepps, Louis Crosley—she looked up from the registry book, her swimming Swedish eyes stern and distrusting, as if there was something untruthful about Americans and no one could fool her.

They each had a leather suitcase. And since I was sometimes required to take the Sports' luggage to their rooms, for which I'd be given a quarter, I stood by the wall with the picture of Queen Elizabeth on it and waited.

Mrs. Gedins told them the two of them would be sleeping in the Overflow House (my shack), because the hotel was full. (It wasn't.) She'd arrange for Charley to take them when they were ready. This was the first indication that what Charley had told me was correct: that the two men had come from the States, that they'd been identified and were expected. I'd halfway believed the story was untrue—something Charley had cooked up for his own fantastical reasons to frighten me. But the two Americans announced names they'd been predicted to have—Jepps and Crosley. They said they were from "The motor city"—in the States. They were in good spirits and made no effort to disguise who they were. They seemed to have no idea anyone would recognize them or know why they were in Fort Royal. It's possible even Mrs. Gedins knew who they were, so that everyone knew, except the Americans themselves.

"We're going out to the west coast of Canada," Jepps, the older one, the former policeman, said with a smile. He was red-faced and wore a toupee made of some slick black hair material that sat up on his round head and looked not the least natural. It imparted an air of foolishness to him, because he was short and round and wore his trousers pulled up over his belly, and had on brown wing-tip shoes that looked as big as a clown's. He didn't say what they intended to do on the west coast of Canada. Crosley was younger and well groomed, with precise, sharpened features and short, black, barbered hair. He smiled a lot also; but his eyes were alert to here and there, and he was darker complexioned. He wore a gold ring on his little finger that he twisted at nervously, as if he was putting on being jovial. Later, when Jepps had been shot and was dead on the floor of my shack and I was terrified but nonetheless involved in moving him, I had to pick up his toupee, which was an awful thing to do. (It had come loose from his head when he was shot.) I hadn't seen a toupee before, but recognized it. I was surprised at how flimsy it was, and small. It ended up in the burn drum, with the goose entrails and feathers.

Crosley asked Mrs. Gedins if there was food they could eat; they hadn't eaten since breakfast, in Estavan. Mrs. Gedins frowned and said lunch (which she called "dinner") was finished long ago (it was almost three) but the Chinaman would fix them something down the street. I could show them where it was—which alerted them to my presence. They said Fort Royal wasn't such a big place ("burg," Jepps called it in a nasal voice that was like Remlinger's). They could find the only Chinese "eatery" in town. In Detroit there was a whole Chinaman town, they said. They often went there with their wives. They were eager to compare Canadian Chinese to their Michigan variety.

They asked to leave their suitcases in the lobby and wondered to Mrs. Gedins if there was any goose shooting to be done. On their drive up they said they'd seen thousands of geese in the air and occasionally one had fallen out of the sky, obviously shot dead from the ground. They had their shotguns, Crosley said, but seemed tentative about that. Possibly they might arrange for some shooting in the next two days. They wanted to see the sights, take the rides—as if visitors came to Fort Royal, Saskatchewan, in the blustery cold of early October to enjoy its attractions. This wasn't a believable thing to say and made them seem even more to be who Charley said they were.

Mrs. Gedins told them they would need to talk to "Mr. Remlinger," who owned the hotel and did the organizing for the shooting. He would be available in the dining room and in the bar tonight. There were other hunters in the hotel, she said. There would probably not be places unless someone woke up drunk or sick.

Standing behind them in the shadowy lobby I was alert to their reactions to Mrs. Gedins speaking "Mr. Remlinger's" name. It was Mr. Remlinger they'd traveled two thousand miles to observe—to conclude if he was a murderer and decide what they should do about it if he was. By what means they'd conclude this, I couldn't fathom, since Remlinger, as Charley said, would never admit to the act, and almost no one still alive knew about it. I'd already wondered that day: what would a murderer look like? Once you committed one—no matter if you intended to or didn't—did you forever have the act written on your face? Did Jepps and Crosley assume it would be simple to detect? And did you have "murderer" written on your face *before* you committed the crime? I'd seen pictures of murderers—again, in old movie-house newsreels. My father was fascinated by them and their adventures. Alvin Karpis and Pretty Boy Floyd and Clyde Barrow himself, and John Dillinger. They'd all looked like murderers to me. Though they'd already committed their murders by then, so there was no doubt. Plus, they were dead. Shot to death, many of them, and laid out for their pictures. My parents, I'd decided, could've been recognizable as bank robbers long before my father entered a bank and robbed it. My sister and I would've been the only ones not to know it.

But the sound of Remlinger's name, uttered in the quiet of the overheated Leonard lobby, excited no change in either Jepps' or Crosley's facial expressions. As if that name meant nothing. "Possibly," Jepps said—his fat thumbs hiked his trousers up over his belly lump—"you could ask this Mr. Remlinger to speak to my friend and me. We'd like to shoot some geese if it can be arranged. We'll come in the bar tonight. Tell him just to introduce himself. We're friendly Americans." They both laughed at this—though Mrs. Gedins didn't.

The Americans walked off together down the windy little main street to find the Chinaman's. But I hurried around to the back of the Leonard to see if a black Chrysler New Yorker was there, bearing a Michigan license plate. If they had asked me to have a meal with them, I would've gone for sure, though I'd already eaten. It seemed adventurous to get to be near them and know who they were, but for them to have no idea I knew. As if *I* was the one disguised. This excited me. I could've found out things about them, their plans, for instance—although I'd been forbidden to speak about this and didn't, in fact, know what I'd be able to say or to whom. Anyone can see how a fifteen-year-old boy would be attracted to such possibilities.

The two Americans, however, barely noticed me and walked straightaway down the street toward the red WU-LU sign. I stepped outside to watch
them. Jepps put his short arm around the shoulder of the younger man
and immediately began talking seriously. "This is the way we want it," I
thought I heard Jepps say, his nasal voice catching up in the cold breeze.
"Okay, I know. I know," Crosley said. "But. . . ." I didn't hear the rest,
though I thought I knew what they were talking about. And I was right.

WHEN I GOT AROUND to the dirt yard behind the Leonard, the hunters'
cars and the cars of the other guests were there, with Remlinger's big maroon Buick parked and cold. Wind and tiny snow flakes were being pushed
through the air. The CP yard was fifty yards across a long vacant lot. A
switcher was nosing a single red boxcar along an empty rail, switchmen
hurrying in the cold with their lanterns, throwing switches and hopping
on the car as it passed. There was a job I would do, I thought, since I liked
working, and if school never began for me again, and if I didn't go to Winnipeg, as Florence wanted me to. Plans didn't always work out, as Arthur
Remlinger had said. I was finding this was true.

At the end of the row of parked cars sat the black New Yorker—a
two-door, dirty with road grit, and with its green-and-yellow Michigan
license plate. "Water Wonderland." I envisioned green-carpeted forests
with expansive lakes on which someone—myself—could paddle a canoe.
A thing I'd never done. I'd imagined there would be a boating club in the
Great Falls high school, and a chance for me to paddle out onto the Missouri. I put my hand onto the Chrysler's hood and it was warm, although
cold was filtering down into it. This car came from America, from the
place it had been made. It represented whatever my father (and I) associated with America. The melting pot. The world drawn closer. I advocated
these values. My parents had instilled them in me and my sister. It made me
feel again that Jepps and Crosley, and their mission in coming to Canada,
were upstanding and right—though I didn't want it to succeed and for

Arthur Remlinger to go back to America to jail. I've already said it's a mystery why we affiliate ourselves with the people we do, when all the signs say we shouldn't.

Yet, standing in the car lot, I experienced a great confusion. I might have been near the point of a breakdown of my own. My temples tightened and ached, and my chin and nose got numb (possibly with the cold). My hands tingled. My feet seemed unwilling to move. As odd as he was, and in spite of what I knew about him, Arthur Remlinger didn't seem like a man who'd transport a bomb and set it off and kill someone. He seemed the last person to do that. Again, Charley Quarters could more easily have done it. Or the murderers in the old newsreels. In my view, Arthur Remlinger didn't have "murderer" written on his face.

What he had on his face was "eccentric," "lonely," "frustrated"; and also "smart," "observant," "worldly," "well dressed." All things I admired (though I'd denied admiring it). So that what I decided—which was why I was able to move, and feeling came back in my face, and my hands quit smarting—was that Arthur Remlinger was *not* a murderer. Possibly these two Americans, in spite of their names and their car and being from De-troit, were not who Charley said they were. This was my habit of mind. My mother had written in her chronicle that to me the opposite of everything obvious deserved full consideration. The opposite could turn out to be the truth. Given my recent personal experiences with the truth, it might've seemed obvious that sooner or later everybody committed crimes, no mat-ter how unlikely a person was. But I wasn't ready to believe it. I didn't know where I would fit into the world if that was true—since I didn't want to commit crimes, myself, and fitting in was the thing I wanted to do most. So I tried hard to believe that Arthur Remlinger was innocent of what he was supposed to have done—since in all ways it seemed better to think that.

6 0

I PERFORMED MY STANDARD DUTIES THAT DAY. I TOOK a shorter nap because I'd lingered in the lobby, then gone out to inspect the Americans' car. The days now held less light, and Charley and I went out nearer to five to drive the fields above the river and find where the geese were using, and instruct the Ukrainian boys to site the pits. These farm boys—two of them, brawny and large limbed—were brothers and kin by marriage to Mrs. Gedins' deceased husband and were silent and unsmiling, as she was. They said nothing to me when Charley told them where to go and dig. They looked at me contemptuously, as if I was a privileged American boy who had no business even knowing them. I thought I wasn't privileged at all, except that I had the strange privilege of having no real place and purchase on things and could leave, whereas they believed they couldn't.

Arthur Remlinger put in no appearance during the day. Typically I would see him pass around through the hotel. Occasionally, as I said, he would grab me and put me in the Buick on some made-up proposition, and we'd drive off down the highway to Swift Current or toward the west, while he talked on animatedly about his subjects. None of this happened. And in spite of what I'd "decided" using reverse-thinking while standing in the cold behind the hotel (that he wasn't a murderer, etc.), I believed his absence was related to the Americans' presence. I suppose I knew my reverse-thinking about the Americans was wrong.

Charley Quarters, I knew, had led the Americans out to the Overflow House. Their suitcases were gone when I came downstairs, and their car was no longer in the parking yard. I thought Charley would make some remark to the effect that he'd been right in all he'd told me. But he had become tight-lipped and irritable, and didn't say even the belittling things he routinely said—that I knew nothing; that I was feeble; that life was too difficult for me there; that I never would go to school again. The little he did talk in the truck that day had only to do with knowing about geese and shooting—the things he'd already said to me: that geese fly high with the wind but will sometimes fly under it; that they are smarter than ducks, though it wasn't truly smartness but having good instincts; that Specklebelly geese liked the wheat but snow geese didn't; that a goose could fly a hundred miles in a night; and that you really didn't need decoys—a "fat farm girl in a black dress" would do as well if seen from the air. I had the feeling that when Charley rehearsed these things, what he was saying had nothing to do with me, but was taking his mind off something he didn't like to think about. I thought that had to do with the two Americans.

I ATE DINNER as usual in the kitchen, then came out into the bar at seven to mingle with the Sports the way Charley had told me to and to listen to the jukebox and talk to the bartender, and to Betty Arcenault about California, where Berner was, and listen to her stories about her boyfriend who she said treated her cruelly. The Sports were drinking and laughing and telling stories and smoking cigars and cigarettes. Two of the groups were from Toronto, and one was Americans from Georgia. These men had accents like my father's when he "talked Dixie." The two Americans from Detroit were in the bar by then, seated at a table to the side of the room under the large oil painting of two bull moose locked in combat, their antlers tangled in a way they'd never escape. *Their Fight to the Death,* this

painting was called. Above it was a black-and-white sign that said GOD
SAVE THE QUEEN, which people had written profanities on. The painting
was a favorite of mine—more than the dancing bear in the dining room.
Once, years on, I saw this very painting, or one exactly like it, on a wall
in the Macdonald Hotel in Edmonton, Alberta, and sat marveling at its
mystery for hours.

The two Americans stood out in the smoky roomful of hunters and
railroaders and detail men. They each drank one beer apiece, which they
sat beside the whole time they were there. They had on clean shirts and
nice trousers and regular brogan tie shoes, whereas the Sports all wore
their hunting clothes, as if they were planning to go straight from the bar
to the goose pits. The Americans also seemed ill at ease, as if the younger
Crosley's nervousness had overtaken the older man. They talked only to
each other and frequently looked around the room—at the tin ceiling,
across to the lobby door, toward the kitchen, and at the closed door to the
gambling den. Arthur Remlinger was who they were waiting for. They'd
said for him to find them to talk about goose shooting. But he hadn't
appeared—which signaled something important: possibly that Remlinger
wouldn't allow himself to be observed and had run off—which would've
meant he was who they were looking for.

I stayed near the jukebox, watching, expecting Remlinger to stride in
and begin circulating the way he did, joking and buying drinks around
and promising everyone good shooting—behavior that never seemed
natural to him. Florence's car hadn't been in the parking lot. I assumed
she was away looking after her mother and managing her shop. Though
conceivably Arthur didn't want her there where the Americans were.

I, of course, didn't know what the Americans had planned once they
laid eyes on Remlinger and had to make their conclusion. Possibly they
would see him and—I'd wanted to believe—realize he was the wrong man
to set off a bomb and kill someone. In which case they could drive back
satisfied and forget about it all. Though if they decided he *was* the mur-

derer, then what would be their plan of action? It excited me to be in the noisy bar, where the Americans' brains were teeming, and to know who they were when they had no idea I or anyone else knew, and to have that advantage over them. But there was also going to be an outcome to these events. Charley hadn't said that, but it was clear he thought so, and that the outcome might turn out to be bad.

I experienced a second strong urge to talk to the men—although it wasn't my nature to do such a thing. It was as if I wanted to move close to something risky and dramatic. I wanted to tell them I'd been born in Oscoda, which might mean something to them. Whatever I'd felt when I'd stood beside their car and touched the warm metal—the sensation of satisfying solidity, even of liking the men (who I didn't know), of sharing something secret with them—all that, I wanted to feel again and believed I could at no threat to anyone. I would never tell them what Charley had told me. And I still thought they might accidentally reveal something important about their mission—what they thought about Remlinger, what they hoped to do depending on what their observations of him made them think.

But just at that moment, before I could bring up my nerve to speak to the Americans, Arthur came into the bar through the lobby door, and the two Americans seemed instantly to know who he was—as if they had a picture of him in their heads, and he looked exactly like they knew he would.

The red-cheeked, round-faced toupee man—the former policeman— immediately said something to the younger Crosley, and nodded and looked at Remlinger, who was talking noisily to a table full of Sports. Crosley turned and looked and seemed suddenly very serious. He nodded and turned back and put his hands around his beer bottle, and said something brief. Then the two of them sat facing each other in the coarse bar light, under the clashing-moose painting, and didn't speak.

Remlinger had on the brown felt fedora he often wore, and one of his expensive Boston tweed suits that made him look strange in the bar. His reading glasses were hung around his neck. He was wearing a bright red tie, and his tweed trousers were pushed down in the tops of his leather boots. I didn't know this at the time, but later I understood he was dressed like an English duke or a baron who'd been out walking his estate and come in for a whiskey. It was the kind of disguise to prevent the people he'd been expecting for fifteen years from recognizing him—even though he hadn't changed his name, and anyone could know him who wanted to. Possibly he wasn't even hiding, only distracting himself while he waited for this day to come.

Crosley watched Remlinger as he worked his way through the bar. Jepps didn't turn to see, only sat and stared across at Crosley, as if he'd begun calculating something. As if he'd become a policeman again—friendly at first, then unfriendly. I wondered if they were carrying their pistols, since Charley said they owned them.

Remlinger saw me by the jukebox. "Well. There's Mr. Dell now," he said, and smiled and waved a hand indifferently. In a moment, he would come to the two Americans' table. I wanted to be there to observe that. I wanted to know what would happen when the three of them met, with Arthur Remlinger knowing exactly who they were, but they not knowing he knew, and the Americans needing to decide if he was a murderer. Anybody would've wanted to see that. It possessed the possibility for danger—if they all three had their pistols and had decided this could go no further.

I saw Remlinger's eye fall on the two men and stay on them a moment, after which he went back talking to the table of Sports from Toronto. One of these men put his hand beside his mouth to say something, as if he was telling a secret. Remlinger looked at me quickly, then leaned toward the man, who whispered something more that made them both laugh. Remlinger looked at me a third time as if they were discussing me—which I didn't think they were. Then Remlinger turned toward the two Americans and moved in their direction.

The nervous one, Crosley, got immediately up on his feet, wiped a hand against his trouser side, smiled broadly, and extended that hand toward Remlinger, as if he was relieved for this moment to finally take place. I heard Arthur say his own name as he shook hands. I heard "Crosley" spoken. The older man, Jepps, got up and shook hands with Arthur and said his name and something else that caused them both to laugh. I heard Jepps say "British Columbia," and "Michigan." Then Arthur said "Michigan," and they all laughed. Arthur was like an actor playing the part of the last person you'd suspect to detonate dynamite and be a murderer. In most ways I don't believe things like this are true, but his entire life in Canada must've been a rehearsal for this moment. If he was successful—as he thought he should be, since he believed he'd suffered enough—then all would be fine and life would go on. If he wasn't, and he was identified as a murderer and had to face even the thought of going back to Michigan, then no one knew what would happen, but we would find out.

I couldn't hear what else the three of them said. The two Americans sat down. Arthur pulled a chair to their table and sawed at his trouser legs and sat straddling the chair in an unnatural way but did not take his hat off. I was sleepy from being up most of the day, and from feeling apprehensive about the Americans. But I stayed where I stood. Remlinger sat and talked animatedly to the two of them for fifteen minutes. He ordered them beers, which they didn't drink. He looked toward and past me several times as he talked. The Americans smiled a lot about whatever they were saying. At some point Remlinger—in a manner that wasn't like him—said, while laughing, "Oh, yes, yes, yes. Yeeees! You're right there." They all three nodded. Then Remlinger sat up straight and extended his arm and seemed to stretch his back and said, "We'll get this all set for you men tomorrow." Which I believed referred to goose shooting and nothing to do with recognizing him as a murderer. I felt the Americans may have individually arrived at the conclusion that he was not the man they were seeking. Or, if he was, that he'd become so unrecognizable he should be left out on the empty prairie at peace. (I've already said I was experiencing great confusion about what was happening, having had no experience like this in my life. I should not be faulted for not understanding what I saw.)

THESE LAST THOUGHTS comforted me when I climbed the stairs to my room under the eaves and locked the door and got in my cold bed with the red Leonard sign tinting the air. My shack in Partreau had had no locks, and I was happy to have them, with people roaming the halls at night. I thought everything would be fine now. Arthur had seemed relieved to meet the two Americans. He'd been hospitable, as if the Americans were not who they were, but were the goose hunters they pretended to be, and would leave for British Columbia once they'd had their morning of shooting Charley and I would provide. I understood why Charley had said Remlinger was "deceptive." He'd deceived the Americans by not acknowledging who they were. But I'd already concluded being deceptive was necessary in the world. Even if everybody didn't commit crimes, everybody committed deceptions. I'd been deceptive when I failed to alert the Americans I knew who they were. I'd hidden the money from the police. I'd committed a deception about my identity from the moment I crossed the border and sat in Mildred's car and said nothing. The person I was now was not the person I would've been in Great Falls—even though my name was the same. It was unclear if I would ever be that previous boy again, but would just go on deceiving all my life, since I felt I would soon go to Winnipeg and start a whole different and better life there, with everything including the truth left behind.

As I drifted to sleep, I tried to picture a young, tall, blond, awkward Arthur Remlinger putting a bomb in a garbage can, in some place I imagined to look like Detroit. But I couldn't make the thought stay in my mind, which was my way of detecting if something was important. (I couldn't imagine, for instance, what a bomb looked like.) I tried to think of a conversation between the Americans and myself. I pictured us walking down the main street of Fort Royal, not in the cold, batting wind of October, but on a sunny, blue-sky day in late August—the way it was when I arrived. Jepps had his large hand on my shoulder. They both wanted to know was I related to Arthur Remlinger; was I an American; why was I all the way in Canada, and not in school where I belonged; where were my parents; what was this Remlinger about; was he married; did I know his background; did he own a pistol.

In my last wakeful minutes, I didn't think I knew the answers to these questions—except for the pistol—and didn't worry about them. And, as often happened to me, I was asleep but didn't believe I was asleep for quite a while. Though late at night I suddenly "woke up" and heard cows in the abattoir pen, groaning and waiting for morning, and a truck growling and downshifting at the traffic light in front of the hotel. All things seemed as they should be. I went back to sleep for the few hours I still had.

61

T HE NEXT DAY, FRIDAY, THE FOURTEENTH OF OC-
tober, will never seem like anything but the most extraordinary day of my life—for the reason of how it ended.
Much of it, however, happened the way other days happened in that period
of time. All morning, I thought about the Americans out in the Overflow
House, and later of them being in Fort Royal, wandering through the cold
day during which it snowed, then rained, then snowed again. The wind
slapped against the hanging traffic light and ice crusted the curbs and citizens stayed indoors if they could. I had no idea what the Americans would
be doing, or what would take place. In the red-smudged light of early
morning I completely gave up on my reverse-thinking—that they were
not who they were, or that Remlinger was not who he was (a murderer),
or that the Americans would give up their mission to identify him as the
fugitive, and then act on that. I didn't know whether, in one fifteen-minute
encounter in a crowded smoky bar, they could make the determination
they wanted (see if "murderer" was written on Remlinger's face, or if it
wasn't); and then decide what they should do. I remembered Charley saying the Americans didn't expect Remlinger to be who they were looking
for. So, likely they didn't specifically know *what* they should do if they
believed he was guilty. They might've been trying to decide at that very

moment. Charley had implied—at least I'd thought he had—they might decide to kill him and had brought pistols for that; or abduct him back to face a Michigan judge. But that didn't seem to fit with their natures and the goodwill the three of them had shared in the bar. None of this made a clear picture, though I thought about it constantly during that day. The thought set a continuous whirring going in my stomach and up under my ribs, which let me know it was significant, and I should pay attention.

Charley and I took out our groups of Sports to the wheat fields before dawn. I sat in the truck and counted the falling geese from the three decoy sets. Charley visited the pit rows and did his calling, although the low sky and snow and wind made the geese come low off the river and distinguish the decoys less sharply, and many were shot. Charley and I stood as always and cleaned dead geese in the Quonset. I noticed the Americans' black Chrysler was not parked at the shack. Which indicated to me that they might've left and driven away.

Charley, however, told me that Remlinger had said we would take the Americans to the pits the next morning and should put them in good places. One of the Toronto groups had left, and there was room now. They'd brought their guns and shooting paraphernalia and wanted to go. I didn't ask any details about the Americans: what Charley thought about them on the basis of taking them to the Overflow House; or what Remlinger might've revealed when he instructed Charley about the shooting. Charley was in a morose humor and made several strange remarks in answer to statements I made while we cleaned and gutted geese. One of his remarks was, "A lot of brave men have head wounds." Another was, "It's hard to go through life without killing someone." As I've said, he was often in a bad humor for reasons he didn't divulge, except to complain about his terrible childhood and his bowel problems. It was best not to provoke him, since I wanted to keep my own view and opinion of things, and his bad humor and odd pronouncements could overpower everything I thought. All I believed, from what little he said, was that if we took the Americans shooting the next morning—like they were any two Sports—shooting geese was not all that would happen. There would be other things, because the Americans were not just Sports. They were men with other intentions.

ONCE AGAIN, I failed to see Arthur Remlinger during the middle of the day, which was noticeable under the circumstances. I saw the two Americans eating lunch alone in the dining room, where the other Sports were congregated talking about their morning's shooting. I ran one errand to the drugstore to get a bottle of Merthiolate and another to the post office to purchase stamps for postcards to reach America. The two Americans engaged in an intense conversation and took no notice of me or anyone. It felt ridiculous that they would be passing the day talking, in full view, when so much was known about them—their intentions; that a man had been killed; that Remlinger was aware of them and was possibly in his rooms imagining what he would do about them; that they had pistols and were possibly expecting to use them. The prelude to very bad things can be ridiculous, the way Charley said, but can also be casual and unremarkable. Which is worth recognizing, since it indicates where many bad events originate: from just an inch away from the everyday.

The only thing I did to make myself visible to the Americans—because I still believed it would be an adventure to talk to them—was to ask the Sports at the next table (who I knew from the morning) if they had enjoyed themselves. I would never otherwise have asked that, but I hoped the two Americans would hear my American accent (which I assumed I had) and say something to me. However, neither of them looked around or stopped talking. I heard one of them—the intense, black-haired Crosley, who seemed to take things more seriously than the round, bald-headed Jepps—say: "Nothing's foolproof. That's just a fucking story." I assumed they were talking about what they should do, and that it posed them a problem. But I didn't know what those words really meant and didn't want to seem to be eavesdropping—though I was. So I left them alone and went to take my nap.

62

I BROUGHT YOU THIS GOOD BOOK." FLORENCE WAS standing in the shadowy hallway outside my room, at the opposite end from Remlinger's rooms. I'd been taking my nap and was startled, and had answered her knock wearing just my underpants. I instantly believed she'd come from Remlinger's apartment. "This one's got some nice maps inside," she said. "We talked about it. So . . ." She looked down at the heavy book, then put it in my hand and smiled.

A single bulb lit the hallway behind her. Only Charley Quarters ever came to my door—to wake me up early. I wouldn't have opened it undressed in front of him. "You need to put some clothes on." She turned to go, as if I was embarrassed.

She'd said she intended to bring me a book on Canada history. This was it. It had white library markings on its spine. "Medicine Hat Public Library" was stamped on top of its pages. *Building the Canadian Nation* was its title, by Mr. George Brown. We'd already discussed my going to Winnipeg to live with her son, and possibly becoming a Canadian. I'd been considering it. It would be better for me, she felt. Though I hadn't been in Canada long—six weeks was all—and I knew almost nothing about it. I'd need to learn the basic things—the national anthem and the pledge of allegiance (if they had one), the names of the provinces and who the president was. In most ways I thought I still wouldn't have said I liked it, since I hadn't chosen to be here. But being a Canadian didn't seem very different from Berner and myself saying we "lived" in any of the towns where we'd moved and gone to school, then moved away. I'd lived in Great Falls for four years and never felt I belonged in it. The length of time you stayed in a place didn't seem to count for much.

"Just give it back to me when you're finished," Florence said. She stepped back into the hallway, the light making her soft, rounded features indistinct. "I didn't mean to catch you unawares."

"Thank you," I said and held the book across my front. I felt like all of me was visible.

"I've got kids," Florence said and waved her hand. "You're all the same."

She left then. I closed my door back and locked it. I could hear her weight on the stairs all the way down to the bottom.

63

REMLINGER FOUND ME IN THE LEONARD KITCHEN, where I was waiting for Charley, so we could go out for our evening scouting. I was drinking a mug of coffee with sugar and milk, a habit I'd taken up from being cold in the truck every morning. I was dressed in my warm clothes—my L-jays, my plaid wool jacket and cap, my wool pants and my Daytons. I was already too hot in the steamy kitchen, where the stove was going. It was no bigger than a kitchen in a family's house—with an old Servel, a wood cookstove, a rick for kindling, a table to prepare the food, and a pantry. Mrs. Gedins tolerated me because there was no other place for me to go, except to be in my room alone. But she never talked to me. She was boiling vegetables and filling tins with meat loaf for the oven. She frowned at Remlinger, as if they'd been having a row—which possibly they had.

"I want you to come with me now," Arthur said to me. He was very intent and seemed certain about something—different from how I'd been used to seeing him. He hadn't shaved, and his eyes looked tired. His breath had a vinegary smell. He was wearing his fancy leather jacket with the fur collar, and his brown felt fedora. He'd come in from out of doors and his cheeks were red. "We have to go on a little drive now."

"I'm waiting for Charley." I was sweating in my clothes. I didn't want to go with him.

"He's left already. I talked to him. He'll do his scouting with the other boys."

"Where're we going?" I knew, or generally knew, so it wasn't really a question. We were going to do something with the Americans, who'd no doubt made their minds up now. I was happier to stay in the kitchen, waiting for Charley. That had already become usual for me, and I liked it. But Charley wasn't coming, and I didn't think I had a choice.

"These two Sports are needing to talk to me," Remlinger said, his eyes flickering. He seemed to be in a kind of motion, though he was there in the kitchen with us. He never talked to the Sports except when he circulated in the bar and the dining room. Charley did it all. "You might've seen them last night," he said. He unexpectedly smiled, and turned his smile toward Mrs. Gedins, who simply gave her back to him and attended to the stove. "It'll be good for you to go. It'll widen your outlook. Be a part of your education. These two are Americans. You'll learn something valuable."

He was speaking in his declamatory way, as if other people could hear him—more than just me and Mrs. Gedins. Or as if he needed to hear himself. No one said no to him, except Florence, who could've kept me from having to go with just a word. She was older than he was. But she wasn't there. Everything in the kitchen suddenly was intensified—the heat, the whirring under my ribs, the light, the bubble of boiling vegetables. I couldn't say no just on my own.

"Are these the two men from Detroit?" I said.

Remlinger cocked his head to the side and looked down at me, his smile vanishing, as if I'd uttered something surprising. I hadn't revealed anything I shouldn't have. I'd been present when the Americans arrived and knew what I knew from that. But he didn't know it. It seemed to alarm him. He looked at me strangely. I'd only wanted to have something to say.

"What do you know about it?" he said. "Who did you hear from?"

"He vas dere ven dey got here," Mrs. Gedins said, her back to us. "He heered dem." She was stirring a pot.

"Is that right?" Remlinger pushed himself up very straight and set his handsome head back, as if that would elicit the truth. "Vas you dere?"

"Yes, sir," I said.

"Vell," Remlinger said. He gave a look at Mrs. Gedins' back. "If you zay zo."

"I have to use the bathroom," I said. I'd become extremely nervous all in one instant.

"Use it, then," Arthur said, stepping past me. "I'll meet you in the lot. The car's running. Hurry up."

He went out the back kitchen door, letting in the cold, and slammed it closed, leaving me in silence with Mrs. Gedins, who didn't say another word.

I DID NOT NEED to use the bathroom. I needed to think something clearly, which I'd suddenly found I couldn't do in Remlinger's presence. I'd had plenty of time since the day before to route everything through my mind, and observe the things I needed to know, and be satisfied with not knowing all that was true, and to feel that probably not the worst was, and that in all likelihood nothing bad was going to happen because of the two Americans. "Our most profound experiences are physical events" was a saying my father often pronounced when my mother, or when Berner or I, was tortured by something we were worried about. I always took it as true—although I hadn't known precisely what it meant. But it had become part of my sense of being normal to believe that physical events, important ones that changed lives and the course of destiny, were actually rare, and almost never happened. My parents' arrest, as terrible as it had been, proved that—in comparison to my life before, where there had been very little physical activity, just waiting and anticipating. And in spite of believing what my father said about the importance of physical events, I'd come to think that what mattered more (this was my child's protected belief) was how you felt about things; what you assumed; what you thought and feared and remembered. That was what life mostly was to me—events that went on in my brain. This wasn't so strange, given the recent weeks—being alone, in Canada, without a future to act on.

Therefore, I'd tried to make my thinking in the last day be the force that determined what would happen—as a result of the Americans' arrival—and to believe the result would be nothing at all. I'd thought, for instance, that because Arthur had been expecting "these two" (he now called them) and knew about them in exaggerated detail—their names and ages, the car they drove, the fact that they were armed but not much committed to their mission—that he would be in complete control of the situation and could make it end the way he wanted. I'd also believed the Americans would never be able to determine anything important about him—not from only looking at him. Murder wasn't written on his face, or on anyone's. I'd considered how it might be possible to approach a total stranger on the subject of that stranger's being a murderer, and had decided it would be very difficult. Which was what the Americans had undoubtedly been realizing when I eavesdropped on them in the dining room. It seemed to me that the Americans would act toward Remlinger in a way that was consistent with their natures. Uncomplicated. Sincere. Goodwilled. They would need to address him, exert their reasoning on him, explain their conclusions, present a plan—after which Remlinger would deny knowing anything, tell them they were completely mistaken, which was what "the interests" back in America believed was the right thing to say. In that way everything would be settled. Whether they believed Remlinger or didn't, the Americans would be forced to accept his denial and—again, consistent with their characters and the small enthusiasm they felt—go home to Detroit. What else could they do? They weren't the kind of men to shoot him. Possibly they would go goose hunting with Charley and me in the morning.

I had even thought of how the Americans might approach Remlinger (since he wouldn't approach them). A word with him in passing in the hotel lobby; an approach by Jepps as Remlinger walked out to his car. "Can we two have a private talk with you? We have something to tell you." (Or "ask you," or "ask about.") As if the two of them were arranging for a girl to visit their shack, or to know more about the gambling. Arthur would've been confident, evasive. "Not in my rooms. In your place. In the Overflow House. We can have privacy."

I had thought it all through—the force of thought working against physical events. But now, it seemed, physical events were beginning to take place. Whether my thoughts were accurate or not was no longer worth asking. My father, it seemed to me, had been right.

I looked down through the second-floor bathroom window, my chest still whirring. In the parking lot, in a swirl of wet flakes and rain falling together, Remlinger stood beside his Buick, its headlights shining, the wipers flopping, the engine spewing white smoke into the night. He was speaking to a man I'd never seen—a tall thin man wearing a wool cap and a tan windbreaker and street shoes, hugging his shoulders as if he was cold. The man's cap caught the snow the wind was driving. Remlinger was talking seriously to him, his left arm sweeping first toward the Leonard, then in the direction of the highway toward Partreau, as if he was giving instructions. They didn't look up at me. At a certain point, Arthur put a hand on the tall man's shoulder—the man seemed to me to be in his thirties and was Arthur's height, but thinner—and pointed with his other hand again toward the highway. Both of them were nodding. I assumed it had to do with the Americans we were going to talk to.

Which made me wonder why I had to be involved, why Remlinger would take me, and what my being a part of it—a point of reference, Charley had said—could mean. Remlinger, just at that moment, turned and frowned up at the bathroom window. The big flakes and cold rain vanished for that instant, like a hole in the storm, and revealed me. His mouth began moving, saying something that seemed angry. He made a wide hailing gesture with his arm—a signal to me that was unusual for him—then said something else to the man in the cap, who looked up at me but made no gesture, then turned and began walking away across the lot into the dark. Whatever I should've been paying attention to for weeks and had ignored was shouting at me. I wished Florence would arrive. I wished I'd taken my saved-up money, which I kept in my pillowcase, and climbed on the bus and gone far away from Fort Royal and Arthur Remlinger, the way Charley had said. I even wished I'd saved back twenty dollars from what I'd given to Berner. I felt trapped and unable to resist. I moved away from the window and started down the stairs to where Remlinger was waiting for me.

64

"T O SAY SOMETHING'S FOUNDED ON A LIE ISN'T RE-
ally alleging very much," Arthur said as we drove. More
fat flakes were dancing in the headlights, the highway
stretching out ahead like a tunnel. He was talking animatedly, as if we'd
been having an exhilarating conversation. "I'm much more interested
in how those lies hold up. You know?" He looked at me, his big hands
with his gold ring on top of the steering wheel. I knew he intended to go
on speaking. The radio's light was on, but the sound turned down. "If
they hold up for your entire life. Well. . . ." He jutted his chin forward.
"What's the difference? I can't see one." He looked at me again. He
wanted me to agree. Under his felt hat brim his features weren't distinct
in the shadows.

"No, sir," I said. I didn't have to agree in my heart.

We weren't driving as fast as customary. He seemed to want to talk,
not reach Partreau.

"You can't leave it all behind," he continued. "Once, I thought that
you could. Crossing a frontier doesn't really change anything. You might
as well go back. I would if I were you. Everybody should enjoy a second
chance. I've certainly made some mistakes. We both have."

I couldn't follow what he said. I assumed I'd made mistakes because my father used to say "Man comes to trouble as the sparks fly upward," which was about mistakes. But I didn't know what mistakes of mine Remlinger knew about. I almost said, *I haven't made any mistakes that you know.* But I didn't want to be argumentative.

"Of course, it bothers me that I'll die up here," he said. "I will tell you that." He was still speaking in his declamatory style. "You ask yourself, 'What am I living for? Just to get old and die?'"

"I don't know," I said.

We passed two doe deer on the highway side, their fur and faces and eyes glistening in the blowing snow. They didn't move when we passed, as if they didn't see the Buick or hear it. Remlinger was still in the intent state of mind he'd been in—different from how he'd been around me up to then. It made me wonder how he felt. I hadn't spent time thinking about how other people felt—only Berner, who always told me. He hadn't mentioned the Americans while we were in the car. It was as if the meeting was unimportant, and there was nothing to say about it.

He looked over at me again, driving us through the blizzard. "You're a secret agent, aren't you?" He seemed about to smile under his hat brim, but didn't. "You don't speak about it, but you are."

"I speak," I said. "Nobody asks me anything."

"Parrots speak, too—only out of despair," he said. "Is that why you speak? I'm interested in you. You know that, don't you?"

"Yes, sir," I said, though I didn't know what "secret agent" meant.

"Now." He straightened his arms and took a firmer grip on the steering wheel and stared ahead into the snow whirl. "You may hear some things said tonight—when we get out here—that may surprise you. These two may say I've done things I haven't done. Do you understand? That's probably happened to you before. Somebody thought you did something you didn't do. That's what all secret agents have to live with. I'm one myself."

I felt I had to say yes or he would suspect I knew what he'd done—which could turn out badly for me. Although I was going to hear the story anyway. Knowing it beforehand couldn't make a difference now. But I said, "Yes, sir," though it wasn't true. I'd never been accused unjustly.

"Now, if you hear me say to these two that you're my son," Remlinger said, "just don't contradict me. Do you understand? Is that satisfactory? Even though I'm not?"

We were in sight of the Partreau elevator, prominent in the snowy dark, the familiar vacant buildings all but invisible along the highway frontage. Charley's trailer sat beside his Quonset, inside light visible through the cracks in the paper window coverings. His truck was missing. The Overflow House also had lights on inside. The Americans' Chrysler sat in the crumbled street, snow accumulating on its windshield and hood. We were going in there.

But I was shocked that Remlinger would say I was his son. I'd entertained my private thoughts of that nature, but they'd vanished when Charley had said what he'd said in the truck the day before. Remlinger saying such a thing was outlandish and made me begin to feel sick in my stomach, and not able to concentrate on what else he was asking me. No matter what I'd half imagined, Arthur Remlinger wasn't my father. My father was in jail in North Dakota. He wasn't this man in the hat in the dark.

"You don't talk enough. Charley said that." Remlinger looked at me sternly. We'd turned down South Alberta Street, the Buick bumping and swaying over the potholes and chunks of pavement the elements had ruined. The vacant houses were ahead of us in the headlights; the broken carnival rides, the caragana row. "Have these men spoken to you?" We were coming to a stop behind the Americans' car, its license plate covered in snow and ice. It was no longer raining, only snowing.

"No, sir," I said. I hadn't said it was agreeable for him to say I was his son. Everything about him was a deception. I didn't know why I had to be a part of it. He, of course, didn't care if I agreed or didn't.

"See here now," Remlinger said, shutting the motor off, then the headlights, making himself an imposing figure in his hat. He took a heavy breath. His jacket squeezed together and gave off its leather odor. "There's no reason for you to get all upset. Just let me show these two yokels the kind of man I am. You don't have to say anything."

He was no longer pretending being here was about hunting or gambling or girls. He hadn't told me anything, but he was admitting I knew— since he knew.

I took in a deep breath of my own and tried to work the sick feeling down out of my throat. The whirring under my ribs hadn't stopped. I wanted to say that I wouldn't go inside. I didn't want to breathe the spoiled smells and rotted plaster dust, have its ceiling press on me, the gloomy, shimmering fluorescent ring like a jail cell. I barely knew how one thing "meant" something else. But the shack, with the two Americans waiting inside for us, *meant* something bad I didn't want to get close to again.

Except if I didn't go, there'd be a ruckus. Remlinger had a violent temper—Charley had said so—made up of his frustrations. And while he'd never done anything bad to me, he could turn against me if I insisted on staying. His interest in me was nothing. That's how human beings were, I thought—unattached to most of the things they said or felt.

It would just be easier if I went. The Americans could explain their position in the reasonable way I believed was natural to them. Remlinger could deny everything and deceive them. Then they could leave. Tomorrow I could tell Florence I was ready to go to Winnipeg. Remlinger, I thought, would do nothing to stop me. Altogether, it would save me from something worse.

"I'm not upset," I said, the nausea gone out of my throat, banished by realizing I'd make everything easier by going inside.

"I thought you were experiencing an unsteady moment," Remlinger said. His face was in shadow. He shifted in the car seat, scuffed his boots on the floor.

"I didn't have that," I said.

"Well, good. Because there's nothing to be afraid of with these two.

They don't know a thing. We don't have to be in here long. Afterward we can go have supper with Flo."

"All right," I said. I thought how happy I'd be if Florence was here. She would have something to say to keep me in the car with her. But I was by myself, and that was how it would be. Remlinger got out of the car, and I got out, and we started toward the shack together.

65

REMLINGER KNOCKED ON THE SMALL DOOR INSIDE the windowed vestibule. I was behind him. The door opened almost at once. The older man, Jepps, was there smiling, wearing his toupee and a green plaid shirt and wool pants that looked new. Crosley sat on one of the two cots in the shadows, wearing a heavy wool coat because it was cold inside, the way it always was. He stared at us intently. They seemed like different men from the Americans I'd watched register-in the day before, and later speak to Remlinger in the bar. They seemed to have a purpose that the tiny room barely held, as if it had gotten smaller. Though it was the same kitchen where I'd slept. Everything the same. The cold-dirt odor that made you think bare ground was directly beneath the linoleum, mingled with the lavender-candle scent I'd introduced. One of them had been smoking a cigar.

The hot-plate burners were turned on and bright red to create heat. The fluorescent ring glowed, giving off poor light. The stuffed coyote still stood on top of the ice box, and the door to the back room—where I'd moved cardboard boxes—was shut. (A third person might be there, I thought. I didn't know who.) The Americans' suitcases were all that was different from when I'd lived there. Standing behind Remlinger, I wondered what the Americans were expecting to do, how they would bring up the subject they were there to bring up, having driven so far. They believed he was who they were looking for. Where were their pistols kept?

"I thought I'd bring my son along with me," Remlinger said loudly. His voice and accent had become different—more at ease. He had had to stoop to come in the low door. He put his hand on top of his fedora to keep from dislodging it. We instantly filled the room up and I felt not able to breathe naturally.

Jepps looked at Crosley on the cot with his two knees together. Crosley shook his head. "We didn't know you had any son."

Remlinger reached his hand around to my shoulder where I stood behind him, nearer the door. "It might not seem like it at first, but it's a good place for a boy to grow up, up here," he said. "It's safe and clean."

"I see," Jepps said. He had a loose jaw when he talked, which made him seem to be always smiling.

Remlinger let several seconds elapse. He seemed completely at ease.

Jepps stuck both his hands in his trouser pockets and wiggled his fingers inside. "We need to talk about something, Arthur."

"That's what you said before," Remlinger said. "That's why we're out here tonight."

"It might be better if we talked about it alone," Jepps said. "Do you know what I mean?"

"Is it not to talk about shooting geese?" Remlinger said, acting surprised. "I thought that's what you cared to do. Possibly there're other things you want me to arrange for you."

"No," Crosley said. The cot was down in the shadows beside the cold window on which sat my lavender candle.

"We don't want to cause any trouble for you, Arthur," Jepps said and sat down on the old straight-back chair where I'd hung my shirt and trousers. He leaned forward and put his hands on his knees. His belly was tight and hard under his green shirt. Underneath my cot were some of the postcard pictures of the naked women that I'd left behind. No one would find them.

"I truly appreciate that," Remlinger said. "I do."

"We think . . . ," Crosley said. He paused, as if the next thing he was going to say would be significant and he wanted to think it over a last time. He looked up at Arthur and blinked several times. "We think . . . ," he said again, then paused again.

"I used to be a police officer," Jepps said, interrupting him. "I arrested lots of people. You can imagine—in Detroit." Jepps smiled in his loose-jaw way that wasn't smiling. "Many of the ones I arrested and who went on into jail—for years, sometimes—didn't really need to go. They'd only done one thing wrong. And because I caught them for it, and they could explain to me what they'd done, I knew they would never have crossed that line again. Do you know what I mean, Mr. Remlinger?" Jepps for the first time appeared to give us his serious face. He looked right up at Arthur as if he—Jepps—was used to being paid attention to and wanted to be paid attention to now. They were to the serious purpose they'd come all the way out here to act on.

"Yes," Arthur said. "That makes sense all right. Must be common."

(When I think back on it now, fifty years later, from another century, I might've sensed then that Arthur could shoot both Jepps and Crosley but hadn't formulated the idea fully and was still carrying on as though he would deny everything. But he was listening to them. People sometimes speak and mistakenly believe they are the only ones listening. They speak only for their own ear, and forget that others hear them. Jepps and Crosley were following a path they believed to be one of reason and that had their purpose in mind. That's how they'd decided they would succeed. They didn't know that Arthur had given up on reason long ago.)

"What we believe," Crosley began deliberately, "is that the only right and good that can come out of this is to put the record straight, Mr. Remlinger. We have no force to bring against you here. It's another country. We understand that."

"Maybe you could tell me what you're talking about. Couldn't you?" Arthur said and adjusted his boot on the cracked linoleum. His leather jacket rubbed against itself again. He still had his hat on over his fine blond hair. The kitchen was airless and overheated.

"You could put your life in order just by talking plainly to us, I think," Crosley said and nodded at Arthur. "We came here not knowing what we'd do. We don't want to cause trouble now. If we just went back knowing the facts, that would be plenty."

Remlinger pulled me nearer to him. "What would I agree to?" he said. "Or what would I have to tell you? You can plainly see I don't know. I'm not a mysterious person. I'm not impersonating anyone. My birth records are on file in the Berrien County Court House, in Michigan."

"We know that," Crosley said. He shook his head again and seemed frustrated. "This is not a thing your son should hear."

"I don't know why not," Remlinger said. He was making a fool of them. They knew it. Even I knew it. They probably knew I wasn't his son.

"You can aerate a bad conscience," Jepps said. That was the word he used. *Aerate*. "The people I arrest—or that I did—always felt better making a declaration, even if they feared it. Sometimes even years later, like you. We'll go home and you'll never see us again, Mr. Remlinger."

"I'd be sorry not to see you again," Arthur said and smiled. "But what would I need to declare?" No one so far had said the words that told the reason for our being there. No one wanted to, I believed. The Americans, Charley said, lacked conviction for their mission and probably wouldn't say them. Remlinger wouldn't. We could've left then and nothing would've gone on further. A Mexican standoff. No one had any stomach for the words.

"That you set off an explosion . . . ," Crosley said abruptly, and had to clear his throat right in the middle of what I thought he wouldn't say and may instantly have regretted saying. "And a man died. It was a long time ago. And we're . . ." Here he lost his air as if the whole thing was too much for him. I hated to hear those words, but I also wanted to hear them. The tiny room was charged by them. Crosley seemed like a weakling for being afraid.

"We're what?" Remlinger said. He was haughty, as if he'd gained a great advantage over Jepps and Crosley and they were of much less consequence for having revealed themselves. "That's laughable," Remlinger said. "I did no such thing."

I was at that moment thinking—feeling the weight of words: Had they ever even known the murdered man? They'd come there on no more than a notion, and now, without conviction, had accused a man of murder, a man they also didn't know, and whose only connection to the crime was that he'd done it. Though importantly—to him—he hadn't meant to. Remlinger, however, had no intention of "aerating" his conscience. The contrary was true.

Jepps and Crosley had forgotten about not wanting to say this in front of me. Though I knew everything and wasn't shocked and knew shock wasn't in my face. Remlinger was not acting like a man who knew nothing about a murder, only like a person *claiming* to know nothing about one. This would've been the thing they'd come so far to observe. He'd as much as admitted it by saying, "I did no such thing." Each one was sacrificing something—a strength—to achieve an advance toward a goal. Remlinger had told the truth when he said I would learn something valuable. I learned that things made only of words and thoughts can become physical acts.

"We thought an honest way of doing this would be the best," Jepps said. "Give you the chance to liberate your heart."

"What if I have nothing to tell you? To liberate?" Remlinger said derisively. "And if this idea is groundless?"

"We don't think it is," Crosley said, having recovered his air but still sounding weakened. He had taken a handkerchief out of his pants pocket, spit something into it, then folded it away. He was very afraid.

"Yes," Remlinger said. "But if I say it is, that's because it is. And if you two're not able to go back to wherever you live, satisfied, then what's going to happen?'" It was just a matter of their wills now. No facts were in contest.

"Well, we'll have to talk about that," Jepps said. He stood up. I thought about the pistols—possibly already taken out, loaded, and put away close by. No one was telling much of the truth here: that Jepps and Crosley had no intention to come this distance and then go away; that they had more conviction than was believed. It was only a matter of deciding on what basis they would do what they meant to do. My presence was possibly the only reason they didn't do it at that moment. That was my use—to keep things in their places, provide a pause for Remlinger to be able to see his situation clearly. I was his point of reference.

"I admit I have something I can tell you," Remlinger said. He sighed deeply, in a way calculated for Jepps and Crosley to hear. "Maybe it'll satisfy you."

"We'll be glad to know about it." Jepps looked approvingly at Crosley, who nodded.

"You're right that Dell doesn't need to hear it. I'll put him in the car." Remlinger was talking about me without the slightest acknowledgment that I was there beside him. Whatever he hadn't formulated in his thinking before (but that I'd sensed he soon would), he had now formulated. What was in his mind was settled. It was one more use he needed to put me to.

"Very fine," Jepps said. "We'll be waiting right here for you."

"I'll be just a moment," Remlinger said. "Is that all right with you, Dell? You can wait in the car?"

"It's all right with me," I said.

"I won't be long," Remlinger said.

ARTHUR MARCHED ME out into the cold to the silent Buick, his grip tight on my shoulder, as if I was going to be punished. Snow was settling down in larger flakes. The wind had gone off and it was colder. Charley's truck was parked in front of his trailer. Light seeped under its door. Mrs. Gedins' white dog sat on the truck's hood, for warmth.

"These two are ridiculous," Arthur said. He seemed angry—a way he hadn't been inside. He'd seemed resigned, and before that haughty. He pulled open the car door and pushed me in behind the wheel. "Start it up," he said. "Get the heat going. I don't want you freezing." He reached in and pulled on the headlights, which shone through the drifting snow toward the house relics down South Alberta Street.

"What are you going to tell them?" I thought for an instant he might slide in beside me. I moved toward the passenger side.

"What they need to hear," he said. "They'll never leave me alone now." He reached a hand up under the driver's sun visor and took down the small silver pistol I'd seen in his rooms. It wasn't in its shoulder holster. It was there by itself. "I'll try to make this plain to them." He breathed in, then out. It was almost a gasp. "Just stay where you are," he said. "I'll come right back. Then we'll go have supper."

He closed the door, leaving me in the cold car with hot air blowing under the dash. Through the driver's window—snow turning to water on the glass—I watched his hat move back through the dark toward the shack's door, which was ajar. He didn't look around, or seem in any way hesitant. He had his pistol down at his left side, not hiding it, although it was small and the light was poor, so it might not have been noticed. I thought Jepps and Crosley might have their own pistols out and be holding them when Remlinger came inside. It made sense they wouldn't have believed him, would know what was going to happen—if they knew what they were doing.

Remlinger walked in through the mud vestibule—the glass panes of which were gone. He stepped to the door and pushed it open with his boot foot.

Jepps, I could see, was still standing in the shallow light just as he had been. Crosley's legs were all that was visible of him from where I was. He was still sitting on the cot. They only expected to be spoken to. They were the uncomplicated men they'd been described as being. Remlinger had misjudged the kind of men they were. He stepped forward into the lighted doorway. I saw Jepps' face acknowledge him. And Arthur raised his silver pistol toward Jepps and shot him. I didn't see him fall. But when Arthur advanced into the kitchen—to shoot Crosley—I saw Jepps lying on the linoleum, his big feet apart. *Pop* was the sound the pistol made. It was not a large caliber. A lady's gun, I've heard such guns called. I heard no shouts or voices. My window was wound up, the heater blowing. But I also heard the shots that killed Crosley. One *pop* went off, and I saw Crosley moving clumsily to his right, trying to go behind the cot. Arthur stepped closer to him. I saw him very plainly point the silver pistol down to where Crosley had gone behind the cot to find protection. Arthur shot two more times. *Pop. Pop.* Then he looked around at the floor, almost casually, to where Jepps was, his left foot agitating up and down very fast. He aimed the pistol almost considerately at Jepps' head or his face and fired another time. *Pop.* Five shots in all. Five pops. All of which I heard and saw through the open doorway from inside the Buick. Arthur looked down at Jepps as he put his pistol in the side pocket of his jacket. He said something very animated. He seemed to make a face at Jepps, and pointed a finger down at him, and thrust the finger at him three times, and spoke what were for me soundless words (though Jepps surely wasn't aware). Words of reproval that expressed the things he felt. He turned then and looked out the open door, across the dark, snowy space separating us—my face framed in the car window, containing an expression I cannot imagine. He said something else then, directed at me, his lips moving vociferously, his big fedora still on his head, as if his words put right what he had just done. I felt I knew what these words meant, even if they never reached my ears. They meant, "Now, then. Now, that's settled, isn't it? Once and for all."

66

WE BURIED THE TWO AMERICANS THE NIGHT they were killed. It is a measure of the kind of man Arthur Remlinger was that he forced me to help Charley Quarters and Ollie Gedins (Mrs. Gedins' son, the tall man in the cap and the windbreaker I'd seen in the Leonard parking yard) with the removal of the bodies out to the holes dug in the prairie where—should they have lived—the Americans would've shot geese the next morning with me as their "guide." It is a second measure of him that he did not in the least take care of me, nor was he at all interested in me, nor did he have a better plan for me than what the spur of that moment provided; certainly not for widening my education other than for me to find out (all over again, in a much worse way) how many more things are possible than my fifteen-year-old mind could've imagined. When he thought of these events later, if he ever did, he would not have entertained a thought of me, might have forgotten even that I was there—like a hammer left in a photograph, present only to provide the scale, a point of reference, and that exhausts its value once the picture's taken. He had, after all, given up on any scale he himself might've provided for himself, just as he'd given up on reason. He did only what he wanted to do, within limits he alone recognized. If you say he should never have brought me there that night, that he changed if not the course of my life, then at least the nature of it; risked my life (I might as easily have been shot and killed had things gone differently)—if you say these things, you would be correct. And it would've been entirely irrelevant to him. Things happen when people are not where they belong, and the world moves forward and back by that principle. Other people were for the most part dead to him, as dead as the Americans we lumped in Charley's truck that night, while Remlinger stood in the snowy shadows and smoked a cigarette and watched us. Put all these elements together and you'll make as much sense as can be made.

67

YOU WOULD THINK THE REMOVAL OF THE TWO dead bodies out of the Overflow House and into the bed of the pickup would be the most memorable event of that night, and possibly the most memorable action a person would ever perform—the sudden weight of them, whereas in life the bodies seemed not to have weight; the awfulness of that; the realization of what a change death brings. As I said, I was the one who picked up Jepps' toupee where it had fallen onto the linoleum and lay in his dense, drying blood. But this is what I most vividly remember—the flimsy lightness of the strange, blood-soaked little topper. I don't remember what the bodies themselves looked like, or how they smelled, or if they were loose or stiff, or what evidence there was of bullets being fired into them, or the smell of the powder (which must've filled the room), or even whether we carried them out like bundles, or dragged them by their hands or by their heels like the cadavers they'd become.

I do remember very well how fast the shooting and the killing took place. There were no dramatics to it, as in movies. It happened at once— almost as if it didn't happen. Only then someone's dead. I sometimes believe I was in the room when it happened, and not in the car. But that isn't true.

I remember after the moment the shootings took place, the look on Arthur Remlinger's face, talking to the dead men—the look of reproval—and then the look he gave me through the door to where I was watching, purely astonished. It was a look (I believed then) that meant he would kill me, too, if the spirit moved him, and I should know that. Murder *was* written on his face, the look that Jepps and Crosley had been seeking, but only saw in their last moments.

I remember that when the shooting happened and Remlinger looked at me, saying whatever he was saying, I—out of instinct—looked away. I turned my whole body from the window and saw through the other car window Charley Quarters, standing in his trailer door, the light behind him. He was wearing just an undershirt and his underpants in the cold. He was leaning on the door frame, watching. Perhaps he knew everything and was only waiting for his duties to take up.

The final thing I remember was that when we buried them—naked of their clothes, their suitcases and belongings bound for Charley's burn can, their pistols and rings and shotguns bound for the South Saskatchewan River—we folded them into their holes, dug deep enough that coyotes and badgers wouldn't reach them. It was relatively easy. I stood above them looking down—each man in his separate hole, several yards apart—then looked out toward the dark prairie, above which I could hear a goose up in the snowy sky, making the screams they make. And I could see—it was to my surprise, but I saw it—the red Leonard sign off in the night, where Fort Royal was, closer than I would've thought, the butler offering his martini glass. For a moment it seemed as though nothing had happened.

CAN I EVEN SPEAK of the effect of witnessing the Americans' killing—the effect on me? I'll have to make the words up, since the true effect is silence.

You might think that over the years I thought a great deal about

Arthur Remlinger, that he was an enigma, a figure worth long consideration. But you would be wrong. He was not in the least an enigma. I had
believed for a while that he possessed significance, a rich subtext that
was more than merely factual. But he did not, other than as the cause of
three men's deaths. He *wanted* significance, there's no doubt (Harvard,
for example, and the first murder he committed). But he couldn't overcome the absence that was his companion in life and that led him everywhere. Reverse-thinking, the habit that had me believing there was
significance when there was only absence, may be a good trait in the
abstract. (It made me seem more interesting to my mother than I was.)
But reverse-thinking can be a matter of ignoring the obvious—a grave
error—which can lead to all manner of treacherousness and more errors,
and to death, as the two Americans found out.

Much more, though, than I've kept Remlinger in my memory, I have
tried hard to keep the Americans—Jepps and Crosley—alive there; since,
inasmuch as they disappeared forever and without a trace, my remem-
brance is the only afterlife they are likely to have. I've thought, as I said,
that their deaths seem connected to my parents' ruinous choice to rob a
bank—with me as the constant, the connector, the heart of the logic. And
before you say this is only fiddling, fingering tea leaves to invent a logic,
think how close evil is to the normal goings-on that have nothing to do
with evil. Through all these memorable events, normal life was what I was
seeking to preserve for myself. When I think of those times—beginning
with anticipating school in Great Falls, to our parents' robbery, to my
sister's departure, to crossing into Canada, and the Americans' death,
stretching on to Winnipeg and to where I am today—it is all of a piece,
like a musical score with movements, or a puzzle, wherein I am seeking to
restore and maintain my life in a whole and acceptable state, regardless of
the frontiers I've crossed. I know it's only me who makes these connec-
tions. But not to try to make them is to commit yourself to the waves that
toss you and dash you against the rocks of despair. There is much to learn

here from the game of chess, whose individual engagements are all part of one long engagement seeking a condition not of adversity or conflict or defeat or even victory, but of the harmony underlying all.

Why Arthur Remlinger shot the two Americans I can only guess by trying to hold close to the obvious. Nothing was settled by it—only some time given back to him, postponing until later his disappearance into even profounder obscurity than Saskatchewan—the "foreign travel" he mentioned.

It's possible he had thought it through. Not the way another person would think something through—measuring pros and cons and letting your thoughts and judgment guide your acts with the understanding that they might guide you *away* from those acts. Possibly he believed the Americans would eventually shoot *him;* and if not, then they at least would never let him rest (as he said), never go away, never *not* return; that they were more committed than he'd been given to think. Thinking something through, for him, was much more a matter of shooting them unless something unexpected made him *not* do it. Who knows what that something might've been, since it didn't occur? Probably many people's vision of "thinking something through" is of this nature: you do precisely what you want to do—if you can. Possibly he simply *wanted* to kill them: because they came to him *at all* and tried to reason with him; because the idea of *talking* made him furious—after years of silent frustration, longing, disappointment, isolation, waiting; possibly to be talked to by two ordinary nonentities from nowhere, who also meant him ill, might've infuriated him, since he possessed an elevated sense of his own intelligence; possibly to hear words like 'aerate' and 'liberate,' and to have it implied that the two Americans sympathized with him—all that might've made him suddenly approachable and then lethal. He may have long known unreason was his great failure. And he might simply have quit caring, accepted he could do no better, that unreason was his nature, and he deserved whatever he wanted from it. He was a murderer—just like, in a smaller way,

my parents were bank robbers. Why hide it, he may have believed. Glory
in it. Any time you murder two people there must be a quotient of insanity
involved.

WHAT WAS THE OUTCOME of it all—two murders? Little, that I personally know about. The Americans' Chrysler was hidden in Charley's
Quonset, then driven down to the States by Ollie Gedins and one of his
cousins, using the Americans' identification, which no one at the U.S. border would've been careful enough to notice (it was Canada, it was 1960).
The two Canadians checked themselves into the Hi-line Motel in Havre,
Montana, using the names Jepps and Crosley; then quietly disappeared
into the Montana night, leaving the car parked in front of the room, and
the authorities to search for the men, believing they'd left Canada, gotten
into Havre, then mysteriously gone out of sight. It's possible the RCMP
came to the Leonard later on, asking questions, showing photos. No one
connected Arthur Remlinger to the deaths, just as they didn't connect
him to the bombing years before. In the case of Jepps and Crosley, buried
out on the soon-frozen prairie (the ground had been just soft enough for
the holes to be opened), there was never proof their deaths had even occurred. If someone came looking more closely—a wife, a relative up from
Detroit—it would've been long after the time I'd taken the bus to Winnipeg.

Something certainly must've passed through the electrical currents of
the Leonard in the days after the murders. Charley Quarters, however,
continued taking Sports into the fields each morning. Remlinger continued circulating spiritedly through the dining room and the bar at night. I
was forbidden to take part in anything, as if I was no longer trusted. But I
was still allowed to eat in the kitchen, and stay in my room, to be at loose
ends around the Leonard, or to roam the wintry streets of Fort Royal as I
had in the warm days of September. I saw Charley Quarters' half-ton on
the street and in the parking yard behind the hotel. Once I encountered

Arthur Remlinger in the lobby where the Americans had registered in. He was reading a letter. He looked up at me in a way he hadn't ever before. He seemed energetic, as if at that moment he wished to express something to me he also hadn't expressed—though his face quickly changed and seemed almost stern. "Sometimes, Dell, you have to cause trouble for things to be clear," he said. "We all deserve a second chance"—which he'd said the night of the murders. What he said didn't make sense, and I didn't know what to say back. I'd seen him murder two people. I was beyond words. He put his letter in his coat pocket, and just walked away. I believe that was how he understood shooting two men and burying them in goose pits on the prairie: it was in behalf of a certain clarity he sought, and of relieving his suffering. I tried to understand it and reconcile it with how I felt—which was mortified and ashamed, as if some part of Remlinger's absence had opened in me. But I never could.

I don't know what Florence either did or didn't know about the murders. My private view is that she knew about them, and at the same time didn't. She was an artist. She held opposites in her mind. So much of life fits into that category. Marriage, for one thing. To do that was consistent with the little I knew about her.

On the fourth day after the murders—the eighteenth of October—Florence came to my room and woke me. She'd brought a pasteboard suitcase with leather latches, and stickers on the side that said PARIS and NEW ORLEANS and LAS VEGAS and NIAGARA FALLS. She set this on the dresser and said I couldn't go the rest of my life with my belongings in a pillowcase. I could return it when I saw her again. She had a bus ticket, which she gave to me, along with a small oil painting she'd made, showing the caragana row at the back of the town of Partreau, the white bee hive boxes beyond, the prairie and blue sky fully painted in. "This is a better view than previous," she said in a business-like way. "This'll make you remember things more optimistically. The town is out of sight." (This, as much as anything, made me think she knew about the murders.) I told her

I liked the painting, which I did very much and was astonished to believe it was mine. It was what I should've told her about her other painting, and hoped this would compensate. I put my few clothes, my chess pieces, my *Chess Fundamentals* book and my roll-up cloth board, my two *World Book* volumes, the *Building the Canadian Nation* she'd given me, but not my *Bee Sense* book, which I'd given up on—all inside the suitcase. Which made it weighty. Together we walked downstairs, out of the hotel and down the blustery main street of Fort Royal, to the barber shop where I'd gotten my hair cut in those last days, as if I knew something was going to happen to me. We stood inside the glass door, and Florence told me she was putting me on the bus, and I should stay on until Winnipeg—a distance of five hundred miles, which would take until early the next morning. Her son Roland would meet me there. I would live with him and be put in school and taught by the nuns, until things could be "properly sorted out." It would all be fine and dandy. It was good I was leaving before the winter took its grip on life. There was really no use, she said, in saying more about things. She hugged me and kissed me when the bus arrived— things she'd never done, and that she only did then because she felt sorry for me. She would see me again, she said. I did not say good-bye to anyone but her. It was as if I'd already left some time before and was just catching up with myself. Ideas about parting, in which kind formalities are observed all around, turn out to be an exception in life rather than a rule.

I was, of course, very, very happy to be leaving. When I'd sat in the car after the shootings, and before the removal of the Americans, I'd looked around out Remlinger's car windows at the Americans' car and at Partreau, there in the dark and snow, and had decided it was a place made for murders, a place of absence and promises abandoned. I had almost escaped it, I thought, but finally I hadn't. This, I felt—in my seat on the bus, rolling out of Fort Royal and Saskatchewan—seemed to be my last best chance.

I had very few looking-back thoughts as the bus plowed eastward. I have never been good at that. Events must sink into the ground and percolate up naturally again for me to pay them proper heed. Or else be forgotten. I didn't for an instant think all the things that had happened to me would color how I thought of my parents and their much smaller crime. Neither did anything enhance my belief that I would ever see them again—though I wanted to. The uses that Remlinger had put me to—to be his audience, then to be his supposed source of interest, then to act the part of his son, then to be his surety, his witness and accomplice—were not things I was glad about. But they hadn't, for all of it, kept me from climbing the steps on that bus, or kept me from a future I wanted to have.

Did he not think I would tell what I'd seen? I'm sure there was never a moment when he thought I would speak about what I'd seen and participated in—no more than the two Americans would in their poor graves. Some things you just don't tell. I feel in fact a small satisfaction to realize he knew me at least that well, that ultimately he'd paid some attention to me.

Mildred Remlinger had counseled me to try to include in my thinking as much as I possibly could, and not let my mind focus in an unhealthy way on only one thing, and to always know something I could relinquish. My parents for their part had by turns counseled me in favor of acceptance. (*Flexibility* was my mother's word.) In time, I would be able to explain it all to myself—somewhere. Somehow. Possibly to my sister, Berner, who I knew I would see again before I died. Until that time, I would try to mediate among the good counsels I'd been given: generosity, longevity, acceptance, relinquishment, letting the world come to me—and, with these things, to make a life.

Part
Three

6 8

I HAVE ALWAYS COUNSELED MY STUDENTS TO THINK on the long life of Thomas Hardy. Born, 1840. Died, 1928. To think on all he saw, the changes his life comprehended over such a period. I try to encourage in them the development of a "life concept"; to enlist their imaginations; to think of their existence on the planet not as just a catalog of random events endlessly unspooling, but as a *life*— both abstract and finite. This, as a way of taking account.

I teach them books that to me seem secretly about my young life—*The Heart of Darkness, The Great Gatsby, The Sheltering Sky, The Nick Adams Stories, The Mayor of Casterbridge*. A mission into the void. Abandonment. A *figure*, possibly mysterious, but finally not. (These books aren't taught now to high school students in Canada. Who knows why?) My conceit is always "crossing a border"; adaptation, development from a way of living that doesn't work toward one that does. It can also be about crossing a line and never being able to come back.

Along the way I tell them if not the facts, at least some of the lessons of my long life: that to encounter me now at age sixty-six is to be unable to imagine me at fifteen (which will be true of them); and not to hunt too hard for hidden or opposite meanings—even in the books they read—but to look as much as possible straight at the things they can see in broad daylight. In the process of articulating to yourself the things you see, you'll always pretty well make sense and learn to accept the world.

It may not seem precisely natural to them to do this. One of them will often say, "I don't see what this has to do with us." I say back, "Does everything have to be about you? Can you not project yourself outside yourself? Can you not take on another's life for your own benefit?" It's then that I'm tempted to tell them about my young life in its entirety; to tell them teaching is a gesture of serial non-abandonment (of them), the vocation of a boy who loved school. I always feel I have a lot to teach them and not much time—a bad sign. Retirement comes for me at a good moment.

It's well and long accepted that I'm American, though I've been naturalized and have held a passport for thirty-five years. I decades ago married a Canadian girl, fresh from college in Manitoba. I own my house on Monmouth Street in Windsor, Ontario, have taught English at the Walkerville Collegiate Institute since 1981. My colleagues are polite about my forsaken Americanness. Occasionally someone asks if I don't long to "go back." I say, Not at all. It's right there across the river. I can see it. They seem both supportive of my choices (Canadians think of themselves as natural accepters, tolerators, understanders) but also are impatient nearly to the point of resentment that I even had to make a choice. My students, who are seventeen and eighteen, are generally amused by me. They tell me I talk "like a Yank," even though I don't, and tell them there's no difference. I tell them it's not hard to be a Canadian. Kenyans and Indians and Germans do it with ease. And I had so little training to be American anyway. They want to know if I was a draft dodger long ago. (Why they even know about that, I can't fathom, since history is not what they study.) I tell them I was a "Canadian conscript," and Canada saved me from a fate worse than death—which they understand to mean America. Sometimes they jokingly ask me if I changed my name. I assure them I did not. Impersonation and deception, I tell them, are the great themes of American literature. But in Canada not so much.

After a while I don't chime in anymore. Canada did not save me; I tell them it did only because they want it to be true. If my parents hadn't done what *they* did, if they'd survived as parents, my sister and I would've both gone along to fine American lives and been happy. They simply didn't, so we didn't.

Over the years my wife and I have taken an occasional vacation "down below." We have no children and represent, in a sense, the end of our respective lines. So we've gone only where we've wanted: skipping Orlando and Orange County and Yellowstone, tending instead toward the significant historical and cultural sites—Chautauqua, the Pettus Bridge, Concord, and D.C., which Clare considers "a bit much," but I consider to be fine. I've enrolled in summer institutes taught by Harvard professors, visited the Mayo Clinic once, and we've often driven down-and-through on our trips back to Manitoba.

I have never been back to Great Falls, but have been told it's a friendlier town—still a town, not a city—much better than when we lived there in 1960 and I was whisked away forever. None of that—taking me over the border—could happen now, since the towers, and with the border being sealed. It is a long time ago. My parents assume an even smaller place in memory. I often remember Charley Quarters saying to me, as we sat in lawn chairs watching geese, that something "went out" of him when he drove back to Canada from the lower forty-eight. I feel the opposite. Something always feels at peace in me when I come back. If anything goes out, it's something I want to be out.

On a driving trip to Vancouver we did once stop in the town of Fort Royal, Saskatchewan. My wife knows everything about those days and is sympathetic and slightly curious, since I don't repeat the stories over and over. I told it once when we were young, assuming she should know, and since then have not much revisited it.

Fort Royal itself was scarcely there. The drugstore, the empty library, the empty brick school—all gone. No trace. Two rows of empty buildings, a co-op gas station, a post office, the disused elevator. The train yard was in operation, but seemed smaller. Oddly, the abattoir (called, now, "Custom Prairie Meats") persisted. And the little Queen of Snows Hotel with a portable sign out front, saying GOOSE SHOOTERS: FALL'S COMING. BOOK YOUR HUNTS! The Leonard itself was among the missing—its space at the edge of town disclosing no sign of it. It was summer—early July—and the harvest hadn't yet commenced. Most of the town residences were still there, on the short squared streets, many with the Maple Leaf flying— nonexistent fifty years ago. But there seemed to be no place for someone to work. Everyone drove, I supposed, to Swift Current or farther.

Partreau, which we later drove past, was altogether gone. Even the elevator husk. It was as if a great vengeful engine had come through and plowed it under and salted the earth. I drove us out into the wheat fields— the crop thick and undulant. The sky was high and clear blue, the hot wind gusting and dusty and dotted with snapping grasshoppers. Hawks patrolled, lazing in the great warm dome or sitting sentry in a single tree, here and there. I didn't say so, but I drove us—to the extent memory could lead me—near to the place we buried the Americans. It's odd how a piece of ground can hold so little of its meaning; though that's lucky, since for it to do so would make places sacred but impenetrable, whereas they're otherwise neither. Instead, it all becomes part of our complex mind to which (if we're lucky) we can finally assent. The great fields of grain swayed and hissed and shifted colors and bent and lay back against the wind where we stopped our car. I got out and breathed in the rich odors of dust and wheat and something vaguely spoiled—a thin seam only. The Americans lay under their ground, as they would've by now, even had they lived on longer. I stood, hands in my trouser pockets, toes in the dust, and tried to make it all signify, be revelatory, as if I needed that. But I couldn't. So I walked back to the car, my wife waiting in the heat, watching me curiously. We turned back toward the west and the distant, invisible mountains and left that place forever, once again.

69

LAST FALL, BEFORE MY SISTER DIED, I WENT TO visit her in the Twin Cities. It is only an hour's flight from Detroit Metro, which we all use as if it were ours. I hadn't known she was there. In planning a party for my retirement, my students "looked me up" on the computer to find out what they could—something embarrassing or touching; someone who might've been looking for me; an old girlfriend, an army buddy, a police warrant. You can't keep much a secret anymore (though I've done better than most). They found a "looking for" message "posted" on some site. It merely said, "Looking for a Dell Parsons. A teacher. Possibly living in Canada. His sister is ill and would like to be in contact. Time is a consideration. Bev Parsons." A phone number was given.

It was a powerful shock to me to see my father's name on the sheet of paper the students rather solemnly handed me, wanting me to know they'd had lighter-hearted intentions, but obviously understanding I should see this.

I had never seen my father again, or my mother, once they went away to prison. The day in the Great Falls jail was the last time. There were letters—one or two from Mildred—that found their way to me. One telling me, also shockingly, that my mother had committed suicide in the

North Dakota prison for women. (I was by then at St. Paul's High School, in Winnipeg, and can't remember much of what I felt.) But there was never anything from him once his prison term was over—if he survived it. I concluded he must've felt I was better off wherever I was, and nothing could be gained by revisiting a life that was over long ago. Which I came to believe was true, though it was not that I forgot him. In a previous visit with Berner, in the town of Reno, Nevada, in 1978, she'd told me she believed she'd recognized our father in a service station casino in Jackpot, Nevada, perched on a stool, feeding quarters into a slot machine with what Berner said was a "Mexican girl" sitting beside him. He'd had a mustache. She admitted she sometimes confused this sighting with a man she'd seen in a bar in Baker, Oregon, and who had been alone. "But either way he was still handsome," she said. "I didn't speak to him." Berner was a drinker and such stories from her were not unusual.

But the thought that my father—at age ninety—could be at my sister's side, seeing her through a bad time, and seeking me out in the world to ask assistance, was tantamount, and surprisingly, to feeling my whole life was not only under assault but in jeopardy of never even having been lived. They were all still there, waiting for me, numinous, obstinate, staring, unerasable. It made me realize how much I'd wanted to erase them, how much my happiness was pinioned to their being gone.

Berner and I had seen each other only three times in the fifty years. These elliptical family relations are possibly more typical in America. I can't generalize about Canada and Canadians—feeling that I am barely one of them. But we saw a lot of my wife's parents before they died. We still see a good deal of her sister, in Barrie. Canadians and Americans, however, are alike in so many ways, it's probably an unfair distinction to insist on.

I'd always felt I *should* see more of my sister, and if you'd asked me I'd have said I was that kind of brother. But it simply hadn't happened. Her life turned out to be different from mine. I have had one wife and been a high school teacher and sponsor of chess clubs through my entire working years. Berner had had at least three husbands and unfortunately seemed able to please herself only on the margins of conventional life. I lost track of most of it. She was a hippie until that played out. Then the wife of a policeman, who treated her badly. Then a failed late-in-life college student. Then a waitress in a casino. Then a waitress in a restaurant. Then a nurse's assistant in a hospice. Another husband was a motorcycle mechanic in Grass Valley, California. No children were involved. And there was more that made her life seem not a good one, though she never said that.

When we visited her in Reno, she was with a man named Wynne Reuther, who said he was related to Walter Reuther. They were both drunk. We ate dinner in a rathskeller place at a casino. Berner, whose freckled skin was puffy and her flat facial features exaggerated, had acquired a sneering, raspy laugh that revealed too much of her tongue. Her narrow gray-green eyes were hawkish and cold. She treated my wife sarcastically and didn't seem to remember or to take in that we were Canadians. She possessed the same wrangling strangeness that always fascinated me—her "hauteur" our father called it. When we were children, we were always two sides of one coin. But now, at dinner, talking noisily over this Reuther fellow, she seemed to me just another extra human being, in spite of mannerisms and hand gestures and an occasional ghostly "set" to her features that I recognized. Eventually she said that I—not Clare—talked like a Canadian. Which didn't bother me. She said Canada was "nondescript," which annoyed Clare. She finally said to me that I'd left my country behind to fend for itself. After that I had a displaced argument with Wynne Reuther—something about Iran—which cut the evening short. The last thing Berner said to me, as we stood in the dark, sweltering, desert car park—Interstate 80 full with its burden of trucks banging above us in the orange sodium lights and the bright casino glow—was: "You gave up a lot. I just hope you know that." She knew nothing about what she was saying. She'd drunk too much and was bitter about the "substitute life" she'd led instead of the better one she should've led if it had all worked out properly—our parents, etc. Of course, she was right. I *had* given up a great deal, as Mildred told me I'd need to. Only I was satisfied about it and about what I'd gotten in return. "It's so odd what makes people different," Clare said, almost whimsically, when we were in the car and all of that was behind us. "Nature doesn't rhyme her children," I said, happy to remember the line of Emerson's, and to have a place for it to fit perfectly. Though what I felt that night was impermanent, incomplete, and sad. I thought it was possible I'd never see Berner again.

I ARRANGED TO MEET HER at the Comfort Inn that is by the huge mall near the airport in the Twin Cities. There was a polite disagreement on the phone over who would come to see who, and once that was settled, whether I would drive to her house in a rental car or she would drive to get me.

"I have to be able to go home when I get tired," she said on the line to Windsor, her voice sounding worn but positive—as if I wouldn't be able to take her home when she was ready. She had a small, harsh cough and sounded hoarse. "I'm doing my chemo on Tuesdays," she said, "so I wear out fast."

"Is Dad there?" I said. "Bev Parsons" was stitched into my brain. I didn't want to see him. But if he was alive and looking after her, I didn't very well see how I could deny it.

"Dad?" Berner sounded incredulous. "*Our* dad?"

"Bev Parsons," I said.

"Oh, for goodness sake," she said. "I forgot. No. I finally decided to jettison my old awful name. Berner." She said it ruefully. "All those years with that being me. Like bad luck. His name seemed better for me. I always envied it. I could keep my luggage—if I had any."

"I always liked your name," I said. "I thought it was distinctive."

"Good. Then you take it. It's unoccupied. I'll will it to you." She laughed again.

"How sick are you?" Suddenly, because of the telephone, and not being face-to-face, it was as if we were not young, but adults who could ask such questions. Twins of another, better kind.

"Oh my," she said. "I'm just taking chemo for something to do. I've got two months. Maybe. A lymphoma you wouldn't want. Really." She breathed audibly into the receiver. A sigh. She'd always sighed, though never resignedly.

"I'm sorry," I said. And we were back being near strangers. Of course, I meant it.

"Well, me too," she said and seemed in good spirits. "The cure's all that really hurts. And the cure's not even a cure. You'd better come on, though. Okay? I want to see you. And give you something."

"Okay," I said. "I'll come next weekend."

"Are you still Mr. Teacher?" she asked.

"Still till June," I said. "Then I retire."

"I'll have to miss your graduation, I guess." She laughed the harsh sneering laugh I remembered from the last time, when she'd told me I'd given up a lot.

"SHE JUST WANTS to see if you'll come." Clare shook her head resolutely. She was helping me pack a small bag. I intended only to be there a day and a night. "And, of course, you will."

I said, "If your sister was sick and dying, you'd go." Our house on Monmouth Street sits beside a small park and has vestigial elms, front and side. Both were in clamorous gold display. It was October, the time you live for at our latitude.

"I would," she said, and patted me on my shoulder and kissed my cheek. "I love you," she added. "Whatever she wants, you give it to her."

"She doesn't want any more than my coming," I said. "She wants to give me something."

"We'll see," she said. My wife is a chartered accountant and tends to see the world beyond her small circle of intimates and close family as a dedicated negotiation, pro versus con, profit versus loss, give versus receive—though not evil versus good. These views have not left her cynical—only skeptical. In her heart she's generous. "You'll get whatever's coming to you, whatever it is," she said. "Tell her I send her warm wishes—if she remembers me."

"She does," I said. "She'll appreciate that. I'll tell her."

IT WAS COLD in Minneapolis, a city I have always liked from afar for what seems to be its down-to-size, polished and sturdy optimism. We occasionally routed ourselves through there on the way to Clare's mother's in Portage la Prairie, taking the ferry across the lake to Wisconsin.

I was outside the Comfort Inn in my overcoat, looking up to a few squads of hurrying southerly ducks, when Berner drove up in a dented blue Probe, rust adhesions scabbed around its wheel wells and across its hood and roof. She rolled down her window. "Hey, big boy. Got time for a quickie? A quickie's all I've got." She looked terrible. Her face, smiling up through the window, was mustard color. The puffiness from thirty years ago was gone, as was the girlish down on her jaw. Her eyes looked played out behind a pair of oversize red-frame glasses—the kind older women wear to look younger. She was thin—almost as when we'd been young. She looked like an elderly woman whose teeth were large for her mouth. Her flat face appeared to have fewer freckles because of her makeup. Her once frizzy hair was gray and sparse.

"I just have to drive back by the house," she said, once we were going. "It's not far. I forgot my oxy-whatever. Then I thought we'd go to Applebee's. I'm comfortable there. You know?"

"Wonderful," I said. She wore a clear shunt taped on top of her right hand—for her chemo. Everything she did was requiring a large effort and difficulty—including seeing me. Her car was a jumble inside. A dirty green chenille bedspread covering the bucket seats. The radio was taken out. A strip of duct tape was patched over a gouge in the dashboard vinyl. The back seat held a tire and some jack equipment. Berner had on a long quilted purple coat that wasn't new, and white furry boots. She gave off a pronounced hospital smell—rubbing alcohol and something sweet. She was clearly very sick, as she'd said.

"I'll take my pill once we've eaten." She was negotiating Saturday morning surface-road traffic near the mall. "I'll have thirty good minutes. Then I'll have to get home. Get you back to the hotel. Or else I'll start driving backwards and upside down. I'm an addict now. I never was before. It's cured my allergies. That's pretty good." She smiled. "Did you recognize me? Yellow's my new fall shade. It's 'cause my liver's snafu'd. That's what's going to escort me out, I guess. It's supposedly okay."

"I recognized you," I said. I didn't wish to seem sober sided if she wasn't. "Is there anything I can do?"

"This." She leaned back in her seat as if something in her middle had bitten her. She breathed in deeply, then out deeply. "Unless you want to teach me math. I thought it'd be good to learn math again before I died. I used to be good at it, remember? It's all different now. Dying must make you thirst for knowledge. As well as other things." She smiled. "I've missed you. Sometimes."

"I remember," I said. "I've missed you."

"Of course, you *have* a memory. I can't seem to find mine." She turned and looked at me seriously as if I'd said something I hadn't. Her look was meant to represent warmth toward me. To welcome me and make me know she missed me. "I remember *you*, though," she said and raised her chin in a way that was like our father more than her. It was a gesture of mine, as well. I experienced a sudden pang of longing then—to be young, for all of life to have been a dream I would wake from on a train to Seattle.

"So you like being Bev?" I had not touched her yet, but I clumsily reached and patted her shoulder, which felt thin under her quilted coat.

She coughed harshly and fanned her face. "Oh, yes," she said and swallowed what she'd coughed up. "I've *been* Bev fifteen years. It's my normal. Poor ole Berner fell down under the bus someplace. Couldn't keep up with my pace."

"I like it," I said.

"Dad didn't do so good with Bev. I thought I'd give it a try. They were just kids, you know? Both of them."

"No, they weren't," I said, not expecting myself to speak to this so harshly. "They weren't at all. They were our parents. We were the kids."

"Okay. Touché," she said, driving. Her hands were red and raw looking. "Don't you say that? Touché? Touché olé?"

"Sometimes."

"Touched," Berner said, and nodded and smiled tolerantly. "I'm touched. I'm touched in the head. So are you. We're twins. The zygote doesn't forget."

"That's right," I said. "We are."

BERNER'S HOUSE was a newer white double-wide down a straight, narrow lane of other double-wides, most newer with neat, tiny yards and single saplings wired to the ground and sporty cars parked in front on the curbless hardtop, and TV dishes on all the roofs. Children were out on Saturday morning. Enormous silver jets rose into the fall sky a mile north of us. Their engines made little noise as they disappeared.

Berner pulled into a paved drive. A small man stood at the end of the trailer, feeding lettuce leaves into a raised wire rabbit frame inside which several fat gray and white rabbits pressed forward into the little opening.

"There's the most patient white man in the world, *and* the world Scrabble champion. He's tending his flock." She opened her door out and encountered trouble moving her legs from under the steering wheel. "Just give us a little push, hon." Berner looked pained and was straining. "Hard to get me going once I'm stopped. I won't be a minute." She'd begun speaking with a soft southern accent as we got close to her house. "We're not married," she said back down inside the car. "But he's the best husband I never had. I had to get a good one once, right? He's shy." She stood up stiffly and looked toward the man, who was latching the pen door. He wore cowboy boots and jeans and a nylon windbreaker and the kind of bright red cap my students wore, but his was on straight. "I forgot something," she called out to him. He looked at her but didn't answer. "My fix," she said and with difficulty began walking toward the front steps to get her medicine.

Down the lane in the chilly sunshine, many of the other trailers, which were long-side-face-the-street, had American flags flying on aluminum poles in their yards—as if someone had sold everyone a flag. Berner's yard lacked its flag. Some lawns had paper placards in the grass advocating whatever the residents believed in. ABORTION KILLS. MARRIAGE IS A SACRAMENT. NO TAXES. It was all catching on in Canada—with the government: the nervous American intensity for something else. The inevitable drift northward of everything.

The small man in the red cap and boots stepped to a second rabbit cage and began feeding in more lettuce from a silver mixing bowl at his feet in the grass. His windbreaker had a Confederate flag stitched to its back, and some lettering underneath that I couldn't read. He was shrunken and tough and angular and dried out—older than Berner by a lot. A religious person, long saved, I imagined, watching him through the windshield's sunny glare. Somewhere would be a motorcycle. A giant TV. A bible. Everyone had stopped drinking years ago, and were now waiting. It's what happened to them, I thought. Ending here, this way. It had become my habit to champion my own course in life, as if mine could teach everyone something. It wasn't so admirable, since it couldn't. Least of all my sister, who'd taken her life into her own hands, and accepted it. I didn't know what to call her, I realized.

The small man closed the second pen and carefully latched it. He bent and picked up his silver bowl and looked at the car while he was leaning. Then he stood up and stared straight at the reflecting windshield. Possibly he could see me in the seat, waiting for Berner—waiting for Bev. He raised the bowl in a gesture of greeting, smiled an agreeable smile I didn't expect. He turned and walked in a stiff, dignified way to the corner of the trailer and was gone. He didn't see me gesturing back. He didn't want to meet me. I understood perfectly well. I was late on the scene.

IN THE CAR headed to Applebee's, Berner seemed improved. She'd put on more makeup and exuded a cherry smell and had begun chewing gum. She'd brought back to the car a Cub Foods plastic grocery bag with—I guessed—whatever she planned to give me inside it.

She turned on the heater and informed me she was cold all the time, couldn't get warm to save her life. She scratched at the clear tape keeping the shunt fixed to the back of her hand and shook her head when I noticed it. She seemed to want to push her wide tongue out between her lips, which I took to be a manifestation of the drugs. She also spoke less in her southern accent now that we were away from the trailer. "He's from West Virginia," she said. She was thinking about the man who was not her husband, and being amused by him. Ray was his name. He was a dear. He knew everything about her and didn't care. He'd been in the U.S. Army a long time, but was retired. She'd met him in Reno and he'd moved her out to the Cities a decade ago. He'd had a brother here. The trailer was her almost wedding present. He raised the rabbits "for the table," and cried every time he had to harvest one. They went to a church. "Of course, I don't believe anything. I just go to humor him and to be nice. He knows I'm officially Jewish on our mother's side. Though I'm non-observant."

She said she'd become interested in China and its growing dominance; was worried about "illegals," taxes, 9/11, "the threat." She remembered Clare's name and that she was an accountant. She said she wished she could visit us and knew Windsor wasn't that far from the Cities. She said she and Ray had both been for Obama. "Why not? You know? Something different." She asked me if I'd voted for him. I told her I would've if they'd let Canadians vote. Which made her laugh, then cough, then say, "Okay. You're right. There's a good point. I forgot you left our country behind. I can't blame you." Once again, she knew nothing about my life, wouldn't have cared to at that point. She was working steadily to cling to some semblance of herself for me. All we had together were our parents—fifty years ago—and each other, brother and sister, which we were trying to make the most of, at least one morning's worth. She seemed, for that time we were in the car, to be able not to seem sick, not bitter that our lives had gone so askew and unfairly for her (now, especially). She seemed to locate an old self, to look at me with her former skepticism and love, which made me feel young and naive compared to her old and wise. I liked it. I was glad Clare hadn't come. Though it was not how I'd featured things. I'd thought of a trailer; but after that, a sick room with lowered lights, a TV without sound, a dresser top filled with medicines, oxygen, the haze and aroma of death all around. This was better. Under different, more promising circumstances we wouldn't have cared to spend a day together. It was death's lenience.

"You know"—we were turning into the Applebee's lot, crowded with Saturday mall-goers in and out of big SUVs, and motorcycles and pickups—"I always tell myself, 'Remember this. It may not be this way in six months.'"

"I'm not so different from you there," I said. "We're still the same age."

"But you don't know how many times that's turned out to be true. In my life? Six months has been a lifetime." She looked at me stonily, her jaw muscles working under her beige flesh, her tongue restless in her mouth.

"I do know," I said.

"Well," she said and sighed again the resigned way. Once when she'd sighed, it had always been with impatience. "I'm trying very hard to resist this gradual dying. It may not seem like it. But I am. I feel like"—she stared down at the keys in the ignition, reached one finger and gave them a pointless jingle—"I feel like, sometimes, my real life hasn't even started yet. This one hasn't been up to standard, you might say. Which is nothing you caused. I walked off down that street all by myself that summer. Remember?"

"I do," I said. "I remember it clearly." I did.

"Do you regret not having any kids?" She'd begun staring out at the traffic on the access road. A large bus pulled past, bound for the mall, its windows full of women's faces, all framed by short haircuts. She clicked off the engine and the heater. Outside the noise was muffled but constant.

"No," I said. "I never thought about it. I guess I see enough kids."

"It's the end of the line, then," she said, triumphantly. "The Parsons line ends here in the Applebee's lot. Almost."

"Clare and I say the same thing."

"You feel like you've had a wonderful life? Now that I've told you about how I feel? It's okay to say you have. I'm glad." She turned her face toward me and for that instant showed no sign of strain, only relief. Her face would look that way to me forever.

"I accept it," I said. "I accept it all. I married the right girl."

"We *all* accept it. That's not an answer." Her dry lips wrinkled and she looked with displeasure back at the bus gone past. "What choice do we have?"

"Then, yes," I said. "I have had." Though I wasn't sure I thought that.

"I'm your big sister." She sniffed in mindfully. "You have to tell me the whole truth. Or I'll come back and haunt you." She smiled to herself, pulled up her door handle and began again to move her feet painfully out. "I can do it myself this time," she said. We stopped that talk then and never returned to it.

* * *

IN APPLEBEE'S we sat by a big window that looked out on her rusted car, which was more battered than I'd thought, with its bent Minnesota license plate and its rear bumper snapped off. No other cars in the lot looked like it.

Berner seemed jolly, recovered from our grave talk, as if this clamorous, TV-distracted, kitsch-cluttered jangle was just what she needed and knew its mission was to make the terminally ill forget their woes. She kept on her purple coat, which needed dry cleaning.

She took her gum out, wrapped it in a paper napkin corner, and set it on the window sill. She ordered a martini and encouraged me to, but said she couldn't drink it with her medication. She just liked seeing it in front of her, like the old days, all set to do its little magic. I ordered a glass of wine to make myself relax and to be in the spirit.

"Did I say," she said (she had the plastic grocery bag beside her in the booth), "that I'm *not* going to commit suicide? I forget what I told you. Chemicals is the shits."

"You didn't mention that," I said. "I'm glad to hear it though." I held up my wine to toast her.

"One suicide's enough for a family of four," she said. We'd only been sixteen then, and in no position to take command of much. The site of our mother's resting place was one more thing I'd relinquished. "I'm not really fixated on them much," she said, letting one finger—on which was a tiny, badly faded tattoo of a cross—stroke the stem of her glass, as she perused the menu, which showed bright-color pictures of the things you could order. "Sometimes I think about them and their big *robbery*." (She emphasized the word.) "I have to laugh. All of us just spinning off like that. It was the event of our lives, wasn't it? A great big fuck-up, and everything piled on top." She squinted behind her glasses and leaned up on her elbows and stared at me to let me know precisely what it meant to her that she was on the way out of her troubles. I felt awful about her, and for her, and I couldn't do anything to fix anything.

"It leads you nowhere to think about it," I said, which was the minimal truth.

All the young waitresses had begun raucously singing "Happy Birthday to You"—to some elderly customer across the restaurant. Other customers had begun rhythmically clapping. The University of Minnesota football team was playing on twenty TVs. There had been occasional cheering, then groaning about that.

"No," Berner said. "It truly doesn't." She looked away from her martini, as if she'd just heard the singing and clapping. "It's a secret we share, isn't it? With the whole world. Letting things slip. It connects us up to the rest of humanity. That's my take." She smiled for no apparent reason. I remembered her writing to me as her life was commencing: *We feel the same and see things the same.* She'd already begun sharing the world then, whereas I hadn't. I'd been abandoned in it. I wondered if I was somehow deceiving her now, in some way that mattered. Was I giving to her my real, most genuine self? Was it true what I'd said about my life? I wanted not to deceive her. It was all I had to give her, and it had always been a preoccupation of mine—given my past, and that I'm a teacher, where you're always acting but trying not to. It's never clear, since we all have selves to choose among. "Maybe you have a hidden wild streak," she said. "And maybe I have a hidden regular one. A tame one." She'd let her mind stray onto some interior conversation we weren't exactly having.

"Probably," I said and sipped my wine, which was stale. "At least half of that's maybe true."

"Okay." She lowered her eyes. She'd caught herself straying off. Her brown-and-gray hair was thin in front and brushed severely back. She'd applied rouge when she'd gone inside her house. Her ears were pierced, but she was wearing no earrings. Her lobes were pale and softened. "And are you still the chess man?" she said and smiled at me to designate she was paying attention now.

"No," I said. "I teach it. I was never good at it."

She looked around suddenly as if our food was arriving. Her soup. My salad. Though it wasn't. "Speak of the devil," she said, and lifted the Cub Foods sack and set it on the table. "So." She sighed and took out of the sack a sheaf of white notebook pages that were dry and hole-punched and tied together with what looked like stiffened bits of shoelace that were a color not so distant from Berner's skin. "I didn't want to send this to you." She set her hands down on top of the pages to keep them close, then looked at me and smiled. "I didn't know if I'd like you. Or if you'd like me, and would even want it." She sighed again, this time very deeply, as if something had defeated her.

"What is it?" I asked. Faded, ink handwriting was on the top page.

"It's just her 'chronicle'—she calls it. Or did. She wrote it in prison when she was first there—looking at the dates. She sent it to Mildred, whose son I happened to meet once. Out west. Mildred sent it to me. A long time ago—whatever degrees of separation that is. She should've sent it to you. But mother-daughter must've made a difference to her. I guess. There's nothing in it to disturb anybody. No great revelations. But you can hear her—which is sort of nice. You should have it." With her two bruised hands she pushed the pages across the table top, inching her martini glass to the side, dampening the edge of the bottom page.

"Thank you," I said and took possession of the pages.

"She calls it the chronicle of a weak person. Which she was." Berner bit a flake of dry skin off her lower lip, as if the pages' contents interested her again, now that she'd handed them over to me. Now that I'd come all this distance to get them. "She says things like, 'You're only good if you can do bad and decide not to.' And, 'We were a failure at marriage,' which we all can agree. 'What makes life better is the essential question.' And, 'You can not know your life's intolerable until you see your way out of it.' She speculates about leaving Dad long before, and about their holdup. She writes letters to us. And she has some lines of poetry she liked. I memorized them once. '. . . Through what crime. Through what fault have I deserved my weakness now?' She always wanted to be a writer. I've read it over the years. It could make me cry. He couldn't help himself. But she had a lot better sense. At least that's how I remember her." Berner shook her head and looked again out at the busy Applebee's parking lot. "I wish I wasn't sore at her. Now, especially. I'd like to be like you. You accept everything. It'd make better sense all around."

"I am, too," I said—which wasn't the reply she'd wanted. I was looking at the fine, precise, faded words running minutely along the pale blue line, not in her favorite brown ink.

Berner had begun drumming her fingers on the table top. When I looked at her plain, waiting face, it was without expression, though her jaw muscles were agitating. Her eyes had grown shiny. We looked nothing like each other now in a different way.

"Do you remember Rudy?" She pursed her lips in.

"Yes," I said.

"Rudy red-head. Rudy Kazoot. My first great love. Isn't that funny?"

"I danced with him," I said.

"You did?" Her expression briefly brightened. "Where was I?"

"You were there. We all three danced. It was the day they went to jail."

I wanted to say her name. For my own sake. Her real name. "Berner," I said softly.

"That's my name." She said this hoarsely, as if someone at the next table had whispered it.

"Do you need anything?" I said. "Is there anything at all I can do for you?"

The crowd on the TV made another swelling roar. People in the restaurant clapped listlessly. She didn't say anything for a moment, as if the other conversation that had been going continuously in her head, the one we'll all eventually have, had become irresistible. "You've done everything," she said. "We all try. You try. I try. We all do. What else is there?"

"I don't know," I said. "Maybe that's right," which did not seem enough to say.

WE ATE A LITTLE of our lunch when it came, but not nearly all of it. She wasn't hungry, and I'd had my breakfast in the hotel. At a given moment, when we'd sat a while with not much to talk about, she said, "I'm not feeling perfect." She'd gotten restless, sitting. She'd taken her pill. I'd put the pages back in the plastic sack. We were finished.

I went to the bar and paid our bill and helped her up and out to the front door. I couldn't see how she could drive us anywhere, and I didn't know her way back home. I asked the hostess to call a taxi, which came more quickly than I imagined it could. We rode silently together in the back seat, with Berner staring out the window at traffic, and me watching out my side. A place I didn't know. She hadn't minded leaving her car behind for Ray to get later.

Finally we came to her paved lane of mobile homes with their flags and saplings and snazzy cars and children, and jets rising into the sky not far off. Ray was there inside. He seemed glad to see her back. We shook hands and said our names. I mentioned we'd left the car. He seemed embarrassed and laughed for some reason he was probably sorry about later. He knew what to do, though. Berner seemed to be feeling not good at all and needed help coming up the steps. Ray asked me if I wanted to step in. He said coffee was always on. I said I didn't, but thanked him. I said I'd call tomorrow. When I said good-bye in through the doorway, where a big TV was going—the game again—Berner turned and smiled and said dreamily, "Okay, dear. Good-bye. It was nice to see you again. Tell them I said hello, will you?"

"I will," I said. "I love you. Don't worry." She didn't have the dissatisfied look on her face that our mother had hoped she wouldn't.

I went back to the hotel in the taxi, which had waited. In the morning I flew back to Detroit.

* * *

THERE'S LITTLE ELSE to say. I have that as my satisfaction. I *am* blessed with memory, just as my sister Berner came to be blessed with less of it. Though she was right; it *was* the event of our lives, since it began in our family, and its consequences ran far but never outran their source. The week after Berner died, which was the week after the American Thanksgiving last year, 2010, I said to my students—very unexpectedly: "Do you ever have the odd feeling that you've somehow escaped punishment?" We were talking about Hardy again. *The Mayor.* They only stared back at me, perplexed, having recognized I was distracted, and was speaking about myself. I immediately realized it was an alarming thing to say to them. Although one boy, whose family are Kosovars, said yes, he did.

I did not see my sister dead. Though Ray telephoned me politely on the day and called me Dell, and Berner "Bev." He said they had gotten married the week before. I told him that was wonderful, and thanked him. Not being there didn't matter, since I don't believe I deceived her on our visit and that she understood I didn't. Although in the days after her death I had the odd feeling—a sensation I'd never had—that our father was still alive somewhere, living on at a great age, and might've wanted to know about her, and even about me. I purposefully tried to forget that thought, and soon did. It was just a fantasy, having to do with being abandoned once again. Although I myself, now, occasionally have Berner's dream— the one she wrote about in her letter from San Francisco, fifty years ago: that *I'd* killed someone, and had forgotten it; then the crime had risen up, a terrible specter, and been divulged to everyone I knew. My students. My colleagues. My wife. All of whom were horrified and hated me for it.

Only I hadn't killed anyone—neither in my dream nor out of it (although I did help bury the two Americans and somewhere have a debt to pay for that).

Our mother's chronicle was much as Berner said: bits, uncompleted thoughts meant for a later time that never came, her view of the robbery, opinions, rationalizations, trivialities, harsh words about our father. Someone could make a complete story up from it. Again, Ruskin says composition is the arrangement of unequal things. And the contents of her chronicle qualify as unequal things. But at my age I'm uninterested in such a duty, since neither are those things equal any longer to the matter of my own remaining life—as sorry as I am for that to be true.

Though there was one thing she wrote that might've been what Berner most wanted me to read and why she gave the pages to me.

"I think," our mother wrote in her fine hand, in the blue ink she would've gotten in prison, and that had grown invisible in places, "that when you're dying, you probably want it. You don't fight it. It's like dreaming. It's good. Don't you imagine it feels good? Just giving in to something? No more fighting, fighting, fighting. I'll worry about this eventually and be sorry. But right now I feel good. A weight's off of me. Some great weight. Nature does not abhor a vacuum, as it turns out."

This was dated, Spring 1961. Berner had put a pencil check beside it. It meant something to her. Possibly it will someday mean something to me, something more than the obvious.

SOME DAYS I DRIVE through the tunnel into Detroit—the city that used to be there, now only acres of vacant lots, with the great glistening buildings along the riverside, like false fronts, a good brave face to our world on the other side. I drive up Jefferson along the river and eventually out into the exurbia toward the Thumb and Port Huron. I always think I'll drive north to Oscoda, where I was born, see what it is today, the remnants of the air base—of which I would remember nothing. But when I see the great welcoming Blue Water arch, eight hundred and seventy feet back across to Sarnia, I lose my need, as though I was trying to possess something I never had. "You should go, sometime," my wife says to me. "It'd be interesting. It would help you, put things to rest." As if I hadn't done that.

Of course, it's not lost to me that I live across a border from the place near my birth, and from the place where Arthur Remlinger's devilment started, and from where the two Americans departed on their way to meet their fates. In a sense, its significance weighs on me, and I've thought often that where I live here, now—in the screwy way of things—was meant to be, and that the weight was the weight of consequence. As if I expected to preside over both sides of something. But I simply don't believe in those ideas. I believe in what you see being most of what there is, as I've taught my students, and that life's passed along to us empty. So, while significance weighs heavy, that's the most it does. Hidden meaning is all but absent.

My mother said I'd have thousands of mornings to wake up and think about all this, when no one would tell me how to feel. It's been many thousands now. What I know is, you have a better chance in life—of surviving it—if you tolerate loss well; manage not to be a cynic through it all; to subordinate, as Ruskin implied, to keep proportion, to connect the unequal things into a whole that preserves the good, even if admittedly good is often not simple to find. We try, as my sister said. We try. All of us. We try.

ACKNOWLEDGMENTS

THERE'S NO ONE I'M INDEBTED TO MORE THAN KRISTINA FORD, for helping me, encouraging me, extending her intelligence, goodwill, and patience to this book's completion, and for being on the case.

A great many others acted generously toward me and toward this work, none more conspicuously than Dan Halpern, who bet on an old friend. I'm extremely grateful to my dear Amanda Urban, who was my first outside-the-house reader and who has encouraged me forever. I wish to thank, as well, my great friend Janet Henderson, who assisted me inestimably in editing and in reading this book in the early going as well as the late. My thanks, too, to Philip Klay, who volunteered precious time to help me research this book. My thanks to Ellen Lewis, for teaching me about *The Haggadah*. I'm grateful to Scott Sellers and to Louise Dennys, remarkable publishers, whose enthusiasm for this book helped me to finish it. I'm grateful to Alexandra Pringle, my friend for decades, and to Jane Friedman, for their faith in these efforts. I'm grateful as well to Dale Rohrbaugh, who generously dedicated time beyond-the-call, as well as vast goodwill, to seeing this book to completion. I'm grateful to my friends at the University of Mississippi, who welcomed me home and gave me a quiet room in which to finish this novel. I thank my friend Dr. Jeffrey Karnes, at Mayo, for his clear insight into the writer's peculiar dilemma. And thanks, as well, to Dr. Will Dabbs for his spirited help when it counted—at the end.

Certain books and certain writers, in ways both apparent and less obvious, were instrumental in writing *Canada*. My great friend Dave Carpenter first took me to southwestern Saskatchewan in 1984. My friend Elliott Leyton took me goose hunting there. Guy Vanderhaeghe has written eloquently about the border region of Saskatchewan and Montana, as did the great Wallace Stegner. William Maxwell's presence will be obvious by any reader. All sparked this book's conception. I profited by two histories of Saskatchewan, *Saskatchewan: A History* by John H. Archer and *Saskatchewan: A New History* by Bill Waiser. Lynda Shorten's remarkable book of interviews with native people, *Without Reserve*, taught me much. A constant charm and resource in my revisions was Blake Morrison's superb memoir *And When Did You Last See Your Father?* I was aided by generous assistance from Rachel Wormsbecher and Lloyd Begley at the Swift Current Museum in Saskatchewan, and from Libby Edelson, and from Laurie McGee, who copyedited the manuscript. My old and dear friend Craig Sterry gave me comfort and a house to write in, in Great Falls. The writer Melanie Little read this book and gave me indispensable and savvy advice about fixing its flaws. Sarah MacLachlan was my advocate from this book's beginnings. And at the very end, Iris Tupholme and David Kent generously agreed to publish *Canada*, in Canada. I thank you every one.   RF